Bethesda's Child

Bethesda's Child

a Novel

To Alice, who was nice
enough to come to the wonderful
event at the Kirwins on 5/7/11,
in hopes that we meet often on
the streets of San Miguel,
and for the joy of friends &
family & books.

John Warley

To order additional copies of this book, contact:
Xlibris Corporation
1-888-795-4274
www.Xlibris.com
Orders@Xlibris.com
74505

Dedication

To Barbara, for her steadfast encouragement.

And to Caldwell, Nelson, MaryBeth and Carter, Warleys all, who have endured "the background" and who make it all worthwhile.

Preface

by Pat Conroy

In the late winter of 1965, I retrieved a thrown-away baseball glove from the trash can in the Romeo section of Fourth Battalion at The Citadel. The glove was cheap and ugly and worthy to end its life in some county landfill project. But there was serendipity at work in the discovery of this homely, misshapen glove and it led directly to my introduction to John Warley, who was destined to become the best friend I made at The Citadel. Though I had played on the freshman baseball team, I could not try out for the team my sophomore year because the glove I'd used since eighth grade had disintegrated in my hand as I drifted for a fly ball in center field. The happy discovery of the homely glove allowed me to resume my spot in the outfield and led me to the training mess where I sat directly across from John Warley.

Though I had known John by sight and we always exchanged greetings when we passed each other on campus, we had never engaged in a single conversation. My classmates and I admired John and long before we became friends, he looked like a squared-away Citadel cadet who embodied the whole package of military and academic virtues which would insure his success in the barracks. John was bright, well-spoken, and as handsome as an emperor on a coin and his toughness had earned the respect of his football teammates. He played center on the football team and his "centeredness" was one of the qualities that attracted me to that shining path that led to our lifelong friendship. He was a political science major who planned to attend law school, enter the army and then test himself in a political career. It seemed that his life would roll out with the unalterable pattern of a master plan. As we drifted around the South playing baseball games, John described the life he had sketched out to live then had the discipline to connect all the dots and follow the roadmap he had created with great success and precision. John left just one thing out—he never told me he was going to become a novelist.

That first night on the baseball mess would prove clarifying and definitive. It would also change our lives forever. My junior year had not proven very much to me except my limitless capacity for unhappiness as I duck walked my slovenly way through a Citadel education. I did not seem to be making as much of a mark at The Citadel as I had hoped to in college and felt inert and trapped in the horse latitudes of my own inert, windless interior. I couldn't have sworn if I was popular or distained by the Corps, but I knew that I thought I had not been recognized or appreciated by either the Corps or the faculty. Even to myself, I served as an enigma; an ambiguous and shadowy figure still searching for an identity in an environment that felt hostile to me. That would change forever on the night I ate dinner across from John. John has always displayed inerrant powers of scrutiny, but this was the first time I had witnessed them working overtime as he turned those powers on me. I was in the middle of a ceaseless monologue, making fun and openly mocking the entire Citadel world as it presented itself to me. Everything about The Citadel appeared silly and preposterous to me and I didn't quite care who either approved or disapproved of my running commentary about the tomfoolery I met each day as I walked around the campus. On this night I had found a witness to my troubled passage at last.

I heard Warley turning to other baseball players at the table and saying, "Is anyone listening to this guy? Is anyone listening to Conroy? This guy is a riot. He's hilarious. Anybody hear this guy? Anybody?"

John was listening and he kept listening for the next forty-four years. During that entire baseball season, John and I roomed together as we played for our hilarious hall of fame coach, Chal Port. The road trips were marvelous that spring. Playing baseball from West Virginia to the Florida state line was a time of pure pleasure for both of us. On the first trip we found we liked to read and talk about good books. John had just completed *The Second World War* in six volumes by Winston Churchill. I had just finished Faulkner's *Light in August* and it remains my favorite of his novels. By that time I'd become the poetry editor of The Shako and I used to tell John the only way I could get a poem out of a cadet was to hold a gun to his mother's head.

Toward the end of that season, we played a road game at Old Dominion in Norfolk and Coach Port allowed us to spend the night with John's family in Yorktown. Previously, John had made the error of telling his mother and father that I was the only person he had ever met who actually believed in the integration of schools. His parents were Southerners from a very old school and I remember both of them arguing politics with me with some gusto and a trace of ire. But I came to love John's family on that visit and it gave me some small comfort that John and I seemed to spring out of that same modest section of the American middle class. I could not have been more completely wrong about that.

In our senior year we became almost inseparable friends. On weekends we drove through the city of Charleston in his old MG. Neither of us remember having many dates that year, and we still haven't figured out where we went wrong in that department, but I can't remember the name of a single girl he dated in college and he can't pull out the faintest recollection of any girl I took to a hop that year. In June 1967, we found each other after we had graduated and promised to be each other's friends for the rest of our lives.

We were as good as our word.

It has been a friendship that has flourished over long distances and many late night conversations. Because we are human we have endured much suffering, reversals and setbacks as we both succeeded and failed in our careers. We talk about The Citadel and our years there as though it all happened in some whirlpool of lost, unsustainable time. The stories still retain their power to make us laugh out loud. We have compiled a hall of fame of jerks among our contemporaries and also a list of men who seemed remarkable when we met them in college and strike the same sense of wonder in us today. But the sense of fraternity and loyalty for each other we carried out of our Citadel lives has proven both everlasting and an unshakeable bond between us.

There have been three great surprises in my long friendship with John Warley. In 1989, I moved to San Francisco to help another friend with his devastating battle against AIDS. I was living in a house on Presidio Avenue when I answered a phone call from John. What he had to say remains shocking to me even today.

"Pat, I just finished a novel. Do you think you have time to read it and let me know if it's any good?"

"Just a minute, John," I said. "Do you remember ribbing me about those 'things' I used to carry back and forth across the Citadel parade ground?"

"What things are you talking about?" he asked.

"Those 'things' you and the other dimwits I went to college with liked to make fun of."

"Oh, those things. You mean books?"

"Yeah, those things. Books. You used to read a lot of nonfiction, John, but I never saw you reading a novel."

"I didn't see the point of reading novels back then," he said. "So kill me. I was an idiot."

"What's the name of your book?"

"Bethesda's Child."

"Good title. Send it right away," I said.

In the life of a writer, some of your most fearful moments occur when a relative or friend writes a thousand page first novel and sends it to you for approval and validation. Many of these books arrive at your doorstep with the stench of the amateur clinging to the first page and hanging on for dear life to the last chapter. I worried about how John would handle criticism but because of his seriousness and sheer native intelligence, I trusted him to hold his own as he embarked on his maiden voyage on the high seas of fiction. On the day I received the manuscript, I went up to my office with its view of the Golden Gate Bridge and I read the book in one sitting. I found it good, then very good, then took note of the fact that I could not set the book down, and then I had to finish the book because I found myself swept away in the narrative drive. When I finished, I called my agent, Julian Bach, in New York City and told him about *Bethesda's Child*, suggesting that he represent John as his literary agent. When Julian received his copy of the manuscript, he was as excited by the book as I was and soon John and I were represented by the same literary agency. Many publishers showed interest in *Bethesda's Child*, and a few came close to publishing it, but the science seemed so far-fetched that it scared off all major publishers when they had to come to a decision. What was far-fetched back in the early nineties is now part of the cutting edge of scientific research today. John's writing was not only ahead of his time, but he displayed an eerie talent for prophecy which informs the soul of this novel.

Bethesda's Child is a beautifully written and composed novel. Its main character is Senator Martin Harmon of Virginia, who assumes center stage in the first sentence and makes his final appearance in the brilliant, chilling last sentence of the book. John's description of the inner workings of Capitol Hill captures the essence of an insider's view of how laws are made and deals are cut with astonishing accuracy. Since he worked as a lobbyist in Washington when he was fresh out of law school, he learned to navigate the halls of Congress and all the intricate ways and means to get politicians' attention and then their vote.

In every good novel there is a love story and *Bethesda's Child* contains a great one. In all love stories there is a touch of agony and betrayal, and *Bethesda's Child* will make you hurt in those parts of the soul where the tissues are softest. Carson Cox is an easy woman to fall in love with, but it is a matter of need and ethical clarity that makes her a great one. All the main characters are sharply drawn and John's development of these personalities seems both clear-sighted and sure-footed. From Dr. Max Grunfeld to Jean Harmon to Dennis Rancour, John demonstrates great skill in moving his acting troupe around his fictional stage. The story builds with an innate naturalness rare for a first time novelist then explodes into fury and epiphany and a sadness almost too great to bear. John lets the reader off gently with one of the most satisfying endings I've read in many years.

The writing of Bethesda's Child was John's first great surprise in our friendship. The second followed several years later when he called to inform me that he was taking a sabbatical from his law practice in Newport News, Virginia, and moving with his family to San Miguel de Allende in Mexico. In a man of his conservative temperament, I could not have been more surprised if he had called to tell me he was having a sex change operation. It sounded as if the spirit of Jack Kerouac had body-snatched my roommate on the Citadel baseball team.

In the long trek from the coast of Virginia to the hills of central Mexico, my house on Fripp Island became a pit stop on the journey. John had married one of the most beautiful women of our generation and Barbara Warley had served as a head cheerleader for my books since I first published *The Boo* in 1970. She has a rare gift for encouragement and she had pushed John to complete his first novel and to start on a second. Barbara and I had instantly liked each other when we met in Arlington, Virginia, in a neighborhood I once lived in as a boy. In the first ten minutes of our meeting, we discovered we were both battle-tested veterans from dark and roiled childhoods. We joined each other's fan clubs that very day. Mexico would deepen my friendship with the Warleys. During their stopovers I could feed them well and get to know their four children; Caldwell, Nelson, MaryBeth and Carter—splendid creatures but so were their parents and they brought me news of Mexico and of the new, exhilarating life they had chosen in a town famous for its elaborate doors. I began seeing John more than any time since college.

In the first year of his life south of the border, I sent John a box of books, carefully selected and cherry-picked from the shelves of the Old New York Bookstore in Atlanta. I wanted him to have available some of the books that had proven invaluable to me over the course of my reading life. I sent him *The Portable Graham Green, For Whom the Bell Tolls, Daniel Martin* by John Fowles, *Glory* by Nabokov, *The Long Patrol* by Norman Mailer, *A Death in the Family* by James Agee, and *The French Lieutenant's Woman*. There were more, but those are the ones we remember. By this time, I knew he had purchased The One Hundred Greatest Books of All Time from the Franklin Library and that he was working on these shelf-by-shelf in his rigorous and methodical way. I like writers to approach their own country of art fully armed with the glittering weapons of the great books at hand. John received these books and read them all. He wrote and thought hard about writing and joined other writers in long conversations about books and work. Mexico changed my friend forever and turned him into a deeper writer than even he could imagine. He remained in Mexico until he was called back to the law in 1995.

At that time, I was in the middle of a titanic effort to finish my novel *Beach Music*. The book was proving too much for me and I despaired over ever finishing it. I was going through a terrible divorce, had recently cracked up and came close to being delivered to the entrance of a mental hospital. Each day was a struggle to even force myself into the writer's chair and I was several years behind on the book's delivery. In looking up notes on a character named Jordan Elliot, I had purchased a family history of the Barnwells who had frequently intermarried with the distinguished Elliots. I was chasing down a line of Elliots when I stumbled across a photograph that both astonished me and furnished the third great surprise. I was staring at a stunning young woman: John Warley's mother, Susannah. Without thinking and on pure impulse, I called Mrs. Warley's phone number. She answered on the first ring and I said, "Mrs. Warley, this is Pat Conroy and I'm looking at a photograph of you in a book about Barnwells."

"It's a rather nice photograph, isn't it Pat?" she said, pleased.

"Nice? What a babe. What a dish. What a knockout," I said.

"I was rather cute, wasn't I?"

"Cute don't cut it. It's breathtaking. Mrs. Warley, I had no idea you were a Barnwell."

"Tuscarora Jack was my great-great-great-great grandfather. Didn't John ever mention it?"

"He most certainly did not," I said. "Barnwell is one of the most distinguished names in the history of Beaufort, South Carolina. Your ancestors are all buried at St. Helena's."

"The Barnwells come from a very aristocratic line," she said.

"What about the Warleys?"

"My husband came from an aristocratic Charleston family. Both families played great roles in the history of South Carolina."

"A personal question, Mrs. Warley. Why did neither family, the Barnwells or the Warleys, embrace your wonderful son when he was a cadet at The Citadel? He should have been going to debutant balls and society parties every weekend and if he went to a single one I didn't know about it. It's worse than I thought. Poor John was with me every single weekend after we started playing baseball together. Why would they ignore John? Who could ask for a nicer young man?"

It was somewhere during the middle of this speech that I realized I had hurt Mrs. Warley's feelings and hurt them badly. I tried to back off and change the subject, but she returned to it because it troubled her.

"Pat, you don't know much about old Charleston families. They are very, very proud. They can forgive almost anything but they can't abide anyone who is without money or social prestige. Mr. Warley did not make a lot money during his lifetime. But both of us thought our families would do right by our son when he attended The Citadel. They did not. It hurt us more than words can express. They acted like they didn't know he was in town."

"Their loss, Mrs. Warley," I said. "I'm going to call John in Mexico tonight and I'm going to tell him he should join the St. Cecilia Society. I've been researching this stupid book for two years and I guarantee he's eligible."

And so, my dear friend the aristocrat, John Warley, joined the St. Cecilia Society at the urging of his peasant manservant, Pat Conroy. When John was getting his membership papers in order, I made a single request as he was about to be admitted to one of the snootiest and prestigious societies in the American South.

"Warley, if you're accepted, I'd like to be your guest when you attend your first ball."

"Consider it done," he said.

Several months later, he called to inform me that he had submitted my name, but discovered that the Society had firm policies where it came to twice-divorced writers who lived close to Charleston.

"Warley, Warley, this hurts. But you have to admire any society founded in 1762 that figured out how to keep poor riffraff like Conroy out of their dance over two hundred years in their future."

John attended his first St. Cecilia ball in 1997 and escorted his mother. When I called later, she told me it was one of the grandest occasions in her life and that she and her son looked like a million dollars on the dance floor. When I asked John if he could take MaryBeth, the beautiful Korean daughter he and Barbara had adopted as an infant, he told me he wasn't sure. But the question caused a divine spark that ultimately produced *A Southern Girl*, a novel that deals brilliantly with this dilemma. I think it is a finer work of fiction than even *Bethesda's Child*, which I find wonderful. It will be published next year.

I love how story works, and how they form in the bright markets of the mind. This one started long ago when I spotted a cast-off baseball glove on top of the trash.

Author's Note

If you are reading front-to-back, you have just finished Pat Conroy's generous Preface. Following Pat with words printed on a page is not easy. I don't remember who followed Ted Williams in the Boston Red Sox lineup, but Williams was such a splendid hitter that whoever did was reminded four or five times a game that by comparison he looked like a butcher hacking away at a grisly side of beef. I now sympathize with that player.

In the Preface, Pat recounts the box of books he sent me in Mexico, a gesture I've never forgotten and so typical of him. What he omitted was the check he also sent during a rough patch when the Warleys were dining on too many tortillas and frijoles. The check for $800 represented a portion of Pat's Dutch royalties on the *Prince of Tides*. He had endorsed it over with no mention of loan or repayment. I stand whenever I hear the Dutch national anthem played at the Olympics.

With me with and with countless other writers, Pat has been generous to a degree that defies belief and in some cases logic. He comes naturally by this generosity of spirit. At The Citadel, most of his conflict with the chain of command amounted to nothing more than his sympathy for the knobs (freshmen), for unlike some he remembered what it was like to be at the receiving end of a tirade unfurled by a newly minted corporal. Most amazing is that in our cynical and often grouchy world, he has not lost his gift for giving, the will to help, the hand extended to those whose hands are full.

I've wondered if I write because of Pat, and I've answered with a firm no. Writing is too personal, and the journey from Chapter 1 to "The End" too long to satisfy anyone other than the man or woman holding the pen. But that is not to say that Pat has not affected my writing, as he has the work of so many others who have come to him for blurbs, encouragement, advice, and courage. I can't speak for them, but Ben Meecham spoke for me when he extended to the dying Dave Murphy "my thanks, my thanks, my thanks."

I began this book in 1990, inspired by a newspaper article speculating that Abraham Lincoln suffered from Marfan's Disease, a genetic disorder characterized by, among other things, elongated limbs and fingers. Although it is difficult for me to believe that twenty years have passed between writing and publication (2010), the math is irrefutable. Even more difficult to believe is the advance in genetics and genetic engineering during those two decades. My story forecasts scientific breakthroughs that seemed light years away in 1990, yet Dolly the Sheep was introduced to the world in 1996. Rather than try to adapt my story using the clarity of the rear view mirror, I am publishing it very much as I wrote it, with a minor concession to cell phones.

My foresight in 1990 has become hindsight. Such is time. But a good story remains a good story, and I hope your pleasure in reading it matches mine in putting it to paper.

I am indebted to Robert Shapiro, whose fine book, *The Human Blueprint* (1991 St. Martin's Press), taught me much of what I know about genetics.

John Warley

August 21, 2010
Beaufort, S.C.

Now there is at Jerusalem by the sheep market a pool, which is called in the Hebrew tongue Bethesda, having five porches. In these lay a great multitude of impotent folk, of blind, halt, withered, waiting for the moving of the water. For an angel went down at a certain season into the pool, and troubled the water: whosoever then first after the troubling of the water stepped in was made whole of whatsoever disease he had.

John 5:2-4

The Responsibility in Eugenics Act of 1999 (REA)

The Secretary may not conduct or support any research or experimentation in the United States or in any other country, on living human tissue, cells or other organic components of the human body unless such research or experimentation is designed to prevent or cure disease, deformity or other conditions known to constitute a health risk either for the individual or society in general.

BOOK 1

WASHINGTON, D.C.
MAY, 1999

Chapter 1

United States Senator Martin Harmon emerged from the shadow of the Capitol's dome into the sunshine of a bright mid-morning. Below, on the final tier of steps leading to the mall, a bank of microphones stood silhouetted against the white marble, and beyond these milled reporters, camera crews and tourists eager for a glimpse of open-air democracy. He paused to let his eyes adjust to the light and to take in a view that, more than any other, reminded him why he had come.

The Washington Monument gleamed white, its luster enhanced by new leaves on old trees, and beyond it the Lincoln Memorial rested with the enduring mass of a pyramid, timeless and solid in its promise that "government of, by and for the people shall not perish from the earth." Across the Potomac, he saw Arlington with its sad flame amidst a silent population. Washington at his feet, but only in the literal sense. He knew his place, and that place suited him just fine. For the moment.

He descended the steps with agility uncommon in a man of fifty-two. A reporter spotted him and extended an arm upward, seeming to draw with it the faces of the crowd, squinting and shielding their eyes. They followed his progress to the microphones, which he approached with unhurried certainty and no hint of being winded.

"Good morning," he said, smiling. "Today I have the pleasure of announcing that we have secured the votes necessary to pass the REA in the Senate."

As he cited the private commitments of three "previously undecided" colleagues, spectators ringing the press corps edged forward, knotting the throng in front of the microphones. At the outer fringe lingered a woman, trim and tanned, in running gear. A wide yellow sweatband wreathed her forehead and dark sunglasses shielded eyes which tracked every movement and gesture made by the senator.

Her first glimpse of him, two years before, had been at roughly this distance. Physically, he seemed to her an impersonator, a college kid in a play, dressed for the part of a senator. Boyish, with a smooth, unspoiled forehead and cheeks slightly more dimpled on the right than left. Light, even facial hair which, because he shaved religiously, never appeared as the gray stubble that lay beneath the surface. His eyes brightened in sunlight, green to greener, and the nose would have been straight but for an errant baseball that hit it flush his junior year of high school. His hair, tousling in a faint breeze off the Potomac, had an adolescent fullness despite its silver flecked with black. The animation of his hands and arms, the athletic shift of toned muscles inside his suit, the restless choreography of a tightly harnessed energy—all suggested a fine young actor.

"Senator, how do you answer critics who say your anti-science agenda is a giant step backward—the Scopes monkey trial?" Brad Simpson of the Detroit *Free Press*, a consistent Harmon detractor, pecked his pen against his note pad but failed to hide the scorn in his smile.

Harmon chuckled softly. Simpson was baiting him, but he'd been through too many press conferences to be provoked. "I'd say they've never read the bill and that backward is the best way to step when you're about to walk off a cliff." Simpson sighed and jotted.

"Jill, you were next." For emphasis, Harmon pointed toward Jill Blanchard, political reporter for the Chicago *Tribune*.

Blanchard: "Would you comment on the possibility of a veto if the REA passes in the Senate?"

Harmon answered confidently. "I don't believe the president will veto this bill. It's in the country's best interests, as shown by support in the House and what we believe will be passage by the Senate."

"Senator," Blanchard pressed, "some are speculating that this legislation is part of the escalating war with the Republicans leading to next year's election. The word is that you are being courted as a candidate for vice president. Would you comment on the connection between your bill and the presidential race?"

Harmon grinned. "Now, Jill, you know better than to try to pin me down on that." Laughter rose from the crowd. Turning serious, he continued. "This bill is not about presidential politics but about the alarming trend in unrestricted genetic engineering, a growing concern to thinking Americans. Abuses in genetic testing and research which began in the mid-90's are now, in my judgment and the judgment of a majority of my colleagues, very real threats to the moral and ethical values of most. If the president chooses to thwart the will of the majority through a veto, this issue could surface in the next election, but that is up to the president." Traces of a grin returned. "Personally, my ambition is to be the best representative I can be for the people of Virginia."

With a dismissive thanks and wave, Harmon ended the formal press conference. The crowd thinned, some moving closer for a better view of the man still taking questions. The runner in dark glasses turned toward the Lincoln Memorial and was soon on a steady pace of eight minutes per mile.

*   *   *

On the following morning, Carson Cox overslept. In a dream she rode a massive bull, gripping its tufted hair as it bucked, writhed and flared in a raw potency. Through a dusky haze of illogic, she saw herself arguing with the beast, yelling to calm itself, to settle, to nuzzle her instead of tossing her violently to the ground. The bull twisted its head, wild-eyed. She reached for the next pillow and opened her eyes.

Across the room, Martin Harmon stood at an oak bureau, putting on his watch. "I'm going down to get dressed. I'll call you as soon as I get settled in at the office." Moments later she heard the apartment door close with its metallic clank.

"Get settled in . . . ," Carson thought through stirring consciousness. Martin used the phrase often and it meant to expect a call somewhere between three and four in the afternoon. Martin, it seemed, took a while to settle in.

She arose. Black coffee and her ritualistic chocolate chip cookie in hand, she sauntered into the breakfast room to read The Washington *Post*. The lead story would be Harmon, she predicted. She opened the front page to find:

HARMON ASSURES REA WILL PASS

Washington, D.C.—U.S. Senator Martin Harmon (D. Va.), leader of the coalition in Congress opposed to unrestricted genetic engineering and recombinant DNA research, announced today that his forces had secured the necessary votes in the Senate to assure passage of the controversial Responsibility in Eugenics Act, the REA.

The bill restricts research on human tissue to experiments designed to prevent disease, birth defects and other threats to health. It pits conservative religious groups and the right to life movement against pro-choice forces and those who support unrestricted freedom of scientific inquiry. The final vote, scheduled for next month in the Senate, is expected to be close and is seen as a major test of Harmon's legislative influence at a time of increasing speculation that he may become a candidate for vice president.

In his second news conference this week, Harmon cited the private pledge of three senators as "the last votes needed to create the majority necessary to carry the measure." Sen. Harmon deflected questions as to the identity of the three, saying only that any announcement should come from the senators. Speculation centers on Senators Grasso, Baine and Santiago, but none has been reached for comment.

The *Post* was right about two of the three, she thought, allowing herself the satisfaction she always felt when she knew the inside details. Grasso and Baine, both first term senators due up for reelection next year and feeling heat from deficits in the polls, had given Martin their hard-earned commitments.

And Martin had hammered on Santiago, who wobbled but would not fall, not yet convinced that the REA'ers could beat him. Two terms in the Senate further reinforced his confidence. The third convert was in fact Senator Marybeth Richmond, a tough business woman from Colorado where REA'ers were "frothing at the mouth," as one of her aides put it. The chime of the telephone interrupted.

"Hi, Sis," Carson answered.

"I saw the news last night," Kathy said. "Your man is a hot item."

"Physically or politically?"

"Both. How in hell are you guys keeping the lid on this thing? I've never seen you linked publicly, but I worry I'm going to see my baby sister's picture in the tabloids."

"God, I hope not," said Carson.

"I mean, with Martin getting to be such a big deal, not that he was ever small potatoes, isn't he attracting hordes of reporters? I can't believe this won't leak out."

"Sis, I'm scared to death, if you want to know the truth. It would be complicated enough if we were just a couple of people in Des Moines, but with his position, our family and all the rest, it's pretty overwhelming. I'd like to come up if you have some time to talk?"

"Sure I do. How's Saturday? And the kids will love to see you."

Kathy, mother of five, lived in a world regimented into quarter-hour blocks of insufficient time. She was also the sole person Carson had confided in regarding her affair.

"See you Saturday," Carson agreed. Relieved, she hadn't been conscious of needing to talk that badly, but the relief was short-lived. Kathy's comment, "I can't believe this won't leak out," replayed in her mind, where she too knew it was true.

When she had finished the paper, she moved to the adjoining room which doubled as a spare bedroom and an office. For two hours, computer humming, she labored over a report that had occupied her professional time for the past four weeks. The volume of work escalated monthly, but her income reflected the growth of her consulting business. The House Ways and Means Committee paid her well for her research on the demographics of single parent households.

When she had met her goal for that morning's production, she left the work in place and went to her bedroom, where she showered and dressed. She was a striking woman people invariably remembered. In dark glasses, worn only while running, her appearance suggested, almost demanded, a scarf drawn tightly around her auburn hair and a trench coat with turned up collar. With the eyes hidden, she looked cold, aloof, unapproachable. But unobscured, warm hazel eyes softened lines and angles, dissolved mystery, and waltzed away any semblance of haughtiness.

She looked in the mirror as she left her dressing room and regretted not being able to attend yesterday's press conference dressed as she was now. It was not the last concession she would have to make to be Martin's lover, which Carson Cox had been for almost a year.

*　　*　　*

Maximillian Grunfeld, Ph.D., snubbed his cigar into the sooty base of his favorite ash tray, simultaneously reading the Los Angeles *Times* account of Martin Harmon's press conference. "Nonsense!" he muttered. A shaft of morning sunlight warmed his head and shoulders, playing upon the haze of lingering smoke. He finished the article, then re-read it to satisfy himself that he had missed no details.

Grunfeld, Professor of Biomedical Engineering at Caltech, tossed the paper onto his desk. His office adjoined his laboratory. Behind him hung framed testaments to his genius: his diploma as a Senior Fellow of the National Academy of Sciences; the coveted Faulkenberg Award, given for lifetime achievement in biomedical research; honorary degrees from Harvard and Columbia; the certificate commemorating his 1987 selection as "Scientist of the Year" by the National Science Foundation; "The Order of Public Merit" from the Brazilian government for his work in identifying a rare genetic leukemia which had plagued certain tribes along the Amazon. His wife had framed and hung these tributes, knowing that waiting for him to do so would have meant permanent consignment to the umbrella stand where he had stored them for years. While they imparted portentousness he did not feel, he had grown accustomed to them now.

Down the hall a door slammed. Someone like me, he thought, here early when the mind is fresh and reflections of the previous evening shape a new experiment, suggest a novel protocol or demand the repetition of an old test, the results of which were never satisfactorily explained. Grunfeld extracted a cigar from a drawer, struck his lighter, and puffed until the end glowed. His aging lungs rose up to meet the smoke as he inhaled. He had given up red meats, French sauces, whole milk and real butter. But a man of seventy-four, he reasoned, had to balance threats to his longevity against assaults on his spirit, and so he drew the line at further deprivations, telling his health-conscious colleagues and friends who demanded to know why he stilled smoked that it was "one of the great imponderables." He said it gently, with his engaging wink and the hint of mysticism that drove him even now. He had made a career of imponderables, pondering them, shaking them, picking at them, holding them up to the light, tasting, smelling and, when they refused to yield their secrets, cursing them and starting over in a relentless pursuit of genetic unknowns.

He looked down at the newspaper spread before him. He didn't know Harmon, or any of the others mentioned. "Morality sheriffs," he called them, bent on arresting scientific inquiry and slapping the legislative cuffs on researchers like him; pandering to the agenda of the Flat Earth Society. A few months before, he would have dismissed them as nuisances, pesky mosquitoes buzzing about the collective head of twenty-first Century science. But no longer. Recent events in his laboratory had startled even him, making Harmon and his allies pivotal in Grunfeld's quest for the ultimate imponderable, the solution to which not only guaranteed him a summons to Stockholm but would cast his shadow long upon generations of scientists to come.

He lifted the page, took a long draw on the cigar, and pressed the ember end to the article. Harmon's reported prediction charred instantly into indecipherable ash.

Chapter 2

Martin Harmon left Carson's apartment on the seventeenth floor of the Westchester, walked briskly to the stairway at the end of the hall and descended five flights to his apartment. He encountered no one; virtually none of the Westchester's residents used these stairs. This location had been carefully chosen six months before. He had been living in Alexandria and Carson had lived near the Capitol when they agreed to set up house, although clearly their "house" would have to be separate units.

The Westchester had been Martin's idea. Most men and women with public profiles as high as his tended to tryst as far from D.C. as possible. The Virginia hunt country around Warrenton and Upperville was especially popular with non-couple couples, and for this reason he ruled it out. Besides, no one escaped the prying eyes of Washington's professional gossips by putting a few miles between the fox and the hounds.

The Westchester, a one-time bastion of the political elite, offered quiet conservatism. The tenants, mostly elderly, stuck to patterns and schedules. In the first week Martin had twice left Carson's apartment at 7:15 a.m., only to meet the same woman in her sixties on the stairs. She walked for exercise, so thereafter he either left at a different time or used the other stairwell. Since that first week, he had encountered only two others, neither acknowledging him as they passed.

But security absorbed him more with each passing day. Newspapers recounted his official comings and goings with increasing frequency.

He was nearing the stage at which reporters might stake out his home overnight, as they did to Gary Hart in 1988. He could feel it.

At the twelfth floor, he changed, grabbed his athletic bag, and called for messages. In less than five minutes, he entered the elevator for the lobby. The doorman, "Mr. Wayne" to the aging population of the Westchester, greeted him with the standard, "Good morning, Senator" as he emerged from the huge brass entrance doors. The faded green of Mr. Wayne's uniform seemed the exact shade of the lawn and neatly trimmed hedges surrounding the apartment, as though fertilized, pruned and watered as part of the landscape by an indiscriminate groundskeeper.

Mr. Wayne ushered Martin down the canopied walkway to the cab he had hailed and opened the door without flourish. "Have a great day, Senator," he said as Martin ducked in.

The very black driver overheard "Senator." He sought Martin's eyes in his rear view mirror, asking in a lilting British accent, "The Capitol, sir?"

Twenty minutes later, Martin hurried into his office at the Russell Senate Office Building. "Good morning, Ellen," he boomed. "How's your cough? You didn't sound so good yesterday." Ellen Fry brought coffee. A portly woman in her late fifties with perfectly coiffed gray hair, she had been his secretary since his election to the Senate.

His desk mirrored those of a hundred other lawmakers on Capitol Hill: framed pictures of his wife Jean and their three children, Edward, Jack and Allie; a gold-plated pen and pencil set, larger and more baroque than he would have selected for himself, but a gift from his staff many years ago; and an assortment of paperweights and mementoes. On a typical morning he began his work day by absorbing news stories, correspondence and memos compiled by his staff since the previous afternoon. But today, he was preoccupied. "Ellen, send in Dennis."

Dennis Rancour, age forty-two, had been Martin's administrative assistant, or AA, for two years. When Dennis came to the Hill in 1979, his organizational skills and personal drive made him a comer. He had advanced quickly, aided by an eager network of young female staffers who found irresistible the combination of his Mediterranean skin, taut body and sultry eyes. But dissipation, a failed marriage, and an expanding midriff had dulled the luster, although his political savvy had grown with experience.

He knew instinctively at the moment of Ellen's summons that his headache, already the target of six aspirin although it was not yet 10:00

a.m., was about to get worse. With resignation, he pushed away from his desk and headed toward Martin's door.

Martin, seated at his desk, looked up as Dennis entered and with a flick of his wrist pointed to a chair. Dennis sat, then stretched with studied casualness to observe the status of Martin's coat, difficult to see because Martin's arm blocked the view. An unbuttoned coat invariably signaled a friendly, collegial talk. Martin was unaware of this barometer of his moods. The coat, Dennis noted when Martin moved his arm, was buttoned.

"Dennis, help me clear something up, will you?"

"What's that, Chief?"

"I don't have to tell you how jumpy the REA Coalition Committee has been this past couple of weeks. Since you sit in on the meetings, you know the pressure we've all been under to pull out this vote, which is going to be close no matter what we do."

"Sure, I'm aware of that."

"Remember that meeting the Coalition had at the Commonwealth Club two weeks ago?"

Dennis nodded, his eyes pensively focused on the picture of Thomas Jefferson hanging behind Martin's desk.

"Then you remember that when we divided the list of undecided Senators, it was agreed that I would approach those on my list in a specific order. That order was dictated by the people we were lobbying. We knew we probably wouldn't get Ed Santiago so we wanted to hit him last. And we also knew that Larry Grasso follows Bill Baine's lead about one hundred and ten percent of the time so we had to see Baine first."

"I remember," said Dennis.

Martin leaned forward. "Well, I sit down at this private meeting with Grasso and the first thing out of his mouth is 'I hear I'm number five on your hit list, but if you think I'm going to make this decision based upon what any other senator does, think again.' Needless to say, I had to spend some time assuring him of his reputation as an 'independent statesman' and all that horse manure. But I was immediately on the defensive—it was like he had read the minutes of our meeting."

"Minutes weren't kept, were they?"

"No, but some AA's took notes and I heard Barbara Clark from Commerce took unofficial minutes."

"But Marty, what makes you think that the information came from our office? You've just identified about twelve potential sources of the leak to Grasso not counting some of your esteemed colleagues."

Martin noted that he had not mentioned he thought the leak came from his office. To give Dennis the benefit of the doubt, perhaps it was implied from the tenor of the conversation.

"I'll tell you what makes me suspect it. At the end of my meeting with Grasso, he said, 'Well, you got Baine to come over, so I guess I would make the fifty-first vote, eh?' I think he was just making a big deal of the fact that his vote could get us over the top—you know, IOU's and all that. But the point is, how did he know we had gotten Baine? I had met with Baine only two hours earlier."

"Maybe Baine picked up the phone and called him. They're fairly close. Or maybe Baine made up his mind to support the REA before he met with you and indicated to Grasso that that's what he had decided."

"Possibly, but Baine was paranoid about this getting out before he had the chance to do his own damage control. He swore he wasn't even going to tell his wife and he made me take a blood oath to keep it under wraps. I just can't picture him, within minutes of our conversation, calling Larry Grasso to tell him he was committing his vote. As you know, I was pretty fired up at getting Baine to come over and you're the only one I told about it before meeting with Larry."

Dennis gradually lowered his eyes to meet Martin's gaze. "I don't know what to tell you, Chief, except it didn't come from me. Baine must have told someone, because I didn't tell a soul."

"Fair enough," said Martin, standing and unbuttoning his coat in the same upward motion. "I'm relieved to hear that. Sorry to have to put you on the spot, but there's too much riding on this to screw around, and I needed to hear what you've just told me. Let's consider it ended here."

"Fine with me, Chief. No hard feelings."

When he was alone, Martin turned and looked out toward the Capitol, quite unsure the matter ended here. He wished he could put his finger on what was bothering him about Dennis. He seemed loyal, but who knew where real loyalties lay in this town. A man like Dennis, on the Hill for so long serving a number of different masters, was bound to have developed strong ties to a host of people.

"Senator," Ellen called on the intercom, "the Bennett delegation is here for its appointment."

Martin hurried into the adjoining room, a well-appointed conference area where he usually met with small groups. He shook hands with their leader, Earl Bennett, and in turn with five others, all constituents from in and around the Roanoke area that had given Martin his start in politics as a thirty-two year old member of the Virginia House of Delegates. This would be an easy meeting; the shepherd talking to his flock.

"Gosh, it's good to see you, Earl. How long has it been, anyway?" asked Martin.

"I expect a year and a half maybe," responded Earl. "Must have been at Eddie Waters' funeral and that was a ways back." Eddie Waters, a longtime Harmon supporter and business partner of Earl's, suffered a fatal heart attack after eighteen holes of the best golf Eddie had ever played. "God, if I could play like that every day I'd die a happy man," Eddie had said prophetically in the clubhouse after his round of seventy-eight.

"Yep, I expect you're right," said Martin, slipping faintly into a Piedmont brogue which life in Washington had all but purged from his speech.

Talk continued around the table as Martin brought the conversation to each member of the delegation. This habit, common to good politicians, came easily to him, as did remembering names. More difficult was idle chatter itself. Martin liked issues. Small talk had never been his forte, although he wasn't bad at it.

At a lull, Earl announced their purpose. "We just want you to know what a fine job we think you're doin' on this REA bill. We think like you think. This bill has to pass for the survival of everything this country stands for.

"Ya know, Marty," continued Earl, asserting his standing with the group by addressing a U.S. Senator in the familiar, "we're representing the Free Will Baptist Church. We've got a huge congregation there, as I guess you know since you've come to worship with us several times. The Lord's been good to this great country, and sure, we've got some problems right now, but we've searched our hearts, Marty, and we at Free Will believe that a lot of those problems are of our own makin' and that if we would all just follow the words of our Savior Jesus Christ, we'd see our troubles clear up. Now you take all this genetic tomfoolery. God's not smilin' on that work. I know He's not. Some mysteries are meant to remain mysteries and what makes people tick is one of 'em. If a young 'un is suppose to have blue eyes, we think it's a sin for some test tube clinker to give him brown eyes or change him from a boy to a girl. I know you're with us on this Marty, so I'm preaching to the choir."

As the last person was about to tell Martin exactly the same thing the other five had said, the door opened and Ellen's head appeared.

"Senator, I hate to interrupt, but you're needed in the other room."

Martin excused himself with, "Folks, I have to cut this short. Apparently, there's a fire to put out around here." He gave Earl's shoulder a squeeze as he walked past.

"What's wrong?" asked Martin as he reentered his private office.

Ellen nodded toward the phone. "It's Anne Harborfield at NIH. She says it's urgent."

"Hi, Anne, what's up?" asked Martin when Ellen had closed the door.

"Senator, I've just come across something I think you need to know about. It's a research proposal—"

"I know, Anne," said Harmon. "I've heard that NIH has been flooded with applications. Apparently there's hope the REA will grandfather any research proposal submitted before it's passed. I guess all the science people are trying to get in under the wire."

"That's true—they've been bringing them in here by the truckload—but I ran across one in particular."

"Who's it from?" asked Martin.

"A man named Max Grunfeld. Have you heard of him?"

Martin brought the fingertips of his right hand to his temple, searching for a name. "Max Grunfeld," he repeated. "No. Who is he?"

"A genetics engineer at Caltech. Big name in the field."

"What's so special about this research grant?"

Anne lowered her voice, making it inaudible over an unrecognizable din in the background.

"Anne, speak up, can you? I can't hear. Where are you?"

"I'm at a pay phone in a convenience store in Bethesda. This grant request is unbelievable. The instant I read it, I thought of you and the REA. Dr. Grunfeld claims to have cloned a mouse from the cell of a fully grown mouse; what we would call a 'fully differentiated mouse.' He wants millions to follow up his discovery." Her voice dropped again, prompting him to ask why she had not called from her office. "Because I wasn't sure I should make this call. These grant requests are confidential."

"I see," he replied. "Thanks for thinking of me, Anne, but I would hate to see you get yourself in trouble."

"I don't mind," she said, rasping into the receiver. "If it hadn't been for you, I would never have landed this job."

"I appreciate your gratitude. But what exactly ties this grant request in with the REA?"

She again lowered her voice. "That will take some explaining; explaining I can't very well do from a pay phone. I'd be glad to come to your office."

"No, don't do that. Why don't I have Dennis Rancour, my AA, call you, and the two of you can go into it. Speak with him as you would with me."

After noting Anne's home number, Martin hung up. He thought back to the day, two years earlier, when Anne's mother had come to see him. At first, he thought she was just another job seeker, one of hundreds the continuing recession brought to his door annually. In a controlled tone, she had described her struggle to put Anne through college and graduate degree programs. Widowed twelve years, she worked as a branch manager at a bank. Then, when her income from the bank proved insufficient, she took on preparing tax returns, and when that wasn't enough she added bookkeeping for three small corporations. She had wanted to avoid selling their modest home in Lynchburg, Virginia, but then sold it when it became clear the equity would be essential to assure Anne's Ph.D. When, at last, her newly graduated, fully qualified daughter had been unable to find a good job, her despair became complete, so she came to see him because she had heard he got things done.

She seemed small and alone as she faced him across the wide desk, but if she felt intimidated by the flags flanking his credenza or the framed photographs of presidents shaking his hand or the thick carpet bearing the Senate seal beneath her feet, she didn't show it. Her face, thin and weathered and somewhat dour, held no makeup, and her hair, a grayish copper pulled back severely in a bun, imparted a certain rural majesty to her frailty. Martin guessed that she had come for the only purpose her pride would accommodate: her daughter's future. Her steely dignity compelled him, so he picked up the phone and with three calls found Anne a job, a very good job, at NIH. Some days as a senator were better than others, he thought, and that day, when his power and his influence and his connections enabled him to replace despair with joy, had been one of his best ever.

Chapter 3

"Jesus H. Christ," Randolph R. Cass, Ph.D. muttered to no one in particular. "What are we, the Library of Congress? It'll take two months just to index all these damn things. Every research university and think tank in the world must have submitted five." He gazed over the sea of research applications stacked on the floor of the receiving room at The National Institutes of Health (NIH) in Bethesda, Maryland. "I'm going to quit this job and go into the copier business." Unlikely, since Cass, Director of the Division of Research Grants, had been at NIH for almost 30 years. He turned to a receiving clerk. "Get me Anne Harborfield. Extension 420." Moments later, he heard Anne's cheerful voice.

"Anne, have you seen this?" he asked, spreading his arm in a flowing motion as if she could see over the phone.

"Yes, sir. I was down there this morning. It's unbelievable, isn't it?"

"Damn right it is. How do you suggest we handle it?"

"I've scoured our neighboring agencies for some loaners plus I've called in some temps to begin tomorrow morning. We can handle the processing, receipts and logging but who knows when anyone will get around to reading these. Temps and loaners aren't much help there."

Cass agreed. "Stop by my office later today, will you, Anne? We need to go over this in some detail. I have a feeling the vultures on the Hill will be circling if we screw it up." He hung up thinking that he always felt better after talking with Anne, even if the subject was burdensome. She attacked problems with spirit. He liked that.

Anne hung up the phone, fully aware that the proposals stacked before Dr. Cass were one short of the total received. The Grunfeld grant request was locked in her top desk drawer to which she had the only key. She had instinctively secured it, a needless precaution. As executive secretary of the Genetics Study Section, she had every right to possess, study, and even copy it. On the other hand, divulging the contents to Martin Harmon could be a felony.

She wondered if she had technically broken the law. True, she had disclosed the existence of the request, and mentioned the name of its sponsor, but not the detailed contents. There had been no time for that, and besides, a pay phone at a 7-Eleven was hardly appropriate for discussion of a scientific concept so revolutionary. She worried that someone had seen her leave NIH earlier that morning. "Don't get paranoid," she instructed herself. She opened the drawer again. Yes, there it was, in the same spot she had put it before heading out to call Harmon.

At 3:00 p.m., she went to Cass's office. Barely five feet tall, her shoes only lightly touched the carpet when she was seated. Her face, somewhat square, she framed in a boxy hair style, with medium brown hair hanging to her shoulders. She wore bangs, again out of favor despite a brief resurgence of popularity in the mid-90's. Nor did her glasses, rounded frames of dark plastic, accent her eyes, which were as dark as the frames. She moved in quick spurts, gesturing often with hands small and dexterous.

Cass appeared to be nodding off at his desk when she knocked on the jamb of the open door. She startled him, causing him to rise with an exaggerated vitality. For the next twenty minutes they discussed the specifics of accommodating the overflow in the receiving area. When they had finished, he went to his large plate glass window and scanned the grounds below. He was tall, having played pivot for his college basketball team in the days before the game soared above the rim. His pants were belted high on his waist, so that his modest pot belly supported his belt at an upward tilt, and his long, willowy trunk bent concavely from the waist, forming a subtle, elongated "S" in profile.

Anne couldn't help noticing how round-shouldered he was. She observed posture, her own having been ruthlessly shaped by her mother, who viewed her failure to "throw those shoulders back" as a sin almost as grave as failing to "keep those knees together" in the presence of boys who, as her mother constantly reminded her, were bent on separating them. Since high school, Anne had equated slouching with sex, and she rarely engaged in either.

"You know, Anne, I'm beginning to feel my age. Sometimes I find myself longing for the leisurely pace of the '70's, or even the '80's. Looking back, I can see how simple life was compared to what we deal with now."

Cass described a rather typical bureaucracy operating as a separate kingdom off the beltway. Most Congressmen had no idea who headed NIH or cared. A few patron saints on the Hill saw it got the funding needed; pretty tame stuff as politics went.

"You know what changed everything?" he asked, shifting his weight to the other foot, hands in his pockets. "AIDS. That's when all the political dog fights began. All of a sudden—it seemed like overnight—people began to care who ran the agency and the Institutes."

Anne unfolded her hands. "I've only been here eighteen months, but NIH is far more political than I thought it would be. I guess I was naive."

Cass shot her a rueful smile. "You weren't naive, just late. Ten years ago we were mostly science with a little politics thrown in and now we seem the reverse. After AIDS came the flap over fetal tissue research, which of course threw us into the middle of the abortion wars. It's been one thing after another. Now it's genetic engineering."

"It's such a shame," she lamented. "Politics is so . . . so ugly."

"Precisely why I've promoted you, Anne. We need more people like you who'll put science first." At the reference to her progress since coming to NIH, she smiled inwardly. For someone professing to be apolitical, she was climbing the bureaucratic ladder at record pace, thanks in large measure to Cass. "Who knows? Perhaps one day you'll be in my position, having to deal with all the politically correct administrators the Congress has taken to sending over here. If that happens, you'll have my sympathy."

Dr. Cass returned to his desk, where he leaned back in his chair philosophically. "Anne, where do you suppose Senator Harmon is going with this REA business? I guess you read in the *Post* this morning that he thinks he has the votes to pass it. At the mention of Harmon's name, Anne's face flushed noticeably. "Is it too warm in here?"

"A little, yes. I'll be fine. I think I have a touch of something."

"Well, as I was saying, the Harmons of this world have to realize they can't turn back the clock. DNA research is a fact of life and to think they can slow it down is just crazy. It will result in a massive exodus of scientists to Europe and Asia and why they don't see it is beyond me."

"So why are they doing it?" asked Anne, hoping to steer the conversation away from Harmon.

"Because neither the pro-life nor pro-choice folks will give up. I don't think about abortion much, in that I'll be sixty in July and have certainly fathered all the children I'll ever father. But I do think about DNA research, and this crazy bill hits me right where I live on that one. Why are people so afraid of research?" he continued rhetorically. "Look at the progress we've made. Do you remember cystic fibrosis? Probably not, but it used to do a lot of damage before the defective gene was discovered. The last statistics I saw on it showed there were maybe twenty-five cases of it reported in the entire country last year. All due to DNA. You can go right down the list . . . Alzheimer's, SIDs, Tay-Sacks, and on; all reduced or eliminated."

"Still, there are a lot of unknowns," offered Anne meekly. "I suppose a lot of people are never really affected by those diseases anyway, but they might be impacted by some of the more experimental research." With her ankles crossed and swaying slightly under her chair, she more resembled a child in a backyard swing than the very bright scientist she was.

"You mean the behavioral stuff. Sure, there are unknowns. That's why we need research." He paused for a moment. "One thing's certain. If that bill passes, I'll be on the retirement list before the ink is dry on the president's signature."

"Will you really retire?"

"I'll quit because they'll throw me out anyway. There is no way Harmon and his crowd are going to leave me in charge of this department. My views are well known and my opinions, I'm proud to say, are universally disliked by those people. I'll go out on my own terms."

"I'd be sorry to see you go."

He smiled the affectionate smile of a grandfather. "Why, thank you. I'd be sorry to leave. I've had a most rewarding career here and it has been a real pleasure working with a young lady with such a bright future in this field."

"Thank you, Dr. Cass," she said with the hint of another blush. "I've been so happy here I'd hate to think of anything happening that would change it."

As Anne walked down the corridor toward her office, Dr. Cass congratulated himself on the wisdom he had shown in advancing her career. He marveled at her willingness to work; she was invariably there when he arrived early in the morning and still there when he left. Weekends, too. A single woman as young as Anne should have some social life, he thought, but who was he to reorder her priorities. She seemed fulfilled by her work.

Anne genuinely liked Dr. Cass, but her debt was to Martin Harmon. Her future was with him as well, and she reminded herself again that her call to him that morning had been the right thing to do, regardless of the risk. And if, as she expected, he became vice president, then her future at NIH could surpass anything even Cass envisioned.

Chapter 4

Twenty miles from NIH, the president of the United States was having a bad day, again. In what must have appeared an endless string of bad days, his chief of staff, Nancy Allenby, publicly acknowledged that the country was experiencing "some turbulence," as if the dying economy was a New York to L.A. plane ride. Republican leaders in the Congress, anxious to support their president, characterized it as "a down cycle" in diminishing hope that the upswing was close at hand. Democrats called it further evidence that the U.S. economy was headed for oblivion.

Historically, most presidents have enjoyed their job. This president, in the beginning, had been no different. He would whistle down the corridors leading from the family quarters of the White House to the Oval Office, pausing to wink at a portrait of one of his predecessors. Such communes with bygone leaders charged his batteries, sending him into his hectic work schedule with the energy of a man half his age.

That was in the beginning. As it turned out, even he had underestimated the burdens despite spending a lifetime preparing for this job and personally serving a number of men whose portraits he passed daily. The confidence instilled by his dramatic upset victory in the 1996 election dissipated quickly after his inauguration. By now, three years into his term, the president was far more apt to walk the passage to his office looking neither right nor left, ignoring people as well as portraits.

The nation he presided over faced financial problems of numbing severity. The fundamental causes were as well known as the governmental impotence which confronted them. One such cause was the flight of capital from the United States. It had begun with the Japanese, whose incredible growth after 1970 attracted gigantic amounts of the world's available capital. In 1990, when the economic bankruptcy of communism had been laid bare before the world, various governments seeking a better standard of living had little trouble reaching the proper conclusion. Given a choice between an East Berlin or a Tokyo; a Bucharest or a Seoul, even governments not known for foresight and gone by the next monsoon season got the right answer. Countries such as India, Indonesia, China and the Philippines became committed to the capitalist model, and this commitment survived the countless political intrigues which plagued these and all governments. Expansions in these emerging economies likewise required huge financial resources.

Exacerbating the problem of capital flight was the U.S. debt, trillions of dollars past any meaningful reckoning. Deficit piled upon deficit brought the arrival of the "mortgaged future," which everyone had predicted and no one could avert.

On this day, the president held a meeting with Republican Congressional leaders, the official purpose of which was to find a successful legislative strategy for getting his economic reforms passed in the House and Senate.

The president said, "We've put an awful lot of time and energy into this package. Give me your candid assessment of our chances."

Florence Rogers, Minority Whip in the House, spoke up. "Mr. President, I've spent the last month canvassing our people on it. The votes just aren't there. As always, we need too many Democrats to make it fly, and election politics have already begun. They're not about to cooperate."

"Then we'll just have to make a campaign issue out of their stonewalling. The Democratic candidate will have to take some heat on this too."

"Do you think they'll nominate Bonner?" Rogers asked.

"I don't have the slightest doubt of it. All my sources tell me he won't even have serious opposition. Unfortunately for us, they may have finally learned that they don't have the money or the candidates to keep chewing them up in the primaries. And folks, for what it's worth, I'll have one hell of a time beating Bonner. And I won't beat him unless we get this economy turned around, so let's get back to business."

They discussed alternatives, but to the mounting frustration of the president, the verdict did not change: "it can't be done," "we don't have the votes," "that dog won't hunt." Two hours later, the doors to the Oval Office flew open and the president emerged, a grim set to his jaw. He walked briskly toward the hallway leading to his private quarters. As he turned a corner leading to the White House elevator, he came face to face with the portrait of the beaming countenance of fellow Texan LBJ.

"Oh, shut up Lyndon!" the president muttered as he passed.

* * *

His Excellency the Governor of Illinois, Justin Alexander Bonner, paced, a sure sign that his mind was in overdrive. Occasionally, as an insight or rumination coalesced, he paused abruptly on his path by the floor-to-ceiling window which separated this large conference room from the smog above Chicago's Loop. Bonner radiated optimism, the upturned corners of his mouth giving his open, friendly face a built-in smile. He could be tough as iron when crossed, and then the mouth went flat and the jaw protruded and the offending party found nothing whatsoever friendly or optimistic about him. But today, he was his gregarious self, optimistic that in eighteen months he would be elected President of the United States.

Seated at the elliptical mahogany table was his attorney, friend and advisor of long standing, Matthew R. Morgan, Esq. Morgan studied ceilings. He could study a ceiling as abstractly, as reflectively, as philosophically as any lawyer in Chicago. He tended to lean back in chairs, thereby reducing the strain on his neck produced by long periods of vertical contemplation. Independently wealthy, he vacationed as much as he worked, and his leisure supplied the perpetual, deep bronze tan he wore like a name tag. Governor Bonner was his only client, and had been since Bonner's first race for mayor of Chicago, when Morgan served as finance chairman. Morgan's law firm tolerated his sporadic productivity: if a partner was going to restrict himself to one client, the governor of the state was the one to have.

Russell Carrington sat opposite Morgan in the law firm's conference room, staring at the polling results spread before him. Carrington's bull neck made him hard to fit for shirts and hard to beat in a street fight like Illinois politics. He grew up in the projects, flirted with jail, then joined the Marines, where every single military instinct in him sprang to life. An inexplicable pattern of vertigo had prompted a medical discharge, but his love for the Corps was undiminished. He had already dictated that Semper Fidelis be inscribed on his tombstone.

Bonner leaned on the judgment of both advisors. He could turn to Carrington, whose crew cut head seemed a blunt extension of that massive neck, for the kind of advice to be found on tables: polls, charts, graphs, memoranda, studies. Or he could turn to Morgan for the insights found on ceilings: the global picture of some problem whose solution required the foresight of a stargazer. Each man would play critical roles in a Bonner administration, but first he had to get elected.

"So, Russ," called Bonner from the far end of the room, "what's the latest from our illustrious Democratic National Committee? Is Pearson going to make a run for the nomination or not?"

"My sources say no. He doesn't think he can raise the dough. Also, his wife's surgery did not go well and he wants to be available if she gets worse. They don't think he'll go for it."

"So we still have the field to ourselves," observed Bonner. "Amazing but evidently true."

"Yep. It's a nice spot to be in. We better not fuck it up. What about the v.p.?"

"Yes, let's talk about that. After all, that's why we're here. Matt, what are your thoughts?"

Morgan's head inclined upward. "I have two thoughts. First, we need to pick the man or woman who will help the ticket in the south. Second, we need to designate him or her early so there are no surprises. Even though the convention is still a year away, the sooner the better."

"No argument there," replied Justin. "Russ, let's go over the list."

"The short list stands at five. Howard Smith's polling was an eye opener. I've got the results here if you want to see them, but the bottom line is easy to read. Claudia Raines got the best overall response, but Martin Harmon helps us the most where we need it."

"Where does Allen Sutcliffe come out?" inquired Bonner.

"Right behind Harmon. His numbers are almost as good, but like Claudia he's no help where it counts most."

The three men absorbed this information in silence; Carrington looking down, Morgan looking up, and Bonner looking out at the lake.

Morgan spoke next. "What's your feeling, Governor? I know how close you and Allen are. You think he would make a good vice president?"

Bonner nodded. "I do. He's an old friend, it's true, and I'm trying to keep that fact from coloring my judgment. I just happen to think Allen would make a fine v.p."

"What about Harmon?"

"A good man. All my dealings with him have been very pleasant. He was a great help on that Great Lakes legislation a few years back. He's well thought of, bright, energetic. His politics are to the right of mine on most issues, but he wouldn't be doing so well in the South if they weren't."

Morgan chuckled.

Carrington spoke next. "I'll be real frank with you on this, Justin. I know when all is said and done it's your call, but I think Harmon's our logical choice."

"I think you're selling Allen short. He has twenty-four years in the Senate. He knows government inside and out. And we will need help on the West Coast, too."

"All true," injected Morgan, "but we can't beat an incumbent president without getting some southern states. We've got to have a few. We don't have to have Oregon. Secondly, Harmon's hot. This genetics bill he's spearheading is on the front page every other day. With all due respect to Allen, who's a great guy, he's not terribly controversial."

"Matt is being diplomatic," said Carrington, fingering the edges of a report in front of him. "Allen is boring, politically speaking."

Bonner, who had resumed pacing, threw his next comment over his shoulder. "I can't believe Harmon's going to sell the Senate that bill."

"Don't be too sure. He says he has the votes."

"I know what he says. I still don't believe it."

Morgan spoke. "You have to give him credit, Governor. He has worked like a dog on that coalition."

"I give him full credit, but he'll come up short. Allen tells me there will be defections and I trust Allen when it comes to counting noses in the Senate."

"Well, if Allen is right, Harmon may go back to being a Joe Schmoe senator. But if the REA passes, he may stay hot, which could help us at the polls. You should think about it, Justin. It could make or break us in a tight race."

"I have thought about it," declared Bonner, "and I think Allen Sutcliffe will make a fine vice president."

"Have you approached Allen?"

"No. I won't do that until I'm sure."

"When will that be?"

"Not today, and probably not until after the REA vote. I haven't closed my mind to Harmon. If he can ram that bill through, I may reconsider. But right now, Allen's my man."

Chapter 5

"You mean you've settled in?" Carson asked when she returned to her apartment late that afternoon, the phone ringing as she entered.

"Into a hornet's nest," Martin said. "It's been a wild one around here. How's your day been?"

"Great, actually. That consulting contract I have with the Hooper Institute? I've spent days looking for some old financial data and today I hit the jackpot at the library. I just might meet my deadline."

"Great. Listen, I forgot to mention I have a speech in Memphis tonight so I won't be up. I'm bolting for the airport in twenty minutes. I need to talk with Jean so I'm going to fly to Roanoke from Memphis. I should be back by Sunday afternoon. Do you have plans this weekend?"

"As a matter of fact, I'm going to Kathy's on Saturday. I owe her a visit and I want to see the kids. I'll put up in the guest room and come back Sunday."

"Great. See you then. Give Kathy my best . . . love you . . . gotta run . . . bye."

Within an hour, Martin was at thirty-five thousand feet heading west toward Memphis. His mind wandered to the morning's phone call from Anne. She had shown loyalty by calling, but had she also put him on the spot by divulging confidential information? In his position, he had to be careful, even when the extent of his sin was listening to an unsolicited call.

He lowered the tray table, intending to make some notes for his speech, but found it hard to concentrate. From his window he saw in the great distance dark clouds of a storm front massing, and it occurred to him that his future was not unlike this trip to Memphis; he flew now in calm, clear weather while ominous turbulence lay close at hand. But the pilot would guide the plane around the storm whereas he, Martin, seemed determine to ride this foolish affair into the very teeth of danger. He should know better, he told himself daily. He reminded himself of the hazards, the probability of exposure, the stakes for both his career in Washington and his family in Roanoke. He repeated it all like a mantra, hoping some combination of self-interest and indwelling guilt would correct his drift. But nothing changed. He wasn't listening to himself anymore.

Had he sensed it from the start? No, he didn't see a threat, only a pretty woman walking toward him at a reception given by the National Association of Manufacturers for its new executive director. She had stopped, extended her hand, and said, "Senator, I'm Carson Cox. I know your reputation but we've never met."

He took her hand, at first by rote as though it were another anonymous offering in a receiving line or from the crowd along Harkins Street in Roanoke during the Fourth of July parade. Then he smiled, his grip firming.

"And what is my reputation, or should I ask?"

"Quite good," she said easily, maintaining the clasp and smiling back.

"Really? My children say I'm no fun." He released her hand.

"I meant at your job . . . quite good at what you do. I can't say I've ever heard your reputation for fun discussed."

"Because I have none. The kids are right."

"No fun or no reputation?"

"Neither," he laughed. "In this town one quickly follows the other. And you, Ms. Cox, what do you do for fun?"

"Tennis, and sailing every chance I get."

"I haven't sailed in years," he said wistfully.

"Then you should follow Melville's lead: 'Quietly take to the ship.' I'll invite you some time if you're interested. We're just coming into the season."

To such overtures, from time to time made by friends and colleagues, Martin served up a pat response, pleading workload. So ingrained was this reaction that he had come to decline automatically, without weighing the merits of invitations. But not that day. The healthy young woman before him, quoting Melville and gently needling him about his image, fit precisely into his memory of sailing, a memory he treasured.

Camp Seagull on the Chesapeake Bay had employed him for two summers as a counselor. There, he taught camping and hiking to pre-teens, drawing on his years of scouting and his love of the wooded Roanoke hills. He arrived at Seagull convinced that he had almost served youth's indenture and that he had taken from that time the lessons needed for life. From two Baptist parents he had learned that God controlled his life and would bless him for as long as he obeyed ten rules; from his paper route he learned that some people paid promptly, a few not at all, but they all wanted their papers early and on the porch when it rained; from school he knew that he did best when he studied hardest and that boy friends were easier to meet and keep than girl friends; from sports he learned that winners gave parties and losers gave explanations.

He spent hours in the woods near his home. On fallen pine needles along the paths he could walk for a quarter of a mile without making a sound. The air was fresh and suffused with the antiseptic aroma of pine, and the sterility of sound and smell somehow accorded his observations on human behavior. Life was really very simple, and he resolved to do well at it.

Camp Seagull gave him his first extended absence from Roanoke. When his official day ended, he joined other counselors for late afternoon or evening cruises south toward Old Point Comfort or north as far as the Rappahannock. In the process, he learned to sail.

And, he met Marci Hall, a tawny wisp of blonde loveliness in the way only sixteen-year-old girls can be lovely. Her rich tan, like butter just beginning to brown, accented Caribbean-blue eyes. Round, full breasts virtually exploded from last year's top, and Martin caught himself staring at them whenever she wasn't looking and always when she raised herself from the water after a swim, for then the nipples stood out as though there were no top at all and Martin would feel aches within and a longing all mixed up with the awe he felt around her. By the middle of the second summer, with Marci then seventeen and Martin a virginal Eagle Scout one year younger, he could think of nothing but her, that buttered body, her white teeth behind the go-to-hell smile and those perfect tuminescent nipples. Nothing he had learned in Roanoke prepared him for Marci Hall.

They sailed up the bay, usually with a crew of four or five and a firm breeze out of the southwest. But three times that summer Martin and Marci went alone. They took turns at the tiller. Spray broke over the bow onto his face and lips and the taste of the Chesapeake mingled with the sunlight and together they seduced him out of his adolescence. Until those afternoons with Marci, he did not know that the briny hint of oysters in the spray carried with it the salty essence of the world he was about to enter. Marci danced lightly on the deck as she moved to adjust the jib. He watched her crouch low to avoid the boom as they came to, her breasts seeming to offer themselves as pressure against her knees thrust them toward him. He discreetly adjusted himself inside his shorts. Their tack completed, Marci sprang forward toward the hatch, turning toward him the rounded buttocks that seemed both muscled and infinitely soft while the horizontal line of her suit rode down to expose the beginning of that cleft leading toward things he had only imagined. The unspeakable excitement of wanting her and fearing her merged with the spray and the sun and the briny taste of oysters and he knew they were one and the same and that manhood would hold not only the duties and responsibilities for which he had prepared but also the salty terror of forces against which he felt powerless and short of breath.

"Let's anchor," Marci suggested. "I feel like a swim."

He tacked toward a cove and lowered the sail, allowing the boat to drift. Turning aft, he reached into a storage hatch, retrieved the anchor, tossed it over, held the line to feel it bite, and turned toward the bow in time to see Marci, naked, dive overboard. Moments later she surfaced, laughing and pushing the hair from her eyes, her teeth gleaming white in the sunlight.

"Come on in," she urged. "No jellyfish."

He dove over the side, hunching noticeably. In the water, he surprised himself by shedding his shorts, careful to hold them and intending to toss them into the boat. But Marci took three or four strong strokes at him and, panicking, he dropped them.

She stopped in front of him, treading water. "You look nervous. Haven't you ever been skinny dipping?"

"Sure," he said, and of course he had—with boys. He sensed that his voice was an octave too high.

"You are naked, aren't you? I love swimming naked."

"I'm naked," he said, hoping to hell he sounded husky and bored.

She laughed, splashed water at him, and sculled backward a couple of body lengths. "If you catch me you can have me," she said playfully.

He swam after her with every atom of strength and determination within him, as he had been swimming since. Now his seductress was high office, and he was poised to capture it as he had captured Marci that afternoon in the Chesapeake. In the clutter of thirty-something years, memories of those cruises had long since faded and curled at the edges. He remembered sailing back to camp with Marci teasing him about the loss of his shorts, but he no longer recalled how he had compensated when they reached the dock, nor what they said to each other that night or any other night, nor why he never saw her again.

Martin shifted in his seat as the pilot announced their descent into Memphis. Yes, it must have been the sailing. With his life all business and the most serious kind of business, there had stood this young woman named Carson, lingering in her handshake for just an instant more than necessary and quoting Melville and asking him to go sailing.

"Yes," he heard himself reply, "I would love to go."

They went, but after their relationship had begun, and only after a series of chance encounters both realized were not chance at all but the product of hints about their respective schedules lobbed during a prior encounter. By then, he certainly knew the danger. He heard the thunder, saw zig-zag lightning, sensed the precipitous barometric drop that confirmed the storm into which he was headed.

Yet only once did he attempt to veer. On the night she called to invite him over for drinks, he insisted on checking his schedule and calling back. During that hour, a very sober hour, he catalogued all he risked by accepting, having no illusions about where drinks would likely lead. There was much to lose, including his loneliness.

With his wife unalterably rooted in Roanoke, Martin had been forced to develop, from his earliest days as a senator, a formula for avoiding the pitfalls inherent in being an attractive, powerful man but essentially alone. Its elements were exhausting work, long hours, and vigilant circumspection in situations likely to lead to compromise. It had been that circumspection which had led, over the years, to the rote rejection of social invitations not related to his work.

And it worked. His fidelity to Jean had been total, although whether from conviction or habit he could not say until Carson came along, and even then the source of his monastic discipline blurred. Much of it stemmed from his essential honesty, the guileless Eagle Scout who did not drown with Marci in the Bay but merely baptized himself. Vows tested character, and vows made twenty-eight years before no less so. He could not bear the thought of letting anyone down, particularly in a commitment as solemn as marriage, where a bargain was kept or it wasn't.

Or, did it have less to do with noble character and more to do with the cold realities of reaching for national office? He had seen colleagues fall from high perches for peccadilloes with women they couldn't name after a few drinks. Perhaps ambition explained his dogged determination to stay above the temptations to which Washington exposed senators on a routine basis and for which the penance exacted by voters could be harsh.

At the end of his very sober hour he had called her back. By the time he showered and shaved, it no longer mattered whether his idealism or his pragmatism died in the interval. He was going because he was going, because he was lonely, and because he liked Carson. Very much.

The plane touched down. A welcoming delegation whisked him from the airport to the downtown Hilton, saturated with the badges, hats and hoopla of the American Legion convention he was to address. His host, a very fat Legionnaire named Mahoney, warned him that expectations for his speech were high.

"The place is buzzing, Senator, so lay it on us good and thick. The boys will respond. You speak anything like Ron Reagan?"

"No," said Martin with a grin, "I'm no Ron Reagan."

"Well, that's too bad. I suppose they told you I'm going to introduce you. Do you mind if I mention those rumors about you running for vice president? I figure it'll spice up my opening; you know, make it sound like you're real important."

"You handle it any way you see fit. Those rumors are circulating, so I can't deny them."

"Then you're going to run?"

"Whoa! I didn't say that. I merely admitted that there are rumors. I'm hardly the only one being mentioned."

"Why don't you announce tonight, Senator? Get a jump on the others. If you did that, I might find myself on national TV. Hell, they might elect me president of this outfit."

"I wouldn't do that to you, Mr. Mahoney," said Martin with a wink.

Martin's speech began in his practiced, low-key manner. From the audience, restless and distracted, a low but persistent undercurrent surged toward the podium. But he built momentum, and soon a noticeable concentration gripped the crowd. He spoke of his concerns for a government no longer serving the citizens who depended upon it; of a political process aligned against the very people most in need of a friend. For twenty minutes he laid the groundwork, sensing a building collective focus in his audience, and when he had brought them to rapt attention, the point at which they were with him mind and heart and could feel a patriotic surge welling up inside, only then did he thunder home his message with a force which daily drove him closer to national prominence.

"I come before you today with a warning of yet another threat to our freedom and the American way of life. I speak of biomedical engineering. Medical research has done wondrous things in this world and I'm proud to say that Americans have been for decades in the forefront of that research. We are why most of the world lives free of the threats of yellow fever, polio, and a host of other terrible diseases. Key to this progress has been our increasing knowledge of human biology. As that knowledge accelerates, as it surely will, profound ethical and legal questions will arise.

"Consider the tip of this iceberg as represented by in vitro fertilization, a practice developed in the 80's. When this technology first appeared, the assumption was that it would give barren couples the chance to produce biological offspring, and so it has. But along with this intended benefit have come surrogate parentage among related parties, surrogate parentage among unrelated parties, custody battles among people related only by contract, surrogates for profit, custody battles over embryos, over sperm, over eggs and most recently over genes themselves.

"I am sure you have all read the recent story of the homosexual couple in Seattle who is now raising a 'customized' infant the media has nicknamed 'Petri.' Petri was created—I say created because the word 'conceived' hardly seems applicable—from sperm selected by the couple and purchased from a celebrity in need of money. Because that celebrity was also homosexual and the couple preferred a heterosexual, a gene splice was performed before the sperm was mated with an egg purchased on the black market. This couple then paid a surrogate mother to carry the fertilized egg to term and produced a healthy, genetically customized child related by blood not remotely to any party to the transaction. Thus what started with the best intentions and which has admittedly produced biological children for barren couples has spawned complications beyond the imagination of those who began it.

"This is but one example of the problems we can expect to confront as research multiplies geometrically. The point is that science is doing what science wants to do and what science can do, often without forethought by science or anyone else as to whether any of this is in society's best interest.

"The REA will put a stop to the headlong plunge into this technological genetic abyss. It will stop us from unleashing forces which, like surrogacy, can quickly spread beyond society's control. The bill prohibits government-funded research on human tissue unless such research is for the demonstrated advancement of the fight against disease and birth defects. Projects which promise the eradication of disease, the cleanup of the environment and the efficient production of food and water, will find a receptive ear. But I can promise you that genetic engineering projects which seek to alter and in many cases counteract God's plan for man on this planet will find reason prevailing over scientific thirst for knowledge for the sake of knowledge. Those projects will not be approved. Heavy criminal fines and sentences await those conducting unapproved research with taxpayer dollars. We are going to shut the lid tight on this Pandora's Box, and you can take that to the bank."

Deafening applause greeted this last pronouncement. In summation, Martin said, "We had better wake up to the crisis we face. None of the problems I have outlined for you tonight—not prayer in school, not abortion, not crime, not surrogacy and not genetic research—taken alone, will sink us, but the combined weight of all of these confronted by a government which is no longer our friend, will do just that. We can, as a people, no longer protect ourselves from ourselves, and the government which we have set up to do it apparently can't either.

"But I remain hopeful. We cannot give up. The REA is but one step in turning our government from an enemy into a friend again, but it is an important step. I urge your support for it and that you let that support be known in Washington. Thank you."

Martin turned from the podium in time to see Mahoney rushing toward him, grabbing his hand and pumped it wildly as he yelled, over the roar of applause, "Hell Senator, you're better than Ron Reagan! Sign me up." The foot—stomping ovation below confirmed Martin Harmon as a political juggernaut.

Chapter 6

On Saturday morning, Carson swung her late model convertible onto I-70 for the forty-five minute trip to Frederick, Maryland. Traffic was light for a change.

As she pulled into Kathy's spacious driveway, Timothy, Kathy's youngest child, came bounding out.

"Aunt Carson! Aunt Carson! Come see my new rabbit." Tim grabbed her hand, pulling her along the walkway leading to the house with all his five year old might.

Carson laughed as she breezed by Kathy, who emerged from the kitchen just in time to glimpse her being dragged toward the back door. "Hi, Sis!" Carson called over her shoulder. "I'm on rabbit watch. See you in a few."

"Tim, that is just about the nicest rabbit I've seen," said Carson when Tim had finally come to a stop in front of the hutch in the back yard.

"His name is George cause he's a boy," said Tim. "But I would call him Carson if he was a girl, but he's a boy."

"That's very thoughtful of you, Tim. I'm thinking of getting a dog and if I do and if he's a boy, I'm going to name him Tim."

Tim turned to run after a playmate who had just entered the yard, giving Carson a moment to survey the area. It never failed to prompt nostalgia for her own back yard growing up. Her Dad had spent his entire vacation one summer constructing a set of swings and slides for his children, who had spent countless hours on them, in them, and under them. Kathy's jungle set was manufactured but it still provided that focus for childhood energy that Carson remembered so fondly.

She left her spot at the hutch and sought out the other children. She found Andrea, Mark, and Jason, smothering each with kisses and ignoring the protest of the twin boys who were entering the age at which being kissed by their aunt, even Aunt Carson whom they thought of as "ok," was not high on their list of favorite things. Cindy was at cheerleading tryouts, so her greeting would have to wait.

Carson walked into the house to greet Kathy more leisurely. "You look wonderful," Kathy said as they embraced. Following a custom that went back to high school with them, each rested her chin on the other's shoulder for a few seconds before unclasping their hands.

"And so do you," Carson said. "Have you ever known a relative to come without saying 'the kids have grown so much!' Well Sis, the kids have grown so much!"

They laughed as Kathy launched into a good natured diatribe on the cost of clothing children. "And food!" she said. "Those twins can eat their weight in pizza and be hungry in an hour."

"Frog had to go to his office to answer some correspondence which piled up during his stay in Denver, but he promised he would be home by 1:00," said Kathy as they re-entered the kitchen. "Frog" was Kathy's nickname for Bill, acquired during their dating days at college. When Frog arrived, only thirty minutes after his promised deadline, he took over the parenting while Kathy and Carson spent the afternoon shopping. They returned in time to sit down to a family dinner catered by the local Chinese food carryout.

Kathy began the meal with a prayer, followed by a command for a "best manners alert." The children stiffened slightly, as if being graded, careful to place napkins on their laps, hold flatware properly, and keep their elbows in. Carson restrained a grin until Jason asked if he could please throw an eggroll at Tim. She asked lots of questions, many of which were answered by two or three children simultaneously. She had a knack for meeting children on their level; of making each feel as though her full attention was focused on that child, and they responded accordingly.

After dinner, as Kathy supervised the younger children getting ready for bed, Carson took a walk with Cindy, whom she had hardly seen since her arrival. Her selection that morning as a JV cheerleader for the Fighting Falcons of Conover Junior High put her in an ebullient mood. Cindy was a vivacious, outgoing girl whose accounts of boyfriends and social jealousies brought back bittersweet memories of the awkward years which fourteen year old girls go through.

It was nearly 10:00 p.m. when Kathy and Carson adjourned to the den with a couple of glasses and a chilled bottle of chardonnay.

"Cheers," they said as they sank deep into overstuffed armchairs. "So talk to me." Kathy laughed. "You know . . . real talk. The good stuff. And don't skip over your sex life."

"Well, you certainly eased us into this discussion, didn't you? As I said on the phone, I'm getting pretty tense. Love on the sly is not something that I ever pictured for myself. It's bound to get out sooner or later and when it does it will make quite a splash."

"Are you thinking of calling it off?" asked Kathy.

"I'm not thinking." Carson raised her hand slightly before letting it fall limply, impotently into her lap. "I guess because I'm so unsure about how I ever got in this, I'm just as unsure how to get out."

"What's he like, Carson? All I know I've gotten from the papers and a few magazines articles. Plus what you've said, which hasn't been much."

"I haven't meant to be secretive—"

"I didn't mean you have," interrupted Kathy. "I just meant we haven't had many real chances to discuss it and the phone doesn't work very well for this sort of thing."

"Part of it is just not knowing what to say. I mean, here I am, lover to a man eighteen years my senior who may end up as vice president of the entire country and who is definitely married to a wife named Jean and definitely has three grown children. It doesn't make any sense on paper."

"So what's paper?" asked Kathy, her eyebrows arching. "Life isn't paper and neither are relationships. This man obviously brings you pleasure and sometimes that's enough, isn't it?"

"Yes," said Carson, lowering her voice and her gaze, "sometimes it is. You know, Sis, something in me died after Richard. Maybe died isn't the right word, because I don't feel dead or even depressed. It's just that after Richard and I broke it off, I had to readjust all my thinking, all the goals I had set since I was Cindy's age."

Silence fell over them. Richard was a painful topic even five years later. Carson had met him while working for the House Ways and Means Committee. Their mutual interest had been immediate. As Shelly Connors, Carson's best friend at the time, had put it after seeing them at lunch together the day after they met, "Bingo." Richard, an attorney just hired onto the staff of a California Congresswoman, was, according to Shelly and an equally envious pool of committee women, "a definite hunk." Carson, while not unmindful of his physical attractiveness, found him warm, loving, and funny.

She was then twenty-nine and had dated almost constantly since coming to Washington. She thought she had been in love once before but grew bored and broke it off. She knew she would find the right person eventually, and when she did she would set about to build for herself and her husband a life very much like the one which Kathy and Frog enjoyed, and which she had cherished as a child: a warm, loving family with the controlled chaos created by a house full of children. There was, she knew, a wrinkle in the part about the children, for as much as she loved them she could not bear them because of her one, hopelessly damaged ovary. But the prospect of an international adoption particularly interested her. She had done some part time volunteer work for an international adoption agency in Crystal City and knew the process from A to Z. She knew the countries which would be her top three choices.

Her relationship with Richard, intense from the beginning, deepened each day. In three months, she moved in. As AIDs was still a threat at that time, they discussed sex and birth control. Carson chose not to tell Richard about her sterility right away. She rather told him she was on the pill. She viewed this as a modest deception which could be forgiven under the circumstances. She knew that pregnancy was no threat; in fact, far less than her representation. Also, she was reluctant to disclose what she considered very personal information to a man who might or might not become her husband. If their trial period worked out, there would be ample time for full disclosure. She was sure he would forgive her fib and appreciate her reasons for protecting her privacy.

After an intimate dinner at Alex, a posh Washington restaurant, he had shocked her with a diamond and proposal. Although she would have preferred more time she said "yes." She said it unhesitatingly; a confident, heartfelt "yes." She loved him and was ready to begin the rest of her life with him.

In the days following their engagement, it dawned on her that she still had not told Richard about her medical condition. She looked for an appropriate opportunity to raise the matter, finding it one evening after a particularly succulent bottle of cabernet. In a tender, straight-forward declaration she confided her sterility, asked his forgiveness for the ruse regarding the pill and explained to him her reasons for protecting her privacy. She had planned to tell him but his proposal took her by surprise and now that they were engaged, he certainly needed to realize that she would not be able to bear his biological children. She hoped with all her heart it wouldn't matter to him.

Richard cast a distracted stare into the distance for a very long time. When he cast it back toward her, she knew before he spoke that something had changed. She panicked, repeating all of her assurances, her apologies, her love for him.

It was not the deception, she later concluded. He had understood that. It was the children. "I don't think I can handle adoption," he said. "I could be happy with you if we had biological children or no children, but I don't think I can handle adoption." Distraught, she pressed. He wouldn't say why, and never did. A week later she moved out. Richard took a job on the West Coast.

Kathy lifted the wine bottle from the end table and refilled Carson's glass. Carson did not appear to notice. "Do you ever hear from Richard?" asked Kathy.

"No . . . no, I don't," Carson replied distantly. "We exchanged Christmas cards for the first year or two; since then nothing. A guy I know on the Hill said he heard he moved to San Diego." Her eyes darted back to Kathy's. "Martin is a complex man. He takes his work very seriously and he loves the Senate. I guess he has as much ambition for higher office as anyone else in the Senate. He says national office is out of his control."

"What does he mean by that? Whose control is it in?"

"His theory is that you put yourself in the position to get there, but that is about the best you can do. After that, it's a matter of breaks and world events beyond your control. If you get a break or two, or latch on to the right issue at just the right time, you can make it all the way. Otherwise, you're just another politician. Fortunately for him, he likes where he is and what he's doing. I don't think he will shatter if he doesn't go higher.

"For a serious man, he has a warm side. We have a lot of common interests but of course we don't always get to pursue them together in Washington. We take weekends to some very out of the way spots, which is pretty safe unless we run into someone we know, which thank God has never happened. I think he loves me. I know I lighten him up and he knows he needs that. And I think he appreciates the fact that I don't pressure him. He gets enough of that from home."

Kathy took a long sip on her wine. "What does he do for you?"

Carson thought for a moment. "The usual things you would expect in a relationship. Companionship, but not too much companionship. He's gone a lot which gives me the time for my work. My consulting is going well and I love the fact that I can put it down for a few days and then pick it back up as long as I'm conscious of my deadlines. Sex of course. No money. I pay my own expenses. Mostly, he puts me in the middle of things, even though somewhat vicariously. You know, I've loved the excitement, the electricity of D.C. since the day I arrived. Getting the straight dope on what goes on in the Senate is a rush."

"Do you love him?"

Carson paused again, then said very deliberately as if measuring every syllable, "I could love him if all the hurdles were out of the way."

"By 'all the hurdles' you mean his wife?"

"Well, yes, I guess you'd have to call her a hurdle, wouldn't you?"

"I sure would," said Kathy with conviction. "What's she like?"

"I've never met her. She never comes to Washington and he rarely goes home; three or four times a year at most. He says she hates politics but otherwise he doesn't talk about her much, which is fine with me because sleeping with someone's husband is one thing and listening to all the problems of a marriage is another. That's the pits."

"Yes, but don't you have to know about them to know . . ." Kathy groped for words.

"Where I stand?" Carson asked.

"Yes."

"It's funny, Sis, but I don't worry about that. I'm living very much for the moment. If he wants to divorce his wife, I can't stop him but I don't want him to do it for me. If he does, I guess I'll have some decisions to make. But right now I don't. The risk is all his . . . he's the one with a career and a political future on the line. The most I risk is some potential embarrassment if it hits the papers."

"Aren't you worried about getting hurt?"

"I've been hurt. I can handle it."

"Just because you've been hurt and can handle it doesn't mean it's any fun."

"Of course it doesn't. It just means I'm not in over my head. I won't drown."

"Still, I worry about you," and then Kathy added, almost as an afterthought, "and Mom worries about you."

"In some ways that's the worst part. Mom doesn't call much. After Dad died she took over as 'the Great Protector' but she doesn't know how to deal with this. She's sure that condemning me is not the answer but she doesn't know what is the answer, so she keeps her distance. It could be worse. Some mothers would run to Washington every two weekends to save my soul or go the other way and wash their hands altogether. I wonder what I'd do if it were my daughter."

"I know what I'd do if it were mine," said Kathy with feigned conviction. "There's an excellent convent right here in Frederick and the nuns turn out some wonderful hand crafts." They laughed at the thought of Sister Carson.

"Wouldn't that simplify things!" Carson grinned. "There are days when you think you would trade everything for the peace of a small church on a weekday. You must have some like that."

"Do I ever," nodded Kathy. "Have you met his kids?"

"No. They rarely get to D.C. His daughter is a freshman at Hollins and his sons have graduated. The older son is in Atlanta with a law firm and the younger one is in computers in Richmond. He talks about them and they talk on the phone some. Apparently they're all pretty bright, hardworking kids. I have the impression they are closer to their mother, but I don't know that to be true. I often wonder if meeting them will be awkward when and if the chance arises. It shouldn't be; I'm hardly their contemporary. Still, I know myself well enough to know that if one of them looks at me sideways I'll burst into tears. Wouldn't that be mature of someone thirty-four years old. I keep putting myself in their place: 'Allie, Jack, Edward I'd like you to meet the woman I've been living with who is largely responsible for my current indecision regarding the continuation of my marriage to your mother.' 'Oh, Carson, so nice to meet you. Dad's told us nothing whatsoever about you but from the accounts in The New York Times we feel like we've known you all our lives.'"

Kathy howled with laughter, and Carson could not suppress a grin. "Oh, that's wonderful! But it would be nothing like that and you know it. You have a natural talent for putting people at ease and Martin's children would be no exception, even if the circumstances were strained."

"Just keep those confidence boosters coming, Sis. I need every one I can get. Now, if you'll just assure me I'm doing the right thing with this entirely crazy affair I will be forever grateful."

"You know I wouldn't try to make that judgment. But you have one of the most level heads of anyone I know and you'll do the right thing. I just don't want you hurt."

By 11:00, the wine had long since vanished and Frog had gone to bed. In the next room, a TV droned on to an audience of empty chairs.

The sisters said good night at the door of the guest room. Carson grasped Kathy's hands in her own and rested her chin on Kathy's shoulder. "You have no idea how much it means to me to be able to unload," she said in whispered relief. "Thanks so much for being here."

Early the following morning, Carson was awakened by the sudden awareness of a presence in her room. She opened her eyes to find Tim standing next to her bed, his sad face only a short distance from Carson's pillow. Big crocodile tears rolled down his cheeks. Carson bolted upright.

"Tim, what's wrong? Are you hurt?"

"It's George," said Tim.

"George?"

"George, my rabbit. He won't wake up. I went out to feed him and he was asleep so I shook his cage and he was still asleep so I poked him with a stick and he still wouldn't wake up. Can you come help me wake him up?"

"Let me get on a robe." Carson held Tim's hand as they made their way through the still dark house into the back yard. At the hutch, they found the motionless George, Tim's stick still pressed against its downy underside. Carson turned to Tim, kneeling to level her eyes with his.

"Tim, I'm so sorry. I'm afraid George is dead. That happens to animals sometimes. They look healthy but there is something wrong inside that we can't see. Don't blame yourself . . . there was nothing you or anyone else could have done for George. Sometimes these things just happen and we don't know why. You took wonderful care of him and gave him the best life he could have had while he was alive. Why, I'll bet he had the best, most fun life of any rabbit ever because he had you to take care of him."

"So you can't wake him up, Aunt Carson?"

"No Tim, I can't. No one can. George is dead. Get me a shovel and we'll find a nice spot where we can bury him."

Tim walked into the garage and returned with a hoe.

"No dear, I need a shovel. Let's go find one together."

They found a pleasant spot in a rear corner of the yard where Carson dug a shallow grave. She then went to the hutch, returning with George inside a plastic bag she had located in the garage.

Tim stared at the amorphous bag. "Goodbye, George" he said, seeming to comprehend the fact that George was about to be interred even if he had not yet assimilated the fact that George was not asleep. Then he turned to Carson and put his arms around her waist, burying his head in her side. Carson groped for words that would comfort a small boy who knew only enough to be dreadfully sad.

"Tim, nothing can take George's place, but I know a pet shop in Washington where they have some terrific rabbits. Perhaps you and I could go there and get one sometime. Would you like that?" She thought she detected a slight nod of the young head still pressed painfully against her robe.

Chapter 7

By the time Martin arrived at his home in Roanoke, he was ready for a short, stiff drink and a good night's sleep. The house was dark as he entered from the garage which comprised the western-most reach of his spacious, split level home. It was after 11:00 p.m.; he assumed Jean would be in bed. As he approached the library door, he saw a light and heard a voice, shrill and slightly slurred.

"Could that be the junior senator from Virginia, home to polish his image as a family man for, oh, twelve hours or so?"

Martin stopped, shaking his head slowly. Damn, he thought. Twenty-eight years of marriage had made him all too familiar with this tone. It was going to be a rough evening following a rough day. For a moment he considered turning on his heels and going straight to the bedroom upstairs. But when Jean had something on her mind, and when that something had been marinating in scotch, ignoring her was not an option. Besides, he wanted that drink, even at the price of Jean's verbal abuse. Recovering his stride, he entered the room, looking neither right nor left, his chin protruding.

At the bar he loaded a cocktail glass with ice and two inches of scotch. Without looking up he asked, "Why start? We've been down this road hundreds of times. So why start? What perverse thrill is there in ending up at the same dead end?"

"Speaking of perverse thrills, how is Washington?" she asked.

Martin raised his eyes to stare out the bay window which bordered the bar. The pitch-black Virginia night stared back at him, a reflection of the emptiness which crawled into him when he tried to make sense of this depressing ritual. After a time he turned to look at Jean slumped in a chair, her preferred position when drinking. Casually dressed in a faded blue blouse and dark slacks, she looked tired. For the first time, he could envision her as old, and the thought unsettled him.

"Notwithstanding your sarcasm, we do a lot of important work in Washington."

"Important to whom? Did I read somewhere that this was declared National Potato Month? Tell me, Senator, did you stand tall on that issue, shoulder to shoulder with those other patriots who believe in the need for recognizing the contribution which spuds make to this great land of ours?"

"By trivializing my work, you trivialize me. I know that game. But the fact remains that the country looks to the Senate for leadership on some important issues."

"Ninety percent of them couldn't follow a cow to pasture, much less lead one, present company excepted, of course."

"There are many capable people in the Senate," Martin replied with measured patience, one of his low-key responses that always drove Jean crazy. He took a long pull on his scotch and studied his wife. She sat near the fireplace, an arrangement of magnolia leaves where logs would have blazed in winter. Jean wore a certain slouch on nights committed to serious drinking, and with each succeeding drink her slump became more pronounced.

"What do you hear from the children?" asked Martin with an outside hope of changing the subject.

"Allie said she was coming home for the weekend but at the last minute she and her roommates got an invitation to spend the weekend at U.Va., so it was no contest. She called last night to tell me that she would slip by for a few hours on Sunday after they got back."

"How are her spirits?" asked Martin.

"Oh, what you would expect from Allie. Still wildly excited about the whole college experience, which I find remarkable. I mean, here she is as a freshman at a school thirty minutes away from home in a town she's lived in all her life and you'd think she was at the Sorbonne, for God's sake. I suppose a lot of her enthusiasm comes from being surrounded by new friends from all over the country. She loves her high school friends, but it was time for a change." Jean straightened slightly. "I'm sure she would have come home had she known you were coming."

"How did you know I was coming?"

"Dennis the Menace called this afternoon. He wants you to call him. He said it was important, of course, but would keep until tomorrow, of course."

"You really don't like him, do you?" Martin accused.

"Well, I don't despise him, but then I hardly know him. I'm sure that once I got to know him well, I would despise him."

"That's my girl. Often wrong but never in doubt."

"To that charge, my dear," said Jean, taking a long sip at her drink, "I freely plead guilty; at least to the part about seldom in doubt."

"I said 'never in doubt.'"

"Never, seldom, whatever. I can't help it, I'm just that way. I meet someone and I react to them. It's a reaction, my reaction. It's either instinctively positive or instinctively negative and once in a while distinctly neutral, but it's mine and it's a reaction. And you know I'm right most of the time. This guy Dennis is a goat jockey . . . he may be disguised in a coat and tie but he's still a goat jockey."

Martin chuckled in spite of himself. Jean could be vividly malicious.

"Jean, the man came highly recommended. He's a pro; by and large he's done a good job."

"Goat jockey," she said, with a knowing nod.

Through silence broken only by the gentle tinkle of ice cubes, Jean said, "Why did you come home this weekend?"

"To talk. It appears more likely that I will have to make some major decisions in the next few months; decisions I can't make alone. I need your thoughts if you'll share them with me."

"These decisions wouldn't have anything to do with your career by any chance, would they?"

"Of course, but I don't want to get into it tonight. We'll both be more up to it in the morning."

"By all means in the morning," replied Jean. "And perhaps while we are at it we can discuss my career or lack of one or my life or lack of one."

"Perhaps we should," said Martin with tired resignation. "Yes, let's discuss both. But Jean, surely you knew it would be an adjustment with Allie leaving. Don't all parents eventually face the day when the last child leaves the nest?"

Her eyes cut toward him and narrowed. "Only widows face it alone."

Martin looked away, then toward her, "It's been your choice to stay away from Washington, and Washington happens to be the only town on God's green earth where a U.S. Senator can do his job. I didn't make that rule but I have to live with it if I want to do this job. We've talked about this a thousand times and it always comes out the same . . . you prefer Roanoke to Washington."

"The kids were happy here and I was happy here, at least happier than we would have been there. But now they're gone and you're always gone so where am I?"

"Hasn't it gotten any easier since Allie left? I mean it has been eight or nine months."

"Harder. Of course I miss her terribly but I really have adjusted to her not being here. What I haven't adjusted to is waking up in the morning without any real need to get out of bed."

"What about your painting?"

"I'm too depressed to paint."

"I thought painters needed to be depressed."

"I'm sure many do, but not me. I don't think I've been to the studio since just before Allie left for school, and that was only to get a painting she wanted to hang in her room. No, I do my best work when I'm happy, which seems to be a very rare condition these days."

"Maybe you need to take a trip," offered Martin. "Lie on a beach somewhere for a couple of weeks."

"Goddamnit, Martin!" Jean exploded. "I don't need a trip, I need a life. If I get any more relaxed I'll scream."

"You just did."

"And I will again if it helps me feel better. I don't ever remember feeling so empty."

Martin rose from his chair, setting his drained glass on the bar. "I wish I could help. Perhaps I can. We need to talk tomorrow and all the decisions I must make affect you, so keep an open mind. I'm dog tired. I've got to get some sleep. See you in the morning."

Jean sat motionless as the silence of the house enveloped her. She thought of an artistic conceptualization of the solar system she had admired recently in a National Geographic—the earth a dot in celestial vastness. We are all so feeble, she thought . . . struggle our entire lives with problems which seem monumental, seldom stopping to think how petty it all must seem to those who behold the universe; to some artist in a distant galaxy whose rendering would not be altered in the slightest detail should the earth and all its problems evaporate into thin air. Too depressing, she thought as she stood up, only to lose her balance momentarily and fall back into the chair.

"The moral is now clear to me," she said under her breath. "I need a new planet," and tottered off to bed.

*   *   *

At mid-morning, Jean entered the breakfast room where Martin sat with coffee and a stack of newspapers. The Roanoke *Times* was delivered that morning as it had been for twenty-five years, but The Richmond *Times Dispatch* and Washington *Post* had cost him five dollars and an earlier trip to the Wawa.

"Morning, Senator," the cashier had said as he entered. "You straightened 'em out up there in the capital yet?"

"That's a tall order, Bill," replied Martin, who didn't know Bill but could plainly see his name tag. "We're doing our best." As Martin paid for his papers he thought about how the convenience store seemed to have filled the void left by the demise of the old general stores. He liked to think those who gathered here believed he was doing a good job in Washington. Perhaps he should stick around some morning and find out.

But not this morning. He returned to the house, called Dennis to get briefed on a matter which could have awaited his return to Washington, and sat down to devour his papers and wait for Jean.

She came in with a steaming cup of coffee and three aspirins, wearing the slippers and run-down housecoat which she had had for years.

"Good morning," said Martin, as she entered.

"Yeah, yeah," said Jean. "I had one too many scotches last night. That's the first alcohol I've had this week."

Martin barely raised his eyes. "The Chinese ambassador has accused us of dumping breakfast cereals. Can you beat it? The Chinese accusing another country of dumping is like the Russians criticizing inefficiency."

She opened the "Leisure" section of the *Times Dispatch*. She made no response to the news of Chinese dumping and soon appeared engrossed in an article on a touring ballet company scheduled to appear in Richmond.

Martin waited for her to pour her second cup of coffee. "Jean," he said quietly, "we need to talk."

She dropped her paper and shifted in the chair. Martin was encouraged.

"No doubt you've seen the news stories suggesting Justin may tap me as his running mate."

"Of course. Don't take this wrong, but why is he interested in you?"

"It's a fair question, and the answer has a lot to do with the direction of the Democratic Party."

"Oh? I didn't think your Party had any direction."

Martin laughed. "Precisely the problem. You know the old expression, 'A clear picture of a fuzzy image is fuzzy'? Well, it seems that the national people feel that I have a message which isn't fuzzy. They don't all like it, mind you. Some positively hate it, but it's a clear message. A high-level delegation of Democrats from the Congress came to see me the other day. They want me to accept if Justin makes the offer."

She stared into her cup for a while. "What's Justin's position? Does he want you?"

"We haven't talked about it. Dennis has had some very preliminary discussions at the staff level but nothing concrete. I know Justin fairly well, as well as you get to know people in this business. We worked together on the Presidential Commission for Health Care back in '95 and I helped him two years ago on some Great Lakes legislation which would have hit Illinois pretty hard. But how he feels on something this big I can't say. Justin is one smart politician. His whole career proves that. You can bet he'll take the person who will help him most even if that turns out to be the donkey himself."

Jean smiled. "No comment."

"One of those on the polling list was Allen Sutcliffe. He and Justin are old friends from way back. It's enough to make me question Justin's judgment because as nice a guy as Allen is, he is one of the laziest members of the Senate and what he does for the state of Oregon I have yet to discover. But Justin likes him so he's on the list."

"How do you feel about it; running, I mean?" asked Jean.

"Well, naturally I'm flattered and I'm certainly interested. Since I've been in the Senate, I can count on one hand the number of members who didn't harbor further political ambitions. It's like minor league baseball. If you went into the dugout of the Richmond Braves and asked for a show of hands of everyone who wanted to make it to the major leagues, how many hands do you think would go up?"

"It's a good thing you admitted your interest," said Jean, "because if you had denied being interested I'd have been forced to laugh in your face."

"I didn't think my aspirations would shock you."

"Where does it go from here?"

"I told the delegation I'd think it over and I meant that sincerely. Despite what I know you regard as my unbridled ambition, I want to make sure we have a good chance of winning before I say 'yes.' But assuming the odds are good, I still have to be selected to run with Justin. All kinds of pressure to name others will be brought upon him by forces I can only guess at. Of course, I'll have my groups in there lobbying for me as well, but who knows who will get in the last word.

"Then, of course, I have to assess it from a personal standpoint. A run for national office is unlike anything we've ever seen here in genteel Virginia. The strain on all of us—you, me and the kids—will be severe; just ask Kitty Dukakis. I need to know how you feel about it. I don't think I'd be much of a candidate without my family's support."

Moral support, on the other hand, was less critical, as they both knew. Martin was by nature independent, a trait acquired both by heritage and the paper route, after-school jobs, and Eagle Scouting which comprised so much of his youth. He grew up in Salem, a small community just outside Roanoke, the only child of Glenn and Marjorie Harmon. His father was a career employee of Sears and his mother taught school. Upon graduation from Salem High, he entered Virginia Tech, where he immersed himself in the politics of student government, making no secret of the fact that he viewed the entire exercise as training for a larger political arena. During their junior year, he met Jean, a native of Richmond and the daughter of a dentist whose shrewd speculation in suburban real estate had brought him a small fortune.

Martin liked her at once. An art major with zero interest in political intrigues, campus or beyond, Jean surrounded herself with friends who shared her creative spirit and prized her friendship because of her sensitivity and the entertainment value of her biting sarcasm. Martin found her honesty disarming and engaging.

Jean's attraction to Martin, she realized early in the relationship, was her fascination with how seriously he took himself, but without being pompous. Still able to laugh. She enjoyed the shared limelight in the close-knit campus community. Underneath a facade calculated to convey indifference to her popularity, she loved the feeling of inclusion and the wider audience for her dark humor.

They married in the summer following graduation. Neither could say they went into their marriage with eyes closed, but each could say that in the long run the differences between them proved far wider, far more intractable than could have been imagined on cold, autumn Saturdays in the rosy glow of a big football victory shared with friends.

In September, they moved to Williamsburg, where Martin began law school at William and Mary and Jean went to work. The following spring, Jean became pregnant with Edward but continued to work until the last possible moment. They struggled. Martin finished near the top of his class, served as an associate editor of the law review, and made numerous friends who were to prove helpful throughout his professional and political life. Upon graduation, he secured a position with the top firm in Roanoke, and the couple, now expecting a second child, Jack, returned there to set up house.

But after their children were born, Martin and Jean gradually found themselves in separate worlds. Jean raised the children, did substitute teaching, and immersed herself in what cultural pursuits there were in rural, southwest Virginia.

Martin was gone most of the time. As an associate attorney he generated at least one hundred forty billable hours each month, as required by the firm. After a time, he delegated some of the routine work to younger associates, affording him an opportunity to interact with clients, which in turn threw him into United Way campaigns, hospital drives, and all types of civic involvements. Thus his time became split between his firm and his pro bono work, stretching him thinner. Shortly after he made partner, several prominent business leaders, clients of the firm, asked him to run for the legislature, adding a third commitment. Because he was not a wealthy man and the Virginia General Assembly was in session only a few months each year, his election in his first campaign did not relieve him of the burden of generating billable hours.

The onset of his political career established a pattern of life with Jean which did not change appreciably until his election to the U.S. Senate. The nature of their lives was never clearer than on the weekend in April when he acquired Allie's rock. Years later, when for both Martin and Jean it became essential to reach definitive conclusions about their relationship, they returned magnetically, inexorably, to the events of that fine spring weekend. For Martin, it was proof positive that the fatal flaw lay not within himself but in Jean, who offered it as irrefutable evidence of precisely the opposite.

The final session of the General Assembly session was set for Friday, April 25th. In accord with steeped custom, the governor, whose mansion flanks the Virginia capitol at a distance of some one hundred yards, issued invitations to his annual leadership luncheon, always held at noon on the day following adjournment. The delivery of these invitations was a highlight of the session, for tradition required that a fife, drum and bugle trio, dressed in authentic colonial garb, escort to the capitol a liveried employee of the mansion. This servant, always black before the 1975 session but now white, carried inside an antique mail pouch the calligraphic invitations. As he made his way through the House and Senate chambers, legislators celebrating the end of months of arduous, often acrimonious, debate applauded wildly, some rising to slap the messenger on the back as he passed.

Those invited to the luncheon were preordained; that is, protocol required invitations to the Speaker, the leadership of both Houses, and all committee chairmen, plus wives or husbands of those members. The governor could invite members unqualified by title, but no one could remember the last time a governor had done so. For this reason, members of the House broke into spontaneous applause when this messenger walked to Martin Harmon's desk and delivered, with an underscored flourish, a pale white invitation. When the final gavel had sounded and Martin returned to his office, he called Jean.

"I couldn't believe it! It's an unprecedented honor, from all accounts."

"Why did he invite you?" she asked.

"Why did he invite *us*. According to his legislative aide, who called me a few minutes ago, the governor wanted to show his appreciation for my support this session. And listen to this. He says there's talk of drafting me for the Attorney General race next year. Not bad for a country lawyer, huh?"

"No, it's all very flattering, but the timing couldn't be worse."

"Why?"

"Martin, have you forgotten? We're scheduled to spend tomorrow at Natural Bridge: you, me and the children. It's Family Day and we committed weeks ago. The kids have talked of nothing else."

"But Jean, that was planned before I knew this would happen. An invitation from the governor is a command appearance."

"Oh?"

"Absolutely. We have to go."

"We do not have to go."

"Jean, be reasonable. This is the kind of recognition that any politician would kill for."

"Martin, listen to me. You left for Richmond the first week of January. You remember January, with the snow on the ground? Well, it's now almost May. The trees are in full bloom. That's how long you've been gone. In all that time you've been home only a few nights and you've seen hardly anything of the children. I've had all the car-pooling, all the homework monitoring, all the ball games, all the trips to the emergency room, all the teachers conferences, all the meals, all the laundry and all the rest of it. For four solid months. I don't see how you can even consider pulling out on us tomorrow."

"Jean, I'm as disappointed as you. I have been looking forward to Natural Bridge. How was I to know this would happen?"

"You always say that. And it's always something out of the blue; unexpected clients or committee meetings running over or God knows what else. And every time there is a blip in your schedule, the children and I get rescheduled."

Martin paused, stunned. Recovering, he said, "You're right. I know what a load you've been carrying. But the session is over now. I'll be home, and I can give you some relief. I promise, but this luncheon is critical."

"I don't give a damn about the luncheon and you said the same thing last year about spending time with us and it didn't happen."

"Well, pardon me for working hard to support this family. And as for the luncheon, it doesn't surprise me that you don't give a damn. You wouldn't come if you had nothing planned."

"Perhaps you're right," she admitted. "I have no intention of driving all the way to Richmond to have lunch with a group of blowhard politicians."

"I'll tell the governor you said that."

"Tell him anything you want. Good-bye."

At noon the following day, Martin entered the foyer of the Executive Mansion. The governor greeted him warmly, sympathetic at his explanation of Jean's disappointment at being unable to attend this special occasion. He passed through the receiving line into the living room, so was in no position to overhear the First Lady lean toward the governor to whisper, "I told you so."

One hundred fifty miles west of Richmond, the Harmon children accompanied their mother on the long awaited Family Day outing. Allie, only five, asked again about her father's absence, to which Jean snapped, "He didn't want to come," before softening to, "He had business in Richmond." At the base of Natural Bridge, a wondrous geologic enigma, Allie found a stone which she discerned, by some instinct rooted in childhood sorcery, to be a good luck piece, and she put it in her pocket. That night, after Martin had arrived at home and his tired family had readied for bed, Allie brought it to him. "It's your lucky rock," she said, kissing him on the cheek. He picked her up and carried her to bed, but did not return to the den where he and Jean had been sitting when Allie made her gift. Jean found him in their bedroom, the rock still in his hand. She thought she detected a fleeting distortion in his face, but he turned away at once and she was never sure.

In consequence of their fundamental differences, Martin had long since become self-sustaining in his career. He ran for office alone, served alone, and kept his own counsel. On the rare occasions Jean accompanied him to an event, the result was the total opposite of that intended. Rather than a loyal wife supporting an up-and-coming husband, the picture which emerged was that of a nervous husband supporting a wife who felt distinctly ill at ease. They learned to avoid these situations entirely.

But the step Martin now contemplated he could not take alone. A major party candidate for national office lived under a microscope. The country wanted to know his family almost as much as it needed to know him. Jean would be conspicuous by her absence. Was she at home? Was she ill? Did she stay away because her views on XYZ are different from his? Is your marriage in trouble? The questions would be endless.

"What would our support entail?" asked Jean. "I suppose you mean whistle-stopping, the rubber chicken circuit, that kind of thing. Don't forget, Martin, your children have lives of their own now. They would all have a very difficult time working in a long political campaign even if their father is the candidate."

"I realize that," replied Martin nodding his head. "I don't want to disrupt their lives and I don't think that will be required. There will be some impact just because I'm running. They'll have to deal with the Secret Service until the election and thereafter if I'm elected. No, I don't want them up to their eyeballs in this, but a few well-timed appearances would be most helpful."

"Well, of course they'll do that," stated Jean.

"What about you?" asked Martin.

"Oh yes, me. What would you like me to do?"

"I think you have a pretty fair idea of what's involved."

"Yes, I suppose I do." Martin felt it coming. "I guess I need to dress up and get political. It shouldn't be too tough . . . all I have to do is make friends with 250 million people, remember all their names, smile until my lips fall off, answer questions about the first time we had sex and agree with everything you say, even when you're wrong. Does that about sum it up?"

Martin laughed. "Yeah, I guess so."

"Seriously, I don't know. This is not a game I'm good at."

"There's a first time for everything. Maybe you'll surprise yourself. Besides, look at all the women who have done this kind of thing successfully, and they were no more political than you are. People like Pat Nixon."

"Are you like Dick?"

"I don't know. You never know how you'll perform in that arena until you get there. Look, it's tough. I know it's tough. But it's terribly important. You said last night you needed a life. If we win, life could become pretty exciting. The v.p. goes to funerals all over the world. With Allie at school, you can travel anywhere."

"Yes, that could be a bright spot," Jean reflected. "But so much of it is mudslinging. They ask you all these bizarre questions about your family and your health and your drinking habits and every other goddamn thing they can think of. And when you lie to protect your privacy, they ask you about your honesty. Campaigns are always so horribly ugly."

"All of that is true. I can't deny it."

"Of course you can't deny it. And you can't protect us from it either. And you never know when some lunatic is planning to shoot his way into the history books."

"Yes, I'm afraid it all comes with the territory. We knew that when we signed up."

"Wait a minute, Martin. We didn't sign up. You went off to practice law and somehow a three month commitment to the General Assembly in Richmond has turned into your life's work and now it threatens to turn into my life's work. We haven't signed up for that yet."

"Why don't you think about it," suggested Martin. "I feel sure that, despite the delegation's support, my chances are riding on the REA's passage."

They agreed that Jean would think it over. Martin flew back to Washington knowing that he would run if the spot were offered, Jean or no Jean, and take his chances with the electorate. He had yet to lose an election; perhaps his luck would hold. Jean stayed in Roanoke knowing two things: that she wanted no part of the campaign, whether she ended up telling Martin yes or no, and that he would run regardless of her answer.

Chapter 8

Upon her return from Kathy's, Carson craved a hot shower. As she stepped onto a thick bathmat, she heard the front door open. Wrapping her hair in a small towel turban-style, she donned a larger one before going to greet Martin.

"You look good enough to eat," said Martin as he pulled her to him.

"Don't," she giggled. "You'll pull my towel off."

"Is that bad?" he asked.

"It's not well-timed. Take me to dinner and we'll discuss it."

Martin relinquished his hold. "What sounds good?"

"Soft shell crabs at Poor Boys."

"Great idea. We haven't done that in a while."

They drove separately to a shopping center some miles from the District where Martin parked and got into Carson's car for the trip to Poor Boys, outside Annapolis, Maryland. She drove, on the assumption that any routine stop for a license or alcohol check would not involve a passenger.

The hour travel time offered the chance to catch up on events of the past several days. Martin focused on the reception he received in Memphis; Carson related the trip to Frederick.

"Kathy is dying to meet you," she said. Martin smiled.

Poor Boys was a seemingly deserted one story building of cinder block on a meandering creek. They had first gone there on the recommendation of the senior senator from Louisiana, whom Martin reasoned should know good seafood if anyone in the Congress knew good seafood. Although Martin had not questioned him about its "privacy factor," the directions for finding it were enough to give Martin comfort that he would not be exposed to prying eyes. The food more than compensated for the wrong turns (it seems wine clouded the senator from Louisiana's memory of milestones and turnoffs).

It was as safe a public place as Martin had found, if public was the right term. The unpaved road winding to it was a mile and a half diet of mud holes and jagged ruts. Anyone attempting it within twenty-four hours of hard rain, in anything other than a tank or jeep, was in decided peril of arriving on foot. The creek afforded an approach by water but the crumbling pier was hardly an invitation to boaters.

If Poor Boys had ever enjoyed a "prime," it had passed decades before. Tables and chairs looked as though they had been gathered from a series of garage sales up and down the east coast. The cash register had far more value as an antique than as an accounting device. The juke box, an original Wurlitzer, appraised higher than the building. But for those reasons, and the succulent soft shell crabs, it was an ideal get-away.

On this evening, the lack of rain eliminated the threat of being stranded, but the dust made them cough even with the windows rolled up. Feeble light from a single hundred watt bulb, on a post near the entrance, welcomed them. Carson, in their pattern, waited in the car while Martin entered through a screen door, dubiously hinged, and momentarily paused to survey the crowd. No familiar faces. He returned to the car. A half dozen couples, dressed in offhand attire, took slight notice as they walked toward a table in the far corner.

Carson sat down while Martin proceeded to the bar for beers to wash away the dust. He returned with two frosty mugs from which beer dripped and splashed. "Cheers," they said, clinking together the tops of the nearly frozen brew. After ten minutes, a young girl appeared in an apron which looked as if it had undergone countless laundering in the strongest of soaps.

"We don't need a menu," offered Carson. "We'll take the soft shell crabs and a bottle of California chardonnay."

When they were alone again, Carson said, "You haven't mentioned Jean. How is she?" Traces of the beer's foam lingered at the corners of her mouth.

"She's well enough," replied Martin. "Having something of an identity crisis with Allie off at school and the house empty, but she'll be ok. We talked about the v.p. nomination. I didn't spend much time with her on the politics; the in's and out's bore her. But I tried to spell out the risks, and the impact if it all happens. She didn't make any commitments but I didn't press. My guess is that if push comes to shove she'll try, but I share her pessimism that she'll be no good at it. And for certain she won't like it. We agreed to talk again."

"It will be awkward without her, that's for sure," offered Carson. "If you were divorced, people would understand and after they asked the usual questions it would be behind you. But if she just sits out the race, questions will be raised over and over."

"So true," said Martin, staring at her pointedly. "Of course, if I was divorced I could always remarry."

"Oh . . . Martin!" she stammered, blushing. "I didn't mean—I wasn't suggesting—"

"You were pointing out what is patently true; that a divorce would be much easier to handle politically than a wife who won't campaign or one who campaigns so poorly you wish she had stayed at home."

"Yes, exactly, that's all I meant. I hope you believe that." She reached across the table and took his hand. Then, remembering they were in public, she withdrew it quickly with a nervous glance aside, but not before he returned a reassuring squeeze.

"Of course. Don't give it another thought. Besides, it's not a taboo subject, at least as far as I'm concerned. But we've never discussed it, have we?"

"No, we haven't." She said it abstractly, as she might have responded to his familiar inquiries as to whether they had seen a particular movie. Martin could never recall movies, and Carson never forgot them, even the bad ones.

"Perhaps we should, Carson. Suppose I run and win."

"For what it's worth, I think you will. As much as I think you would make a great v.p., or president for that matter, I think whomever wins the nomination will be elected because I can't see sending the Republicans back for another four years."

Martin idly fingered the salt shaker, bracketing it between his thumb and forefinger while attempting to balance it on its edge. "The polls clearly agree with you, but you never know. Don't forget, there are eighteen months until the election and we are dealing with a man who stood little chance of being elected four years ago but managed to find a way to win. In that I happen to belong to a political party which could screw up a free lunch, nothing is certain. Nothing, that is, except the inescapable fact that my running will have a dramatic impact on our relationship, win or lose." The salt shaker teetered before coming to an upright rest.

"What do you think the odds are Justin will pick you?"

He shrugged as if to signal the futility of a guess, but then said, "Fifty-fifty, which may not sound all that strong until you consider that none of the other names being floated rate better than about four to one. But odds won't mean a damn thing in the end if Justin decides he wants someone else badly enough."

Carson asked him about the "myth" of "geographical balance" in the selection of vice-presidents and he assured her that the perception of its demise was itself a myth—it still mattered.

"Very interesting," she observed, "but Clinton and Gore were both from the South."

"True, but the '92 results are discounted as aberrational. Democratic pollsters still think a North-South balance is a winner if the right two are on the ticket."

The clatter of their waitress's tray interrupted. The crabs were as good as they remembered, but Martin was thinking less about food than about how wonderful it felt to be with Carson; to talk with someone like her who knew and understood politics.

As they awaited coffee and dessert, Martin said, "This REA issue just gets hotter and hotter. If we can get the bill passed, my stock is going to rise dramatically. Not only will it show leadership in the Senate, but it puts me firmly in the forefront of the national debate on eugenics. Every time I go to places like Memphis, I come back more convinced that people want this stopped before it's too late. This is going to turn into the hottest scientific debate since Copernicus argued that the earth revolved around the sun."

That same sun, Carson noted, was setting over her shoulder, a shard of slanted orange piercing an unclouded spot of the windowpane behind her, coloring his eyes as green as she had ever seen them.

"Did you know," he continued, "that some of our scientists have been routinely splicing animal and human genes together, more or less for grins. What are these clowns thinking about when they use tax dollars for that kind of nonsense. I read that one of these eggheads claims to have discovered a combination of genes responsible for reclusiveness. Can you believe it? So next they'll establish a test for it that costs fifteen hundred dollars and gives wealthy young couples the opportunity to make sure their child won't spend all his time in one corner of the kindergarten. And if the test is positive they'll just pull the plug and try again. Where does it end? Maybe the kid would have been better off in the corner. Maybe he or she's over there learning the fundamental structure of building blocks. Maybe he finds it hard to concentrate in crowds." He brought his palm down hard on the table. "You know, there was a time when you watched your child grow up to find out what he or she was like. It was part of the thrill of having kids. Now, these genetic engineers have come up with so many tests we can write a book on the kid's personality while he's still in the womb."

"Come on," Carson said gently, "it's not that bad."

"But getting there fast. I have sources in places where this research is being done. Have I ever mentioned an Anne Harborfield to you?"

"The name doesn't register."

"No reason why it should. I got her a job in NIH a while back and she looks out for me. Anyway, she called a few days ago to report some revolutionary new finding by a man named Grunfeld at Caltech."

"What is it?"

"Who knows? It was too complicated to explain, and literally, I'm afraid to ask these days. I told her to call Dennis. In Miami—there's an in-vitro fertilization clinic there—a woman calls me from home because she doesn't want them to know I know. Anyway, the other day a client had them run a genetic profile on a fetus she planned to have implanted. Tests were negative for diseases or deformities, but she specifically wanted to know the hair color. When they told her 'brown,' she said, 'but I want black.' You can guess the rest."

"That IS horrible," said Carson, "but that woman sounds like an extreme case."

"Perhaps, but I would bet that and worse goes on more than we realize."

"But the REA bill doesn't address that, does it?"

"It's very frustrating. These clinics are private, so there are no federal funds to cut off. And you know how hard we've tried on the abortion end of it, but the Supreme Court has frustrated every effort to get it outlawed. So the only avenue left is to curb the genetic research that is producing so many of the problems."

"I'm not on top of genetic engineering," she allowed. "I've done some reading lately because of all the controversy. During the 70's there were fears that some mutant strain of genetically engineered viruses would take over the earth. A real sci-fi scare."

"That's true. When the first wave of gene experiments hit, there was panic that some guy in a lab coat would create something no one could control. What has happened is far more sinister. While we slept, these guys kept cross—breeding their fruit flies and splicing their genes so now they can do just about anything. It's got to stop somewhere or we will wake up and find our grandchildren come from the home shopping channel."

"But they have made so much progress on diseases . . ."

"That's the worst part, and why it is so difficult to stop this stuff. Proponents point to the good work they've done, but the diseases and deformities are only the ticket to the show; once inside, anything goes. When I was a kid, we had an expression about a bullfrog with wings. I can still hear Frank Taylor in that hill-billy twang of his; 'Marty,' he'd say, 'if a bullfrog had wings he wouldn't bump his ass.' I'll bet you dollars to doughnuts one of those kooks is out there right now trying to engineer that frog."

"Yes, but if you're a mother pregnant with a Down's Syndrome child, you'd want to know it, wouldn't you? Then, depending on your view of abortion, you could make the decision you had to make. Either way, there's plenty of adversity."

"What would you do?" asked Martin. "Would you abort a Down's Syndrome child?" It was an insensitive question, which Martin instantly regretted.

She looked away but recovered quickly, answering evenly. "That's a difficult question. I honestly don't know. I'm not opposed to abortion in all cases, but I have not spent much time trying to draw the lines. I have empathy for women faced with that choice."

"You and I will have to agree to disagree on that, my dear. I strongly believe it is society's obligation to draw the line and protect that unborn life."

"I know you do and I admire your conviction. I wish I could be as sure."

"Such a serious mood," Martin said. "We might as well discuss what I alluded to earlier; winning, I mean. Two years ago, the prospect of this race would have put me on cloud nine. This is the Super Bowl. I should be fired up, but I'm not, and you have everything to do with that. I have no regrets: you've been the best thing that has happened to me in a long, long time. I had come to view myself as some machine; well-oiled, highly efficient, and totally mechanical. I had forgotten what love was like, if I ever knew. Then, this past year, I discovered how wonderful it can be to be comfortable with someone you're crazy about."

Martin looked away for several seconds. "Running for v.p. will mean giving you up—I'm not sure I can do it. We've been taking quite a risk these past few months. Frankly, we've beaten the odds. But this arrangement will soon be impossible, as we both know. The press will follow me everywhere. My life will belong to the Democratic Party and Justin until the election. After that . . . ?"

"Martin, are you telling me goodbye?"

"No. God, no. I can't. But neither can I ignore what is plainly on the horizon. I don't see any way to avoid both of us getting hurt. It's such a screwy predicament. Here I am pleading with my wife to do something she'll hate doing and I'll hate doing with her at the same time that I'm confronting the probability of losing the very thing I want most."

"Martin, be honest. I'm not what you want most."

"You—"

"Wait," she said. "You're a professional politician. You have given it your whole life. You haven't come all this way without a fierce ambition; ambition which is still very much alive and well. You want to see where it goes, to see how high Martin Harmon from southwest Virginia can climb. That's what you want most and there is nothing wrong with that. It doesn't make me feel any less wanted or loved."

Martin stared at her intently. "It's things like that which make me appreciate you so much. If you have a selfish bone in your body, I haven't come across it."

"Thank you, love, but you give me too much credit. I have selfish bones and more than one. But it is pointless to deny what is clear, and equally pointless for me to take it personally. I understand how you feel. I appreciate your dilemma, or should I say our dilemma."

In the ensuing silence, the last couple in Poor Boys was leaving, pausing at the oversized cash register.

"So, what do we do?" asked Martin.

"It's your call, Martin. I'll do what is best for you. If that means leaving your life now, I'll do that. If it means leaving later, I'll do that. Just be honest with me and let me know what you want."

"What I want," said Martin, placing his hand on her thigh under the table, "is you at home, without the towel."

She laughed, a little giddy at their mutual reprieve. "It seems we want the same thing then. Can the free world afford for us to put off these decisions for another day?"

Back at the Westchester, their lovemaking fell short, victim to a hurried distraction, as though they were availing themselves of a conjugal privilege soon to be withdrawn, and the shuffling of events outside the room was palpable. But after, he studied the silhouette of her profile against light filtering through the curtains: Could he, at any cost, give this woman up?

BOOK 2

MAX

Chapter 9

In his role as conservator of the land, Gustaff Grunfeld took his son Max outside one spring morning in 1931 to plant an oak. Wildflowers, new and faintly rippling in a breeze off the plains, stretched from the house to the edge of cornfields which would, with rain, swell with their bounty.

"Why are we planting a tree, Papa?" inquired six year old Max, using the old world salutation preferred by his father.

"For many reasons, Max." His father's voice still held the guttural authority of his Teutonic ancestors. "The first is that by the time this tree is big enough to climb, you will be big enough to climb it."

"I'm big enough now!" countered Max. "The Olsens have a big tree in the back yard with limbs up to the roof. Sam Olsen climbs it all the time and he lets me climb it too. We can see his farm and all the animals, but the animals look small up there."

Gustaff chuckled. "I am certain they do. Be careful to hold on tightly or you will discover what it means to fall." He laid his hand, delicate for a farmer's, on Max's shoulder. "We plant trees for other reasons; to hold down the soil so it will not blow away. And for shade when it becomes too warm in the house. And because trees are beautiful to look at, are they not?"

"Yes Papa, they are beautiful. But how do you plant a tree?"

"It is quite simple. You put a hole in the earth, like so," his father instructed, auguring a large hickory stick into the ground. "Then, you drop in a seed. You see the seed here in my hand, Max?" His father opened his fist to reveal an acorn. "The tree will grow from this."

As his father bent to the ground to deposit the acorn, Max, his eyes fixed on the seed, said, "Wait, Papa! Let me."

"Hold out your hands," directed his father, tilting his open fist to allow the acorn to roll into Max's cupped hands.

Max stared at the acorn, then up at his father. "Do you mean, Papa, that this little seed will grow a tree?"

"Yes, Max. Is that not grand?"

"But what kind of tree will it be?"

"It will be the same kind of tree it fell from," replied his father patiently. "It will be an oak."

"But how does the seed know to grow an oak?"

His father laughed. "I cannot answer that one. Nature knows. God made the oak and He will make the oak make more oaks. That is His way."

"Oh," was all that Max replied as the acorn rolled around in his hand. "May I plant it?"

"Of course," replied his father, and Max carefully dropped the acorn into the ground.

The oak which sprouted and prospered did indeed provide the benefits cited by his father as justification for planting it, but it furnished an additional benefit which could not have been foreseen by Gustaff Grunfeld; a constant and growing reminder to a supremely intelligent boy of a question which had not been satisfactorily answered: how does the acorn know to grow an oak tree?

In the Grunfeld's Iowa farming community struggling with the Depression, no one was very far from the edge. Max's parents, second generation Germans, both traced their origins to families who immigrated to Minnesota in the late 1800's from Cologne, where they had farmed fertile plains along the Rhine. Martha Grunfeld, buxom with Nordic blonde hair, blue eyes and disarming strength of body, received little formal education, in the tradition of the times. It was from her that Max inherited his superior intellect. Max's father, on the other hand, received proper instruction through high school and would have joyfully pursued college had not the family's fortunes dictated that he put in eighteen hour days on their small farm. But his love of learning endured. Intellectually, he was no match for his tragically undereducated wife or for Max, but his thirst for knowledge, quenched by voracious reading, drew Max to an early love for books.

Growing up on a farm where animals bred provided Max with a steady stream of genetic demonstrations. At school, he found still more in a class which covered rudimentary concepts of biology. The subject was roses and the process by which a knowledgeable breeder could produce white, red and pink roses, and shades of each, on command. The prodigy in Max began to emerge. He devoured lessons on dominant and recessive colors and characteristics, later winning a local science fair with an exhibit which celebrated his new-found interest. By age fifteen, so insatiable was his appetite for biology that his high school teacher arranged for him to audit a course at a college thirty-five miles away.

Max arrived for his first class of Introduction to Biology after the semester was underway, and brought with him an understandable apprehension that for all his renown at high school, he might not comprehend a word. Fortunately for Max (as well as the regular students) Professor Alden Carter's gift was the ability to take the most complex process and reduce it to simple terms, often by analogy. On the annual occasion of his lecture explaining the origin of life on earth by comparing it with an old family recipe for lentil soup, the lecture hall filled to capacity. Years after leaving Iowa, Max could close his eyes and picture the thin, mustachioed wisp of a man sitting contentedly on his desk, like a lizard on a rock, delivering his fateful discourse, his dry wit spread evenly throughout.

"What you must understand is that genetics is an invisible science." He looked over the rim of his glasses at a mammoth football player struggling to remain awake, then added, "And some of you, I predict, will make nearly invisible marks in this subject." The football player jolted as laughter arose around him, but settled back into his trance.

"Not only is it invisible to the human eye," he continued, "but much of its elaborate physics and chemistry is invisible to our most sophisticated microscopes. But before you become discouraged, consider that the 'father of genetics,' a European monk named Gregor Mendel, used his own eyes to make his more important observations. Mendel had a fondness for the peas which he tended on a small plot of land in one corner of the monastery. For eight years he planted, bred and counted, keeping careful notes. When he had finished, he had formulated the fundamental laws of heredity.

"Mendel's peas bred true, which is to say that in nature, the offspring mirrored the parent because each pea flower fertilizes itself in a closed environment, free from exposure to pollen from other plants. Mendel introduced to the closed pea flower the pollen from another variety of pea and recorded the impact of this second parent on the plant produced.

"He concluded that something specific, something tangible passed between the plants which controlled their heredity traits. But what? Mendel did not know, but theorized that these messages or units came in pairs which separated when sex cells were formed inside the peas and then recombined when fertilization took place. For example, a pure strain of yellow peas contained a pair of units controlling color, which can be designated as YY."

Professor Carter turned to the blackboard and drew two Y's. "The capital Y indicates that yellow is a dominant characteristic. That plant is then fertilized with the pollen from a pure strain of green peas, whose units can be designated as gg, the lower case illustrating that the color green is recessive to yellow. The offspring from this process will all contain color units of Yg, with one characteristic contributed by each parent. These offspring will all be yellow, because yellow is dominant over the color green. The green message or unit is still present in the offspring, but is not visible. Mendel confirmed this fact by producing succeeding generations of the Yg offspring, a mathematically predictable number of which turned out green, proving the absence of the Y unit and the presence of the gg pair. Had Y been present, it would have dominated as I have noted."

Professor Carter left his desk to wander toward the hulking athlete. "I, like Mendel, have made some observations over the years, one of which is that in the species known as football playerottus, the learning instinct is recessive to sleep." The snore of the football player competed with the general laughter.

"Had Mendel's rules, probabilities and theories been confined to peas, his work would hardly have earned for him the title of 'father of genetics.' The first milestones for human inquiry came later in the century. A young German physician, Friedrich Miescher, investigating the chemical structure of human cells, discovered a large molecule in the nucleus which he termed 'nucleic acid.' Before he died, he speculated that such a molecule could conceivably carry the message of heredity from parent to child.

"As the world prepared to enter the 20th century, the state of human knowledge as to why we resemble our parents could be summarized as follows: Living things duplicate themselves in their own images by tangible messages or units which pass from parent to child; these units come in pairs and behave in accordance with certain immutable and predictable rules; and theoretically, a single molecule within a cell could carry such messages or units in human beings.

"Beginning in 1900, the pace of development quickened. For starters, Mendel's messages or units were termed 'genes.' But what were genes? What were they made of? How were they structured? A German professor of physiology named Albrecht Kossel provided some of the answers, for he dedicated his efforts to continuing Miescher's investigation into the chemistry of the human cell. His findings were monumental to the fields of genetics and biology. He found that present in nucleic acid were four substances called bases. These four, adenine, cytosine, guanine and thymine, are universally abbreviated as A, C, G and T. In identifying them, Kossel discovered the alphabet of heredity, for the combinations of these substances make up the genetic code within all plants, animals and humans. Kossel's work earned him a Nobel Prize in 1910.

"Thomas Hunt Morgan, the next giant in genetics, spent years at Columbia in a lab filled with fruit flies feeding on rotten bananas in an attempt to settle the debate over whether acquired traits or characteristics could be inherited by subsequent generations. His research employed fruit flies, Drosophila, because their exceedingly short ten day gestation period yielded results quickly. Remember that Mendel spent eight years on his peas. But testing his theory required a mutated fly, something not readily available nor easily produced. For months Morgan inflicted all manner of indignities on the hapless flies, from acids to x-rays, in his effort to produce a weirdo. Eventually he stumbled upon a white-eyed fly unique among the thousands in his lab. Here was a mutation of eye color. Would it show up in subsequent generations? It did, giving Morgan the momentum he needed to produce flies with a dazzling array of mutations. His work confirmed Mendel's experiments and went significantly beyond by linking certain fly characteristics to specific chromosomes within the fly. Fruit flies have four chromosomes, as opposed to the forty-six possessed by humans. These chromosomes in flies are large, facilitating study. Morgan and his assistants used the linkage data to chart a map or guide to the fly chromosomes. Like all maps, this helped point researchers to the specific area of a specific chromosome which controlled or influenced a particular trait.

"Well, enough about the mating of fruit flies. Now we turn our attention to the mating of humans, a subject of intense interest on most campuses." A titter of laughter went through the room.

"As I mentioned, we humans have forty-six chromosomes, twenty-three of which are furnished by the mother's egg and twenty-three of which are furnished by the father's sperm. At the point of conception, these chromosomes pair off instinctively forming twenty-three pairs. One of those pairs determines the sex of the child. A female egg always contributes an X chromosome, and if the sperm fertilizing the egg also contains an X, the result will be a female offspring. If the sperm contains a Y, then a male is produced."

Carter continued. "Human life begins when a male sperm fertilizes a female egg, producing a zygote. A zygote is a single cell which, within hours of fertilization, begins to divide, forming first two cells, then four, then eight etc. as each cell divides and makes a copy of itself. The zygote contains a full set of chromosomes. Within each chromosome is carried one molecule of DNA. The DNA carried in all forty-six chromosomes constitutes a detailed set of genetic instructions on how to make ourselves, right down to the last pore in our skin. It is the human recipe, formulated by our ancestors and their ancestors and passed to us through DNA.

"There are those," said Professor Carter gravely as the hour was almost up, "who believe that DNA will ultimately prove we all descend from a common ancestor." He looked contemptuously at the football player—head back, mouth open, eyes closed. "I pray to God that is not true. Are there any questions?"

A hand went up.

"Yes, you young man. State your name."

"Max Grunfeld, sir."

"What's your question?"

"Can you explain how DNA passes the human recipe from generation to generation?"

Carter's eyes narrowed. "Mr. Grunfeld, aren't you the high school student auditing this class?"

"Yes, sir."

"Well, that's quite a question coming from a high school student. No, I cannot explain it, nor can any other human being so far as I know. It is an unsolved mystery of towering significance, and the person who solves it will be a unanimous choice for a Nobel Prize."

*   *   *

By the time Max accepted a full academic scholarship to CalTech in 1942, at 16, he was a confirmed prodigy. Martha and Gustaff worried about a boy so studious. His rural naiveté left them confident of his ability to comprehend the molecular structure of hydrocarbons but apprehensive of his ability to take a bus across town.

They need not have worried. No sooner had he settled in his room when his roommate, Eric Walsh from Portland, Oregon, introduced him to some activities which had received sparse mention in the college handbook, namely the three B's of beer, "broads" and bridge, in that order. Eric, a math major who could perform virtually any college level mathematical function in his head, did not purchase a course book in his major until the second semester of his junior year. With such audacious proficiency in his chosen field, Eric found himself with time on his hands. He and Max hit it off at once, not because of what they had in common but because of what they would come to have in common.

On his second night at college, Max reluctantly accepted an invitation from Eric to go to The Oasis. Max had purchased his biology text book that morning, consuming five chapters despite the fact that his first class in the course did not meet for another two days. He looked forward to getting back from dinner early to finish chapters six and seven, which looked particularly interesting from the description in the index.

"Fuck it," said Eric. "Let's go to The Oasis. They have live biology experiments going on there."

So Max went. Upon arrival, Eric ordered Max his very first beer, a tall one. Max admitted it tasted very good, an admission he repeated after the third, fourth, and fifth beers as well.

"Where's the biology?" asked Max in glassy-eyed innocence.

"Look around you, Max. The place is crawling with it," said Eric, alluding to several women near the bar. "I'm surprised you didn't meet a couple of these girls on the turnip truck when you came west."

Max grinned a toothy grin, not over the comment about the turnip truck—he wasn't sure what Eric meant by that, but he sure felt good right now and that beer was just great.

The next morning, Max paid the age-old price for the ten beers he drank before Eric carried him out.

"God," moaned Max, opening one eye, "what hit me?"

"A turnip truck," said Eric, who whistled as he dressed for a tennis match.

"I'm not sure I can go to class. This head—I really feel horrible."

"If it's any consolation, you look horrible too. Don't worry about class, they have them here all the time."

Max stayed in bed all day. By early evening, he felt well enough to go to the cafeteria for a light meal, after which he returned with the full expectation of relapsing into bed. But he found Eric there with three other boys, none of whom Max had met. They were playing cards.

"Max, you have to learn bridge," said Eric as Max entered. "Come sit by me. I'll teach you."

Within days, Max was sitting in for the regulars and within the month he was a regular. They played for hours, days, entire weekends. Max displayed a fine aptitude for the game, which pleased Eric immensely. Truthfully, his aptitude for all of the three B's caused Eric to revise his original estimate of Max's potential.

Max and Eric roomed together for the next three years, sharing not only Eric's natural affinity for college life and Max's acquired one, but academic interests as well. Max's personal development did not follow the well worn path of the naive young innocent who, away from home for the first time, burns himself up in self-destructive overindulgence. He was too much a student for that. Rather the exposure to the larger world tempered his academic single-mindedness, giving him a human dimension he might otherwise have lacked. So while hangovers occasionally kept him from class, or a long weekend with a brunette or bridge disrupted his routine, he was hardly on the road to irretrievable ruin.

Which is not to say that he acquired his lighter side at no cost. Perhaps it would have happened anyway. During college and the post-graduate years that followed, the burning curiosity which characterized his high school career dissipated. Because he was brilliant and applied himself with reasonable diligence, he acquired vast knowledge in his discipline. But the creative thrust was missing. The drive to break through barriers, as predicted by his mentors, simply wasn't there.

After securing his Ph.D., he went to work for a small research laboratory in what became Silicon Valley. His work was competent, at times distinguished. As time went by, he found himself overtaken by the gnawing sense that he was drifting, looking without really seeing; interested without being consumed.

A month before his twenty-eighth birthday, his life changed. A recurring pain in his arm prompted him to see a doctor, who ordered tests and eventually a biopsy. The diagnosis was cancer. In the next year, it spread to other parts of his body. He grew weak, unable to work. He took a leave of absence from the lab, visited Eric in Los Angeles, toured some places he had intended to see, and prepared for the worst.

Cancer research was in its infant stages, with treatments few and virtually ineffective. Max held out little hope.

Suddenly and inexplicably, the cancer went into remission. His treating physician called in colleagues both to marvel at his case history and to suggest some medically plausible reason for the reversal. Max took less interest in his mysterious reprieve than might have been expected from one in his profession. He seemed to care less about how his life had been spared than why.

As is natural for some who suffer near-death experiences, Max found renewed purpose in his good fortune. His inspiration and focus progressed with the renewed strength of his body to a point that one year after tottering at the abyss, he burned with creative energy. To his native inquisitiveness the experience with cancer had added something which Max had lacked and might never have acquired had it not been for the illness: drive; an obsession to conquer; to take full advantage of the second chance he had been so fortunate to get. He absolutely had to make a contribution: a major one.

Max's education and work experience positioned him perfectly to assault the disease which had assaulted him. The ultimate revenge on one of mankind's cruelest plagues would have been to take dead aim at the assassin whose bullet he had just managed to evade.

But retribution didn't interest Max, nor was he spiteful, philosophically assuming the cancer had chosen him randomly and was "nothing personal." Certainly he wished to see it cured, for he was never completely free of the fear that it would recur. But he was not prepared to dedicate the balance of his life to its eradication. He hunted bigger game: the keys to the human race itself, to ALL diseases. That was the biggest prize of all, and he would stalk it relentlessly in the years to come.

Chapter 10

"Incredible!" said Max in slack-jawed amazement. "Absolutely, positively, indisputably incredible."

Spread before him on a desk littered with scientific magazines, three coffee cups (none clean), and assorted lab paraphernalia was the May 30, 1953 edition of the British journal *Nature*, answering the precise question Max had raised with Professor Carter twelve years earlier: how does DNA pass the human recipe from generation to generation? For Max, the article was tantamount to the final chapter of a long mystery novel.

In the decade before the Watson/Crick discovery detailed in Nature, strong evidence suggested that genes were composed of DNA, setting the stage for a fascinating race for glory. On the chemical side, the complete composition of DNA was known and on the biological side it was known that this acid controlled heredity. The billion dollar question was, how? The person answering that question would stand astride the world of genetics.

Francis Crick and James Watson seemed humble candidates for the title of Colossus. In fact, they would have been more aptly described by 1900's jargon as nerds. But very bright nerds. Crick, an Englishman; Watson, an American from Chicago. Watson's path was not unlike that taken by Max Grunfeld in his early years, for Watson finished undergraduate school at the University of Chicago by age nineteen and had a Ph.D. by age twenty-two from the University of Indiana. A fellowship took him to Denmark, but the monotonous work he found there inspired him to transfer to Cambridge, England, where he arrived in 1951. There he met Francis Crick, a more experienced scientist in search of his Ph.D. Teamed up at the Cavendish Physics Laboratory, they set out to build a model of DNA, to demonstrate how it was constructed and how it worked. In short, to answer the billion dollar question.

But others were probing the same question. One was Erwin Chargaff, who had already established certain rules for DNA, one of which was that the amount of adenine (A) in a molecule always equally the amount of thymine (T), while guanine (G) always equaled cytosine (C). This rule was a building block for a DNA model, but Chargaff did not build upon it.

Crick studied x-ray photos of DNA, and from these and from his knowledge he concluded that DNA was shaped as a double helix, two strands of chains coiled around each other in a shape not unlike a spring. These strands are made of phosphorus and it is to these that the bases A, C, G and T are attached. Watson and Crick were very close now. The realization that DNA was shaped as a double helix put them within inches of the finish line.

On the morning of February 28, 1953, Watson was fingering some cardboard cutouts of the molecular structure of A, C, G and T in an effort to fit them together. It suddenly struck him that the geometry of A and T were complementary, as was that of C and G. And hadn't Chargaff shown that the amounts of these substances were always equal? Of course. That was it! The A's are matched to the T's along the double helix, and C's to G's. When the two strands separate during cell division, the new strands form alongside the separated strands, and the order of the bases which form along those new strands is determined by the order in the existing strands; that is, the A's are matched to T's and the C's to G's. The new strands are negative copies of the old, and perfect copies of each other. That's how nature does it! And it was enough to send Francis Crick screaming into a nearby pub, The Eagle, with news that he and Watson had discovered "the secret of life."

Max read, re-read and read again the text, as if he were a dubious lottery winner checking his ticket. "Why, this opens a whole new world!" he said. Two new worlds, actually, for the Watson/Crick discovery was a marriage of biology and chemistry, almost equal passions for Max.

The laboratory at which Max was working when he became ill was only too happy to offer him his job back once he regained his health.

Max hesitated, chiefly because the industrial synthetics project awaiting him there hardly satisfied his new appetite for cutting edge research. But he needed to work, in part to pay off his substantial medical bills, so he returned to his old company.

The synthetics work proved every bit as pedestrian as he had feared. One particularly monotonous afternoon he placed a call to his favorite CalTech professor, Dr. Alvin Wharton, now chairman of the department, seeking advice. Wharton urged Max to apply for a vacant associate professorship, asserting that while the flood of applicants had given the department an excellent pool, he and the other members of the search committee had held out for just the right applicant; the special blend of qualities which Dr. Wharton knew Max possessed.

Max hesitated. He was a "doer" rather than a teacher of doers.

"Don't worry about it, Max," Dr. Wharton said, summarily. "The best teachers we have in this department came primarily for the research opportunities. Once here, they became infected with the curiosity of our bright students. Many of them found teaching far more satisfying than they predicted. Some even preferred it to research. Come give it a try. If you don't like it, the world outside the walls will still be there."

Max's first stroll through his old laboratory, with its creative clatter of glassware and the pungent smell of formaldehyde, convinced him he was home. As Dr. Wharton had predicted, the teaching quickly changed from a necessary burden to a pleasure, although joy was still to be found in his research.

For the next four years, Max reveled in the academic atmosphere which now seemed as natural as air itself. Still a bachelor, he enjoyed the company of women both on and off the campus. The students were a perpetual source of inspiration, amusement, and surprise. The tranquility of peaceful Pasadena belied the ferment of intoxicating theories and forecasts, especially in the physics and astronomy departments, where prospects of space exploration had gripped the collective consciousness.

In 1959, Max took a sabbatical to Harvard to study under James Watson. Here was a chance to labor at the feet of the master after following DNA developments since the double helix discovery.

During his two years there, Max met and married Rita, a shy, clever research assistant in the history department and twelve years his junior. Rita, born and raised in the Boston area, presented Max with a large extended family of in-laws with whom he became close, except Uncle

Eddie, who confided to Rita within earshot of ten or twelve relatives that he found Max "weird."

"Don't worry, Max," advised Rita's Aunt Emma, "he says that about everyone who can read." In actuality, it was Uncle Eddie who was weird, but only by the standards of Rita's family, which placed higher education on a priority level only one notch below salvation. Uncle Eddie had finished high school but resisted all pressure to attend college, shocking the family by taking as job as a longshoreman.

Near the end of his sabbatical, the combination of the rarefied Harvard atmosphere and his new extended family caused Max to consider requesting an extension. He might have done so had it not been for a fortuitous debate with a colleague named Lawrence Mishaw, an associate professor of chemistry with whom Max had become good friends at Harvard.

The debate took place in a tavern just off campus known as O'Malley's, a cramped, smoke-filled den of timeless collegiate nostalgia. Ivy League pennants of faded blue, green, burgundy and gold felts dotted the upper walls, while the lower walls above the booths were dominated by photographs of by-gone athletic heroes. Here was tangible proof that men who now dominated courtrooms, operating rooms, board rooms and class rooms once roamed muddy fields in odd shaped helmets made of near cardboard. No face guards marred their vision nor prevented Yale players from marring their appearance with elbows to the face or nose; blood splattered, mud-encrusted warriors toe-to-toe in the days before the real competition began.

The patrons' booths lined one wall of the narrow, elongated room. Made of hardwood, these booths creaked and groaned with the ups and downs of customers. They were very compact, requiring one who entered to assume a sitting position in the aisle before sliding sideways into the booth, as a key might enter a lock.

The grill and Formica counter lined the opposite wall, allowing a large collection of single diners to sit on round, swiveling seats covered in red vinyl. A mass of people crammed into every corner of the place, especially on weekends. When six or seven occupied a booth near the door and were joined by friends to laugh, drink, and joke, the aisle became virtually impassible, but no one seemed to mind. When reunions were in town, the place took on a time warp. Alumni contorted themselves into the same creaky booths to drink the same cold beer and eat the same meatball subs. A few inches on the waist, a hairline slightly higher on the forehead, but students again for a few hours.

Over the din of noise created by raucous students, clattering dishes and a juke box buried somewhere near the rear by the door to the men's room, someone would yell, "How's O'Malley!", to which tradition required all in the place to answer, in unison, at the top of their lungs,

"O'Malley's Great! O'Malley's late!

A toast to his safe return!"

Failure to join carried a fine in the form of drinks for the house. No one currently associated with O'Malley's knew how or when the responsive cheer began. It had been a part of life there for generations. Whatever its source, a graduate student had established in a paper written in 1948 that O'Malley had never existed. That is to say, the founder of the tavern was not named O'Malley nor were any subsequent owners or proprietors. Not surprisingly, no one who patronized O'Malley's gave a damn.

Mishaw and Max found themselves seated in O'Malley's one dreary spring Saturday. Their plan to catch a Boston Red Sox game had become a casualty of a steady rainfall which began at midday. Rita, who hated baseball, was spending the day with her family leaving Max and Mishaw the luxury of a free day together. The rain drove hordes of people into O'Malley's producing an elbow-to-elbow gridlock. Max and Mishaw had arrived early enough to get a booth at the back where they lunched and talked. Mishaw enjoyed a quixotic, almost poetic imagination for a chemist, a quality some found perplexing in a man engaged in such precise work. Others found him occasionally obnoxious, as he could get carried away with his flights into fantasy. Max appreciated this aspect of Mishaw's personality; it separated him from the majority of his more mundane colleagues.

The debate began innocently enough. Mishaw casually expressed the hope to live long enough to see prehistoric animals again walk the earth. Max laughed.

"Larry, if you want to see dinosaurs, you need to live earlier, not longer."

"Oh, I don't know about that. DNA research may progress to the point of allowing us to resurrect them."

"Resurrect dinosaurs?" quizzed Max. "You're serious, aren't you?"

"Quite serious. I think it can be done in our lifetime."

"And how do you suppose that will be done?" Max was prodding him a bit. He had an idea where Mishaw was headed but wanted to hear his thoughts on the matter. Mishaw, true to form, needed no prodding.

"It may prove to be rather straightforward, actually. All which must be done is to gather sufficient bones, hides, and whatnot from some preserved specimen and diagnose the DNA of the beast. Then, when chemistry advances to the point that artificial genes can be manufactured, we can brew the beast up from scratch, so to speak."

"It sounds so simple."

"Why, Max, you're mocking me. I'm being quite serious. Naturally it will prove a complex process. But my basic thesis is correct, which is that someday it will be done."

"I don't know, Larry. It's an awfully long reach. You're assuming that some method will be found to analyze DNA and that the method will work for dinosaur DNA, even if enough of it could be found to analyze."

"It wouldn't take much, would it? DNA is so prevalent that virtually any trace of the animal should furnish an adequate amount."

"But, Larry, we're talking about dinosaurs here. Not bears or wolves or turtles. Dinosaurs! which haven't been here for millions of years. What do you suppose their cell structure will look like after all the oxidation, deterioration, environmental damage, and the rest. It would be astounding if enough DNA could be harvested to allow analysis, assuming a method for DNA analysis is forthcoming."

"DNA analysis can't be more than a decade or two away, Max. The brightest people in my field are working on it night and day. The benefits to mankind cry out for a solution. One will be found, rest assured."

"I agree with you there," replied Max. "I'm not as confident on the timing, but I agree that a sequencing technique is inevitable."

"And when it comes, a chemist . . . not a microbiologist, will find it," boasted Mishaw.

Max laughed. "Ah, the old inter-disciplinary rivalry rears its ugly head. Alright, you're on. Ten bucks says it's a biologist, not a chemist. Agreed?"

"It's a bet."

Somewhere in the bar someone yelled, "How's O'Malley!" The roar went up:

"O'Malley's Great! O'Malley's Late!

A toast to his safe return!"

"I wonder," contemplated Max as he looked toward the team photograph of the 1932 Ivy League champs on the wall above Mishaw's head, "how much dinosaur DNA could be out there?"

"Well, it would vary tremendously with the species, of course," opined Mishaw, professorial. "Most species, I suspect, are irretrievably lost. But the key factor for those left behind would be the conditions under which they are preserved. If they were interred in dry sand or clay which kept air and water at bay, there's no reason to think we couldn't salvage enough to work with, assuming the DNA analysis technique doesn't require vast amounts."

"Very well," said Max. "Let's assume for arguments sake that enough could be found to support analysis. There would still be huge problems to overcome. Reconstructing a dinosaur's DNA on paper is a far cry from recreating a living, breathing one. For certain we need the ability to manufacture genes artificially, which can't be done now and may never prove feasible. We have to assume that some of those genes are not present in any living organism today, so someone will need to devote a few thousand man-years to producing genes that function only in dinosaurs. Then we need to know how all those genes relate and we have to figure that out without the benefit of one living observable dinosaur for comparison. At least with plants or animals which aren't extinct we have subjects to study. Other than that," grinned Max, "I see no problems."

"As I said," conceded Mishaw, "the idea is fraught with complexities. But that's why we're scientists, isn't it Max? Besides, a couple of decades of DNA research will throw new light on the entire field. Problems we think incapable of solution may be the stuff of freshman chemistry classes a few years from now."

"You mean freshman biology classes?"

Mishaw ignored the jab. "That's always the way it is in science, isn't it? Once the answers appear, they seem so obvious that it's difficult to believe we might have once classified the problems as impossible."

Max made a response that was inaudible to Mishaw as someone had demanded to know, yet again, "How's O'Malley."

The choir of patrons shouted its response:

"O'Malley's Great! O'Malley's Late!

A toast to his safe return!"

For days following his afternoon at O'Malley's with Larry Mishaw, Max reflected on their discussion. Possibilities bombarded his highly developed brain, colliding with four years of cell research and two years of DNA study, like a thousand billiard balls on a giant table, each collision producing yet more possibilities. On the horizon of Max's mind, an image formed, turbid and illusive at first, then gradually taking shape and definition. He watched it intently, knowing all the while it was his future approaching. Slowly, imperceptibly he recognized the outline of an oak tree.

Chapter 11

In the months prior to his 1961 debate with Larry Mishaw, Max, now thirty-six, had hinted that he wished to remain in the Boston area. He had begun scouting research opportunities in the private sector, finding more in the East than he thought available in the West. But following the afternoon at O'Malley's, Max fell uncharacteristically silent. Despite the short duration of their marriage, Rita knew something was on his mind and wisely gave him space.

Max returned from his introspection without fanfare. One evening over dinner he casually noted that he had been giving his career a lot of thought and had concluded that he wanted to return to California. He spelled out his reasons and asked Rita for her thoughts and opinions. To his mild surprise, she expressed enthusiasm. She would miss her family, of course, but at age twenty-four perhaps it was time to spread her wings. Some miles between loved ones and Boston would do her good, she reasoned. Perhaps she was too dependent, anyway. "Maybe I'll learn to surf," she joked. Rita's approach to the impending move strengthened Max's conviction that they were doing the right thing.

At a tear-filled farewell party given by Aunt Emma, Max and Rita said good-bye to her family, with the exception of Uncle Eddie, who claimed he had to work. "Besides, that kissy, kissy stuff ain't for me," he had said.

Max and Rita headed west on a leisurely ten day drive across an America which Rita had never seen outside of TV. The itinerary included a three day stopover in Iowa to visit Max's family, most of whom had met Rita only once, at the wedding. The Grunfeld homestead provided Rita with her first contact with a working farm, prompting dozens of questions which Max's parents answered patiently and appreciatively. Any fear they had ever entertained that Max had gotten himself connected to a Northeastern snob were put forever to rest on the night Rita helped a distressed sow deliver a litter of pigs. It was, for all, a most satisfying visit.

"Would you ever come back to Iowa, Max?" Rita asked as their car left the county line headed west.

"You never really leave Iowa" is all that Max replied.

Upon arriving in Pasadena, Rita applied for a position in the UCLA history department similar to that she had held at Harvard and was hired after a seven minute interview. Her confidence boosted, she quickly embraced her new environment.

For Max's part, the plan of attack he had been mentally sketching for weeks was committed to paper in the form of a research grant request. The official title of his project, which received prompt approval, was "The Extent to which Nucleic Acids Deteriorate Postmortem." Rita lovingly teased him about obtaining a huge government subsidy to study "Why Dead Things Smell Bad." Max countered with the suggestion that Rita use her background to secure a grant to explore "The History of Dead Things that Smell Bad."

Cells, like people, have a life cycle. They are born, mature, and die. Why they die has been a matter of intense scientific interest. Max's prior research had explored but several of infinite possible explanations. The current project broke new ground, for the questions of how, rather than why, cells die had not been explored.

For Rita, the life and death of cells was all so much Greek. She had only a fundamental grounding in the sciences, and had struggled to achieve a B in a course known around campus as "Betty Crocker chemistry." But she was blessed with stalwart tenacity which dictated that she master a working if rudimentary knowledge of her husband's field of endeavor. This determination produced numerous discussions about Max's work, of which he was usually pleased to speak. And in a surprising number of instances over the life of their long marriage, their respective disciplines overlapped, allowing each to impart a beneficial perspective to the other. Rita's study of the pattern of hemophilia among the royal families of Europe prompted one such discussion.

"It is such an awful affliction," she declared one idle Saturday morning. "And they never knew when it was going to strike."

"That's because they never understood what caused it," observed Max.

Rita appeared surprised. "But Max, I've read numerous accounts of their concern regarding certain marriages because they feared the male offspring of those marriages would be hemophilic. They certainly knew it was an inherited disease."

"Oh, it's quite true that they observed the pattern over many generations and that they understood it was a condition inherited by males. I'm speaking strictly in the technical sense. They thought inherited traits passed through the blood, which of course was a centuries old misconception until relatively recently."

"How recently?" she inquired, eagerly.

"Well, it was actually the first half of this century before we began to understand that inheritance is determined by genes and that genes are made up of DNA."

"How does DNA work?"

"It's a fascinating process," Max assured her. He summarized the Watson/Crick findings which explained the essential mechanics.

"What a discovery!" marveled Rita. "They are clearly two very brilliant men."

"You know another remarkable fact about their work? They never performed a single experiment in arriving at their conclusions."

"You're kidding."

"It's true. They studied the pieces of the puzzle which the experiments of others had produced."

"That must have been a first."

"Not really. Just think how many people prior to Sir Isaac Newton must have noticed that objects in trees fall to earth instead of skyward. Thousands? Millions? But no one previously making that simple observation postulated a theory of gravity. To the infinite credit of Newton, and to that of Watson and Crick, they grasped the significance of what they observed."

"I understood your explanation of Watson and Crick's discovery, but I still don't see how DNA works."

"As you can imagine, it's wondrously complex. Let me see if I can simplify it. In almost every cell you have forty-six chromosomes. Yours and mine look pretty much alike except as a woman you have two X chromosomes and I have one X and one Y. Each of those chromosomes is made up of one molecule of DNA. To picture DNA, think of a movie composed of thousands of frames in a set order. DNA works like that, only instead of a series of frames DNA is composed of a series of four chemicals which are abbreviated A, C, G and T."

"Only four? That doesn't seem like many."

"Nature makes up for that by putting those four into some mind-boggling combinations. Suppose," said Max, warming to his analogy, "we could show your DNA on a projector. Would you be interested in knowing what it looked like?"

"I'll show you mine if you'll show me yours," replied Rita with a seductive grin.

Max returned her grin and continued. "If it were possible to project DNA on a screen, it would appear as static for quite a while. That's because the large majority of our DNA is so much genetic babble, or at least that's our current belief. But eventually, we would see a genetic signal that something important was about to be shown, like the credits signal the beginning of a movie. Following that signal, the letters of the genetic alphabet—A, C, G and T, called 'bases'—would appear in combinations of threes with each triplet constituting a formula for an amino acid. For example, the combination GAG indicates glutamic acid. These triplets can go on to specify hundreds or thousands of amino acids. At the end, another genetic signal occurs to mark the return to static."

"So what is the significance of the amino acids?"

"The acids specified, in the order specified, make up a gene, which defines an enzyme or a protein. Your body is made of enzymes and proteins. Now, if you are normal and healthy, it is probable that your amino acids are in the correct sequence, but if even one of them is out of sequence, you and your children could have a problem."

"An inherited disease like hemophilia?"

"Exactly. And the smallest error can create huge problems. Something as terrible as neurofibromatosis, which we know as elephant man disease, is caused by a defect in a single gene out of the 50,000 to 100,000 genes which make up our bodies. That would be akin to a single frame out of place in a feature length film."

"So if you have one defective gene, you're stuck with the disease? That seems pretty harsh."

"Not necessarily. Remember, you are born with two sets of DNA, one set contributed by each parent. If one set contains the defect and the other is normal, you will be fine as long as the disease is recessive. But if the disease is dominant, it will appear despite the presence of a healthy copy. Understand?"

"I think so . . . ," said Rita.

"Makes you thankful for your health, doesn't it?"

"And thankful that my field is history."

*   *   *

By 1969, Max and Rita shared a pleasant, satisfying routine which would have been tranquil had it not been for the turmoil created by protests of the U.S. involvement in Vietnam, which kept the entire university community in a state of anxiety. Max opposed U.S. involvement but opposed the protests almost as much, regarding virtually anything which interfered with his research as unwelcome intrusion.

But a most welcome intrusion appeared late that year with the birth of their first and only child, David Michael. Max received the news joyfully. After satisfying himself that mother and son were in good health and well attended, he celebrated by going to his lab for an entire Sunday free of distractions.

David proved a constant source of pride to Max and Rita. He obeyed the immutable laws of adolescence, so there were the predictable strays from the straight and narrow of perfection, but nothing of consequence. Max would frequently over the years report to relatives that he was "such a good boy. No interest in science, mind you, but a good boy." David possessed a confirmed interest in sports and women. He went on to UCLA where he played varsity baseball, struggled for a C average, and had one hell of a good time.

Professionally, Max redirected the focus of his research to the newly emerging practice of recombinant DNA. While he appreciated from the beginning the subject's potential for controversy, he and many of his colleagues in the field underestimated the furor triggered by this practice.

The controversy sprang from the nightmare of organisms growing out of control, a vision which had some powerful forecasters by the mid-70's. These doom-sayers were alarmed by the prospect of accidental creation of an unknown life form. The structure of DNA is essentially the same for all living things. The four bases that appear in humans are the same that pass genetic instructions in fish, fowl, fleas, and flowers. This fact makes it possible to combine, for example, the DNA of the King of England with that of a king crab or a king cobra or King Kong. It is done by the use of proteins called "restriction enzymes" and "DNA ligases." By employing these in what is tantamount to a cut and paste operation, the DNA of an animal or plant can be spliced into and function as part of the DNA of a human. The concern over this process was that an unknown and unnatural organism, once released, could not be recalled, posing a potential threat to mankind.

By 1976, the furor over recombinant work largely evaporated. The battleground of the future would prove to be intentional alterations and mutations as opposed to accidental ones, and Max would find himself in the middle of that battleground on the eve of his great discovery.

Chapter 12

In 1990, Max celebrated his sixty-fifth birthday. The occasion brought together family and friends from as far away as Seattle, Washington (a former colleague), and Ames, Iowa (a brother). Eric, recently retired from an aerospace design company, brought French champagne and a new wife, the former Mrs. Walsh having died five years earlier. In answer to the age-old question "What do you give a man who has everything?" Rita and David sprang surprises.

Rita's gift characterized the woman to whom Max had been married for thirty years. She presented him with a small brass desk plate inscribed, "I'm not shy and I'm NOT retiring." Rita had noticed that Max became unusually quiet during and after these talks about retirement which, as time passed, Rita took as a sign of reluctance to discuss the matter. Whenever he could be coaxed to talk, his positive observations usually dealt with benefits and enjoyments for Rita, rather than for himself. Max was making it clear, by what he was not saying, that he did not wish to quit his research. Privately, the thought of retirement scared him; he would consider it only out of a sense of obligation to Rita's wishes and only then if she truly wanted it. She didn't. True, she wished to see more of Max than his research had permitted, but not at the cost of making him unhappy. She had a comfortable life, many good friends and rewarding interests, both personal and professional. She was happy. She wanted Max to be happy also, and that meant he had to stay in his lab. The engraved plate said, when read between the lines, "it's fine with me for you to continue working as long as it gives you joy." Max was deeply touched, and prized her gift until his death.

David's was none other than a grandchild, Max and Rita's first. Actually, it was the announcement of the birth still seven months away, but that mere technicality in no way detracted from the celebration. Max showered David's wife Laura with heartfelt congratulations, privately confiding to David, for perhaps the forty-first time, how much he admired his daughter-in-law of eighteen months. Laura was, in a word, an "eyeful" with a rich California tan spread evenly over classic athletic good looks. Young David might not know a test tube from a test drive or science from shineola, but the kid knew women. Laura, in turn, was very fond of her father-in-law. Her news that they had decided on Max as a boy's name was an added thrill.

"And if it's a girl?" inquired Max.

"We still go with Max," laughed Laura, "although Maxine may end up on the birth certificate." Max loved it.

Within days of this celebration that Max received a most unusual telephone call. He had been summoned from his lab by a hesitant assistant to take the call of a Doctor Eason at the University of Illinois. Unhappy at being disturbed, Max briskly searched his mental rolodex.

"Eason, Eason . . . no, it doesn't ring a bell. Tell him I'll call him back."

"I did, Dr. Grunfeld. I'm sorry, he's very persistent."

"Well, I'm going to be persistently mad as hell if this experiment goes bad while I'm on the phone to this Eason." The lab door slammed behind him.

"Max Grunfeld here."

"Dr. Grunfeld!" came a cheerful voice on the other end. "Ben Eason at Illinois. I hope I didn't disturb you."

"You did," said Max flatly, more out of irritation than anger. "I have an experiment running so I can't speak long. How may I help you?" If either Max's comment or tone affected Ben Eason, he gave no hint of it, blithely chatting on in the same peppy, upbeat voice.

"You don't know me. I really don't know you either, but I know your work and it's first rate, but then I don't need to tell you that. Anyway, we here in Illinois are starting a project that I hope holds some interest for you because we can certainly use your help, not to mention your reputation."

"Dr. Eason, I don't want to cut you off but . . ."

"This is a terrific project, I can tell you that, Dr. Grunfeld. The whole country's going to be talking about it. But it will take me some time to explain."

"That's the problem, Doctor. I don't have the time. Perhaps—"

"How would you like to perform a genetic analysis of our sixteenth president, Abraham Lincoln?"

There was a pause on Max's end of the line before Max repeated slowly, "a genetic analysis on Abe Lincoln. Hmmmmm. Give me some details."

For the next forty minutes, Ben Eason outlined the Lincoln project. The idea had originated within the medical community but was now being pushed by some historians as well. The medical question to be answered was whether Lincoln suffered from Marfan's Syndrome, an inherited disease of the bones, joints, and circulatory system. A number of doctors had observed over the years that Lincoln's physical appearance displayed some of the characteristics of Marfan's and historians had wondered if it could provide an explanation for his well documented depression. With the location of the Marfan's gene, it now became possible to contemplate analysis of Lincoln's DNA to resolve the debate. Eason went on to describe the make-up of the team pushing the project as well as the legal, ethical and political considerations.

Eason said, "I do hope the political issues don't erupt on us, or I guess I should say on Lincoln. That's all he needs; political problems 125 years after he dies. Poor guy can't get a break!"

Max could hear Eason chortling.

"Where will the DNA come from?" asked Max.

"Two sources, potentially. One should be fairly simple but there may be hell to pay for the other. By that I mean, you know, taking some tissue samples from the interred body. That's the hard one. We fully expect to hear a chorus of 'Leave him alone,' if that becomes necessary, which we don't think it will."

"What's the easy one?"

"That's very interesting. Lincoln lived for ten hours after he was shot. He was too critical to leave the house across from Ford's Theater but doctors attended him continuously. A Doctor Grossberger, who fully appreciated the magnitude of the event he was witnessing, kept some samples of blood, skin, hair that sort of thing. These samples have been well preserved and carefully safeguarded over the years. They may be available for analysis with no need to invade the crypt, which could spare us all a lot of headaches. Well, what do you think?"

"I may be interested," said Max. "I would appreciate a complete description of the project, in writing if you have it."

"Of course, of course. I anticipated you'd want that. I'll have the full package sent to you right away. Look it over and let us know officially once you're comfortable with the details. If I can help, please call."

That evening, Max shared with Rita the details of Eason's call. Her eyes widened with the revelation that human tissue samples over a century old could provide answers to enlighten twenty-first century inquiries. Then it was Max's turn to be impressed. From her reservoir of history, Rita painted a vivid picture of the man and his times. "You can almost see him, can't you, Max? A rough, unpolished country lawyer bidding his long-time law partner William Herndon goodbye before boarding the train to assume control of a government on the verge of chaos; tagging his own luggage with 'A. Lincoln, The White House, Washington, D.C.'" Max, whose knowledge of Lincoln prior to Rita's discourse was no more nor less than the average person's, was now doubly glad that he had expressed positive interest at Eason's project.

Two days later Max spread the promised package before him and examined it in detail. Rita joined him, asking a host of questions which had not occurred to Max. Her keen interest in the project was evident, and natural in light of her background. Max raised the prospect of their joint participation and pledged to a most enthused Rita that he would call to clear it the following morning. Ben Eason was delighted, assuring Max that the project's steering committee would welcome Rita's participation.

The task force which gathered in Springfield, Illinois, consisted of experts from five disciplines: medicine, politics, history, psychology, and microbiology. The State of Illinois underwrote it for reasons critics charged were far from altruistic. Was it indeed "a re-examination of the man considered by many to have been our greatest president," or a ploy to stimulate tourist traffic in a bad economy by focusing the spotlight on the state's most famous son.

But if the commercialism bothered any member of the task force, it didn't show. A great spirit of camaraderie pervaded the organizational meeting, attended by the ten official members and a host of interested supporters like Rita. After introductions, the effervescent Ben Eason was chosen chairman. Max, embarrassed by the attention heaped upon him, tried to dampen expectations, noting that any analysis of DNA over 125 years old was certain to have its limitations. He prepared them for the possibility that his examination would yield nothing of value. To his conservative admonition the panel paid not a bit of attention.

Three weeks after Max and Rita's return to California, Max received a call notifying him of the arrival of the Lincoln specimens, scheduled for the following day. Max met the plane from Washington, where an employee of the Smithsonian Institute handed him the tightly packaged vials. Max invited the courier to join him and Rita for dinner, but was not disappointed when he declined. The faster Max finished dinner, the faster he could get to his lab.

Rita rarely visited the lab but accompanied Max on this occasion. If the DNA of a man long dead was meaningless to her unschooled eye, Max's reaction would be worth the trip.

Max knew from the briefing in Springfield that there were four vials of Lincoln matter known to exist. All had been gathered by Dr. Grossberger attending Lincoln on this death bed. Max had been entrusted with two of the vials, which he painstakingly extracted from Styrofoam molds custom made to transport the material to his lab.

The sun had set by the time Max finished setting up the initial experiment. Max and Rita sat on opposite sides of a work bench with the glass vials mounted on a rack between them. The tops of the vials had been sealed with wax within days of the assassination and a crude label had been affixed to the vial itself which bore the initials "A.L." in penned longhand and the words "vial#." The numbers themselves were smudged. They looked like a 3 and a 4. Max picked up a vial, cutting away the paraffin to get to the stopper.

"It's the original vial, all right," Max noted casually. "You can't order these from the supply houses anymore."

"Oh Max, how can you be so calm as to care about the vial. Aren't you just trembling inside? I am."

"It is exciting," replied Max, dropping his attempt at indifference. "But if I allow myself to get as excited as I feel I won't be able to work," he said with a wink.

The stopper removed and set aside, Max took a pair of needle nosed forceps and slowly extracted the tissue from its perpetual bath. He followed the prescribed handling procedures designed to minimize deterioration and loss of tissue. After several moments, he looked up at Rita.

"Ok, Mr. President. Let's see what you're made of."

As Max adjusted the myriad of settings of the microscope, which would give him his first look at Lincoln's cells, he paused to deal with a sensation which had overtaken him without warning. Here I am, he thought, handling the part of the scalp near the bullet wound of a man who changed human history; a man considered by many to be among the greatest who ever lived. In moments I will be viewing things that no one who lived in his century could have seen. I may find facts about his health and his heritage that he could not have known himself. He may have struggled with afflictions of mind or body of which he died ignorant, but which I could clear up for him with five minutes conversation.

These realizations explained nervousness, a certain edge he felt as he brought the cells of the slain president into focus. The source of that uneasiness, he now knew, was awe in the presence of a great man. Even a trace of the great man. Clothes, hats, watches, papers, furniture, are also traces which serve to recall memories and images of their owners. But human tissue is more: within the slides of his microscope lay the genetic formula for one of mankind's heroes. He, Max, might not be able to read or decipher it, but it was there. The wonder of that truth came hard upon him.

For the next month Max studied, probed, and learned. The climax of his effort came in the third week during the definitive test for Marfan's Syndrome (Arachnodactyly). The disease Lincoln was suspected of having is an inherited trait produced by a dominant gene. It is almost always produced by an autosomal defect in one parent, although fresh mutations are possible in descendants of families with no history of the disease. It occurs equally in men and women and is degenerative, slowly breaking down connective tissue in the bone and skeletal structure. The gene responsible for Marfan's Syndrome had been isolated in 1989 on chromosome #17. To provide sufficient quantity for analysis, Max employed a technique known as polymerase chain reaction.

As Max watched Lincoln's DNA multiply before the invasive lens of his microscope, he felt a spiritual bond with the lanky plainsman who saved the Union. Late at night, with the darkened lab complex shrouded in shadows, unbroken except for the gleam of light cast out of Max's window, the giant of the nineteenth century communed with an aging prospector of the twentieth. Max could almost imagine himself an old country doctor, calling on the president in the White House. "Stick out your tongue, Mr. President; say AHHHH, Mr. President; How long have you felt this way, Mr. President?" And although the president was unable to answer, the answers could indeed be found.

And Max found them, or at least the one he had been charged with. The news that Max had confirmed the presence of Marfan's Syndrome was applauded by the task force. His final report was exhaustively and painstakingly documented so as to leave no doubt as to his conclusions. He noted how remarkably well-preserved Lincoln's tissue samples appeared. His early work in cell death had provided him with hundreds of specimens of recently deceased tissue which had degraded to a far greater extent. Immediate preservation and the unbroken seals had done their job for the president's physician.

Max's curiosity about Mr. Lincoln's biological make-up was only whetted by his Marfan's analysis. As he was free to examine his tissue samples in whatever depth he desired, Max gave serious thought to a more comprehensive study which might uncover additional facts. Rita had wondered if additional study might shed light on Lincoln's parents, about whom little is known. Wouldn't it be interesting, Max and Rita agreed, to discover some dominant traits which escaped history's notice or some recessive ones that might have put Lincoln only a gene or two away from deformity, mental illness or some other agent of destruction which would have deprived the nation of his talents in its hour of need.

But such a study was premature, reported Max to his disappointed wife. "There are simply not enough data on the human genome to conduct a meaningful analysis," he explained.

"But I don't understand," said Rita. "You performed the analysis on Marfan's; can't you do the same thing for other genetic problems?"

"Well, yes and no. If by other genetic problems you mean the handful of diseases that we know a great deal about, the answer is yes. The only reason I was able to check Lincoln's DNA for Marfan's was because thousands of man-hours were spent figuring out the gene's identity and location. But that background work has only been done on a few genetic disorders and virtually no work has been done on genes that don't cause major problems.

"I don't understand," admitted Rita. "Explain it again."

Max patiently reviewed for Rita the broad rules covering the structure of DNA.

"In other words," said Rita, determined to understand the obstacles confronting a wider Lincoln inquiry, "the order of DNA is so random that these genes could be on any one of the forty-six chromosomes. You found Marfan's on Lincoln's chromosome #17 but if I had it, chromosome #11 might be the location."

"No, no, no," replied Max. "If I gave you that impression I am sorry. No, the defective gene for any of the known diseases is found on the same chromosome. If it's #5 on Lincoln, it's #5 on you and me if we have Marfan's. In fact, about 97% of human DNA is the same for everybody . . . it's the other three percent which accounts for most of the differences among people. Isn't that amazing?"

"So why don't we find out all about the DNA of one person and then we would know 97% of the answers?"

Max smiled a big, warm smile at Rita. "You know," he said playfully, "I've long suspected that you are smarter than I am and that confirms it."

"Oh, Max. Equal maybe, but not smarter."

"Well, my darling, leaving aside the question of our respective IQ's, that was a most astute observation you just made. In fact Congress, which rarely does anything I approve of, just appropriated about 100 million dollars to fund just such an inquiry. It's called the HGP for Human Genome Project. It's quite an undertaking. The best estimate is that it will take fifteen years to complete at a cost of . . . oh, several billion dollars."

"And what will we taxpayers get for several billion dollars and fifteen . . . did you say fifteen years research?"

"Yes, fifteen. That's just an estimate. No one knows how long it will take. There could be sequencing advancements that would speed it up. Fifteen years is the current estimate based upon current technology. As to what we get for our time and money, we get a map of all forty-six chromosomes, which is what we need for the Lincoln project. As you know from listening to me over the years, the human genome is massive . . . about 3 billion base pairs which code for somewhere between 50,000 and 100,000 genes. The idea of HGP is to map each chromosome so we will know the location of the genes. Once we have that map, genetic engineering is going to take off like a rocket."

"Will you get involved or is that someone else's field?"

"It's my field all right, and yes, I probably will do some work on the project. I've had some discussions already with people at the lab concerning a research grant application for the university. But sequencing work is tedious and can be done by graduate assistants with the proper equipment and training. I've done some; it's like watching paint dry. I'd much rather play with the genes that are located."

"So, if we had this map, we could pursue the Lincoln study but without it we're out of luck. Does that sum it up?"

"Yes, but even if the map were available there is only so much we can do. That's because knowing where the genes are located doesn't tell us what function they perform or what role they play in the body's development. Those studies will keep future molecular biologists like me busy for the next few centuries, and even then it won't all be understood." He paused, then added reflectively, "You know, it's nice to know that some mysteries will remain for the next few generations."

"I suppose, but wouldn't you like to know it all now?" asked Rita. "We're not going to live forever. Don't you sometimes wish there was some metaphysical process by which we could know it all before we go?"

"Not really. Science has fascinated me all my life and a lot of that fascination springs from knowing that the mysteries are endless. No, I don't think I would want to know them all even if it were possible to learn them. But I do want to uncover one or two before I go. That would thrill me to no end—to solve a riddle and put a piece or two of the puzzle in place."

"Now Max, please don't sell yourself short. You've already done so much. The Faulkenberg Award, that wonderful work in Brazil; you're a leader in your field. Most biologists would give anything to have made even a fraction of the contributions you've made."

"My darling, you're my biggest fan. Always have been. I'm not selling myself short at all. I've had a very rewarding career; one that has been blessed by some modest successes. All I'm saying is that I would dearly love to cap it off with a home run, you know, something that would have a dramatic impact. Oh well, there's not much sense brooding about it. I've still got a few years of good research left in me. Time to stop wishing and get to work, eh?"

Chapter 13

The spring of 1999 came to southern California much as the summer, fall, and winter had come, with clear, sunny skies and insufficient rainfall. The run-on seasons were Max's least favorite characteristic of Pasadena, but as he aged, he became increasingly grateful for the mildness of the winters. Spring was announced, not by the emergence of leaves or gentle winds void of winter chill, but by his arthritis, which flared like dawn.

But this year, Max's arthritis had come and gone virtually unnoticed. What was a little stiffness in the joints when matters of utmost scientific inquiry were afoot? Max was on to something. He could feel it in his arthritic joints and through his aging body. So strong was the scent of discovery that he resumed the work schedule he had kept while in his fifties. If his long sought goals were denied, it would not be for lack of effort.

Following the conclusion of his Lincoln analysis in 1990, Max had, as predicted to Rita, supervised a CalTech team of twenty researchers doing sequencing studies for the HGP. NIH had awarded the University exactly what it sought: complete authority and responsibility for a single chromosome to be sequenced in a ten year study. At Max's recommendation, his team had asked for and received chromosome #5 (chromosomes are numbered according to size, with #1 being the largest). Max's reasons for selecting #5 were half science, half hunch. Studies showed some interesting activity on it, but the same could be said for others. The determinative factor was his gut feeling that it would be "lively." He was correct.

The sequencing work on chromosome #5 had proceeded on schedule until 1995, when Max found buried in the literature the results of some innovative Japanese experiments on cell differentiation which quickened his pulse. Max was so intrigued by the findings that he and Rita flew there to investigate.

As they flew over the Pacific, Rita seized the opportunity to learn more about the dividends Max expected from the trip.

"Max, you've been so excited about this trip that you've hardly had a minute to explain to me why we're going half way around the world. Not that I'm complaining—I can't wait to see Japan. All I know is that it relates to that study you were telling me about."

"Their studies may be the first step toward genetically grown organs; hearts, lungs and all those other things we now have to transplant from others and hope the recipients don't reject."

"My!" exclaimed Rita. "Are we close to doing that?"

"No. A long way off . . . 75 or 100 years. But you have to start somewhere."

"Would I understand it? The Japanese research, that is."

"Sure. As you know, we all start life as a single cell called a zygote. Within hours of conception, the zygote divides forming two cells, then four cells etc. As these cells multiply, the process of cell differentiation begins. Differentiation is Nature's acknowledgement that the structure of the cells necessary to construct a human being differ from those required to maintain one. It's logical when you think about it. In the very beginning, the infant skeleton must be fabricated. To it must be added the heart, the lungs, the brain, and other organs. The circulatory and nervous systems must be formed. The brain's intricate circuitry must be put in place. All of the instructions for this work are, of course, contained on the forty-six chromosomes. But once these systems have been formed, a host of cells must be manufactured to maintain and repair them. So the same cells with the same forty-six chromosomes produce specialized cells that will insure this maintenance and repair function. You with me so far?"

"I am a veritable sponge. Proceed."

"If you extract a cell early in the process, say at the four cell or eight cell stage, before it differentiates, you can implant it in another egg and grow a genetically identical copy of the original."

"Isn't that cloning?" inquired Rita.

"Exactly. Cloning is quite common now that it has commercial applications, particularly in animal breeding. But cloning works only if you implant the cell before it differentiates. In other words, you can't take a cell from a mature cow and clone it even though that cell contains all the genetic instructions on how to make the cow. Put another way, cloning works in the early construction phase of an organism's life, but not at the maintenance and repair stage.

"We don't know very much about the process by which cells differentiate. The keys undoubtedly lie in the genes contained on the chromosomes. Presumably, a gene or group of genes whose role is to 'build a nose,' is activated, or turned on during the formative stages of embryonic development, but turns off after its job is done. What turns it on and off? Other genes, according to the research done by some teams investigating this switching effect. Several dozen switches have been isolated which can turn off or on certain genes. Those which turn them on are called 'starters' and those turning them off are termed 'stoppers.'"

"So what is so special about this Japanese project?"

"The Japanese team used some early sequencing work on the mouse genome to locate the genes involved in the production of the tail. Mice have forty chromosomes as opposed to our forty-six."

"Are we that close to being like mice?" asked Rita in amazement.

Max laughed. "The size of the genome doesn't always correspond to the sophistication of the organism. If it did, corn would rule the world since its genome is ninety billion bases, or about fifteen times the size of the human genome."

"So continue. What did the Japanese do with these poor mice?"

"Extracted a differentiated cell from a mature mouse to which they added a switching compound known as alpha134, a known starter. Naturally, the mouse genes which held the genetic instructions for the mouse's tail had long since done their work. What the Japanese team wanted to ascertain was whether the addition of the alpha134 could be made to start the process of building the tail all over again, as if the cell was new and undifferentiated."

"Did it?"

"The published reports hinted a measure of success, but that is one reason I wanted to visit. I want some clarification on the results and I want to study their testing methods."

"But why are they fooling around with the tail? Why not the heart or the liver or some vital organ?"

"Good question. The answer is that they know where the genes for the tail are and they haven't located the genes for those organs yet."

"Is locating them difficult?"

"Extremely. Without a complete mouse genome sequencing, finding them is hit and miss. Remember our discussion about the Human Genome Project? Well, there's also a Mouse Genome Project, but unfortunately it's way behind schedule because of budget restraints. Some of my brethren argued strongly in Congress that funding the Mouse Genome Project was even more vital than the HGP, because more risk in research can be tolerated with white mice than can be tolerated in human subjects. The information derived from the MGP could be put to test in free-wheeling experimentation contrasted with the careful control required for any human experimentation."

"That makes sense, but Congress didn't buy it, eh?"

"Nope. The MGP funding didn't squeak by."

Rita turned to look full-face at a grinning Max.

"That was really awful, Max," she said before smiling in spite of herself.

*   *   *

Following the Grunfelds' visit to Asia, the disparity produced by the lagging MGP and the HGP, which forged ahead more or less on schedule, became known as the sequence gap.

Its impact was felt in 1996 when the human genes for the production of kidneys were discovered on chromosome #14. Major players in genetic kidney research chaffed to begin a wide variety of experiments, but only a few could be performed because of the need to use humans as guinea pigs. It was here that the value of the MGP became most evident, for if the work on the mouse genome had been current, these researchers could have searched it for the genes responsible for production of mouse kidneys. They would have started that search with the mouse chromosome which analysis showed to be structurally closest to human chromosome #14. While there would be no guaranty that the mouse kidney genes would be in the same location, that likelihood would make it a logical starting point. Once the mouse kidney genes were located, experiments on the mice could have been performed, thereby gaining valuable insight into the dimensions of human kidney formation. But without current data on the mouse genome, work had to halt.

A variation of this theme occurred in 1998 and involved Max directly. The same Japanese team which had located the genes for tail production in the mouse located those responsible for the mouse liver. Mouse chromosome #12, on which the liver genes were found, corresponded to human chromosome #5, on which Max's team was working under the HGP funding grant. This coincidence was critical. Although portions of chromosome #5 sequences had been published by Max's team as the chromosome was sequenced, the region on the chromosome which contained the liver genes had only recently been sequenced and had not yet been published. That left Max with a monopoly on that unpublished stretch of chromosome #5. After an exhaustive three month study of that segment, Max recognized the sequence of genes which he believed to be responsible for human liver production. As the Christmas of 1998 came and went, he planned a series of experiments centered on the human liver production. Perhaps, he thought, this is the area where my big breakthrough will come. Here was a critical organ, capable of transplant but always in short supply, for which he enjoyed a head start by virtue of his team's work on chromosome #5. All the elements seemed in place for a major scientific conquest.

By mid-March of 1999, Max was ready to begin the experiments he had spent the winter planning. The research protocol dictated that mouse chromosome #12 be extracted from ten cells furnished by the same mature mouse. To these ten chromosomes he added ten different starters, seven of which were being tested in other research reported in the literature and three of which Max had formulated himself based upon his expanding knowledge of the chemical structure of starters. Following treatment with the starters, the ten chromosomes were returned to their respective cells and those cells were in turn implanted in ten enucleated eggs. The ten eggs were then implanted in ten separate female mice labeled A through G for those employing starters which Max duplicated from the literature and H, I and J for the three which employed starters of Max's own creation.

The gestation period for a mouse is three weeks. Max expected spontaneous abortions by all ten mice between the third and seventh day following implantation. Then, he would analyze the ten fetuses for evidence that the liver had been restarted, as the tail had been restarted in the Japanese study. If he found such evidence, his experiment could properly be called an unqualified success. If not, which was the probable result for the first attempt, he would try again.

The first spontaneous abortion was noted at the end of the third day. It occurred in Mouse C, and the autopsy showed no signs of liver regeneration. The next day, Mice A, F, and G aborted. On day five, B, H and I, all negative for liver regeneration. Day six was uneventful. On day seven, E responded as expected, and D followed suit the next day. In each instance, the mutant fetus showed no evidence of liver regeneration.

That left Mouse J, which by day ten showed no signs of distress, for reasons unclear to Max. By day twelve, with J still appearing normal, Max reluctantly sacrificed the animal on the assumption that the implantation had been defective or the abortion had taken place so early as to have gone unnoticed.

The shock which greeted Max's inspection of the sacrificed mouse was profound. He looked up from his microscope, bewilderment spread across his face. "What the . . . ?" His voice trailed off as his eye returned to the lens. This was no mutant. It looked very much like the normal fetus. Having examined thousands in the course of his career, Max could be virtually certain. He groped for explanations. None sprang to him. He retraced his steps. He had enucleated the egg in all ten mice, hadn't he? That would have been a stupid omission, he thought, but simultaneously discarded it as impossible. He checked his notes. Absolutely, for certain, he had followed his prescribed procedures. So what, then? Why was this fetus not a mutant?

Max's befuddlement gave way to genuine curiosity. Most likely, he thought, this is in reality a form of mutation itself, an apparently normal fetus where one would not be expected. Perhaps had the mouse grown to term, the deficiencies would have become apparent. After pondering this theory for several minutes, he rebuked himself. "What kind of cockeyed explanation is that, Max? You're slipping, old boy."

His ultimate conclusion was that he had no explanation. "It just beats the hell out of me how it happened," confided Max to himself. But he would run the experiment again.

The following day he retraced each step, duplicating his earlier effort to the best of his ability. Mouse J had received one of Max's own starters, which his notes revealed to be delta41, a highly complex substance which differed from his others by only a few molecules.

On April 3, he initiated a repeat of the Mouse J portion of the prior experiment. His excitement grew with each day that passed with no sign of distress. By the beginning of the third week he could hardly contain his anticipation.

On the afternoon of April 23, Mouse J delivered without incident what appeared to be a healthy newborn. Max lost no time in extracting some DNA from Mouse J's offspring and running some sequences. His genetic analysis confirmed what he now knew but could hardly believe. The infant mouse was genetically identical to the donor mouse from which the differentiated cell had been extracted. Somehow the interaction between the delta41 starter and chromosome #5 had regenerated not simply a liver but an entire organism. He peered intently at the two cages he had placed side by side, the one containing the donor mouse in blissful ignorance that beside it in the next cage lay itself, at an earlier age.

Max sat perfectly still as the full impact sank in. Max knew the biological name for the phenomenon he had just witnessed. It is called totipotency, which is defined as the capacity of a single cell to develop into a completely differentiated organism. He knew it had been reported in certain species such as frogs, fish, and carrots. But never, he knew, had totipotency been achieved from the cell of a mature, fully grown, freely differentiated organism. If in fact that is what Max had achieved, the consequences were incalculable. For if totipotency could be achieved in vegetables and in animals, what about humans?

Chapter 14

All Max Grunfeld knew about Martin Harmon was, as Will Rogers had put it, "what he read in the papers," which was not much, until the REA surfaced.

The first reports of Martin's proposed legislation had come to Max as little more than a distraction, as a small cloud on the horizon might appear to a fisherman on the bay. The REA restricted human tissue research, and because Max labored in the sanctuary of white mice, the threat to him was of no more than casual academic interest.

Now, overnight, the REA took on the properties of a poison. As the controversy surrounding the legislation and issues raised by it heightened, Max confronted the need to form a judgment about the senator from Virginia, of whose very existence he had only recently learned. It was a short deliberation, a "no brainer," in the parlance of a lab assistant. "He's a menace to society and a threat to science," declared Max.

As the bill wound its way through the labyrinth of congressional committees, Max initially felt sure it would be defeated, an assumption based on his innate confidence that men and women of logic and education, even politicians, shared his view that science could not be stopped or even appreciably slowed. But when the committee reported the bill favorably, he could only shake his head. "Whatever can they be thinking?" he asked over and over to no one in particular.

As the hearings concluded, Max faced the very real prospect that the bill might pass. While there was still much work to be done on his mice—work which might consume the remaining years of his career—there was also the distinct possibility that human tissue experiments would be logical outgrowths of that research. And from what he had read and heard concerning the REA, that was precisely what the bill sought to restrict.

Max mulled over the impact of the REA on his future experimentation for several days before deciding to seek a legal opinion from his old friend and long-time attorney, Morris Sokolman. Sokolman's dream, known to Max and a few others, had been to produce movies, but dressing like a Hollywood mogul, in imported Italian suits with rich silk accessories, was as close as he was destined to come. He consoled himself with a seven figure income from his law firm.

"Morris, I need your help," explained Max as he sank into the sofa in Morris's office.

"That's what I'm here for, Max. That's what I've always been here for. Haven't I always been here for you, Max?"

"Yes, you have, only this time I am not as sure you can help, but I wanted to come see you just in case."

"Whadaya mean I can't help. Of course I'll help. I always help, don't I? What makes you think I can't help?"

"Because I can't tell you the problem, that's why."

"Can't tell me the problem? As in you can't talk about it, is that it, Max? Say, Max, does this have to do with Rita? Is that why you can't talk about it, Max? Is it Rita?"

"No, no, Morris. She's fine, we're fine. It's not that."

"So why can't you talk about it?"

"Because it's incredibly powerful stuff and I'm not sure I should tell anybody anything about it."

"Max, you're really hurtin' me now, you know that, don't you, Max? You're really hurtin' me deep here with this hush hush business. After forty-five years of being your lawyer you don't trust me?"

"Relax, Morris, I trust you." It was pointless to tell Morris to relax once he got going.

"Relax, how can I relax? I got a client here for forty-five years who's trying to decide if he can trust me."

"I trust you, Morris, I trust you. It isn't that."

"Give me a clue," demanded Morris.

"It's complicated. A short time ago I happened upon a discovery. I say 'happened' because it wasn't what I was looking for when I found it. It was an accident of sorts, but a very significant one because it has huge implications for biomedicine and for science. It is one of the most important discoveries in history."

Morris gazed at his client with a mixture of awe and disbelief. He knew Max to be modest, prone to understatement. Max, as Morris had once noted at a social function, was the type of person who might have described the sinking of the Titanic as an "offshore incident." For Max to make the statement Morris just heard was almost as significant as any scientific breakthrough Max had uncovered.

"Is this a positive discovery?" quizzed Morris.

Max hesitated. Was it a positive discovery? He had not put the question to himself. He had assumed so, but that was instinctive for a scientist. Any unveiling of the unknown was hailed by a researcher. That was his job. He was not unlike the defense attorney who secures an acquittal for a guilty child molester. It was the lawyer's job to represent his client, not to compensate for the quirks in the jury system or to expound on the social implications of the verdict.

Max measured his response. "I believe it is positive, although it will raise the most profound ethical questions; questions with which our society has not begun to deal. I suppose it will be like so many things in life—positive on balance but with negative aspects. Like cars, or sex perhaps."

They chuckled.

"What's in this discovery for you?" persisted Morris.

"Oh, not much. Aside from a Nobel Prize, more money than I ever dreamed of, and a permanent place in the history of science, it has very little to offer."

"Ah!" cried Morris. "For a minute I thought we were talking something really big. Seriously, is it that gigantic?"

"It is that gigantic."

"Max, do I need to tell you that you have piqued my curiosity here?"

Max laughed. "I rather assumed that."

"If what you say is true—I believe you, don't get me wrong—then what is your problem aside from some tax and estate planning advice? But you didn't come to me for that."

"True, I didn't. The problem is that I must do research to complete my work. You have no doubt seen the news reports of the bill in Congress they are calling the Responsibility in Eugenics Act of 1999, or REA for short. It's being pushed by some senator from Virginia named Harmon. He's regressive, as best I can determine. My friends at NIH tell me that he's got a hidden agenda that is quite anti-science. It has a lot to do with his political aspirations and his standing among the pro-life zealots. Anyway, he's leading the charge. I didn't think much of it when I first heard about it because it didn't affect me. But that was before my discovery. They say now that it could pass in Congress. I'm worried that it will ruin the research I need to finish."

"I personally am not familiar with either the bill or Senator Harmon. We have several people in the firm here who do a lot of work in Silicon Valley. They stay on top of things like this REA business. I'll see what they know. But I still don't understand your problem well enough to brief the group downstairs. Don't you trust me, Max?"

"You know I trust you. But I must keep this confidential for a while. See if your people can find out about two things: first, what are the chances that current research will get in under the deadline of the effective date. I think the term is 'grandfathered.' Find out what is grandfathered."

"Ok, I'll do it. What else?"

"I need to know very precisely what they consider prohibited under this law. I've read the text of this bill—it is not very long—and I know what it seems to mean, at least to me, but tell me what your people think it means."

"We'll do our best, Max, we really will. But I hope you understand that we don't have a lot to go on. Lawyers deal in problems. Once we know the problem, we shop for a solution. Here we've got to find a solution without knowing the problem. It's a little iffy."

"I realize that. Do the best you can. Maybe the information will allow me to find the solution. Or maybe I'll just have to give you more information if I expect you to help. I'm sorry to be so secretive, but I feel I must."

"We'll respect your wishes, Max. You're a good client as always. I'm so pleased for your good fortune. Does anyone else know the details besides you? Suppose the elevator cable breaks on your way out of here."

"I wrote it all down and put my notes in my safe deposit box. But how is the elevator?"

Morris guffawed. "No problems . . . inspected oh, eight, ten years ago at most."

Morris accompanied Max to the door of the outer office.

"Goodbye, my friend," said Morris. "It's all very exciting. There is just one thing I want to know."

"What's that?"

"Don't you trust me?" asked Morris, as they both broke into belly laughs.

*   *   *

Days later, Morris called with the results of his firm's investigation.

"Our guys studied the committee reports and witness transcripts, but it's difficult to draw conclusions. The key words in the bill haven't been used enough in other legislation to have acquired defined legal meaning so there is always the remote possibility the words mean what they say. But you know how that goes. First the Congress says what it thinks it wants to say, then the litigants in some law suit say how they interpret what Congress thinks it said, and then the courts proceed to rule on what Congress actually said when it said what it thought it was saying. It takes a long time for that to happen and until it does, no one is sure what the language means. So in terms of what kind of research will still be permitted on human tissue, it's anyone's guess.

"We had better luck on the grandfather clause. There was substantial pressure put on the committee to do something about all the projects in the pipeline and on the drawing board. Without some kind of grandfather provision, research universities and laboratories all over the country stand to lose millions of dollars and some valuable research. Some have research grants up for renewal where the failure to renew will negate all the benefits of the prior research. Others have already expended major dollars to plan research projects involving human tissue. The committee never could agree so the bill was reported without any recommendation as to projects in the pipeline. The feeling of the committee staffers is that some significant grandfather amendment will be proposed from the floor and if the bill passes, it will probably survive a conference committee. Everyone wants to see some compromise.

"Max, I don't want to be pushy, but the feeling here is that we could be a lot more helpful if we know your exact situation. Do you feel more inclined to open up a little bit?"

"I just can't now. Thank the guys down stairs for me. I'm sure I don't need to suggest that you send me a bill."

"I'll also send you a written memo of what I've told you. Call me when you've looked it over."

When Morris's memo arrived, Max pored over it. The proper grandfather clause offered the best hope for a way out of his dilemma, but the drafting and ultimate approval of such a clause was clearly out of his control. He would have to wait and to hope for the best.

In the meantime, Max paid a visit to Dr. Nelson Anderson, the head of his department at the university. He needed to lay the groundwork for the sudden submission of a research proposal to NIH in the event a grandfather clause opened a loophole. Anderson understood. He pledged to appoint reviewers, required by university policy, immediately upon being notified of Max's intent to submit the request. They had discussed possible reviewers which had given Max the chance to steer the appointments toward two colleagues whose reviews Max knew would be sympathetic and fast.

One week before Martin's news conference announcing the votes necessary for passage of the REA in the Senate, Morris called advising Max that sources in Washington predicted passage of the REA, although the vote was expected to be very close. Max lost no time in delivering the research proposal to Dr. Anderson, who duly appointed the reviewers Max had requested. By the following week Max had both reviews in hand, enabling Dr. Anderson to sign off on the grant request and ship the proposal to NIH via overnight delivery, where it joined hundreds of others on the floor of the NIH receiving room on the day after Martin's triumphant press conference.

"You're going to have problems with this, Max," Dr. Anderson had predicted upon being shown the grant request. "And the university may have problems as well. Do you agree?"

"Yes, given the present climate. I considered going private with this, you know. I wouldn't do anything to harm the university's reputation."

"Max, if I understand your thesis and if it proves correct, the university's reputation for science will take a giant leap forward. But its political reputation . . . that's what worries me."

"I see no way around it unless I go it alone, which is still an alternative, I suppose. My lawyers tell me that because of the grandfather provision that's likely to emerge in the Senate, what I am proposing should be judged by the pre-REA standards for review. That is the whole point of the grandfather clause. If that's true, the fact that this research would not be funded after the REA passes should be of no consequence. That's the way I analyze it. Of course, if there is no grandfather clause I may have a problem."

Anderson leaned his head back philosophically. "Washington is a funny place, Max. Your logic is sound, of course, but logic doesn't always prevail in our nation's capital. If I were you, I'd plan on a fight, grandfather clause or no grandfather clause. The tide is running against genetic engineering and you could find that tide washing overboard a lot of good proposals, yours included. The university will back you, I want to assure you of that. We still put science above politics here. Still, I'm concerned. With the awful state of this economy and the budget crisis, we need every dollar we can lay our hands on. We don't need to offend the powers at NIH."

"I hope I'm doing the right thing in submitting this request," responded Max. "I hope I'm doing what's best for me and for the university. At age seventy-four, I'm not sure how many fights I have left in me, so I'd much prefer to grapple with science than with the government."

"Perhaps the REA won't pass after all," speculated Anderson. "That would solve our problem."

Max nodded. "That would solve our problem."

BOOK 3

THE REA

Chapter 15

Capitol Hill was Martin Harmon's world. He did not own the Hill as had some of his legendary predecessors. He could not dictate, yet he had influence, hard earned and zealously protected. And ability to build a consensus, a talent the uninitiated assumed of lawmakers but in fact remarkably rare. The REA, which he brought to the floor for final passage on June 17, 1999, required every ounce of his political talent.

His immediate problem was the "hard count," a term used to define the total of those senators who had given their firm, unqualified and unambiguous endorsement. He had fifty-two votes by that standard, and another five votes which he considered "probable," but not hard. Fifty-two hard votes presented a couple of potential difficulties. As his margin was only two, and as the position of the vice president, who would be called upon to break a tie, was unknown, it was critical that all of his supporters be present. And the hard count had to be, in fact, hard.

The Senate committee had reported the bill favorably by a vote of nine to four. The nine affirmative committee members were placed in the hard count, as they could be expected to vote in similar fashion when the matter came before the full Senate. Martin had assigned Dennis the task of monitoring these nine votes against any slippage. He detailed five other Senators to Dennis in hopes of persuading them to join Martin's majority. Martin, Dennis and the rest of the REA coalition met weekly for the purpose of reviewing the list name by name, adding and updating their intelligence base on each Senator.

As the date for the vote approached, Martin had been working night and day on the REA, and had not seen Carson for four days. He placed a call to her shortly before leaving for the Senate chamber.

"So today's the big day," she said, with no hint of remonstrance.

"By sunset I'll know if all this work has paid off. I'm sorry I've been invisible these past few days, but I don't want any surprises."

"Do you expect any?"

"If I did they wouldn't be surprises. If all commitments pull through, we're home free. I feel confident we'll come through."

"I'm sure you will. If you have a chance, call me to let me know how it's going. I'd love to go sit in the gallery, but I guess that's a thoroughly dumb idea."

"Indeed. After this is over I'm hoping we can spend some concentrated time together. How does your schedule look for the next few days?"

"I'm busy, but not that busy. Let's see, I have to go to New York for a day to finish research on my assignment. I have a dental appointment and a doctor's appointment the following day. Other than that, I'm free."

"A doctor's appointment. Is anything wrong?"

"Strictly a routine checkup. I get one every other year."

"How does a few days on the coast of Maine sound?"

"Like heaven. Can you get away?"

"Leave it to me. I've gotta run. Wish me luck."

"I know you'll be terrific."

"Thanks. I'll call you. Bye."

* * *

At noon, the Senate chaplain, Rev. Harrison Logan, delivered the invocation to a Senate chamber more crowded than usual. His melodic tenor, normally soothing to rushed pages and decorous senators exchanging greetings, did little to quell the electricity running along the floor and through the gallery in anticipation of a close vote. As the vice president gaveled order and the clerk read, in his practiced monotone, the perfunctory business of the Senate, Martin surveyed the chamber and, above it, the audience to which he would be speaking. It was, he knew, the most important speech he had ever delivered.

"The chair recognizes the junior Senator from Virginia."

Mr. Harmon: "Mr. President, I rise today for the purpose of urging upon the Senate the final passage of Senate Bill 481, more commonly known as the Responsibility in Eugenics Act. We sail today into uncharted waters. While the health of the human race has long occupied our energies in this deliberative body, we have not previously considered in so direct a manner the future of our species. This bill addresses a fundamental dilemma: shall we control genetics or shall they control us? That is the decision before you."

Martin scanned the chamber. He sensed the attention he commanded among his colleagues; he felt they were listening. In the gallery, all was still, the guards having turned away a dozen with passes seeking admission. It, too, seemed intent on his words.

"We have a sacred kinship with our predecessors on this planet. And so it is that we can read Plato, Aristotle, Thomas Aquinas, Euripides and other ancients and see in their writings and teaching the same human nature with which we deal today; the same strengths of character, the same temptations, the same prejudices and passions. With respect to human nature, the axiom that 'the more things change, the more they stay the same' has been a truism for thousands of years.

"Will it be true tomorrow? The answer may depend on the passage of this bill. If that strikes you as a rather presumptuous importance to attach to this legislation, let's consider some history.

"Eugenics, as we all know, is the attempt to improve qualities through selective breeding. Those of you who represent farming states are fully conversant on the subject as it relates to plants and animals, for I suspect that you, like me, have been to countless 4H and agricultural fairs in the course of your political campaigns. We have all had our share of explanations for 300 pound pumpkins and bulls the size of mobile homes. Invariably, they are the result of selective breeding and crossbreeding to improve the size, taste, hardiness, texture, color, and countless other characteristics of plant and animals, and can be labeled as positive eugenics. Positive eugenics have been around for centuries, and mankind has benefitted from these practices despite the fact that no one has quite understood the scientific basis.

"Negative eugenics imply the attempt to eliminate flaws in plants, animals, or people. Where humans are concerned, negative eugenics is the process with which we have become most familiar in our efforts to control birth defects and inheritable diseases. For most of recorded history, our efforts in negative eugenics have been feeble because we understood so little of the science involved. We passed laws forbidding marriage between brother and sister because we observed deficiencies which resulted from their union. The deficiencies were obvious long before any scientific explanation for them was advanced. Other defects were much more insidious, for the relationship between cause and effect was less predictable.

"Small wonder, then, that the world community hailed the discovery of genetic secrets; that it rejoiced at the prospect of bringing these scourges under man's control."

Martin shifted at the podium, turning slightly toward another group of seated senators, and folded in front of him his hands, which held no notes.

"It was not until the beginning of the century which is about to end that we began to understand genetics. Quite properly, our initial human research was targeted at human misery so as to supply hope and relief to those afflicted. Between 1953, the year in which the structure of DNA was ascertained, and 1999, the current year, we made giant strides in diagnosing, treating and preventing these maladies.

"In 1985, it was proposed that the entire human genome be sequenced and in 1990 we funded the initial year of this long term project. As this project nears completion, and I am told the end is very much in sight, we became aware that the knowledge we have acquired in sequencing the genome has potential for harm as well as good. The dark side of that knowledge is that we now confront the prospect of positive eugenics for people, in much the same way it has been practiced for centuries in plants and animals.

"Positive eugenics in people can be roughly divided into physical and behavioral. There is controversy about both and with good reason. Because deformity and inheritable disease were the early targets of genetic engineers, we know much more about physical heredity. But as we begin to link genes to behavior, we inch toward a precipice which is very dark and endlessly deep. The trend is clear. Several years ago a study of twins was undertaken to measure the degree to which genes control a condition known to psychiatrists as sensation seeking, which creates an inclination toward gambling and alcoholism. A direct genetic link has been established, as it has for inclinations toward prevarication, criminal violence, exhibitionism, and sexual perversion. Where these links are established, can others be far behind? We are daily acquiring the knowledge necessary to engineer musical talent, athletic prowess, mathematical proficiency, to name but a few. Is this a power we want? Is this a tool of creation or a tool of destruction?"

Martin turned to face the spokesman for the REA detractors. "The opponents of this legislation, led by the right honorable gentleman from Missouri, Senator Collins, will bombard you with genetic success stories. They will recite, in glowing detail, the vast improvement to mankind and to the human condition which have been brought about as a direct result of genetic engineering.

"As a proponent of this legislation, it is my job to prepare you for these destructive arguments . . . arguments all the more disingenuous because the evidence cited in support of them is valid. But you should know that it is not the evidence with which I quarrel; it is the conclusion reached in light of that evidence. I do not and will not deny the measure of success which genetic engineering has attained. Alongside my opponents in this debate I applaud the progress made in the fight against cancer; I rejoice with the parents of cystic fibrosis patients for whom hope now flourishes because of this research; I share the relief of diabetics for whom insulin is now affordable and available by virtue of recombinant DNA techniques. With few exceptions, I will lend my voice to the chorus of praise sung by my opponents to the scientists who have brought us these remarkable achievements.

"From what I have just said, I hope and trust that you are persuaded that I am not anti-science, nor are my allies in this fight anti-science. Those who contend that scientific achievements to date would have been impossible had this bill been enacted several years ago are misinformed. Virtually all the progress I have acknowledged would have been possible had this bill become law ten years ago, and will be possible after it is enacted. Valid research and experimentation will go forward as planned. And of course the bill does not affect animal research in the slightest.

"But if I am prepared to concede to my opponents that much genetic progress has been made, my opponents must concede back that not all progress is as progressive as it first appears. Let me suggest one case in point. Surely the inventor of the medical procedure known as amniocentesis assumed he or she had made a positive contribution to the human race. This process allows the diagnosis of over eighty serious disorders affecting the fetus, including Down's Syndrome and Tay-Sacks disease. Do you suppose he foresaw the day when this procedure would be used to determine the sex of the fetus in utero, so as to enable thousands upon thousands of Indian and Asian mothers to abort females in favor of males? I seriously doubt the inventor intended this result or foresaw it as a possibility, but it is in fact occurring today at a cost of millions of unborn children. This is an abuse of an honest idea, and it is my firm belief that genetic engineering is and will continue to be the abuse of an honest idea, but an abuse of such magnitude, of such stupendous consequence, we cannot afford the risks involved.

"Only once in human history has an analogous situation confronted us. When science first split the atom, its potential for both good and evil was duly appreciated. Like the splitting of the atom, genetic engineering has permanent, irreparable potential for damage to our way of life, but unlike the atom, this fact is not generally recognized or conceded by those in the best position to appreciate the risks, by whom I mean the scientists themselves. These genetic engineers seem very much taken with the notion that they can handle or control any risk of harm which presents itself. Viewing risk in its most narrow sense, perhaps they are correct. But when the risk is measured in the broad, global futuristic sense, a different picture emerges. Humans have been 'mutating' for millions of years. For all of that time, nature has selectively controlled that mutation. For all its imperfections, we humans have emerged ever stronger, ever more adaptable and ever more intelligent. The question now before us is whether to substitute man's judgments, or more to the point, man's whims for nature's tried and true method of natural selection.

"My friends and colleagues, genetic engineering is a Trojan Horse. It comes to us as a gift promising wonderful cures for horrible human deficiencies. It is welcomed into the gates of our global city on the premise that all will benefit by its presence. But like the Trojan Horse, it is full of enemies. It seethes with the forces of latent destruction who wait patiently inside for their release by an unwitting and ill prepared population. Send it away, before it is too late." Some members of the gallery looked around, as if to see the Trojan Horse of Martin's warning.

"Let us face facts. We have today the ability to determine by genetic selection the sex of an unborn child, the height, the weight, the skin pigmentation; the color of eyes; and many other physical features. We stand at the edge of control over music ability, artistic bent, athletic prowess and intellectual propensities. We have truly arrived at the threshold of cafeteria plans for reproduction, and I for one think the results will be devastating.

"In the 1950's the most popular name in America for boys was 'John.' By the 1990's, John was far down on the list of names chosen by parents. Such things, it seems, run in cycles. The names of the 1990's are more exotic and not infrequently derived from TV shows or entertainers. Can we afford to have human traits chosen this way? Will not those who select human traits be patrons in the cafeteria? Will they not tend to select that which is familiar, popular and traditional? Or worse, will they not select that which is trendy or voguish? As they do so, and as successive generations do so, will we not lose the differentiation which makes life what it is? What makes us think we can do a better job than Nature has done?

"The selection of human characteristics, both physical and behavioral, is largely determinative of who we are individually and collectively. It is determinative for that generation and successive generations. It is not the choice of a food in a cafeteria, the choice of a hair cut style, a first name, or a new car model. We cannot allow it to become trivialized even by people who mean well. We must leave such choices to nature's random selection and the natural laws of genetics, for we do not and cannot have the wisdom or experience to make the momentous decisions required.

"Americans are by nature a competitive people. If it came within our power to structure our children as we structure our stock portfolios, we will, as always, want the best. That frightens me. There was a man who lived within the lifetime of many members of this body who thought he could create a master race predominated by characteristics he and his evil henchmen considered desirable. That man died by this own hand in a bunker in Berlin in April of 1945, after taking millions of lives in his lunacy.

"In these remarks, I have carefully and intentionally avoided references to any particular religion or deity. I believe it is important that these discussions remain secular as I can think of no recent crisis in which the principle of separation of church and state is as applicable. I have used the term 'Nature' and 'natural selection' as the coins of a higher realm, and I leave it to you, and to each American, to decide for himself what those terms mean. For me personally, they refer to God's plan for man upon this earth; a plan so intricate and carefully woven that we should not disturb a single stitch or thread, much less assign to ourselves the responsibilities which we now contemplate.

"The bill before you today is designed to divert us from the dreadful path I have described. It is structured to permit the continued assault on disease and human misery. It will not inhibit progress nor will it turn back the clock. But it will turn us away from a disastrous course. The cafeteria plan for humans is not yet in place. The biomedical research necessary to put it in place has not yet been completed although, as I have noted, it is well underway. This bill will stop that research before it is too late. An essential ingredient is human tissue and organic matter, and without access to these materials for experimentation, the social engineers who would give us a power we don't seek and don't need will be deprived of their basic tools.

"The citizens of ancient Troy rued the day they admitted the wooden horse to their city. It stands today at the gates of our city. Let us not make their mistake. Let us send it away before it is too late." Martin paused, satisfied with the hush pervading the floor and gallery.

"Mr. President, I yield the balance of my time to the gentleman from Texas."

Senators then arose speaking in support of the bill, one of whom moved to amend the REA by adding the grandfather clause, limiting the bill's effect to projects proposed or initiated after the date of passage.

Martin knew this was coming. He had led the fight to kill a similar proposal in committee. But once the bill emerged, Martin learned his victory had been pyrrhic. As he made the rounds to uncommitted colleagues in the effort to sell the REA, he found support for a grandfather clause. Senators who held the swing votes were being lobbied heavily by major research facilities both within their states and outside. In the end, Martin's agreement to the amendment had been a price he had to pay to assure his majority.

The opponents of the bill then took center stage, making all the arguments which Martin had anticipated in his speech. When Allen Sutcliffe, an "uncommitted" according to Martin's notes and memory, stood to denounce the REA, Martin smelled vice presidential politics at work. His fears were immediately confirmed as other "uncommitted" senators and even the five viewed as "probable" arose, one by one, to announce that after much soul searching, they had decided to oppose the bill. Someone, undoubtedly Sutcliffe, had been leaning on the uncommitted and the "probables" and the pressure must have been heavy because the split which could have expected from the normal laws of probability simply was not holding. After the vote, he thought, he would get to the bottom of it. But at the moment, he was re-counting noses. It would be very close.

The opponents of the REA had almost exhausted their allotted time when Senator Collins of Missouri, leader of the opposition, stated: "Mr. President, I yield the balance of my time to my colleague from the great state of Nebraska, Senator Grasso."

Martin practically leaped from his chair. "The son-of-a-bitch," he said through clenched teeth, his anger palpable at the double cross about to take place. Grasso had promised Martin his support in an eyeball-to-eyeball meeting that admitted of no confusion or misunderstanding. Martin had pressed him, almost to the point of cross examination, to ferret out the strength of Grasso's commitment. It had been solid. Of course, that had been a while back. Grasso was on Dennis's list for reconfirmation before the vote. Had Dennis reconfirmed? Had Grasso misled Dennis in the same way Martin had been duped?

As Senator Grasso intoned in his best baritone his denunciation of the REA, Martin felt a cold sweat permeate his shirt. If Grasso had gone over, what about Baine? Was this another vote in tandem by these two? If so, the vice president could well send the REA to its grave and along with it Martin's national political future. Martin scanned the chamber for Baine, hoping to read his fate in Baine's eyes or countenance. But Baine was nowhere to be found. Damn Grasso.

Minutes later, the debate ended. The "yeas" and "nays" were demanded. After all the months of discussion, the committee hearings, the newspaper articles, editorials pro and con, legislative arm-twisting and back room caucusing, democracy was about to settle the matter. At the last moment, Senator Baine strolled into the chamber looking neither right nor left. With a nonchalance which mocked Martin's dread, he casually recorded his vote as "yea." The REA, as amended on the floor, passed the Senate by a single vote. Two weeks later, the president signed it, making it the law of the land.

Chapter 16

"Mandate Martin," as his friend Fritz Ewing had dubbed him, was every bit as pleased with the one vote margin as he would have been with ten to spare, or so he told those who offered congratulations. Privately, his assessment was more realistic. Clearly, he had come within a whisker of defeat and he meant to find out why. He pondered the effect the pale margin might produce on his image as a senator in control of his legislation and his supporters; as a man who could count votes and deliver in tight showdowns.

Dennis was more upbeat. "Chief, everyone and his brother knew it was going to be tight. We only went in with a two vote spread, for Chris' sake. Ok, we got a rotten break on the uncommitted, but hey! it happens. And Grasso! well, what goes around comes around and we owe him a kick in the ass. But you won! Three weeks from now nobody will care what the margin was. You blew them away on the floor, you held your coalition together and you brought home the bacon. That's called leadership, and that's what the people around here are going to remember."

That was certainly one perspective, Martin concluded. Dennis's words were the tonic he needed and over the hours following the vote he heard much the same praise from others. Not enough to remove his doubts, but enough to permit him to savor the hard fought victory. He would deal with the Grasso matter in good time.

The political dividend from the REA victory was not long in materializing. On the day following the vote, Martin's phone rang.

"Martin, Russ Carrington here."

"Hello, Russ. It's been a while."

"Too long. That's the reason I called. Thought you and I might get together one day this week and talk about . . . well, let's call it politics."

"What kind of politics?" asked Martin, a restrained grin forming at the corners of his mouth.

"Let's call it high level politics."

"Sounds interesting. Will Justin be there?"

"No. We don't think that's a good idea for either of you. How about day after tomorrow? We can meet at Howard Smith's place in Georgetown. R Street. You know where it is?"

"Yes. What time?"

"Eleven a.m. Oh, and Senator, the less said, the better."

"I agree. See you there."

Moments after Martin hung up, Dennis walked in, his eyebrows arched in anticipation.

"Not to be nosey, Chief, but did I hear Ellen put Russell Carrington through?"

"You did indeed," beamed Martin. "Seems he wants to meet with me Friday morning."

"Damn," said Dennis in mock consternation. "Wonder what Carrington could want to see you about?"

*　*　*

Howard Smith's brick home in Georgetown was built decades before by old money, but his new money bought and furnished it with a lavish decor that sought understatement but missed, while making a definite statement about the profitability of polling in general and Howard's firm in particular. He was the best in the business, and still a young man. And evidently a night owl, for when Martin arrived he caught the impression Howard had just gotten out of bed. In a heavily appointed den, Carrington began what he, Smith and Martin knew was a high stakes interview.

"The Governor was impressed. We continue to believe that the entire genetic engineering area holds great promise as a campaign issue next year."

"How do you envision using it?" asked Martin. Carrington had gained weight since their last meeting, Martin noticed. Even more of a rock.

"Clearly, Howard will have a lot to say about that," replied Carrington, bending at the waist to effect a nod at Smith who, with his second cup of coffee, showed signs of coming to life.

"Senator," Smith responded, "the image possibilities with this stuff are endless." His voice carried the weight of tired finality, as if the election was over and his advice had prevailed, as he had no doubt it would. "Remember Willie Horton? The law and order values that Bush was able to invoke with every use of the man's name were worth millions at the polls. I can see the same potential here. It's just a matter of coming up with the best possible symbol and weaving that into the grand design." The "grand design" was Smith's term for his overall campaign strategy.

Carrington cut in. Martin sensed that discussions of the grand design made him edgy. Martin knew, or suspected, that sessions such as this would be held with other prospective candidates as well. In the end, that process was bound to produce one satisfied politician and three or four who were disappointed, possibly angry, at being passed over. Carrington wisely wished those three or four, whomever they turned out to be, to have as little concept of the grand design as possible.

"The point is," said Carrington, his bull neck straining against his collar, "the issue has sex appeal. You're recognized as a leader in the effort to stop scientific tinkering. That tinkering produces stuff we want to run against; new, untested values against old fashioned, down-home values, technology out of control against responsible progress, indiscriminate abortion versus the sanctity of life. It will play well where we need help, in the South, primarily."

Carrington continued, "Senator, there is no desire on my part or the Governor's part to play footsy. We all know why we're here. Now I can't offer you the nomination. Only the Governor can do that, and only after he himself has been nominated. But I can tell you that my boss believes in planning ahead. He has instructed me to investigate five or six possible running mates from a list the Governor, with my assistance, drew up. You wouldn't have been asked to this meeting if you weren't under active consideration. The Governor believes the v.p. nomination is critical, both from the standpoint of the election itself and the well-being of the country after the election. That having been said, I need to ask you some questions of rather obvious relevance to the final decision."

For the next hour, Carrington and Martin discussed Martin's assessment of Justin—a clearly loaded question, Martin thought—Martin's appraisal of his own chances in the South, his views on several issues, his assessment of other people rumored to be in consideration for the nomination, and a number of personal predilections including Martin's drinking habits.

In conclusion, Carrington tendered a carefully worded request. "I'm not going to ask you to commit yourself. It's a big decision. I'm sure you need to give it a great deal of thought, talk to your wife, things like that. But I would ask that you let the Governor know if you definitely have no interest. If you know that now, tell me. If not, please advise me as soon as you reach that conclusion."

The three men stood. Martin shook hands and prepared to leave. Carrington said, "I'll walk you to the door." As he guided Martin toward the exit, he lowered his voice.

"As I said, only the Governor can extend the invitation to join him on the ticket. But I don't mind telling you that your stock with him is high, if you get my meaning. He will be very disappointed if you are not available."

"Please tell the Governor I'm quite flattered. If I can help him or the party, I would be inclined to give it serious consideration."

"Wonderful," replied Carrington. "I assume you can be reached without difficulty in the next few days? I may have some more questions."

"Certainly," responded Martin, before remembering his planned trip to Maine. "I will be out of town for a few days, but I can be reached through my office."

*   *   *

At dinner that evening, Martin related to Carson the details of his meeting.

"How influential is Carrington's opinion?" she asked.

"With Justin? It's critical. I doubt he would go to lunch with anyone Russ didn't approve, and it's certain that if he's elected, all roads to the Oval Office will lead by Carrington's desk."

"Sounds like someone to stay on the right side of. And incidentally, if you want to stay on my right side, you'll keep your promise about Maine, or have you forgotten?"

"Forgotten! Do you have any idea how difficult it was giving that speech and counting votes with thoughts of you and Maine swimming around in my head?"

"Not nearly as difficult as keeping me off you every minute we're there. Can we really go?"

"Let's compare calendars."

They did, each making a scheduling concession to marshal seven consecutive days together. Martin agreed to miss a committee vote he had planned to attend and Carson rescheduled her biennial checkup.

His calendar now cleared, Martin prepared to leave town. He called Dennis in to brief him on the meeting with Carrington and to give him two assignments to be done in his absence.

"First, keep your ear to the ground for any news regarding the nomination. Let me know at once if you hear anything I need to deal with. If Carrington calls, call me at once. Secondly, I want you to meet with a woman named Anne Harborfield. She works at NIH, but call her at home. Ellen's got her number. She's seen a research grant proposal by some Ph.D. at CalTech; Grunfeld, I think. Anyway, she thinks we need to be clued in on this grant and I was going to meet with her but we decided it would make more sense to talk after the REA vote. Go see her. Find out all you can about this grant."

"No problem. Where're you headed, Chief?" Dennis asked as the briefing broke up.

"Out of town for a few days to get some rest. I'll leave a number with Ellen where I can be reached in an emergency. And, Dennis, I mean a real emergency. Otherwise, I want everything to wait until I get back."

"Don't worry about a thing. I'll hold down the fort."

Late in the afternoon, a jet carried Martin and Carson to Maine and seven days of blissful idleness. Martin found it impossible to relax in such a public place. Carson, six rows up on the other side of the cabin, appeared calm and engrossed in a book. They had arrived at National Airport separately; Carson in her car an hour prior to departure and Martin by cab with only minutes to spare. The dentist's work on her teeth had been modest, requiring only a small amount of pain killer. Even so, he had advised her not to drive, "just to be safe." Given the risk of exposure which she and Martin were now taking, the dentist's warning verged on the comical.

As he stared distractedly out the window, Martin convinced himself that he indeed must be crazy. Did he really think he could continue this reckless course? He told himself momentarily that his decision to come had been hasty, taken in the glow of victory, and that given the chance to reconsider, he would have been more prudent. But on reflection, he doubted it, and that fact worried him even more.

Pleasant Point, Maine, is a tiny village on the Atlantic coast two hours east of Bangor. Aside from a commanding view of the ocean, it offers the visitor a choice of two diners, a convenience store, a motel, and a gas station sprinkled among the handful of houses occupied by the hearty residents. The population increases slightly in the summer because the motel, closed all winter, reopens and campers populate the woods surrounding what passes for the town. The grande dame of Pleasant Point is "Miss Ruth," owner and operator of Calm Seas Bed and Breakfast, which she inherited from her mother, the only other grande dame ever to reside in Pleasant Point.

Martin had never been to or near the place. He had learned of its existence because his accountant had recommended it to him as a place "as far removed from Washington as any place you'll ever visit without a passport or a space suit." As this comment came to him early in his relationship with Carson, when his mind had begun to wander to out-of-the-way spots which might serve as a vacation site, he noted it for future reference. Then, days before the REA vote, he had called the CPA to get a recommendation on a place to stay in Pleasant Point.

"There's only one place; one place in all of Maine if you want my opinion: Miss Ruth's. Trouble is, you probably can't get a reservation. The place stays full. With only four rooms, that's not hard, but people come from all over the country to spend time there. Be sure to use my name if you call. Miss Ruth prefers a referral."

Martin decided to try. Initially, Miss Ruth had sweetly but firmly assured him that there was no possibility of a vacancy so close to high season, but on checking her register, she found a recent cancellation, which seemed to startle her. "Imagine that," she had said. "A vacancy!" as if it were a pearl in her soup. "Must be my memory. I forgot all about that cancellation." He made a reservation under the name of "Mr. and Mrs. M. Harman," the subtle misspelling of the last name his only concession to anonymity.

He had given considerable thought to the dilemma of the reservation. Initially, he thought he would use an alias, which he had never done before and was reluctant to do now for obvious reasons, chief among them the need to leave some phone number in case of a true crisis. But leaving a number and an alias with Ellen was clearly not an option. He resolved it by leaving the number with the explanation that he did not wish to be bothered with politics during his vacation, so Ellen was to ask for "Mr. Harmon" rather than "Senator Harmon." She accepted this instruction with indifference. He did not tell her where he was going; he merely left the number with the admonition that only a genuine emergency would justify a call.

For a week Martin and Carson inhabited the isolated world which is Maine. They stayed very much to themselves while in Calm Seas, taking their breakfast in privacy and disdaining the traditional communal gatherings at the cocktail hour. They walked the bluffs along the sea in the morning hours and wooded trails in the afternoons. Their sole concession to tourism was a brief visit to a nearby fishing village, where Carson bought a scrimshaw broach. They rarely ate in the diners, opting for sandwiches and wine on walks along the remote paths leading to the beaches.

As their jet idled on the runway, waiting for the Bangor fog to lift on the morning of their departure, Martin was able to say silently to himself that whatever the consequences of this adolescent recklessness, it had been worth it. Carson, again six rows away, felt the same. Perhaps, she thought, I am a little more over my head than I realized.

*   *   *

Back in Washington, Dennis carried out his assignments. As soon as his boss left town for parts unknown, Dennis contacted Anne Harborfield for an appointment. The best meeting place turned out to be her apartment on the outskirts of Bethesda. After introductions, Anne led Dennis into a traditional den reflecting Anne's conservative taste. Dennis thanked her for her willingness to meet with him in Martin's absence. He was used to dealing with the disappointment which people felt when a Congressman's alter ego stood in for him at meetings.

"That's quite all right," responded Anne. "I know Senator Harmon trusts you or he wouldn't have sent you."

"Anne, the Senator tells me you are privy to a research grant proposal which you think he needs to be aware of. He described it to me in the briefest of terms. I'm not sure he understands it completely, to be honest, so he wants to see if you will explain it to me so I in turn can brief him intelligently. Does all that make sense?"

"Perfect sense. He shouldn't feel badly about his confusion; this is highly technical research data. Without a strong scientific background, and I mean at the postgraduate level, anyone reading these grant requests will think they are written in Sanskrit."

"Have you read them all?"

"Hardly. I read a good percentage of them during a normal month, but the avalanche we received in connection with the REA vote buried me along with everyone else. But I keep an eye out for the requests coming from the major research universities and labs. That's how I ran across this one."

"Did you give the Senator an actual copy? He didn't tell me one way or the other."

"No, I didn't. That would have been very dangerous. I gave him a summary."

"Well, the Senator certainly appreciated your keeping him informed. Now, as I understand it, the request came from a guy named Grunwald, Grunfelt . . . something like that."

"His name is Grunfeld; G-R-U-N-F-E-L-D, but it's not his request. They don't work that way. The university, in his case CalTech, puts forward the request. He is the principal investigator. Essentially, it's his project."

"I see. So, tell me, what's it all about? And remember, that post graduate degree you mentioned a moment ago? Well, I don't have one."

Anne laughed. "Ok, I'll remember," she promised. For twenty-five minutes, she outlined DNA structure and the flash points of controversy regarding recombinant DNA research.

"That's incredible!" said Dennis.

"Yes, it's fascinating, isn't it?"

"No, I mean your explanation. Oh, it's an interesting subject all right, but you summarized it so well I feel as though I actually understand it."

"Thank you," replied Anne, flattered. "But I can assure you that thirty minutes of explanation barely scratches the surface."

"Perhaps I still don't get it. This fellow Grunfeld is doing a project on white mice as I understand it. I mean, how much damage can that do?"

"Listen," said Anne. "Where white mice are today human beings will be tomorrow. Grunfeld's research grant goes on for pages about mice, but his real interest is two legged animals. If you read between the lines of this proposal, it's plain. Why do you think he's rushing to beat the grandfather deadline? If this were really about mice, the REA wouldn't concern him in the slightest. No, I think it's ultimately about humans, and not about human disease or genetic disorders or the betterment of mankind or any of that other smoke." She leaned forward in her chair, her finger punctuating every syllable. "That's why I was sure Senator Harmon would be interested in Grunfeld's grant request. This is what the REA is all about."

"Interesting," conceded Dennis. "See if you can get me a copy."

Anne stared at him before slowly shaking her head. "I really don't think that's a good idea. I could lose my job, or worse." At mention of "worse," her eyes widened.

"I see."

"Don't get me wrong," insisted Anne. "I owe Senator Harmon so much—this job, everything." She related her mother's saving visit to Harmon.

Dennis nodded. "Well, perhaps a copy won't be necessary. The point, from all you've said, is that Grunfeld requires lots of taxpayer money to experiment with mice, but you think he has a hidden agenda involving humans that runs counter to the REA. Is that right?"

"Exactly."

"The Senator will be very interested in this, and I'm certain he appreciates your help. We'll play with it and see where it goes."

"I wish you luck," said Anne, rising to see him out. "Call if I can help. You, ah, won't have to use my name, will you?"

"Not to worry."

"I need my job. I couldn't risk my job."

"Relax," urged Dennis. "This is Washington. This stuff goes on all the time."

*   *   *

Martin's charge to keep a finely tuned ear to the political ground for rumblings regarding the v.p. nomination was something akin to throwing Dennis in the briar patch, for his favorite pastime on the Hill was trading insider gossip with fellow AA's and staffers. Dennis's network of sources had served Martin well. Not many coups caught Dennis off guard. His instincts, sharp and well developed after years of factual sifting and sorting, had saved him enumerable hours of tracking down groundless turkeys. He had come to rely heavily on those instincts, which is why he first dismissed outright the rumor that Justin had all but settled on Phillip Moorehead as his vice presidential running mate.

"Phillip Moorehead?" repeated Dennis. "Naw, not a chance. Wacky idea. Trial balloon, maybe. Some pollster wanting to gage some variable or another as part of some election scenario that would never see the light of day. Phillip Moorehead? You gotta be kidding."

Not that he was any joke. The man had a resume which would have been the envy of the CEO of any Fortune 500 company in America: President's Council of Business Leaders; President of the U.S. Chamber of Commerce; founder of the America 2000 Committee; and on and on. Well liked, highly respected and singularly competent, he was a capitalist's champion; and he was a life-long Democrat; but he was not a politician. This salient fact was, according to the rumor, his chief asset. The word was that Justin wanted to tap the "throw the bums out" sentiment which accompanies any recession. An outsider with no political enemies lying in wait, a dominant force in the business world where funding was so critical, a media draw as a nonpolitical political contender for national office—all of these attributes were reported to have convinced Justin to throw over Martin Harmon in favor of Phillip Moorehead.

Dennis hesitated. It had a tin ring to it, but the stakes were enormous. He could ill afford to dismiss it if the rumor was well founded. Dennis decided he owed it to his employer (not to mention his own future) to check it out.

The source of the rumor was a reporter with whom Dennis had played racquetball back in the days when his physical conditioning had been a source of pride. According to this reporter, his paper was sitting on the story pending confirmation. Dennis moved. First, he called one of the best contacts he had, the political correspondent for a national news weekly. "Have you heard anything very recently about the v.p. nomination?" he had asked. "Nope, too early to matter," was the answer. Next, he called a former AA now employed by the Democratic National Committee and known to favor Martin's candidacy.

"Interesting you should ask," he said. "I started to call you about the same thing this morning. One of our people picked up the rumor yesterday, but the source is pretty shaky and we think it's a bunch of crap. If Justin were even contemplating something like that, we'd know it."

Dennis was simultaneously alarmed and reassured. Alarmed, because the rumor had turned up again; reassured because apparently no one at DNC was taking it seriously. Still, his DNC friend could be mistaken. His assertion that "if Justin were even contemplating something like that, we'd know it," was contradicted by too many examples which disproved it. The DNC might be the last to know. Dennis sometimes thought their building might be on fire without them knowing.

He pondered his next move. Should he call Martin to alert him? If there was any substance to the rumor, Martin was the only one who could impact the situation and the sooner he found out the better. On the other hand, Dennis would look like an idiot if he panicked by calling his boss and the DNC assessment proved correct. Then again, if at least his source and his friend at DNC had heard the rumor, what was his assurance that it wouldn't be a headline in tomorrow's paper in wherever it was Martin was staying. Then he would really look asleep at the switch for not sending an advanced warning.

He decided to get Martin's number from Ellen in the event he needed to call. She handed it to him with Martin's admonition: "don't call unless it's a real emergency." Well, thought Dennis, this is sure as hell an emergency if it's true. But is it true?

"And by the way," said Ellen. "You're to ask for 'Mr. Harmon,' not 'Senator Harmon.' I think our boss is trying to be a civilian for a few days."

Interesting. Dennis did not recognize the area code. To call or not to call?

Waiting proved a good decision. It was not his instincts but cocktails with his old racquetball buddy which led him to the truth. The same reporter who brought Dennis the rumor advised that his paper had confirmed it had no basis.

"Where did the rumor get started?" demanded Dennis.

"You'll love this. A divorce deposition, for crying out loud. Seems one of the vice presidents in Phillip Moorehead's company is being sued for divorce. At the deposition, his wife's attorney is cross examining the guy about the bonus structure in the company. He says, by way of explanation, that he expects no bonus unless he gets promoted to replace Phillip Moorehead. 'Is Phillip Moorehead leaving?' asks the attorney, at which point the guy mumbles something about a possible leave of absence next year to help run the Democratic campaign. The wife reports this over a few cocktails at the country club. It goes on from there. Absolutely nothing to it."

Chapter 17

The Maine respite transfused Martin. Months of tension dissipated on cliffs overlooking the surf before evaporating completely into the star-sprinkled summer nights above Pleasant Point. He returned to Washington eager to deal with the problems awaiting him, known or unknown.

A known problem was the vote giving rise to "Mandate Martin." Martin held Larry Grasso personally responsible for his untimely about face. Grasso's support had been pledged directly and without equivocation. Martin knew from experience that even these commitments were not carved in stone and that circumstances did come up which necessitated a shift. He had encountered such circumstances in his own career. At times these shifts were motivated by political realities which became apparent after the commitment had been given, but more often than not stemmed from a simple change of mind. The cardinal rule, known to Martin, Grasso, and others, was "be up front about it." Do not, as Grasso apparently had done, leave your colleague hanging in the lurch.

Before Martin could deal with his own staff about the surprise on the Senate floor, he needed to speak with Grasso. He called him the day after returning from Maine.

"Larry, Martin Harmon."

"Hello, Marty." The tone was affable, with no hint of strain. "I was wondering when I would hear from you."

"Oh? Something on your conscience, Larry?"

"Not exactly. I've heard you feel I let you down on the REA vote. I guess that's true."

"Larry, you don't need to explain your reasons to me. We all change our minds from time to time. It's just that a little notice would have helped—"

"But that's what I was getting ready to tell you. I tried to let you know two days before the vote. I called but you were in a meeting, so your secretary put me through to Dennis Rancour. I told him I had to talk with you, that very day if possible. That's what I wanted to tell you; that I had reconsidered my position. When I didn't hear from you, I assumed you had enough commitments from the undecideds to bring it home. Next to you, I was the most surprised guy in the Senate at the closeness of the vote. When I saw the final tally, I knew there was a mix-up. I feel terrible about it, but I did try. You can ask your secretary or Rancour."

Martin backpedaled, glad he had not approached Grasso with words he would have to eat.

"Don't worry about it, Larry. I figured it must have been some snafu. We'll consider it history. Thanks for trying to contact me."

"Dennis," said Martin ten minutes later to the man standing in front of his desk, "I just had a most interesting chat with Larry Grasso. He tells me he talked with you two days before the REA vote and left the message that I was to call him; that it was important. Did that happen?"

"Ah, yes and no," replied Dennis, picking up a paperweight from the desk. "Yes, I spoke with him and yes, he wanted you to call, but he didn't say it was important. In fact, he sounded so casual I thought it must have been social or something."

Martin brought his hands to his head as if shielding his ears from an explosion. "Social?" he repeated with incredulity. "Since when have I had any social contact with Larry Grasso?"

"Well, Chief, you keep your own schedule there. I don't know, you could have had something social with him. But I distinctly remember that he did not mention that it was important."

"Ok, he didn't mention the word 'important.' Did he say I was to call him that day, if possible?"

"He might have said that, yes."

Martin let his arms fall limply to his side. "Doesn't that imply importance, urgency, priority?"

"That's certainly one way of looking at it."

"That strikes me as the only way to look at it. What were you thinking?"

"He just sounded so casual. If it had sounded urgent I would have written a note to myself. Then with the push during those two days before the vote, I just got busy and forgot. I'm sorry. I just forgot."

"All right, I can accept the fact that you forgot. But my notes show that Grasso was on your list to confirm prior to the vote. Did you confirm, Dennis? You reported confirming, I remember that. Did you confirm?"

"Sort of."

"You know good and damn well there is no such thing as 'sort of' confirming. What does that mean?" Martin felt the constriction of blood vessels in his temple.

"It means I tried to reach Grasso the morning of the vote. He was tied up. His AA is a friend of mine, so I called to see if he knew of any change in his boss's position. He said he didn't. I know I shouldn't have considered that a confirmation but I did. I blew it."

"You certainly did. Have you considered the embarrassment that I would have suffered if we had gone down on the REA? That's not your embarrassment. I'm the one on the Senate floor and in the papers with egg all over my face. God, what a catastrophe that would have been."

"I'm very sorry, Chief. That's all I can say."

Dennis turned to go, anxious to be somewhere, anywhere that was not in the line of sight of his angry employer. He had almost reached the door when Martin said, with icy deliberateness, "Dennis, your position demands a high degree of professionalism. I won't tolerate anything less. Is that clear?"

"It's clear," said Dennis.

If Martin closed his discussion with Dennis on the assumption that Dennis felt a remorseful mea culpa, he was wrong. Dennis was mad at Larry Grasso but even madder at Martin. Grasso was scrambling, he thought. Yes, he called, but Dennis suspected it was not about the REA. If it had been, why not just tell Dennis what was on this mind? Grasso knew Dennis was tallying votes and monitoring commitments. It was just too offhand to convey the kind of importance Grasso now sought to attach to it. On second thought, Grasso might have said, "Ask him to call me or I'll look him up in the next day or so,"—something like that. True, Dennis hadn't followed the book on the confirmation, but who did? In truth, he had confirmed almost everyone on his list by talking with their AA's. All the others had been right on the mark.

And Martin. That was gratitude for you. Dennis had busted his hump tracking down the v.p. rumor and, if he could permit himself some credit, had done a highly "professional" job of sorting fact from fiction. When he had related the story to Martin on his return, Martin had simply chuckled. No praise for Dennis's follow-up or his sound judgment in not hitting the panic button. Just a chuckle. Then on to other business. Besides, in a vote with a safety factor of two, it was naive of Martin to think there wouldn't be a defector somewhere. It was just Dennis's luck that the traitor was on his list. A thankless job is what this is, he thought. He had worked for tyrants before; Martin was beginning to look like another one.

*　　*　　*

Justin had two pacing styles, both well known to Morgan and Carrington. On this afternoon, they recognized that his gait was not the amble of a man generating options but the stride of one narrowing them. The triumvirate had cloistered themselves for the last hour with a one-item agenda. When Justin Bonner raised his arms in triumph on the podium at the Democratic National Convention a little more than a year hence, one of those arms would raise the arm of his vice presidential running mate. Whose arm would it be?

"So Russ, whaddaya think? . . . straight up . . . need to know." Justin, who could be as fluid in speech as honey flowing from a jar, tended to talk in clipped, laconic phrases when decisions were afoot. Such was his manner as he strode back and forth by the window, head slightly bowed and hands clasped behind his back.

"Governor, we've pretty much hashed over the pros and cons. I've given you a full report from my meeting with the prospects. I want to do more polling but when have you known me not to want to do more polling. My recommendation hasn't changed. You're better off with Harmon than any of the others. Unless you have new prospects in mind, I'd go with him."

"New prospects? Think I need um?"

"I didn't say that. No, I think Harmon has a lot to offer. Remember, he and I are farther apart philosophically than any of the other candidates, so for me to recommend him is saying something."

"Saying what? What's it saying?"

"It says I like the guy, even if I'm not wild about his politics. We're going to take some heat if we go with him, but nothing we can't handle.

We'll have to kiss the majority leader's imperial behind for a few weeks, but he'll come around. The biggest problem, as always, will be the left wingers. You're not exactly their man of the year, and Harmon will raise their blood pressure a few hundred points, but where will they go, Republican? Fortunately, they are so desperate for a Democrat in the White House that I expect them to lay down in front of tanks if we ask them to. What do you think, Matt?"

"I agree completely," replied Morgan, studying the ceiling. "I think we need to be very specific about some liberal appointments in the Bonner administration so they know we have no intention of bringing in people that could be mistaken for Republicans. I'd like to let their main people know which plum we have in mind for them so they feel even more of a stake in our success. Maybe if some of their more tiresome ideologues see a fat federal job for themselves after the election, they'll think twice about rolling grenades onto the convention floor."

"What?" said Carrington in mock horror. "Buy off a liberal. It can't be done, can it?"

Morgan laughed. "It's tricky, but there are ways."

Carrington observed, "My, my, what I am learning about the big world in which we live and work."

Justin broke in. "Back on track." He turned and faced outward, addressing their reflections in the glass. "Looks like Harmon's our man. Hard working guy. I like him, which helps."

Morgan and Carrington exchanged glances.

"What about Allen Sutcliffe?" Carrington ventured.

"Allen's a good man and a close friend, but neither fact should decide this. Harmon got that bill through, and the more I study it, the more logic I see in going with him. Matt, you had your people check him out on the personal side, didn't you? No problems; booze, drugs, skeletons."

"He's got a good rep," replied Morgan. "Takes a drink, but no problems with it. The Senators I talked with say he's honest. Finances are in order. Taxes paid. Kids aren't likely to cause us any embarrassment. His wife could pose a problem. She's a bit on the tart side. Tart, as in her tongue, not tart as in loose. Doesn't care for politics so she stays close to home. Sounds like a marriage where the flame died out a while back. A number of the people I spoke with guessed that he must have someone in Washington, but they admit they're guessing. It figures though; good looking guy, powerful position, wife never around. But he's no skirt chaser, that's for sure. If he's got someone on the side, he's been very discreet about it. We might want to check it closer, though. You know what can happen if the news bloodhounds catch a scent."

"Yeah," injected Carrington, "they get so busy reporting on the indiscretion of others that they barely have time for their own."

"I've met Jean," said Justin. "A nice lady. I think people underestimate her. Still, we owe it to ourselves to ask the right questions. I'll have a talk with Martin; you know, one of those man-to-man's where I ask him to tell me about anything that could blow up in our faces."

"Definitely," said Morgan. "And press him. Lean on him hard. It's important."

"I'll tell you something else that's important," said Carrington, thumping the table. "We need to keep this REA business alive. We can't afford to let it slip off the front page. If Harmon is our man, we can't buy the kind of press we can get for free as long as it stays controversial. You know, talk show stuff, outrageous abuses in science, that kind of thing."

"Perhaps," suggested Morgan to Justin's back, "that could be another agenda item for your meeting with Harmon. I mean, it's his baby. He should have some ideas about how to keep it in the news."

Justin nodded to a skyscraper across town. "I'll do it."

*   *   *

The telephone call which summoned Martin to a meeting with Justin at the Hay Adams Hotel came from Matt Morgan, who gave no detail as to its purpose. There was, however, a need for privacy, so Martin was asked to be as "inconspicuous as possible." Stealth was not that difficult to achieve, for while press speculation over the likely ticket was increasing, no one expected the second spot to be filled a full year in advance of the convention. Martin was being watched, but still from a distance. A visit to the Hay Adams, even at a time when it was known that Justin was in town, would have occasioned no uproar among the media hounds.

In the event, he slipped in and out of the historic old hotel without notice. As he watched the elevator's antique brass floor indicator confirm his ascent, he wondered if he was being brought to another exploratory session similar to that he had held with Russell Carrington weeks ago, or whether there awaited something more. His instincts told him something more.

An hour and forty-five minutes later he emerged from the same elevator, striding across the richly carpeted lobby. Each step exhibited a spring, a dance of purpose and mission. He was, after all, now running for the second highest office in the land if a handshake with the certain nominee meant anything. As he burst from the large double doors of the old hotel, he glanced to his right at the White House, fully illuminated under the summer sky. A phrase from the Bible welled up through his euphoria:

"Many are called, but few are chosen."

*   *   *

Following Martin's return from Maine, a decided strain was evident between Dennis and him, precipitated by the long-standing problem of unauthorized information suspected of coming out of Martin's office and exacerbated by the screw-up in the REA vote count. As a result, both men found themselves increasingly wary of the other.

For his part, Martin began drawing his cards closer to his vest, particularly those political cards which revealed changes in the v.p. situation. He said nothing whatsoever to Dennis about his meeting with Justin, preferring instead to continue to portray himself as one of five or six possibilities. When, from time to time, Dennis brought him news of a rumor or a perceived shift in the presidential currents, Martin would feign interest, ask a couple of perfunctory questions, and resume his business.

Dennis suspected Martin knew more than he was acknowledging, but did not guess how much more. For certain, he knew only that the thin ice he felt beneath his feet needed reinforcement, and the sooner the better.

He saw an opportunity during a conversation with Martin during an increasingly rare lunch with him in the Senate dining room. Martin had expressed, with a casualness which belied the intense need he felt, an interest in some immediate political dividends from the REA vote. Surely, he noted to Dennis, there were opportunities to exploit. Martin observed that a high profile dividend could only boost his v.p. stock. Dennis didn't have the answer at lunch, but his motivation to find one was high, and he did know a place where an answer might be lurking: the apartment of Anne Harborfield.

He called her immediately after lunch. "Say, Anne," Dennis began, "the background you gave me last time has helped more than I can tell you. And the Senator wants you to know how appreciative he is. I wonder if I could impose on your time again. I've got a problem that someone with your background might be able to solve."

Dennis drove to Anne's without knowing precisely what he needed from her. He had no plan—not even the outline of a plan—but he sensed that Anne could help him, especially if her help inured to Martin's benefit. Was there, he wondered, a strategy which might bolster his standing with his boss by aiding Martin's v.p. prospects? It was in this vein that he eventually asked her the process by which Max's grant request would be evaluated. With her usual precision, Anne outlined the process by which grant requests were translated into research dollars.

"It's called 'peer review,' she explained. "The principal investigator, in this case Grunfeld, motivates his university to submit an application for a research grant to NIH. The application is received by the Division of Research Grants (DRG) where it is receipted, date stamped and sorted. My boss is the director of DRG, Dr. Cass, who has ultimate responsibility for this process. The Referral and Review branch of DRG evaluates the requests for assignment to the relevant DRG study section."

With her hands drawing an organizational chart in the air as she talked, Anne outlined her role as a referral officer within Referral and Review. She wore two hats. She assigned appropriate requests to the Genetics Study Section and served as executive secretary of that section. As executive secretary, she selected the reviewers, managed the study section, and prepared summary statements on the proposals coming before the section.

"A study section analysis results in one of three actions: approval; disapproval; or deferral. If approved, a scientific merit rating is assigned on a scale of one to five, with one rated as outstanding and five rated as acceptable.

"Next, the request goes to the National Advisory Council, charged with the broader policy considerations involved in the evaluation of scientific merit, program considerations, and funding availability. It can concur with the study section, modify, or defer the project pending additional review."

Dennis broke in. "Back up a second. Who is on the Council? Is it a collection of big cheeses in the genetics area, or what?"

"Yes, I would say it is. Naturally, they have impressive credentials in science but most members of the council have been active at policy making levels as well. You might think of it as a Board of Directors or the trustees of a university. They provide guidance with one eye on the big picture."

Dennis leaned forward. "How political is the Council? I mean, do their sessions drag on for days with members lobbying for their pet projects and storming out of meetings not speaking to each other; that sort of thing?"

"Oh, of course not. This is science, after all. No, the meetings tend to be highly technical; very boring unless it's your grant that is on the table for consideration."

"But surely it can't be all peace and harmony. Don't they ever disagree?"

"Certainly. But the disagreements usually take place within a narrow spectrum of choices. And, of course, they are scientists, not politicians. They debate, they reason, they decide. A high premium is put on consensus. No one on the Council would be very happy with a one vote victory on a grant request. If they see a truly troublesome issue about to surface, they will usually just defer it for further review."

"The old 'table it until next session' ploy? I've seen that a few million times on the Hill."

"It seems to work. Somehow, compromises seem to materialize which take the Council off the spot, which relieves everyone, of course."

"I wonder what would happen," speculated Dennis, "if a truly divisive issue presented itself and wouldn't go away. Take this Grunfeld proposal you told me about. From everything you said, it's bound to cause a flap when it comes before the Council, isn't it?"

"Without question."

"If it makes it to the Council," Dennis added, smelling the sweet aroma of a plan.

Anne looked at him uncertainly. "I don't understand."

"Well," said Dennis, "you just told me that you selected the reviewers. Could you manage to get Grunfeld's request killed at the study section level?"

Anne swallowed visibly and continued to stare at him.

"Don't be alarmed," Dennis reassured, "this kind of thing is routine. In politics, you always try to play on your home court, meaning that when possible you select people who agree with you."

"Yes," Anne stammered, "but this is science; we aren't like the Congressional committees you deal with."

"C'mon, Anne, get into the twenty-first century. Everything in D.C. is political—everything. When there is a vacancy on the Supreme Court, who does the president pick? Someone who agrees with him, of course. Courts are packed, committees are packed, Congressional offices are packed—everything's packed. This is just a little 'ole science club."

"I don't think I could be involved . . ."

"Look! You told me how much this job means to you. Wouldn't it be great if you could help Senator Harmon become vice president? Talk about payback!"

Anne hesitated, looking down at her hands twisted in her lap. "Of course I'd like to pay him back."

"Here's your chance," Dennis insisted, his confidence rising as he sensed Anne's vulnerability. "Does NIH require you to appoint certain people?"

"No," she said meekly. "It's my choice."

"There," he declared. "You can't be criticized." He stood up and began walking around the room, his forehead furrowed in concentration. Anne actually slumped, as if she was already guilty of some unnamed crime. Dennis continued pacing, fitting the pieces together as he walked.

He stopped suddenly, looking up. "But this study section is just a committee, isn't it? A few people holed up in a room somewhere going over the grant. It could reject Grunfeld on some technicality."

"True."

"That won't do. We need something more dramatic. Something that the press and public can get their teeth into."

Anne thought for a moment. "Well," she began tentatively, "suppose I made sure it passed the study section and went to the Council?"

"And the Council," said Dennis, picking up her thought, "charged with looking at the big picture, turned it down."

For the next twenty minutes, Dennis and Anne brainstormed the idea. When they finished, a strategy known to them, and them alone, as "Axe Max" had been born.

Chapter 18

Three days after the second meeting between Dennis and Anne Harborfield, Martin found an envelope placed conspicuously on the top of his priority mail. It bore no postage and only the words, "Senator Harmon: personal and confidential," in longhand. Inside, Martin found the following:

Memo: 7-29-99
TO: Senator Martin Harmon
FROM: Dennis Rancour

You want to keep the public focused on the issues raised by the REA. This is my recommendation.

I had two meetings with A.H. of NIH in the last thirty days. She is a bright, aggressive, and loyal where your interests are concerned. After talking with her, I came up with a plan.

Remember the microbiologist from California named Grunfeld who submitted the grant request to NIH under the REA wire? A.H. called you about it. If NIH follows its published regulations for review of the Grunfeld grant, it will be assigned to a study section for evaluation. Guess who makes the assignment? Answer: A.H. The study section is composed of science types appointed by the executive secretary of the study section. Grunfeld's proposal will probably end up in the Genetics Study Section. Guess who is the executive secretary of that section? Answer: A.H. The study section either approves, disapproves or puts it on the back burner. Once it acts, the proposal goes to something called the National Review Council made up of scientific heavyweights from all over the country. The Review Council serves as a check and balance on the peer review study section.

A.H. thinks Grunfeld's project is aimed at humans rather than white mice, and therefore violates the REA. If true, a highly visible effort to block funding of this grant could be our vehicle.

NIH is now swamped with requests. In the normal course, Grunfeld's request won't be acted on for months. We need action now, so I suggest we get A.H. to help it along within NIH so that it gets top priority. If it gets through the study section, we should make sure word gets out which focuses the media's attention on the importance of the deliberation at the Review Council level. If we can be seen as leading the charge to kill a genetic monster, and if that charge takes place in the presence of a horde of reporters, the "vehicle" should bring us home. What do you think?

I think, mused Martin as he looked up from the memo, I like it. And what's more, I think Justin will like it too.

*　　*　　*

Anne selected five grant requests for consideration by the study section she formed within days after Axe Max was adopted. Her choice of reviewers was dictated by need for controversy in the Grunfeld debate, but not so much controversy as to defeat the proposal. The narrow vote on Max's grant in the study section, coming after three days of review, showed just how well Anne knew her group. In keeping with the Axe Max script, Anne wrote the summary. In pertinent part, it said:

> The attached proposal, submitted by California Institute of Technology, generated a unusual amount of debate within the study section. Strong positions were taken both in favor of, and in opposition to, funding.
>
> The proposal under discussion outlines a methodology for manipulation of an unspecified gene or genes in the white mice genome with the objective of achieving totipotency

from a mature, differentiated cell. The scientific advancement represented by this research, if successful, cannot be overstated. A majority of the study section felt that the reputation of the principal investigator coupled with the scientific merit of the inquiry was sufficient to sustain the project.

Approval by the study section came at what must candidly be described as vehement opposition by the minority members. The objections of the minority can be summarized as follows:

(a) The aim of the research goes beyond that stated in the application. This is a serious allegation leveled at a researcher with outstanding credentials. The minority cites the timing of the application, made just prior to the well publicized cutoff date for projects to be evaluated under pre-REA standards. The timing of the submission, claims the minority, indicates the researcher's intent to use human tissue in the tests conducted, a fact not disclosed in the methodology described.

(b) If, as claimed in (a) above, the intent is to pursue human tissue testing, the proposed project would clearly not be permitted under the post-REA standard and should not be permitted now on the basis of a technicality in submission deadlines. The minority argues that it has always been the right, and indeed the duty, of sections to disapprove projects which raise serious moral, ethical, or legal concerns, and that the subject project raises such concerns.

(c) Taken to its logical extreme, the minority felt the project could represent an effort to search for human totipotency, a concept with dire social implications.

With the forwarding of Anne's summary to the National Review Council, phase one of the Axe Max strategy was complete. Phase two was not far behind.

*　　*　　*

The ringing of the telephone echoed through the silence of the sleeping Grunfeld household. Max glanced at his bedside clock showing 10:45 p.m. before lifting the receiver.

"Yes?" he said with a tired rasp.

"Doctor Grunfeld? Doctor Max Grunfeld?" came the voice on the other end.

"This is Doctor Grunfeld." He did not awaken well.

"Doc, sorry to call so late. I can see I woke you. This is Gary Lawson at The L.A. *Times*. We're checking out a story that's just come to us regarding a research project you've got going over at CalTech. Sounds like a fairy tale, but the word we get is that you've found some genetic gimmick that can re-create a person from scratch, so to speak. The term is human totipotency, I think. Care to comment on that for me?"

Max fought to clear his senses. Was this a dream or was this reporter waiting for an answer? He shook his head to gain full consciousness.

"Where did you get such a report?"

"Well, Doc, you know, we can't reveal our source. It just isn't done."

Max was silent. Rita, now awake, tried to guess the meaning of his baffled expression.

"Like I say, Doc, I can't tell you where the info came from. Do you have some kind of research application in somewhere? Like Washington?"

"I might. I'm not sure I should discuss it with you, even if I do. Any research application at NIH is strictly confidential."

"Yeah, I'm glad you mentioned NIH. That's it, all right. Well, this one ain't so confidential."

"Are you going to tell me you have a copy of my grant request?"

"No, I don't. Like to have it if you want to give it to me, which I doubt. What I have is a report on your request."

"That is also intended to be strictly confidential."

"Doc, I'm sure you're not pleased at getting this call, but if we limited ourselves to stuff we're supposed to have, we couldn't put out a paper here, you know what I mean?"

"You are certainly correct in your assumption that I am not pleased. I think perhaps I should talk with my attorney."

"Your attorney? Ah, come on Doc. You're not on trial or in trouble or anything. Suit yourself, but I can't see where you need one. So, Doc, what's the story on your science project? What's this human totipotency thing all about? Are you going to invent like a copy machine for people, or what?"

"My application, if I have an application, is not about human totipotency. What it is about, if it exists, is my business and NIH's business. That's all I have to say."

"Ok, Doc, I won't grill you. Thanks for your time. Sorry I woke you. I think we're going to run this though. Probably tomorrow morning. And hey, Doc, for what it's worth it's not my source. They just gave me the story to follow up on. Nothing personal, Ok?"

"Goodnight!"

Despite the hour, Max put in an immediate call to Morris Sokolman who, to Max's relief, had not gone to bed.

"Morris, this is Max."

"Ah, Max, how are you?"

"I'm not sure. I'm sorry to call you at this late hour but I just received a phone call which has upset me. I don't know if there is anything that can be done, but I thought it worth a try."

Max related the call from Lawson. Morris listened without interruption. When Max had concluded, Morris asked: "Is this the same proposal you came to me about several months back?"

"Yes, the same."

"The one we did the research on which involved the grandfather clause?"

"Exactly."

"That wasn't long ago. Do they always act this promptly?"

"No, they don't. I was dumbfounded when Lawson said he had a report on my application."

"What report could he have?"

"It could be the report of one of the reviewers."

"What's that about?"

"The study section. They assign grant requests to two or three reviewers on the section to report to the full group when they come together to decide. It could be the report of one of those reviewers."

"What else? What other report could it be?"

Max thought for a moment. "Theoretically, it could be the summary report that goes to the National Review Council . . . that's the next step in the peer review process. But I doubt he has that report. There just hasn't been enough time for the application to clear the study section. I only submitted the report a few weeks ago and NIH was inundated with requests. It has to be the reviewer's report."

"Does this leak jeopardize your application?"

"I don't see why it would. But then I don't see why someone would leak it either."

"Do you think it may be time to furnish us with some information regarding your discovery, Max?"

"Yes, perhaps it is."

The explanation for the leak was to be found on Max's doorstep the next morning. The caption on the story proclaimed:

> 2nd Bite at the Apple? Calif. Researcher says 'Maybe' The prospect of cloning mature human beings from their DNA has been raised in a research grant application currently making its way through the National Institutes of Health, according to a reliable source familiar with the process and a report supplied to The L.A. Times.
>
> The source, who spoke on the condition of anonymity, said the proposed research deals with white mice but that the scientific techniques employed may be equally applicable to human beings. The principal researcher under the application, which has passed the first stage of NIH's peer review system, declined to comment on his work. Maximillian Grunfeld, a Ph.D. at CalTech, would say only that the contents of the application were "my business."

The article described the development in plant and animal totipotency leading up to Max's application. Max read the column with a distant foreboding. Since the call from Lawson, he had spent the better part of the night in restless recollection of any precedent for this egregious violation of confidentiality. He could think of none. Oh well, he thought, so the public was now aware that he had a grant request pending. So what? The public didn't decide such questions.

*   *   *

Nancy Allenby, chief of staff to the president, ordered the item concerning Grunfeld's application clipped for her morning briefing with the president.

"Mr. President, I don't like the odor coming from this news story. It smells like election year politics a year early."

The president scanned the clipping, concluding with a gentle chuckle. "Oh, it's election year politics all right, but I don't think they're aiming at us yet. Harmon's jockeying for the v.p. spot. Maybe he figures this will put some heat on his rivals who opposed the REA." The president was silent for a moment, then added, "Yep, it's just one pack of Democrats shooting at another pack of Democrats."

"So what do we do?"

"Send them more bullets," said the president with a laugh.

*   *   *

Dr. Randolph Cass had seen the wire service story shortly after breakfast. It nearly cost him his pancakes.

"Oh, no!" he said in a low voice. "How could something like this happen here?" He shook his head as he read the story again. He threw the paper aside and dressed rapidly, so eager to demand answers that he nearly went off without his coat. "And right in my own department. Damn!"

He strode into his 9:00 a.m. staff meeting and looked sternly about at the subdued faces of those present. "Well, I can see you've all seen the *Post*. I've been here a long time, and I don't remember anything like this. I probably don't have to say this to anyone present, but this is a most serious violation of policy. If someone at NIH leaked a report, it is in all probability also a violation of Federal law. Frankly, it is inconceivable to me that anyone here would be involved in such an underhanded thing. Now before I get a phone call demanding an investigation, I intend to get to the bottom of what happened. I'm going to oversee a complete review of the CalTech application from the moment it hit our doorstep. I'm setting up a fact-finding panel whose members are familiar with our process. Frank English, Sylvia Stockton, Bob Ebersole; I want the three of you to be on the panel, agreed? Fine. Anne Harborfield, I want you to head it up. Report to me in two weeks."

*   *   *

Russell Carrington was getting nervous. The newspaper spread before him rang an all too recent bell—NIH, an elderly scientist, a controversial grant application. Surely this was the same "situation" to which Martin Harmon had alluded in their follow-up meeting to the initial Hay Adams conference.

Now, this newspaper article. Leaked reports? Anonymous sources? This was getting messy. And the last thing Carrington wanted for Justin was anything messy. Justin had the nomination won, but there was still time to give it away. Carrington was determined to insure that wouldn't happen. He placed an immediate call to Martin.

"Martin, Russell Carrington. You've seen the story?"

"Yes."

"This business could be a problem. You and I talked about some fireworks in front of an administrative panel of scientists, but leaked reports and anonymous sources weren't mentioned. Have we created some little monster here?"

"I'm as surprised as you are about the report. No one said anything to me about leaked documents. If they had I would have vetoed it. I told Dennis Rancour, my AA, we had to find a way to get the word out that this Grunfeld report was in the mill. Otherwise, no one would have cared what happened when it came before the National Review Council. I don't know who called; I really don't. I left that up to Dennis. We have a strong contact within NIH but I don't even know if it was her. Frankly, I don't want to know."

"I read you. I don't want to know either, and I don't want the Governor associated with any dirty tricks. A PR stunt is one thing; smuggling out confidential documents is another. We can't afford to be remotely connected to it, and we don't think you can either."

"But I'm not. I only expressed to Dennis the need to get the word out. I didn't imply that he compromise NIH and certainly said nothing about reports being leaked. I don't play the game that way."

"I'm relieved to hear that, but you need to get to the bottom of it." The tone in Carrington's voice told Martin that this was a tactfully stated order. "If you've got an overly zealous aide on your staff, I'd advise you to deal with it now. It's a long road to November of next year."

*   *   *

Carson read the story twice, an uneaten chocolate chip cookie on the end table beside her. She wondered about Martin's reaction and looked forward to his call that morning. Since Martin had confided to her the news from the Hay Adams meeting, she had felt the pressure building. Reckoning day was near. Martin knew it, too. He had broken the news to her devoid of the joy he must have experienced at Justin's offer. They had talked into the early hours about the nomination without once addressing the impact of this news on their relationship. Both were reluctant to discuss what each knew could not be put off much longer.

Chapter 19

The uproar ignited by the newspaper report of Max's grant application surprised even the battle seasoned veterans of Washington's political establishment.

The cries of a wounded animal were heard from the religious right. Within 24 hours of publication, Max had been called a lunatic, a slimeball, a madman, a sicko, a devil worshiper, and the antichrist. Max's personal favorite was "an agent of darkness," which carried a degree of demonic dignity.

Visitors and callers besieged NIH demanding confirmation or refutation of the report, to which NIH patiently repeated its policy against discussing pending grant applications with the general public. This facile dodge was not available to members of Congress, to the great regret of many who fielded calls from constituents whose moral and religious sensitivities had been assaulted by the story.

The newspapers, smelling a controversy of lasting duration, jumped into the fray with all the resources at their disposal. Letters to the editor poured in both from organized letter writing organizations and from independent citizens who expressed outrage at this use of tax dollars.

Interviewed on the Today show, a fundamentalist spokesman branded the CalTech laboratory "Satan's workshop" while suggesting that a competent analysis of Max's DNA would show a high correlation with the Devil's own. He did not suggest a source of the Devil's DNA for the comparison.

As taxpayer resentment grew more vitriolic, a predictable counterattack began to coalesce around the more outspoken members of the scientific community. They demanded that peer review, the professional scientific apparatus which had been designed to deal with the problems perceived by the public, be given a chance to run its course. They charged a segment of the public with a lynch mob mentality for its hysteria over an idea that had yet to clear the administrative hurdles for funding. "Let us," they admonished, "wait and see."

The net effect of this conflict was the precise result sought by Dennis: to focus an inordinate amount of attention on the anticipated proceedings before the National Review Council on Genetics.

The National Review Council on Genetics was ill-equipped to deal with the controversy. This scholarly body traditionally made decisions as the local country club might elect a chairman of the annual member guest tournament, with high premiums paid on manners, unassuming deference and collegial good will. The few controversies which had legitimately divided them had been patched over within weeks so as to leave no lasting scars. Its meetings, normally closed to the public, were equally indecipherable to that public, the average member of which might have assumed he had stumbled into a gathering of Talmudic scholars conversing in an ancient tongue.

The chairwoman typified its membership. Dr. Margaret Foxworth, retired professor of genetics at the University of Wisconsin, was a straight-back, no-nonsense scientist who carried a reputation for technical excellence and outstanding scholarship. When one of her former undergraduates observed that she posed no threat to late night television hosts, another had suggested the source of her humorless persona: "They left her out in the cold weather too long."

The first hint Dr. Foxworth received that her chairmanship would be memorable was the call from a representative of a major network requesting the location of the Review Council meeting at which the Grunfeld application would be discussed so camera crews could be set up in advance.

"Camera crews!" she shouted. "There will be NO camera crews at my council meetings and the location of those meetings, wherever they are scheduled, is our business."

"I'm sorry, Mrs. Foxworth. I assumed you had been briefed on this. I have a memo from our news department saying this has been cleared at NIH. Plus I have a copy of your agenda, but it doesn't have the location on it. They told me to call you to find out where you plan to hold the hearing."

"First, young man, my name is not Mrs. Foxworth, it's Doctor Foxworth. Second, I cannot imagine who at NIH would have taken it upon themselves to authorize cameras in my meeting, much less provide you with a copy of my agenda. And third, it is not a hearing, it's a review panel. There is quite a substantial difference. Do I make myself clear?"

"Yes, Mrs—Dr. Foxworth. All I know is what I've been told, which is to set the cameras up for a hearing. Could you be mistaken?"

"Mistaken!?" she shrieked, "Of course I'm not mistaken. It's my hearing, rather my committee. Don't you think I know what's planned for my own committee?" She slammed down the headpiece, breathing heavier than she had in years.

A majority within NIH favored affording Max an opportunity to respond to the minority position of the study section as set forth in the summary report. In that he was being vilified publicly for aspiring to turn his lab into what one commentator called a "little shop of horrors," that majority felt that inviting him to appear before the National Review Council was simple fair play.

Not everyone agreed, fair play notwithstanding. They were aghast at the inquisitional tone of a hearing covered by the media at which the principal investigator was called upon to defend his grant application. It just wasn't done, in their view, nor should it be. If no compromise was found, it was their hope that Max would withdraw his request to save all concerned from a bad moment.

In fact, Max was seriously pondering that option. Initially, he had been stung by the controversy. In the days following the appearance of the story, he had been besieged by telephone calls, requests for interviews and direct approaches by people he didn't know—all annoying. But camera crews and hate mail were distressing.

On the first morning Max arose to find his house staked out by the local affiliates of major networks, he stayed home for an hour after his normal departure time in hopes that they would leave. But they were being paid not to leave. So Max ran the gauntlet to his car and drove to the lab. Camera crews awaited him there, also.

When letters without return addresses began arriving, Max determined to make light of them; to administer to himself the antidote of pitiful humor against the poison contained therein. But after attempting to read the first few to Rita in a lighthearted air, as if to say, "Hey, here's a good one, listen to this," he abandoned the pretext. The language made him blush, for one thing. Some of it was illegible. But it all hurt. He ceased reading or even opening them. Contemplating the inevitable stress on him and his university, he confided to Dr. Anderson, the department head who had encouraged him to submit the request, that perhaps the grant should be withdrawn. "Max," Anderson said, "don't let the bastards get you down."

Though Max was at its center, the storm engulfed his colleagues, who would stop him between classes or during labs, voice their disgust at his treatment, and urge him to fight. On a morning near the end of the second week, Max surprised himself by emerging from his home, walking straight to a doughnut-munching cameraman, and ordering him to "get the hell off my lawn." He had made his decision. He was seeking funds to further a legitimate scientific inquiry, and he was not going to knuckle under to ignorant reactionaries, whatever the personal cost. At age seventy-four, he was nearing the end of his productive scientific run. There was nothing they could do to him and nothing they could dish out he couldn't take, and if they thought otherwise, then bring them on. He would be ready.

As the date for the hearings approached, Max prepared for his trip to Washington. Rita was adamant that he not go alone, while he insisted that he would feel more comfortable testifying if Rita were not present. They compromised: Rita would accompany Max to Washington but not attend the hearing, which was scheduled in a Congressional committee room after it was determined that no facility at NIH was capable of holding the crowd expected.

On the morning of the hearing, Max climbed into a cab in front of the Washington Hilton, where he and Rita had arrived the night before. He gave the driver the destination before sitting back for the brief ride to the Capitol. As the driver pulled up to the Rayburn Office Building, Max wondered who might direct him to the hearing room.

The cluster of reporters and camera people eagerly pointed the way. He entered the hearing room ten minutes prior to the 10:00 a.m. start time, having declined to make any statements to the clamoring media corps. He proceeded to the podium to shake hands with the members of the Council already seated in the chairs normally reserved for the members of Congress. As he turned from the elevated platform toward the witness chair where he would be sitting, he realized the room was packed. There was only one empty seat, conspicuously vacant in the front row nearest the witness table.

Max seated himself in front of his microphone and spread his notes before him in a carefully ordered sequence. He had nearly completed this task when he felt a murmur of unrest ripple through the room. The crowd had turned and fixed its collective eye on the tall, lean figure of the distinguished junior Senator from Virginia, Martin Harmon. In the doorway of the hearing room, Martin gazed around the room. All eyes followed him toward the vacant seat in the front row. TV cameras caught not only the moment, but the juxtaposition of Max and Martin within ten feet of one another. At stake, and beyond the vision of any camera or spectator, were the destinies of both men.

*   *   *

As Dr. Foxworth gaveled the hearing to order and Max began to testify, Carson was keeping the doctor's appointment postponed in order to go to Maine. As she negotiated the traffic between the Westchester and the Chevy Chase offices of Dr. Henry Kiner, M.D., she was conscious of two concerns. The first of these was her perpetual paranoia about her cholesterol count, at risk only because of her penchant for chocolate chip cookies. The other was her recent nervousness, brought on by the dilemma she and Martin could not escape. She wondered to what degree she should confide in Dr. Kiner about Martin. Although he had been her physician since her arrival in Washington, he was a general practitioner, not a psychiatrist. Perhaps she should offer a general explanation: "I'm in a stressful relationship and it's beginning to take a toll on my health." No names, no details. He probably won't need to know anyway.

Her physical was thorough, except for the Ob-gyn work which Dr. Kiner left to specialists. He complimented Carson on her treadmill results, boosting her ego by noting that he rarely encountered women in her age group who were as fit.

As she finished dressing, a nurse poked her head into the examination room and asked her to see Dr. Kiner in his office. He was seated at his desk when she entered. Without looking up from the folder in front of him, he motioned her to a chair opposite his own. Carson sat in silence for several moments. When he lifted his eyes, they were skeptical, foreboding.

He spoke slowly. "Carson, you've been my patient for a good while now. Must be twelve, thirteen years, isn't it?"

"Yes, I believe that's right."

"And as your doctor, I'm aware of your medical history."

Oh God, she thought, it's cancer. Her father had died of it and it ran in her family. Oh, God, no.

"I've just finished looking at your blood work. I know this is going to shock you, but you're pregnant."

So prepared was Carson for the word "cancer" that she showed no reaction for several seconds. Then her eyes widened into a vacant stare.

"Pregnant? But I—that's not—but I'm sterile. I can't be pregnant."

"Your medical history documents your sterility. That's why I'm so perplexed at these results. Of course, it could be a lab error. We'll rerun the test, but the current blood analysis is virtually foolproof. The physical examination also turned up some consistent symptoms, but I didn't want to say anything until I saw the blood work. There's no doubt.

"But . . . how?"

"Carson, the one ovary which you possess . . ."

He detailed a medical theory but she heard nothing of the explanation. His words droned in the distance like an old air conditioner on a summer night. Soon the humming stopped as the room went dark. She had passed out.

*　　*　　*

"Dr. Grunfeld, now that we've all had a chance to get some lunch, we're going to open the hearing to questions from members of the Council."

Max seated himself for the next round. His morning testimony had been uneventful as he led the Council through his application, supplementing it with the results of a most recent German study of some of the gene "stoppers and starters" that he had employed in his own experiments. He noted Martin's absence as the afternoon session began.

Dr. Foxworth used her prerogative as chairperson to pose the first series of questions.

"Dr. Grunfeld, it seems clear from the reports of your experiments that you have achieved, at least in an isolated instance, totipotency of a mouse from a fully differentiated cell. But I note that nowhere in your application or support material do you claim to have found a method for such results. Is that correct?"

"That is correct, and I am glad you have pointed out the distinction. You must realize that this line of inquiry which produced this rather dramatic result was in its early stages. I have had no time to explore fully the very pertinent question of why I achieved what I achieved. Until that can be done, any claim on my part to a method for producing totipotency would be premature, and grossly so."

"Are you saying, Doctor, that your totipotent mouse is essentially a freak, a mutant?"

"To be honest, I don't know. It depends on how you define mutant."

"Would it be more accurate to say that the process which produced it is mutant?"

"Clearly yes, if by that you mean I was not expecting the results I got."

"But can you do it again, consistently, is what I'm getting at?"

"I don't know. That is the essence of my need for the grant. I need to find a scientifically defensible explanation for this mouse if I can. When I do, I will be able to say whether the results can be duplicated."

"Dr. Grunfeld, I found it a bit unusual that you did not describe in detail the chemical agents used in the experiment which produced your totipotent mouse."

"That's true, and it was done purposefully. This work is still highly experimental. Were the results less dramatic, it would be premature to release any information at all, including methodology. But given the realities of research funding and recent changes in the law, I felt it prudent to bring this application forward despite its incipient status."

"That brings us, Doctor, to a troublesome aspect of your work—I'm sure you know what I'm alluding to. The press and TV have been full of speculation that you have found a method by which people can be cloned. Can you address that?"

Max drew himself up in his chair and returned a steady gaze. "Yes, I seem to recall speculation in that area." The crowd behind him laughed with members of the Council. "I believe my research has attracted far more attention than it deserves, at least at this stage of the process. The completion of the studies will take time. The applicability of those mouse studies to humans is entirely speculative."

"It may be, but there can be little doubt that human tissue research will be part of your work if the grant is approved. Was that not the reason you met the grandfather deadline under the REA?"

"It is quite true that I hastened my application so as to qualify for grandfather status, but only as a precaution against the final mice studies showing a possibility of human correlation."

"So you admit that human tissue research done as an extension of your mouse totipotency work would not pass muster under the REA?"

"I admit no such thing. I merely suggest that obviously, with the passage of this legislation—incidentally, in my judgment a mistake—the climate will become more restrictive."

Dr. Foxworth turned her head from Max toward the panel members on her left. "And now, I'm sure other members of the Council have questions for you as well. Thank you, Doctor."

The next several Council members took turns asking perfunctory questions which Max answered sincerely and without strain. But he dared not relax. For the panel held not only friend, but foe.

Max's friends at CalTech had warned him to expect trouble from Arlen J. Ullman, the University of Georgia's professor emeritus of microbiology. Ullman had been something of a whiz kid in his earlier years, with a reputation for incisive thinking, original ideas and a goodly quantity of luck. His participation in the research teams responsible for three significant genetic breakthroughs in a five year period beginning in 1961 had catapulted him ahead of his peers. Thereafter, for reasons no one quite understood, his successes never matched the torrid pace set early in his career. Over time, youthful verve and scientific audacity gave way to a stale rigidity more natural to accounting than science. Conservatism, the handmaiden of age and experience, first slowed his adaptation to change, then arrested it altogether, fixing him forever in a medieval mind-set. He hailed none of the great genetic breakthroughs of the last quarter century, expressing to all who would listen pessimism that men of abiding faith could survive the onslaught by men of infinite curiosity. We would, in the end, he thought, tinker ourselves into oblivion. As Dennis had remarked, Ullman was "not a fun guy."

He was, however, loaded, cocked and ready for Max. After a mere nod toward the witness table, Ullman began. His melon-shaped head seemed precariously balanced on shoulders of average dimensions, and perspiration, collected at his hairline, glistened in the glare of TV lights.

"Professor, with all due regard, sir, to your reputation, I do not see how you can defend this work. Let us leave aside for the moment the technical considerations, such as a conspicuously inadequate description of how you intend to pursue these experiments, and focus, if you will, sir, on the value of a totipotent mouse if you can achieve it."

"With all due mutual respect, Dr. Ullman, I believe that microbiologic inquiry must follow where such breakthroughs as this mouse lead. Otherwise, all science will suffer. To produce an unknown, even accidentally, and not seek an explanation is the antithesis of science." Max knew this general platitude would probably not pacify Ullman, but he saw little benefit in an all out war of words with someone so diametrically opposed in his views.

"But surely, sir," persisted Ullman, "it is well for inquiries to lead somewhere." He cast his eyes over the crowd, as a prosecutor might deliver a summation to the jury, always with one eye on the guilty bastard accused of the crime. "This grant request requires several million dollars to fill; money that is increasingly hard to come by. This council is being deluged with requests it cannot fill. So I, for one, want to make certain that those projects we fund are aimed at targets which need to be hit, so to speak. What I am asking you, sir, is why this target needs to be hit. If you had stumbled upon a mouse who could whistle 'Dixie,' should we spend several million dollars to find out how or why?" Laughter, led by Ullman, rippled through the room.

But Max had not travelled 3000 miles to be blown over by a gust of wind. He replied, "Dixie, no, but the Star Spangled Banner? I believe we should fund it." The laughter of the audience was interspersed with applause.

Dr. Ullman did not laugh. "My question is valid. Please provide a valid answer."

"The answer, Professor, is that the mouse resulting from my experimentation represents a threshold in genetics. To achieve totipotency of anything from a fully differentiated, mature cell is a startling event. It hints at a genetic trigger whereby the life cycle can be re-started at will. I find that possibility intriguing."

"Intriguing, I may grant you, Doctor. But I find it frightening as well. To what end do we pursue such a trigger? What will the public get for this expenditure of funds, aside from intrigue?"

"Specifically, I would think the prospect of biologically generated organs and limbs would be worthwhile. That is just one of a number of examples which come to mind."

"But such work is already underway, Doctor. As we speak, there are advances being made toward that very goal, and none to my knowledge require that an entire organism be triggered."

"Professor, clearly that which triggers the entire organism holds the prospect of valuable insight into the question of how and why cells differentiate. Differentiation is a critical piece of the genetic puzzle. I would think that point beyond debate."

"To the contrary, sir, it is quite debatable. The unavoidable consequence of your work, even if you are successful, or perhaps I should say especially if you are successful, is to make genetic mischief, and little more. You claim that your work may aid others in the search for the biological generation of organs and limbs; you claim the lessons learned will translate into positive progress in understanding differentiation. Perhaps, but it is all speculation. What is not speculation, however, is that you and others in your faction will not be happy until every man, women, and child on this earth is reduced to a chemical formula stored in some computer somewhere." Sweat trickled down Ullman's face in serpentine rivulets, meeting at his chin like ski slopes at the base of a mountain.

Max gripped the edge of the witness table with both hands and leaned into the microphone. "But we ARE chemical formulas, Professor. That is not some theory concocted by me and my faction, as you put it. It is scientific fact. We just don't yet know the formula, but it's there nonetheless. We aim to find it, yes."

"Yes, and what will you do with it?" Ullman let the question hang in the air as he removed his glasses and mopped his face with a handkerchief. "You realize, of course, Doctor, that when you and your colleagues finish, we will all be saddled with genetic profiles that will be as much a part of us as our social security numbers. And do you know what those will show? That some among us are genetically inferior or superior, take your pick. That will not be an assessment upon which reasonable men will differ as it is today and I hope it remains. No, it will be a demonstrable fact. As a civilization, we have worked hard against the concept of genetic inferiority. I shudder to think of a day when a young man shuns a beautiful girl whose genetic profile may not be acceptable; when no job is offered to the man for whom manic depression is predicted by some computer; for families or entire races whose genetic IQ's condemn them to the menial work available in society."

"It seems to me, Professor, that we've gotten very far afield from the subject of mouse research on—"

"But that's just it," broke in Ullman, his face swelling like a balloon ready to burst. "We're not talking about mouse research at all and you know it. We're talking about human beings, Doctor. You know and I know that your totipotency studies are and will be aimed at humans. Why don't we put our cards on the table? You're trying to take God's place, aren't you Doctor?"

"Not at all."

"Certainly you are. And you cited not one valid basis for this work under the newly passed REA, a long overdue restriction which I helped to draft, incidentally."

"The REA doesn't cover this grant request. I thought that was understood."

"Technically, you may be correct. But I'm going to vote against funding your request, Doctor, for the reasons I've outlined and for the reason that the people have spoken by enacting that legislation and some artificial deadline isn't going to save a project such as yours. And I believe," he noted with a confident glance to each side of the Council, "that a majority of my colleagues are in accord."

It was past 7:00 p.m. when the Council adjourned. Dr. Foxworth had been determined to finish the session even at the cost of limiting debate. In truth, the outcome was apparent, and to hold Max over for another day was to compound his defeat. This act of kindness was the least she could do to support a man with whom she agreed but for whom she could not deliver a majority of her associates. Max knew it, too. He made his way from the hearing room, declining substantial comment to the media. "I've had my say," he noted dejectedly, "and it was not persuasive."

He climbed into a cab and searched through his mental numbness for the name of his hotel. Remembering, he was about to relay it to the driver when he changed his mind. He needed some time to collect himself before going to meet Rita; some time to renew the strength and optimism that had never been lower than at this moment.

"Drive, please." he said lamely.

"Where to?" inquired the driver over his shoulder.

"Oh, anywhere. Just drive a while. Take me on a tour around the mall a time or two."

Max rolled down the window despite the air conditioning billowing forth from the front seat. He needed fresh air. The cab made its way down Constitution Avenue, past the Washington Monument toward the Arlington National Cemetery. As it pulled abreast of the Lincoln Memorial, Max called out on impulse, "Wait, stop here, please." The cab swerved suddenly left so as to avoid the wrong concentric circle looping the monument. The cabbie guided the cab to the curb. "What now?" he asked.

"Wait for me, please."

"Fine by me, I'm getting paid just the same."

"I may be a while, but wait, please."

Max walked to the head of the reflecting pool in which the Washington Monument lay in radiant illumination. The stars overhead, normally his friend and ally on warm California nights, twinkled a new message to him tonight. He imagined them flashing a form of celestial semaphore to the earth, to its hills and its oceans, the animals and the elements. The message was simplicity itself: "Our secrets are safe."

As he stood looking skyward, he rebuked himself. What was he, an arthritic old man, when matched against a conspiracy of the universe to guard its ageless mysteries? The totipotent mouse had been part of that conspiracy, an ambush designed to lure him into the trap of self-aggrandizement, a ploy to feed the ego of one who would dare think himself adequate to the task. What he saw clearly in the pool this evening was an old scientist beaten down by the very forces he strove to understand; a tired, spent fossil second by second obeying the rules he had spent a lifetime trying to learn. Perhaps if he had a hundred or a thousand scientists like himself, with unlimited resources and centuries to test and probe, perhaps then he could make some dent in the forces which marched against him on this evening.

As he turned from the Washington Monument, his eyes met the fixed gaze of Abraham Lincoln. And in those eyes, Max found the inspiration he sought.

The weariness that had draped itself over Max's shoulders at the hearing lifted. He walked closer, observing the deep lines in Lincoln's face, testimony to the toll taken by the struggle which characterized his life. He thought back to his analysis of Lincoln's DNA a decade earlier. His microscope had held the genetic agents of that face, noble in its awkwardness. The disease he had confirmed had distorted Lincoln just enough to carve the caricature which at first had been an obstacle to his personal advancement, but had later cloaked him in the humanity beloved by the mass of common men. They loved him because he, like they, were imperfect, rough and original.

His critics had called him "an ape," an easy comparison in light of the distended arms and gangly legs produced by his disease. To such slurs, the great man responded by stretching those same distended arms across the land to embrace those critics, and drawing to him friend and foe alike, spoke to them soothing words of comfort and healing and compassion.

Max wondered what Lincoln would think of the United States at the dawn of the twenty-first century. Could the decades leading up to the Civil War have been any more divisive than the present? The hearing from which he had just escaped was but one example of the friction and discord which now seemed to be the daily diet of the nation.

Everywhere Max looked the politics of anger seemed pitched against the feeble efforts of reconciliation. As in Lincoln's day, a meanness was upon the land, not because the intervening century and a half had allowed hate to grow into a larger measure of the spirit, but because Lincoln, or someone like him, was not here to summon forth the higher virtues people tend to praise but not practice.

How much of Lincoln's greatness was a product of his genetic composition? Any? All? Max had pondered that question often in the past ten years. How much was shaped by his hardscrabble farming, his failure in business, his lost elections or his erratic wife? Would he have been the same man had he been born a century earlier or later? Had the chromosomes under Max's microscope held a genetic recipe for greatness in any age under any circumstances, or for only one precise moment on the celestial time line?

As Max ascended the steps of the Memorial toward Lincoln's granite presence, an inspiration seized him that he suspected had been born a decade ago, dormant until this moment. Why not reconstruct Lincoln's DNA from the tissue still preserved in Max's lab? The technology he had lacked in 1990 had been supplied in the intervening years. No law prohibited him from doing it on his own at his expense. If he could piece together one intact cell from the millions available to him he would set the stage for the drama presaged by his totipotent mouse; the day that would usher into the world the Age of Genetics as surely as Sputnik had launched the Space Age; the day Ullman and Harmon and the rest of them feared but which Max knew was inevitable; the day Lincoln, or any other human for that matter, might arise again, re-triggered from the single cell that he, Max Grunfeld, had reconstituted.

Chapter 20

The sun had nearly set when Martin opened the door of Carson's apartment. The victory over Max had been sweet. Martin had been particularly pleased with the coverage the major networks had given him in prime time newscasts. He looked forward to sharing the accounts of his very busy, highly productive day.

The apartment was in semi-darkness when he entered. The only light was a slim, horizontal shaft of orange sunset which squeezed between the drapes and valance. There was no sound. Martin was groping for a light switch when Carson's voice came to him out of the dusk.

"Martin, please leave the light off."

Martin stopped, startled.

"Carson, where are you? Why the blackout?"

"Just please leave it off. Why don't you sit down."

Martin's eyes, becoming accustomed to the dimness, settled on her amorphous form in a chair, her legs pulled up close to her chest. He made his way to the end of the sofa opposite her.

"Why are you sitting in the dark?"

She did not respond.

"What's wrong? Why are you sitting in the dark?"

"Because I've been thinking, and it was easier to think with the lights off."

"How long have you been sitting here?"

"Oh, since mid-afternoon, I guess." Her voice, weak and reedy, trailed off. Then it returned, stronger. "Martin, what do I mean to you?"

"You mean the world to me . . . I love you."

She said nothing. From the chair Martin heard a muffled sob, barely audible.

"Carson, we knew this day would come. We're both adults, and we knew that there were forces at work here far beyond the control of either of us, didn't we?"

"No. We never knew this day would come."

Martin sighed, then said gently, "But of course we did. We talked about it. We couldn't be sure because we didn't know what was going to happen with the nomination. But we knew it was a possibility, even a probability."

Soft sobs from the darkness continued. Martin got up to go to her.

"No," she said quietly but firmly, "please don't. Just stay over there for a while."

Martin resumed his seat, puzzled.

"Tell me about your children," she said.

"What?"

"What have your children meant to you?"

"Well, you know—"

"No, I don't. Please tell me."

"Well, let's see, my children. We had them early, perhaps a bit too early. They're great kids. I guess a lot of the credit goes to Jean. I was gone a lot; missed a whole bunch of things . . . school, sports, recitals, that kind of thing, that fathers should get to enjoy. But I've maintained a good relationship with them, especially now that they're older. I love them dearly, of course. I guess every father does. Why do you ask?"

"It's important for me to know. Have they held back your career? I mean, if you had it to do all over again, would you do it? The kids, I mean?"

"Why, yes, of course. I can't imagine not having them. I can see you're upset, and I don't know what my children can have to do with the decision you and I have to make, but for God's sake let's talk it through. You know, when we first met, I thought I could keep you at a distance. I was lonely, I'll admit that. And when you came along I saw a chance to ease that loneliness, knowing all the while that feelings can take you in directions you don't necessarily want to go. The last thing I needed, considering the v.p. possibility, was what I got. I wish we had—"

"Martin," she pleaded, "listen to me. There is no way to cushion what I have to say, so I will simply come out with it. I found out today I am pregnant. About six weeks. I can't give you a biological explanation for it; no one can even explain it to me."

The sun had all but disappeared, raising the narrowing beam of horizontal sunset ever higher on the wall to Martin's back. His features, vaguely visible to her when he had first entered, were now invisible. He made no sound as he absorbed her words.

Suddenly, he bolted forward, raising enough for his face to come within the band of light furnished by the dying sun. His eyes flashed desperation; then passed out of the sun's narrow spectrum. He was beside her, kneeling.

"But how could that be!" he stammered. "I don't believe it. It's just not possible. There has got to be a mistake. The test—they can't be sure this early—errors are made all the time . . ." His chest heaved. She cried faintly. Gradually, his head dropped toward the floor, his eyes half closed in a vacant stupor. Silence engulfed the room.

After a time, he arose and returned to the sofa. The darkness was complete. "What are we going to do?"

"I don't know. It's so sudden. I fainted in the doctor's office today. Can you believe it? Thirty-four years old and I fainted."

"Carson, they didn't need to—"

For the first time, her voice carried an edge, a tinge of exasperation unmistakable. "No, they didn't ask about the father. Naturally, I told them nothing."

"How do you feel?"

"Physically, I feel OK. I bumped my head when I passed out, but nothing serious. Mentally and emotionally, it's a different story. When it began to sink in, I was happier than I had ever been. But then I realized what a mess it presents. Martin, I swear I had no idea there was even a remote chance. Honest, I didn't. You have to believe me."

"I believe you," he said somberly.

"Good. That takes one burden off my mind. Only forty-nine to go." She laughed and cried.

"Dr. Kiner called Dr. Short, my ob-gyn, to discuss the results and to schedule an appointment for me. Dr. Short told him the odds of my getting pregnant were about one in two million."

"Did you discuss abortion with Dr. Kiner?"

"Abortion?" Carson asked distantly.

"Well, Carson, surely the thought must have occurred to you in light of our situation."

"No," she said slowly, "the thought did not occur to me. It didn't then and it doesn't now."

"Be realistic." Martin was businesslike. "Surely you're not thinking of bearing this child. It's just not feasible."

"Not feasible!" Her voice rose. "A two million to one miracle not feasible!"

"This 'miracle,' as you put it, is half mine, don't forget. And that's exactly what I mean. It's not feasible."

"I'll tell you what's not feasible," she said, icy in her deliberateness. "Anything which precludes my giving birth to a baby in about seven and half months is not feasible. And to borrow one of your favorite expressions, you can take that to the bank."

"Think about what you're saying." His voice boomed out of the darkness now, insistent and emphatic. "Seven and a half months from now I'll be slugging through the snow in New Hampshire giving speeches for Justin, preparing myself for the very real possibility that I will become the vice president of the United States. What's more, like it or not, I probably will be doing it in the company of my wife. The very furthest thing from my mind would be the birth of a bastard child somewhere around here."

Carson screamed. "That's the most selfish thing I've ever heard in my life. I'm sorry if my child and I will be the furthermost thing from your mind. I'm sorry if you have weighty matters of national importance on your mind and I'm sorry if traveling with your wife is not your idea of fun. Excuse me for living, but I have things on my mind as well, not the least of which is the fact that I have lived my whole adult life hoping to hear the words I heard today in Dr. Kiner's office. I've thought about it and prayed about it and hoped against hope that it could happen, and if you think for an instant that my baby is going to become a casualty to some misguided ambition of yours, you're crazy."

The lamp on the table beside Martin switched on. She blinked. Martin stood up and walked to the door. Placing one hand on the knob, he turned to lock his eyes onto hers.

"And if you think I've traveled all this way to be destroyed by some microscopic freak of nature, you're crazy!" The slam of the door shook the walls.

*   *   *

Carson remained curled up in her chair. She wished the room dark again, but could not find the energy to cross it and extinguish the light. And so she sat, thinking of her eleventh birthday, when a line of dolls appeared commemorating the bicentennial. "Patriot Girls" dressed in the regional fashions of the original thirteen colonies. She had developed a strong attachment to "Peaches," the doll representing Georgia's colonial attire. Rosy cheeks framed by cascading blonde ringlets drew her magnetically at an age when her fascination with dolls should have been over.

Linked forever with Peaches were Carson's first conscious thoughts of womanhood. Kathy had filled her in on the facts of life after it became painfully apparent that their mother, despite repeated promises to "have a girl chat with Carson," could not bring herself to do so. Kathy had worried that the changes overtaking Carson would arrive ahead of the information needed to deal with them. The awful, wondrous truths imparted by Kathy gave the doll a luster which tingled Carson with excitement. When she opened her present to find its blue eyes staring into hers, she imagined she had delivered it with her newly discovered feminine secrets. She soon outgrew the doll, but sensations which accompanied Peaches were with her still.

She must have slept, for she awoke to find a slight crimp in her neck. It was 10:30 p.m., and the nap renewed her. She gazed about the living room, lingering at the sight of mementos of her former life; the life she had been living when she woke that morning. Whatever happened with Martin, that life was gone, replaced by a voyage of deliverance to be shared with what would become, in the coming months, a name and a personality and a being.

She sprang from the chair, as if she had been a frame of celluloid on a video tape, suddenly released from the pause position. She could not remain in the apartment on this night. Within minutes she packed some essential clothing and left her apartment. The laser disc in her car blared an Elvis Presley tune as she headed for Frederick.

Kathy had been the last in her household to retire, as usual. After locking the doors, setting the alarms and addressing the remaining rituals of sleep, she had crawled into bed. No sooner had her head hit the pillow when the doorbell chimed. She got up, putting on her housecoat as she walked. At the front door she turned on the surveillance camera to reveal a smiling Carson. She flung open the door.

"What a treat! What are you doing here?"

Carson entered, clasping Kathy's hands and resting her chin on her shoulder. "Me?" she giggled. "I'm celebrating the most wonderful day of my life."

Chapter 21

In the early years, when his work habits were being molded, Martin unwittingly borrowed a page from Napoleon's book: "Give me the bad news first." The timely disposition of negatives had stood him in good stead. He never understood how colleagues in the Senate bore the weight of mounting, unaddressed difficulties and had come to think of himself as somewhat invincible in this area. While he never came out and said it, he believed the problem had not been fashioned that he could not deal with directly, honestly and with dispatch. Which was not to say that he believed all problems capable of resolution. But even when he could not solve a problem, he dealt with it.

His inability to confront the crisis presented by Carson shook that long-standing confidence. For twenty-four hours after his departure from her apartment, he closeted himself in his office, staring at the phone as if it were a hand-held nuclear device, and debated calling her. Then he picked up a stack of priority correspondence and consumed himself in dictation. After an interlude for lunch or dinner, during which he ate almost nothing, he repeated the process at the cost of mounting frustration.

He knew he had handled it badly. She had been right; he had been selfish. She loved children, and after years of loving other's children she had just learned that, against all odds, she was to become a mother. Was that the time to bring up termination of a pregnancy? He must call her, he told himself. But beyond apology for his insensitivity, there was nothing to say.

He became more convinced that the opinion he had expressed, however tactlessly, represented the only sane path out. The other, he preferred not to dwell on. If she would agree to go away to deliver the child, he would pay her expenses and pray that she would not drag him down publicly in an ill-timed scandal. He could pay child support, and he could continue his life in the Senate and beyond. But dare he run for vice president? If word leaked, he would be ruined, and he could take Justin with him. Surely she would not be so malicious as to broadcast their liaison. She would want to protect the child and herself. Still, he couldn't be sure. And with the stakes so high, the risk was enormous. Too great, in truth.

The other complexities in his life proceeded as if no emergency loomed. Jean called; could he slip home for a day or two to address some pressing personal business? Carrington called; he thought the press on Grunfeld's doomed grant request was terrific and wanted to know what Martin had in mind for an encore. Anne called from NIH; she expected problems as a result of the task force she headed, charged with investigating the leak of the Grunfeld report. The bank at Hollins called; Allie was overdrawn again.

And then there was Dennis. A good Congressional AA is an alter ego, sounding board, confidant and counselor. An AA who is not those things is a personnel problem, of which no Congressman needs more. Had the flaws in Dennis's performance been there from the beginning, unnoticed by Martin, or had Dennis started strong and faded as familiarity set in? Martin didn't know, and it no longer mattered much. What mattered was that the performance improve or the performer be replaced. It was in this frame of mind that he confronted Dennis three days after his blowup with Carson.

Dennis welcomed the meeting. Perhaps, thought Dennis, this would give him an opportunity to clear the air with a man he found increasingly enigmatic. Since the dramatic dismemberment of the Grunfeld grant request, he could think of no better description of Martin's behavior than "strange." The victory celebration he had anticipated not only died stillborn, but the morning after, Martin had looked positively morose. Far from the lavish praise Dennis expected as reward for the coup, Martin had been, if anything, indifferent. His efforts to draw Martin into a discussion of the hearing's dividends to his v.p. aspirations were met with cold disquiet, as if to warn Dennis against making the subject a matter of his concern. What the hell was the matter with the guy? Did he want to be vice president or not?

When Dennis arrived for the meeting, he was struck by Martin's appearance. He looked in dire need of sleep. The close shave and tailored suit could not disguise a subtle tick Dennis had not observed before.

"Sit down, Dennis," said Martin, who remained seated at the desk, his eyes roaming. "We haven't seen much of each other in the last couple of days. I apologize for that; I, ah, have had quite a bit on my mind. How are things with you?"

"Oh, I'm getting by, I suppose," replied Dennis, mildly surprised at Martin's concern. "The Richmond office is a mess. I went down there Monday, kicked some ass, took some names. It will improve."

"Sounds like time well spent," said Martin.

"I think so," replied Dennis, observing Martin closely.

"Dennis," said Martin, suddenly making eye contact, "some questions have been raised about what might or might not have been done in conjunction with the Grunfeld hearing. I need some answers." Dennis felt his grip on the chair tighten.

"I thought you pretty much knew the answers. We pulled it off, didn't we?"

"Yes, but that's beside the point at this moment. I need details on how. The report which found its way to the press is my biggest concern."

"I don't get it. Who is demanding information?"

"I am." Martin pointed his index finger inward.

"No, not you. I thought you said a moment ago that some questions have been raised. Who is raising them?"

"And I repeat, I am." Again, the finger.

"Well, pardon my density, Senator, but I simply don't understand where you're coming from."

"Dennis, let's not make this difficult. I am merely asking for information about the NIH report which was leaked to the press. A simple, straightforward answer will suffice."

Dennis's eyes narrowed slightly, his voice increasingly hard.

"Fine. How about an answer to my question, which was 'who wants to know?' Look, you assigned me a job. You said, 'find some way to keep the REA controversy before the public.' And I said, 'yes, sir.' It wasn't easy, but judging by the ink and air time you've received in the last week, I'd say it was quite successful. And instead of getting some credit, I get the feeling you're building some kind of file on me."

"Yes, I told you to find some way to keep the REA business going, but I didn't say to find any way to keep it going. Are you aware that leaking that NIH report is a criminal act? I certainly had nothing like that in mind when we laid our plans, and I don't recall any discussion of leaking documents. Do you?"

"In the first place, I didn't leak any documents. And I don't know who did. And no, I don't recall any discussion with you about it. But I recall a memo I wrote to you and a discussion following that memo in which you agreed in principle with trying to block Grunfeld's grant at the National Review Council level. You do remember that?"

"Of course. It's a bad investment of tax dollars."

"And while you didn't get involved with the details, it was plain to me that you wanted me to do whatever it took to get the job done. Within reason, of course."

"Did it occur to you that breaking the law is not reasonable?"

"I just said I didn't leak the report."

"You're playing games with me now, Dennis."

Dennis crashed his fist down on Martin's desk.

"The hell I am. It's you who are playing some kind of game. I don't know why you're doing it, but I don't like it. I don't like being used to further your sacred political ambitions and then dragged in here to account for it like some common criminal." He returned his trembling hand to the arm of his chair.

Martin diverted his gaze, staring at a spot on the far wall over Dennis's shoulder. He sighed audibly as he joined the fingertips of both hands in front of him.

"It's quite apparent to me, Dennis, that we cannot work together under these circumstances. I regret it has come to this, but your performance in the past few months has been a growing source of concern to me. I'm going to let you go."

"Oh, yeah? Well, I don't know what your problem is but I doubt it has anything to do with my performance. Whatever it is, I don't give a damn."

Dennis stood up and leaned forward, placing his fists on the desk and looming over Martin, still seated.

"Good luck getting on the ticket," he rasped. "I'm voting Republican."

* * *

The plane returning Max and Rita to California testified to the near perfection commercial flight had achieved by 1999. The silence of the engines and the stillness of the cabin were almost enough to persuade Max that he was at home, in his study, instead of 40,000 feet above the Midwest. He studied the checkerboard farms, calculating the odds of spotting his family homestead. Beside him, Rita read *Canadian Follies,* a novel gracing The New York *Times* best seller list for the fourth month.

For Max, it was the follies in Washington which absorbed his thoughts. The denial of his grant request stung. But each time his mind wandered to his rebuke by the Council, he recalled his inspirational hour at the Lincoln Memorial, holding fast to the feeling of purpose he had derived there. He must look forward, he told himself, for despite the loss of the battle, the war continued.

He would not get NIH funding; that much was clear. He was ever so thankful now that he had been vague about the identity of the "starters and stoppers." Such specificity would not have, he felt sure, saved his grant but would have provided a huge boost to anyone inclined to pirate his discovery.

As Max admired the endless sunset which can occur on afternoon westward flights, he contemplated the task ahead. Some way must be found to continue his search for the microscopic needle in the biological haystack. The odds against him were long, but not nearly so long as those facing his rivals. It was as though he had stumbled into a giant mechanical mouse filled with millions of power switches, only one of which actually turned on the animal. He had found the switch, admittedly by accident, but that accident put him quantum leaps ahead of those who might be experimenting with bogus switches acres from the actual one. His job was to bring his scaled down resources to bear on why this switch turned on the mouse; why delta41 triggered a mature cell to act like a newborn cell, generating a newborn mouse.

Oh, to be twenty years younger! thought Max as he watched the sun's fireball bury itself in the distance. Its transition from yellow to burnt orange was now complete. Full submersion in the horizon burnished the sky with the most radiant array of golds, purples and ambers, as though the plane's path of flight might take it into the furnace of the earth. It was an achingly beautiful sunset; he could remember none more glorious. Nature, he thought, has saved her best for last, perhaps with scientists as well as sunsets. The thought was a pleasing one which comforted him mightily as the plane glided toward the golden coast of California.

*   *   *

At NIH, Anne struggled to organize the special task force to investigate the Grunfeld leak. It would require deft skills bearing little resemblance to those Dr. Cass had in mind when he appointed her. She began with conspicuous activity centered on Dr. Cass's office and areas where her efforts were certain to come to his attention. She would appear with a legal pad replete with scribbled notes, nose around a set of files or an administrative area, ask one or two questions related to the Grunfeld grant request, and scribble more notes. Then disappear for a few days until the process was repeated, with small variations for effect. Her seemingly dogged pursuit prompted Dr. Cass to remind her that he had not intended for her to accomplish the investigation alone, but she waved off his protest as "part of my job."

She interviewed each of her task force members, but always in private. She knew she would eventually have to convene the group at least once, but not until she devised a plausible explanation for the leak. She felt the copying process offered the best prospect for a scapegoat, and if no other culprit surfaced, she could always attribute the leak to an "unidentifiable" clerk. It was an answer, but a weak one; the kind which could prompt serious inquiry if Building 1 became fully engaged in the hunt.

During her second meeting with Sylvia Stockton, a task force member, Sylvia mentioned an NIH clerk who moonlighted by baby-sitting. This clerk, Mavis Bodine, had been scheduled to baby-sit for Sylvia about the time the Grunfeld story broke, and had simply not shown up. Sylvia had called her at home but got no answer, and had learned the next week that she had left the agency. Anne appeared nonchalant as she made notes on her pad, writing at a pace and with an intensity that suggested this was just another detail, among many, to be examined as part of a thorough investigation. But inside, her pulse raced ahead with her mind at the prospect of a culprit with a face and a Social Security Number.

When Anne convened the mandatory meeting of the task force, its first and last, she thanked its members for their "splendid cooperation," in particular Sylvia Stockton, "whose tip led to the source." None of them, including Sylvia, could remember doing very much, but they accepted her praise and readily acceded to her offer to write the final report, which would, according to Anne, contain circumstantial suspicion arising from the departure of Mavis Bodine. Anne had confirmed, she informed her fellow investigators, that Bodine had left NIH without her last paycheck and her apartment without leaving a forwarding address; that she had access to the study section material and "probably" copied some or all of the reports. Anne was unable to hazard a guess to whom the unauthorized copy might have been directed or why: "presumably money."

Bob Ebersole suggested that Anne circulate a draft "so we can see what it is we've concluded," and Anne promised to do so. But she never did, and the task force members soon forgot in the press of their considerable duties in the vast NIH bureaucracy.

Chapter 22

On a wooded trail in the Frederick Park and Recreation Center, Kathy and Carson walked at a conversational pace. On this fourth day of Carson's stay in Frederick, the sisters engaged the topic which had been scrupulously avoided until now. On the night of her arrival, Carson had disclosed her news to a nonplused Kathy but said nothing of the blowup with Martin. She enjoined Kathy not to tell Frog and pleaded for a couple of days to "come down to earth." Kathy battled every curious impulse in her body to honor Carson's request for space and time. As they prepared to leave the house earlier that morning, Carson had said: "Time for the park, Sis. And have I got a tale for us today."

But once on the trail, her mood turned sober, reflective. She related to Kathy the confrontation with Martin, concluding with his stormy exit from the apartment.

"What?" said Kathy. "Martin Harmon suggested abortion?"

"Yes. He was in shock and upset."

"Well, perhaps, but isn't he a saint of the pro-lifers?"

"He has very strong feelings about abortion, or at least he seemed to."

"Well, the jerk seems to have had a sudden conversion."

Carson stopped walking and turned to Kathy. "He's not a jerk, Sis, he's just had a huge shock, like me. He was lashing out against the mess this creates."

"Yeah," said Kathy, "the mess for him."

"No, for us. You have to admit it's logical."

"But to demand it—to ignore your feelings about something so personal—is unforgivable."

"He hasn't had time to consider my feelings. We all think of ourselves in a crisis, don't we? All I thought about at first were my own feelings about being pregnant. Only later did I think through some of the complications from his end."

"Has he thought about your side? Has he called?"

"Well, no, but then I've been up here. I didn't tell him I was coming. For all I know, he's been trying to reach me. I left my cell phone in Washington."

"What will you say to him?"

They resumed walking. "I'll encourage him to sit down with me and discuss it like two mature adults. Then come to a mutual decision, if we can."

"Carson, you're not thinking about going along with his suggestion, are you?"

"I have to think about it, Sis. It solves so many problems."

*   *   *

Martin forced himself, on the fifth day following the blowup, to pick up the phone and call. He left a voice mail, kicking himself for the relief he felt at once again avoiding her. But having forced himself to make the overture, fruitless as it was, he managed to try again that evening. Again, no answer. He walked up the five flights of stairs to her apartment, knocking several times despite possessing the key. He finally let himself in, cautiously poking his head inside before calling out meekly, "Carson?"

The apartment was silent. He walked through briefly, noting evidence of neither presence or absence. He saw her cell phone by the bed, which could indicate a brief absence. He checked the closet in her bedroom, where a set of leather luggage was missing. She owned two sets, the missing one being her favorite. She had taken it to Maine as well as other places they had visited. Martin immediately surmised that she had gone to Kathy's.

Kathy answered when he called.

"Kathy, it's nice to finally talk with you after hearing so much about you from Carson."

Kathy, mildly flattered in spite of herself, grew nervous at the realization that Martin was at the other end of the line. The man she had described the day before as a jerk was still a U.S. Senator, a breed only distantly related to her social milieu. "She's told me a good deal about you, as well."

"Is she there, by chance?"

"Wait a moment, I'll get her."

Kathy walked backed to the guestroom where Carson was curled up with a book. Kathy entered saying, "OK, you win. He did call. He's on the phone now."

Carson picked up the extension and spoke a reserved, "Hello." Kathy lingered at the door.

"Not much, how about you? . . . Yes, last Friday night . . . Oh, they're fine, everyone's fine. Yes, I think we should . . . No, here is fine . . . ten tomorrow sounds ok . . . see you then."

*   *   *

Martin proved taller than Kathy had pictured him, and younger. After greeting him and engaging in a few minutes of small talk, she made her exit.

Martin seated himself in the den. As he waited for Carson, he reflected on the stakes in this conversation: his career, her career, an unborn son or daughter, Justin's aspirations, the country's leadership. He stood up as she entered, extending his hand. She smiled faintly at the gesture of formality. He grinned in response, guiding her toward a long sofa, but she passed it by in favor of a chair. He chose the chair closest, leaning forward as he plunged into the apology he had rehearsed the way he mentally rehearsed all his speeches.

"I want to start by saying I'm sorry for the way I acted the other night. I've been ashamed of myself all week. You called me selfish, and I was. I hope you can forgive me."

"You had every right to be upset. I wasn't exactly a picture of composure myself."

"How are you feeling?"

"Fine. Normal. How about you?"

"It's been a rough week. I had to fire Dennis, which was very unpleasant. He took it like I thought he would. I'm interviewing for a new AA now."

"What will Dennis do?"

"I'm afraid he's in for a rough time if he expects a lateral move to another Senator. I'm not aware of anyone who's looking and I can't give him the kind of recommendation that would help him. It's sad, but he brought it on himself."

"I don't know him, of course, but from what you've told me he was given every opportunity to shape up."

"For a fact. I tolerated more than many of my colleagues would have. But Russell Carrington's comment hit home with me. That was the straw that broke the camel's back."

"Oh? You didn't tell me about that. What did he say?"

"He said was that a presidential election is difficult enough surrounded by people you can trust completely, and there's no room for any question marks."

They stared at each other. Martin said, "The time up here must have given you a chance to sort things out a bit. Tell me what you think."

Carson began, her voice subdued; her tone reflective. "It's easy now, in light of what's happened, to second guess ourselves in becoming involved. The truth is, I've had misgivings from the start—misgivings beyond your marriage." Martin had understood that reservation, but it was apparent as she spoke that she had more. Until her affair with Richard ended, she had pictured a future very much like Kathy's present: a husband, children, and the sense of family. "But at some point, I changed. I don't think I gave up those goals completely, but I stopped viewing every relationship or potential relationship in terms of them. I opened my mind to the prospect of a risk, with more limited objectives, like having fun and living for the moment. The new me. But I'm not sure I believed it. When we met, a real part of me hung back, not sure the new me was a good me. Then gradually, as we got to know each other better and as my feelings for you grew stronger, the new me must have fallen off the cart because I started seeing our relationship in the same way I would have looked at it as a young woman."

"You're still a young woman," he observed.

"Yes, I suppose I am, but I fought the return to the old me; I fought it hard because it was so clear to me that the only future in us, you and me, was the present; the way I became involved in the first place. And now this happens. Who's in charge? Is it the new me or the old me? If it's the new me, I have to consider options I've never dealt with before. I have to behave like the modern girl I was going to enjoy being. I have to be practical."

"By that, you mean terminating your pregnancy?"

"That seems to be the only way."

"Could you handle it?"

"I'll have to, I suppose, if it comes to that."

"Carson, I wouldn't have put you through this for anything in the world. Neither of us dreamed this could happen, so we're both without fault in that sense."

"Are we? Or do we share fault for getting into something with no future and no graceful exits."

"Ok, so perhaps we do. My frustration is the lack of options. If we do nothing, that is, if you take no steps to terminate this pregnancy, I can provide financial support but little else. Although I regret like hell mentioning it the other night, my point about the New Hampshire primary was the truth. I have to be there. But assuming for the moment that the primaries and the election could be managed, what then? If I'm elected, what kind of relationship would the three of us expect to have? Morality has slipped a long way in this country, but not that far. The public would never tolerate my other family. I don't know if it's possible, much less realistic, to think we could keep it a secret for years. And what kind of life would that be for you and our child? I can't picture you in that role, can you?"

"Not easily, no."

"Besides, I have strong views on being an absentee father. In a sense, I've been one for 25 years, but not like we're discussing here. I missed a great deal, but we were still a family, and the kids knew that and Jean knew that and I knew that. It made a difference. I could have been a much better father to my children than I was, but I was still a father. What kind of father would I be now? A source of income visible in the newspaper. That's no way to raise a child."

A moment of silence fell over them, broken by the loud chime of an old grandfather clock in the hallway leading to the den. They each jumped slightly at the sound.

"Martin, what if you lose? What if the nomination falls through or you and Justin lose the general election? Does that change your analysis? It is a possibility."

"I suppose in theory we could live as we have been for a time. As an unsuccessful candidate, I wouldn't have the same worries about intense media scrutiny, but as long as I'm an elected official, even just a work-a-day Senator, the underlying problems will be there with the risk of public embarrassment."

She nodded.

"What about adoption? Have you considered that?"

"I've thought of it," she said, her voice cracking for the first time. "But I don't know if I could do it. It's selfish of me, but I'm being honest. I could say I would, but when the time comes, who knows?"

"So what's the answer?"

"I take it from what you've said that your choice would be to terminate, all things considered."

"Yes, but I don't want to force it. You once said to me, Carson—I think we were at Poor Boys in Annapolis—that it was 'my call'; that you would do what was best for me. Do you remember saying that?"

"Yes, I remember clearly. Obviously, a lot has changed since that night. But I remember the whole conversation that evening, including the part about your strong feeling against abortion."

"I—I guess I did say that," he stammered. His gaze fell to the floor. "I did say that, didn't I . . ."

"Martin, I'm not ready to decide this. I need more time. I recognize that time is limited for one option, and I promise I won't delay my decision. I want to think about what we've talked about today and make certain whatever we do is best for everyone."

"That's reasonable," he said, still staring at the floor. "It's a big decision. Call me if I can help."

They left the den to wind their way toward the front door, where they paused to say good-bye. Lost in the awkwardness of a handshake was the simple fact that, a mere week ago, they had loved each other.

BOOK 4

DENNIS

Chapter 23

The Rancour family had been star-crossed for two generations before Dennis. His grandfather, Mario Rancour, had trained as a boxer before enlisting in the Army at the outbreak of World War II. His weight lifting and conditioning for the ring drew begrudging respect on the tough streets of Philadelphia, where respect of any kind was hard to come by. But he was too slow to make it as a boxer, and being newly married and needing regular pay, he abandoned the fight trade for the fire department, where he saw an opportunity for a man of modest education.

As Christmas of 1946 neared, Mario Rancour counted himself a lucky man. He had a wife he adored, a new two month old son, who became Dennis's father, and a promising job which satisfied his youthful love of danger.

Four days before Christmas, his unit answered a call from a walk-up tenement which had burst into flames as a result of an overloaded electrical circuit. Mario and his mates arrived as flames licked the frozen night sky. Inside the third floor apartment, which held a family of eight, screams could be heard from terrified children. At the window nearest the street, a hysterical woman shrieked for help. Moments later, her nightgown burst into flames as the hideous cries were snuffed out with her life.

Mario and three others charged into the building in hopes of rescuing second and first floor occupants before the fire descended. What happened inside was a tale of confusion. The senior man in the quartet of firefighters, a man named Kowalski, ordered the forcible evacuation of those trapped on the second floor, all of whom were panicked by a dense smoke which thickened by the minute. Mario, certain that he had heard a scream near the landing on the third floor, started up the stairs leading to it. "They're done for!" Kowalski shouted and ordered Mario to abandon his effort to save the third floor victim. But Mario charged ahead, almost reaching the landing before the stairs beneath his feet gave way in a murderous collapse.

The tragedy of Mario's death was compounded the following day with the discovery of a charred body on the second floor. Despite the heroic evacuation of five people, questions were raised as to why the sixth member of the family had perished. A defensive Kowalski explained that, in his opinion, the second floor death would have been prevented had Mario followed orders forbidding his ascent to the third. The surviving members of the dead man's family, while grateful for their own lives, were not too grateful to insist on an official inquiry, which the department reluctantly performed.

Mario's widow attended the hearing, which was inconclusive. Two surviving members of the foursome testified. The first said he was nowhere near the site of the fatal mishap, but the second testified that he was standing near Kowalski, and that he was virtually certain that Mario could not have heard Kowalski's order over the din of panicked shrieks. Further, no hand signals were given in support of the order, according to this witness, whose testimony contradicted Kowalski's on this point as well.

After the funeral this man approached Mario's young widow in the cemetery. "It's a damn shame," he said. "Mario died a hero, and he would have been treated like one if there was any justice in this world. But there ain't."

Mario's widow and her relatives raised his infant son, George, and gave full accord to Mario's memory as a hero. But the homage was coupled with a deep distrust of city hall imparted by his mother, who never reconciled herself to the questions raised about her fallen husband in the hearing, and who spoke often of her cynicism.

George followed in Mario's footsteps, joining the fire department upon his graduation from high school. But awaiting him was a fate not unlike that met by his father—a death of sorts: less violent, slower, but nonetheless a death.

George rose rapidly in the department. An intrepid firefighter, he proved equally adept at administration. He attained a college degree over ten long years of night school, enhancing his reputation for hard work. The word within the department was that, with a few more years of dues paying, George had this ticket punched all the way to chief. But as he climbed the organizational ladder two steps below chief, he perished, as his father had done, in a conflagration known as "affirmative action." He was passed over for the promotion he deserved in deference to a black man who also had his eye on the top spot, and the political realities of the early 1980's in Philadelphia dictated that a black get the job.

George Rancour was never the same man. The inherent unfairness of it all, inculcated by his mother for as long as he could remember, broke his spirit. He withered at the Department, and his career withered with him. He put in his remaining time, retired on the first day of eligibility, and cursed his fate, bitter and broken, until his death.

As a boy, Dennis knew few of the details of the injustice done to his grandfather. He was more familiar with that imposed upon his father, but coming as it did at a time when Dennis was a typical college student with big ideas and raging hormones, he was only dimly cognizant of the extent of his family's misfortune. But as he matured, the depth of his father's bitterness became evident; bitterness all the more galling because history had repeated itself. Dennis had once made the comment to a cousin that if the family had a crest, which it didn't, it would surely have encased the Latin phrase for "It ain't fair."

Dennis observed an additional similarity in the fates of his forebears: no one fought back. While his grandfather had had no opportunity, his grandmother had accepted the verdict of the hearing with stoic fatalism. What was she, a nineteen year old immigrant widow, to do to correct a miscarriage of justice within the gargantuan Philadelphia Fire Department? His father had likewise not resisted, his protests confined to gin-soaked ruminations in a dimly lit den of their modest home.

So when Martin fired Dennis, without cause in Dennis's view, Dennis saw himself as a third victim, and seethed at the thought. He could not stop Martin from firing him, but vowed to break the Rancour pattern of woe. Dennis Rancour would fight back.

Martin's assessment of Dennis's job prospects proved only too accurate. In the days following his dismissal Dennis canvassed his fellow AA's for leads on a similar position with another Senator. He portrayed his parting with Martin in the best light possible, making liberal use of phrases like "philosophic differences" and "conflicting management styles," while the AA's rendered a near unanimous verdict: "Dennis screwed up and got canned." Which is not to say they condemned him or lacked sympathy. They each had a "personality" to deal with and needed no persuasion by Dennis to realize how truly arbitrary, onerous bastards many of their employers could be. As the AA to one notoriously difficult Senator put it, "They are not content merely to shoot the messenger. They insist on torturing him first."

Dennis did not go unarmed. His weapons included an extensive network of contacts in Congressional offices, committees and Federal agencies. He also had a strong resume, unblemished until Martin's dismissal. With these, it was a virtual certainty that he would find a job.

But not necessarily the job he wanted. Having spent years on the Senate side of the Congress, where prerogatives of power and influence take on the characteristics of a narcotic, he was reluctant to settle for anything on the House side. When his canvas of colleagues was complete, however, it was apparent that no AA slots were open, or likely to be until the newly elected crop of Senators invaded the Hill after the November, 2000, elections.

Dennis set his sights on a Senate staff job, to mark time. The staff positions authorized in the Congress far exceed the number of AA slots, which by definition are limited to the number of Senators, one hundred. In addition, staff positions turn over much faster.

But even here Dennis had difficulty. The raging recession had slowed turnover on committees. Where a senior position was available, Dennis obtained an interview without much trouble. But despite three solid interviews, he received no offers. The humiliation left him hurt and depressed. Adding to his anxiety was confusion about why someone so clearly qualified should not be hired.

When the third rejection landed in his mail, Dennis allowed himself several hours to regain his composure, then sought out Harriet Storm, senior counsel to the Senate Armed Services Committee, where Dennis's last interview had been conducted. He had known her for years and dated her following his divorce. Their entanglement, brief and unmemorable, ended satisfactorily by mutual consent, leaving no scars. Since then, they often lunched together, cementing what both considered a good, solid friendship. If anyone on the Hill had an answer, she did, or could find one.

He reached her by phone. She said she had been expecting to hear from him, was glad he called, and wanted to help. One problem, in her view, was his lack of a recommendation from Harmon.

"Wouldn't Harmon write you a letter?" she asked.

"He did, but it's so bland I haven't been using it."

"You may want to rethink that," she said. "With the letter in hand, some committees won't inquire further, especially if they like you and want to see you get the job. But without anything to cover their ass, they're going to call every time." And Armed Services had called Harmon, according to Harriet.

"Who talked to him?"

"Ed Simpson."

"Christ!" muttered Dennis. Simpson was the AA to Senator Clayton Watkins, chairman of the committee, and one of the few AA's with whom Dennis did not get along. "Just my luck. What did Harmon tell him, do you know?"

The hitch in her reply told Dennis she was holding back.

"Ah, c'mon, Harriet, this is important. Don't yank my chain. I hate to put you on the spot, but it's critical that I know what was said. If I call Simpson, he'll tell me to go to hell. Please, I need it."

"All I know for certain is that Simpson asked if you quit or were fired, and Harmon said 'fired.' Then Simpson asked if there were any circumstances under which he would hire you for another position, and he said 'no.' That's all I know."

"Simpson told you that, in those words?"

"Yes."

"That's just swell," said Dennis. "With all the time I've spent on the Hill, and with all the people I've worked with and for, it comes down to an offhand assessment by one unreasonable Senator."

"That Senator may be vice president soon. Between you and me, I'd say that fact had a great deal to do with the attitudes here. But you didn't hear that from me, ok?"

"I get it. Ok, thanks Harriet. I owe you one."

The days following this conversation numbered among the longest Dennis could remember. His daily ordeal began early with a review of advertised positions in *Rollcall*, after which he began his rounds to deposit his resume. Self-consciousness increased with each office he visited. His resume, once a source of pride and security to him, now took on the weight of a confessional, tendered apologetically to people who were still in college when Dennis was earning his spurs on the Hill. The hallways between offices became mine fields, each step exposing him to the prospect of meeting a friend or former associate with whom eye contact felt like shrapnel, burning its way into his brain. He walked these gauntlets in the uniform of a buck private, stripped of all rank, all privilege and all power. And with each step he cursed the man responsible for sending him to this no man's land, and swore revenge.

His worst fears were realized on the day he found himself sitting across the desk from a young woman he had hired. As an AA for Senator Ragsdale (D. Tenn), from whose office Martin had recruited Dennis two years before, Dennis interviewed this woman for her first job in Washington. She performed well, and was lured to the House Agriculture Committee. Her progress had been steady and her responsibilities now included screening job applicants.

To her credit, she perceived Dennis's discomfort, and offered him a job without emphasizing the irony of their role reversal. He was over-qualified, she allowed without condescension, but she hoped Dennis would regain his rightful place on the Senate side.

He accepted the position on the spot, dispensing with any pretext of "considering it with my other options." He had no other options. He knew it, and she suspected it strongly.

A mid-level staff position with House Agriculture was a long way down, but at least it broke his fall, ending the painful job search and providing a pay check. The severance pay he had received on leaving Martin's office was nearly exhausted, and the prospect that Dennis would miss his first alimony payment in seven years loomed large.

On the morning he reported to work at the Agriculture Committee, Dennis organized his desk from the two jumbled boxes he had thrown together in his haste to put distance between Martin and himself. As he sorted, saved and discarded a dizzying number of notes, messages and memos, he happened upon his notes from the Phillip Moorehead rumor. "A damn good job, and as usual unappreciated," he muttered. As he prepared to throw them away, his eye caught the emergency telephone number Ellen had provided for Martin. On impulse, he dialed.

"Calm Seas Bed and Breakfast," an elderly voice answered after a couple of rings.

"Yes—ah, I'm not sure I have the right number—where are you located?"

"We're on Route 204 about—"

"No, no; I mean, I hate to sound dumb, but in what town or city are you located."

"In Pleasant Point. Pleasant Point, Maine."

"In that case, I do have the wrong number. Sorry to bother you."

After hanging up, Dennis wondered if dialing the number had been spontaneous after all. Perhaps the entire episode of Martin's one week absence had been on his mind.

The phrase "bed and breakfast" brightened what had been a black hole since his introduction to Martin, that of Martin's personal life. His confident, assertive employer seemed to evaporate at night and return the next morning, groomed and tailored. It was not unusual for Dennis to see him at a breakfast meeting, observe him execute a grueling schedule of committee meetings, floor votes, constituent briefings and paperwork, and then surface at a diplomatic reception, party function or an evening gathering of the powerful and near powerful. He would walk into a room, arm himself with one drink for the duration, and work the crowd. When he had touched the bases, he left.

But for where? Home? Dennis had been in Martin's apartment any number of times. It reminded him vaguely of a very nicely furnished college dorm, decorated to serve its occupant for a semester or two. There were personal touches—pictures, mementoes—but they seemed more props than possessions. If Martin's body resided there, his soul did not.

It didn't reside in Roanoke, either. Dennis had met Jean on several occasions, always on brief, official trips to Roanoke. He found her a touch on the frumpy side and hard to talk to. He marveled at the union of two such plainly diverse personalities. Either Martin and Jean had an incredibly strong bond which required little nurturing by visits or other contact, or they lived apart while legally married. Dennis suspected the latter, if only because he had rarely seen strong marriages on the Hill. If his suspicion was wrong, and the marriage was solid, Martin's time was accounted for. He probably came home, read a book or committee report until his eyes slammed shut, and got up the next morning to do it all over again.

But, thought Dennis, if his suspicion was correct, what occupied the black hole of Martin's personal life? More to the point, who?

Dennis himself was one of the more active bachelors in Washington, slipping in and out of relationships and living arrangements. His inability to resist this kind of temptation had been a prime cause of the destruction of his own marriage to a woman who tolerated his weakness for years before giving up. He prided himself on knowing who was doing whom. As an eavesdropper to the world's biggest party line, Dennis was in prime position to catch any rumors about Martin's extracurricular activities.

Only there were none. A frequent subject of speculation, Martin was never linked to a face, a name or a place. The only way to achieve that status, in Dennis's view, was to live the monastic life of a saint. And saints were in woefully short supply in Washington, D.C.

To the riddle, "was Martin Harmon a saint or a very discreet sinner?" there were few clues, but there were some. When Dennis joined the Harmon staff, Martin spent most weekends in Washington, confirmed by his presence in the office on Saturdays and Sundays. When he took long weekends, it was usually to Roanoke, confirmed by phone calls to and from his home. On the rare occasions he left town for some other destination, he invariably left a telephone number and address where he could be reached.

But after that first year, Martin's habits underwent a subtle change. Weekend appearances at his office became rare, leaving Dennis unsure of whether Martin was in Washington. When Dennis called his apartment, he usually reached the answering service. Calls would be returned, but Martin rarely said where he was calling from. And instead of leaving a phone number and address, he called Dennis or Ellen at home to check on situations he wanted monitored. And visits to Roanoke seemed less frequent.

Dennis stared at the phone number, thinking back to Martin's week off. That whole scenario rang hollow; Ellen's cryptic instruction about requesting "Mr." rather than "Senator" Harmon. Martin had spent a week at a bed and breakfast in Pleasant Point, Maine, wherever that was.

Alone? That was the question. Any personal or political business of Martin Harmon was now Dennis's business. He picked up the phone, re-dialed, and heard the same elderly voice, who identified herself this time.

"This is Ruth; May I help you?"

"Ruth, this is Martin Harmon. Remember me?"

"Why, Mr. Harmon, of course. Calling to make your reservation for next summer? It's a good idea, you know. We book so far in advance. You remember how fortunate you were to get that cancellation this year."

"Yes, Ruth, that was quite a break. Please put me down for the same week next year, can you?"

"Let me just check to make sure it's not reserved." There was the faint sound of rustling papers for several moments before she again spoke. "Oh, I still have a spot. I can give you the same room if you wish."

Dennis arched an arrow into the dark. "That would be fine. My wife liked it so much."

"And what a lovely woman. Did she enjoy her stay?"

"Oh, absolutely," replied Dennis. "We both had a wonderful time."

"Splendid. Then I'll put you down for your same room. Is there anything else I can do for you?"

"No, I think not, Ruth. You've been more help than you can possibly imagine."

Dennis hung up, a self-satisfied smile spreading across his animated face. He dialed Martin's home number in Roanoke. Thirty seconds later, he had confirmed what he had known instinctively: Jean Harmon had never been to Maine.

Chapter 24

Despite his popularity in Virginia and throughout Congress, Martin had few real friends, and none close enough to share this private agony.

In the early 90's, he had developed a personal bond with the senior senator from South Carolina, with whom he had served on two committees and a Senate-House task force. They shared an enthusiasm for Southern politics and the Senate gymnasium, and had lunched together often. The South Carolinian had invited Martin to dinner parties, his daughter's wedding, and other social events, all of which Martin attended alone. He and Martin had talked of deeply personal subjects, like the time he confided his fear to Martin that his wife might be involved with another man or the time they stayed up all night, in the friendly company of a quart of silky southern mash, and he shared his disappointment in his only son's inability to hold a job. Martin had countered with his loneliness and isolation in Washington; feelings only slightly less strong when he went home to Roanoke. But the South Carolinian had retired in 1996 and left Washington, and Martin had missed him until Carson entered and reminded him that life could be more than just work. He had confided his intimate thoughts to her, but she could not help him at this moment. And he had to talk to someone.

Rev. Harrison Logan, chaplain to the Senate, had held his position for ten years. He measured his success by the number of senators who came to unburden themselves, and by that standard he was perhaps the most successful chaplain in Senate history. He had told his bishop often that this tenure had marked the beginning of his real understanding of human nature, for no other environment, he insisted, afforded comparable exposure to the passions, prejudices, strengths and foibles of such a complex group. Members sought his tempered wisdom, non-judgmental ear, uncommon faith, and his absolute, uncompromising confidentiality. Father Logan never expected to counsel Martin: too controlled, too independent, and quite possibly too proud to check his ego at Father Logan's door. But he had been wrong before.

Martin never expected it either. But during the week after his visit to Kathy's, he encountered Father Logan in the elevator outside the Senate chamber and welcomed the casual opportunity to set an appointment. He had tried to sound controlled, unhurried. But Father Logan had a decade of insights into the demeanor of powerful men and women, and he offered an appointment at nine the following morning, bumping the one already set for that hour with a man whose problem could wait.

Father Logan welcomed him with a firm clasp on the shoulder as they shook hands at the door. From the tension in Martin's jaw, the shaded pouches under his eyes, and the fatigued droop of his eyelids, Father Logan knew that sleep had come grudgingly.

Martin was struck at once by the starkness of Father Logan's office, a twelve-by-fifteen room. On the back left wall hung a modernist print, stark in its contrasts of golds and blacks, and on the right, a pastel rendering of a mountain church. Between and below stood a rectangular wooden table which served as Father Logan's desk. A wooden chair on coasters pressed against this table. Near the desk stood two plain, armless chairs, straight-backed and facing each other. These oak chairs, standing on a stained hardwood floor, completed the furnishings.

High, open windows dominated the wall to Martin's right, and through them he could hear the rumbles and clangs of heavy equipment engaged in street repair below. The high-pitched bleat of machines in reverse pierced through, unmitigated by the naked decor of the office. On the opposite wall, built-in bookshelves, floor-to-ceiling, housed Father Logan's personal library.

"A lot of philosophy here," observed Martin as he perused the shelves. "I just assumed your reading would be more—"

"Religious?" Father Logan scanned the shelves alongside Martin, their backs to the noise coming through the windows.

"Yes, religious," responded Martin, turning toward him.

"Religion is my job, but philosophy is my passion. Have you read any Durst?" Father Logan still faced his books.

"I'm lucky to get through the newspapers and official correspondence."

Father Logan nodded as he turned toward the armless chairs. He motioned for Martin to sit. "Let's talk," he said as they sat down facing each other. "You look tired." Father Logan's warm tenor rose above the industrial racket outside. He nodded toward the windows. "I can close those if you like."

"No. They're fine," replied Martin, slumping against the unyielding oak. "I'll be frank with you, Father. I spent most of last night figuring out how to broach this conversation. About three this morning, I decided to just say what's on my mind."

Father Logan chuckled softly. "Surprising how often that works. What's troubling you?"

Martin sighed as he diverted his gaze from Father Logan's gentle stare. "I am troubled by abortion."

"Many are. What is your specific concern, the morality of abortion?"

"Yes, the morality. As you know, I'm officially pro-life."

"By 'officially,' you imply your personal feelings are otherwise."

"My personal feelings are . . ." Martin paused, looking first at Father Logan, then off again. "My personal feelings are . . . personal."

"I see. You prefer not to discuss them. That's fine."

"I have trouble putting them into words."

"That's not uncommon, even among those such as yourself, who are so persuasive when they speak."

Martin half-smiled at the compliment. Then he lowered his head, fixing his gaze on his legs crossed in front of him. Outside, a jackhammer bit relentlessly into the pavement. "What I meant to say is that my personal feelings are unknown. That's what I meant: unknown."

Father Logan shifted in his chair, causing the old oak to creak under his weight. He sensed Martin would continue. They sat still for a time, Martin staring at his legs, Father Logan appraising him passively, and the insistent hitting of the jackhammer echoing in the spartan room. Without warning, the noise stopped, and Martin began to speak. He talked about Salem, the small town near Roanoke where he grew up, and about his parents, and about his early political races. Eventually, without mentioning Jean, his children, or Carson, he talked about abortion.

"If you are confused," said Father Logan when he had finished, "it is certainly not for lack of understanding the issues."

"True," acknowledged Martin. "I believe I'm well-informed."

"But are you well-grounded?"

Martin looked at him quizzically.

"Durst," continued Father Logan, "uses the term 'well-grounded' to describe the point at which an opinion becomes a belief. Such a point, says Durst, is almost always triggered by trauma, real or imagined. We play with things which amuse us, but we wrestle with things that can hurt us. It is critical to wrestle."

Martin nodded, and he wondered, both then and for days after leaving Father Logan's office, whether his mother or his constituents, whose opinions so mirrored his own, had ever wrestled as he was doing now.

*   *   *

The day following Martin's conference with Father Logan, Carson went for her first prenatal checkup. As she sat in the waiting room, dotted in merciless swatches of pinks and blues, she cursed the uncertainty of her situation. She damned the forces which dictated that she remain aloof and unattached from that which she wished to embrace with all her strength. She had vowed not to become embittered, but keeping such a vow became more difficult each day. If only, she thought, Martin could see their options through her eyes, she would feel comfort that was now absent. Didn't he realize that terminating her pregnancy was in one sense the easier way out for her, too? She had little heart for raising her child alone, and positive distaste for mothering someone whose identity, whose very existence, would inevitably be subject to news articles, snide jokes and cruel gossip. For both she and Martin, the choices were between lesser evils, but he seemed concerned only about the impact on his career. What about her career?

As she followed the bubbly little nurse to the examination room, she smiled in rueful irony at her long held love of being in the center of national politics, and she came to this realization: her decision could determine Martin's fate in the v.p. race, and upon Martin's fortunes could turn the prospects for Justin. She was, she now knew with crystal certainty, more at the center of Washington politics than she ever dreamed possible. And she didn't like it.

*　　　*　　　*

In Bethesda, Dr. Cass was beginning to suspect the soundness of his own judgment, so wrong had he been in recent predictions. For one, he had been certain the Grunfeld grant would be approved by the National Review Council. For another, he had been certain that his superiors at NIH would, within hours of the publicized leak, demand an explanation coupled with an investigation. It was that anticipated demand which had motivated his initiation of the special task force which Anne headed. But the demand never came. This mystified him. Didn't anyone over at Building 1 want to know how this happened? Didn't they care? The agency's integrity for fair play had been called into serious question, but so far Dr. Cass felt that he alone had taken steps to defend that integrity. To stonewall the vultures on the Hill was perhaps understandable, but to fail to make inquiry within the agency was unforgivable, in Dr. Cass's judgment. Perhaps the upper echelons of NIH were afraid of the answers. Well, Dr. Cass was afraid only of not having them, and he was confident Anne's report would supply them.

But again his prediction was off the mark. He re-read the report before calling Anne into his office to go over it.

"Yes, it is frustrating, Dr. Cass. I know you take this security breach very personally, and for that very reason I made a special effort to get to the bottom of this. I ran into one blind alley after another. I would bet Mavis Bodine is the culprit, but as I acknowledge in my report, the case against her is far from airtight."

"I'm afraid I agree with you, Anne. Is there anything else we can do where this Mavis Bodine is concerned? Contact relatives, have her traced, anything?"

"The Privacy Act says we can't access her personnel file for that kind of information unless we have reasonable grounds to believe she may be guilty of a crime. I'm told that generally means the FBI has to be involved."

"The FBI, eh? I hadn't really thought of that. Do you think we should call them in?"

Anne quickly responded, "No, I don't. It's up to you, but I don't think it's necessary."

"Why?"

"Oh, I don't know. Pride, I think. That copying process really needs some work. With your permission, I'd like to restructure it from top to bottom where study section reviews are concerned. Mavis Bodine's disappearance seems suspicious, but it could have been any one of four or five clerks in the pool."

"Maybe the FBI could give them all polygraphs."

"But they may not limit those to copy clerks. They would probably have to take one for everyone with access to a report. That's a lot of people, including some of our most loyal members of the study section. I think it would be terrible for morale."

"Perhaps you're right. It just galls me that someone here could violate a trust."

"How do you think I feel?" asked Anne. "It took place under my nose, within my study section. I'm mortified!"

"You shouldn't be. It wasn't your fault. With the barrage of applications we had, you couldn't possibly keep your eye on every copy of every grant."

"It's true," she conceded. "It's just an impossibility."

The corners of Cass's mouth turned down in an exaggerated frown. "Let's leave the FBI out of it for now. No one in Building 1 is demanding any scalps. In the meantime, Anne, I want you to do everything in your power to get to the bottom of it. If it wasn't this Bodine woman, we may see more leaks."

"I'll do my best," she said, thrusting her shoulders back. "Let's hope it's an isolated instance."

"Anne, I admire your protection of study section members. I hadn't even considered the possibility of the FBI treating them as suspects. It was commendable of you to look out for the welfare of your people."

In the back of Anne's mind, a refrain echoed: "This had better be worth it."

*　　*　　*

At the end of August, David, Laura and their three children visited Max and Rita for a final fling before beginning school.

The relationship which had developed between Max and his eldest grandson, also named Max but known as Maxie to family and friends, was special. The foundation of their bond, aside from the natural affection between grandparent and grandchild, was Maxie's precocious interest in science. From the age of six it had been clear that the Grunfeld scientific genius which resided in Max had skipped a generation to land firmly in Maxie, whose idea of a wonderful day of vacation was to accompany Max to the lab. Now eight, Maxie asked questions about absolutely everything he saw, heard, felt or thought at the lab. Max did not tolerate the boy's questions; he encouraged them, giving answers as concise as possible before the next question arrived. Max understood full well his grandson's inquisitiveness. As a boy, he had felt the same driving need to know the how and why of his surroundings. Nor did Maxie's rapid-fire questions lack quality, but rather reflected an absorption of the information given and its logical employment to formulate still more questions; questions Max knew to be quite astute for a lad of eight.

Max shared with Maxie, during this week-long visit, the particulars of his Lincoln research to the degree Max felt him capable of comprehending. Having studied Lincoln in school, Maxie seemed intrigued from the start while clearly puzzled about the concept of restructuring his DNA. As he often did, Max reduced the complicated to its simplest terms to facilitate understanding.

"Think of it this way," instructed Max. "When the carpenters who built your house started their work, they had a set of plans to show them where to put the doors, how large to make the rooms, how high to build the walls; things like that. If they had a really good set of plans, everything they needed to know to construct your house would be right there in front of them. Now let's say they built your house out of bricks. The plans would tell them where to put the bricks, but the plans themselves would be kept in a trailer or a truck where the workmen could look at them. Are you with me?"

"Yes, granddaddy."

"Well, your body is like your house in some ways and different in some ways."

"How are they alike?"

"The cells in your body are like the bricks. Your body is made of them. Millions and millions of them. And like your house, your body is built according to a plan. That plan determines how tall you grow to be, what color your hair is, and even whether you're a boy or a girl."

"We studied cells in school. They're very, very small," said Maxie, holding up his thumb and forefinger squeezed tightly together.

Max smiled and continued. "The difference is that every cell in your body has the plan in it. It's not in a trailer or in any central place. It's in every part of your body."

"So to be the same," observed Maxie, "each brick would have to have a plan in it."

"Exactly right!" Max exalted. "And that would be impossible, wouldn't it? If a plan was small enough to fit into a brick, it would be too small for the workmen to read, right?"

"But maybe the workmen have some special equipment, like a magnifying glass, to read the plans."

"That's a possibility," conceded Max.

"But granddaddy, why would the workmen need a plan in every brick?"

Max laughed. "They wouldn't. They would need only one or two sets of plans. But your body is different because it is not built by someone outside; it is built from within, so every part needs a copy of the plan. Does that make sense?"

"Sort of," replied Maxie. "What does this have to do with Abraham Lincoln?"

"A very good question," acknowledged Max, thinking it best to continue the analogy. "Suppose bricks did have a copy of the plan inside them and, as you suggested, the workmen had a magnifying glass so they could read the plan. Then suppose a big earthquake came along. You know about earthquakes, don't you?"

"Granddaddy! Everyone in California knows about earthquakes."

"You're absolutely right. I forgot about that. Anyway, suppose this big earthquake wiped out all the houses in the town. Then the owners of the house, who left the town when they heard the earthquake was coming, came back and wanted to build a house just like the one that was destroyed. How would they do it?"

"They could go to their yard and find a brick from their old house and look inside the brick and find the plan," he said triumphantly.

Max smiled broadly at his grandson, locking his arm around his head in an affectionate embrace. "You are one smart kid, you know that?"

"Yep, I'm one smart kid," acknowledged Maxie.

"Abraham Lincoln is a little like that," Max continued. "He died over one hundred years ago, so like the house destroyed by the earthquake he's not around for us to see what he was like. But if we have some of his cells, with the plan inside them, we might be able to build someone just like him someday."

"Do you have some of his cells?" asked Maxie, a touch of awe creeping into his voice.

"Millions of them. They're right over here." Max walked over to the safe where the Lincoln vials were kept. He picked one up and held it to the light.

"Can I hold it?" asked Maxie.

"No, I'm afraid not," replied Max. "It's far too valuable and something might—" He stopped in mid-sentence as he recalled a small boy many years before reaching out his hand to hold the seed of an oak tree. "Sure," he said, "but be very careful."

Maxie took the vial and dutifully handled it as though it were nitroglycerine. "Wow!" he said, studying the opaque substance. After a minute, he returned it to Max with a sigh of relief which said he was glad it was no longer his responsibility.

"So if you have Abraham Lincoln's cells, why don't you look at the plan and make another one?"

"That's another very good question and there are several answers to it. For one, the plan is hard to read because it has been damaged by the passage of time. The plan in your cells isn't printed on paper, of course. It's written in a very complicated chemical formula called DNA. Cells die when the people they make up die, and when cells are dead it isn't easy to read the DNA within them. It would be like finding one of those bricks after the earthquake if a lot of water had seeped into the brick and smudged up the plan."

"So Lincoln's plan is gone?"

"No, it's there, but parts of it are gone in each cell, so we have to find lots of copies of the plan from many different cells to make up a whole, complete plan."

"Then what would you do with it?"

"That's the tricky part. One thing we could do is study it to learn more about how Lincoln was built. Another thing we may be able to do in the future is make an exact copy of him. A living copy."

"Can I meet him?"

"Sure," replied Max, "you'll be first in line."

"What would he be like?"

"He would look like the man in your history book, but he would probably act much differently."

"Would he split rails and stuff like that?"

"There's not much demand for rail splitting these days. His second life would be quite changed."

"Did Lincoln have children?"

"Yes, he did."

"Wouldn't he want to see them? But I guess they're all dead too, huh. Maybe you could bring them back."

Max laughed. "He wouldn't remember his children, Maxie. He wouldn't remember being president or being shot or anything else about his life. His memory died when he did, and even if we found a way to bring back his body, he would be starting over, as if he had never been born."

"My teacher says some people believe they have lived before."

"It's called reincarnation. It is an important part of some religions which believe very strongly in it."

"Do you believe in it?"

"No. Not yet, anyway."

"So if Lincoln came back and had no memory, he would have to go to school to learn about himself, huh. That would be weird. Suppose he failed a test on his own life. Wouldn't he feel stupid?"

"Like a real dodo."

"But granddaddy, I still don't understand something about Lincoln. If his family is gone and he doesn't remember anything about when he was alive, like his friends and stuff, what good would it do to bring him back?"

"That," Max said, as if addressing someone his own age, "I cannot answer."

Chapter 25

Autumnal winds swirled, bent, and twisted through National Stadium on this Sunday afternoon, sending a blustery signal of fall's approach. Dennis was glad he had dressed warmly and remembered to top off the flask of eighty proof antifreeze in his overcoat pocket before starting out for the game. After twenty years of living and dying on the fate of the Washington Redskins, he always bet heavier when the forecast called for a chill in the air. He was never certain the Redskins played any better in the cold, but his luck seemed to run stronger.

National Stadium was packed as it had been for every Redskins home game since it opened in 1995, supplanting the smaller RFK Stadium used by the team for over three decades. His seats at RFK had been marginal, a corner of an end zone where his view of every play was taken at a herringbone cant. In the new arena, 20,000 seats larger than the old, his tenure as a ticket holder landed him on the twenty-five yard line, where he and his date, a Fairfax County schoolteacher, watched the burgundy, gold and white gladiators perform their awesome feats of precision violence. Here, his demotion to House Agriculture was irrelevant, for when the Redskins were in town, a reserved seat in the stadium conferred prestige enough.

A close game against the Eagles almost kept his mind off his obsession with Martin's vacation. By the fourth quarter he had drained the flask of bourbon, and he lamented leaving his backup at home. The crowd pulled him along as it stood, screamed, booed, and sang in frenzied unison. His date, attending her first pro game, turned to him and yelled over the din of the crowd, "Isn't this great?" He nodded, as he would have had she asked if he'd ever had sex with any of the Redskins, for his mind was elsewhere.

Confirmation that Martin's roommate in Maine was not his wife seized Dennis's imagination like nothing he could remember. As a professional student of Capitol Hill gossip and romantic intrigues, he had to determine the identity of the woman.

But it would not be easy. She might live anywhere in the country, or out of the country. If she lived anywhere other than the Washington, D.C. metropolitan area, the logistics of finding her would prove daunting. He had to assume that even small clues would be difficult to come by as Martin could be presumed to use his usual discretion. It had to be an affair of some duration, thought Dennis; the only other explanation would be a one week fling, which seemed unlikely for a man in Martin's position. Dennis reasoned that the trip had been a gamble in light of political circumstances, suggesting the relationship was serious. If he was right, Martin could be expected to pursue the affair, unless the vacation had ended it.

With these thoughts and a headache left over from the football game and the round of victory celebrations, Dennis found himself parked on Northwest 38th St. within sight of the main entrance to the Westchester. His high-powered binoculars afforded him the luxury of observing, from one hundred yards, that the doorman, Mr. Wayne, had cut himself below the left ear while shaving that morning.

Dennis chuckled in the realization that his erstwhile stakeout of Martin's living quarters was possible only because Dennis worked for the House Agriculture Committee with far fewer responsibilities than he had shouldered as Martin's AA.

He had no background in sleuthing and would have hired a detective if he could have afforded one. As it was, Dennis still had two major resources—his modest work load at House Agriculture and a fairly detailed knowledge of Martin's habits and schedule, at least the official elements. That would save him from chasing down too many blind alleys. And a third asset: motivation, which he preferred to revenge.

But there were substantial liabilities. His free time was not unlimited, so coverage of Martin's comings and goings would be sporadic. Martin could take thirty days to make a misstep, but finally do so when Dennis was shuffling papers on the Hill. Also, the hunted knew the hunter. A couple of run-ins under odd circumstances could be rationalized, but eventually, Martin would know Dennis was trailing him and might guess why.

As he nibbled on the remains of a cold grilled cheese sandwich and sipped hot coffee from his thermos, he made book with himself on his odds. Slim, he had to admit, but not so slim as to call off the chase. He was in it for the long haul, and with a break or two he might come up a winner. His best chance would occur either when Martin deviated from his scheduled routine, or during the black hole of his night. The problem was spotting a meaningful deviation from a schedule riddled with deviations. Dennis decided that keeping up with him during his work week was not only impossible but unnecessary. If Martin had been in a relationship which infringed on his workday, Dennis would have spotted it. This affair was being conducted, if at all, on Martin's time, not the government's.

Afternoons and evenings were even trickier. Martin had absolutely no set patterns. At least in the morning he followed enough of a routine to leave the Westchester at about the same time and head to his office. After that, only Martin and Ellen knew his schedule.

The best prospects seemed to be weekends, when Dennis was free to follow and logic told him Martin was most likely to lead. It would put a crimp on his social life, but "no pain, no gain." Perhaps he could get that hot Fairfax schoolteacher to sit in the car with him.

Dennis began his first weekend vigil at 4:45 the following Friday evening. After securing a parking place affording a view of the entrance, he settled in to wait. A light mist fell as the temperature dropped. He couldn't idle the engine for hours, but when he turned it off the windows fogged and the mist obscured his vision. He was cold, so every fifteen minutes he started his car and let it run until he could see and cease chattering.

At 6:30, a cab pulled up and a man who resembled Martin alighted. As this occurred during the latter stages of a fog-up, Dennis did not have the best view of him. But it looked like Martin. Thirty minutes later, a man who was definitely Martin emerged in an overcoat through which a formal black tie was visible. Dennis followed his cab to the French Embassy, where a sizable crowd of limousines and taxis signaled a major reception. Security at the embassy would not let him close enough to observe the arrival and departure of guests. He had no way of following Martin when he left the reception. A blown Friday night, thought Dennis; probably the first of many if he was serious about this.

The next morning, Dennis parked at his Westchester vantage point at 7:30. He could only assume that Martin was inside and only further assume that he would eventually exit the apartment house. At 10:30

a.m., Martin did in fact appear, dressed casually. Dennis was ready. Anything beat sitting still. He pulled in behind Martin's cab, using caution to maintain at least an eight or ten car length distance. The cab headed downtown. A hotel perhaps?

The cab made straight for the familiar confines of the Russell Senate Office Building, and waited as Martin disappeared inside, meaning that his business would be short. In five minutes he returned, clutching a brown bag and a brief case. The cab returned to the Westchester where Martin was clearly visible going inside.

Martin did not leave the Westchester again that weekend, or at least Dennis would have sworn he didn't. Tired, discouraged and sore from thirty-two hours of sitting, broken only by the eight hours of sleep he took at his home on Saturday night, Dennis left the Westchester with nothing to show for his weekend except the completion of twelve crossword puzzles.

The following weekend was even more frustrating, for Martin did not appear. He was, in fact, out of town making a speech, as Dennis learned from the newspaper on the following Tuesday morning. "What a frigging waste of a weekend," muttered Dennis. But on the following Friday evening, again at his cold, isolated post on 38th Street, Dennis realized he had overlooked something so basic it made him scream in anguish. Martin had a car. He kept it in a parking garage for tenants not visible from where Dennis sat. "Great," muttered Dennis. "I'll be out here freezing my ass off and he'll be driving on the New Jersey Turnpike." So he scouted out the entrance to the parking garage and found a space from which he could observe both the front door and the computerized exit to the garage. An hour after Martin's 7:00 p.m. return from the Hill, he drove out of the Westchester.

Dennis acknowledged a tingle of excitement as Martin headed over Chain Bridge toward McLean. Near Tyson's Corner, Martin's car swung onto the Dulles Airport access road. Perhaps he was picking her up after a flight from wherever she lived. Or he was leaving on yet another political junket. Dennis would know soon enough by Martin's entry into either long term or short term parking. The access road for long term parking loomed ahead. Martin turned. Oh well, Dennis could use a free weekend about now. At least he had found out on Friday night this time instead of spending a fruitless weekend staring at the console of his parked automobile. He swung his car around and headed back toward the capital.

* * *

Martin's flight from Dulles that Friday night was exactly what Dennis surmised: a political junket. He flew to Chicago to meet with Russell Carrington and Justin, returning Saturday afternoon. There, he went straight to bed in a vain effort to ward off a flu bug which had caused him chills and nausea on the flight from Chicago. He stayed in bed for the better part of three days, when the bug gave up and went elsewhere. His work week shortened by illness, he stayed late at his office for the next several nights to catch up on paperwork. As he surveyed the stack of priority mail which had piled up in only two days, he said a small, mental prayer for the volume of work which he hoped might distract him from his troubles.

For the first time Martin could remember, he forced himself to go to work. His seemingly endless enthusiasm flagged, victim of a concentration he could not focus. During his tenure in Washington he had witnessed colleagues who, by virtue of impending retirement, mid-life crisis or legislative ineffectiveness, simply went through the motions. He felt that way now, only none of the usual explanations fit.

On the contrary, he was inexorably plunging toward a year which would demand the very best of him; a year in which all his faculties would be tested against every pressure, every pitfall and every gauntlet national politics had to offer. At the end of an eighteen hour day in which he would make appearances in four states, he would be expected to live up to his reputation for oratory by looking and sounding fresh and inspiring. Between campaign stops at which his hand would swell from the incessant meeting and greeting of voters, he would be required to artfully field questions from the media designed to trip him into that one misspoken word or phrase that his opponents could seize upon to hammer him until election day. He would have to monitor every late breaking news event anyplace in the world where U.S. interests were at stake, formulate a cogent political response on a moment's notice, and insure that response was not in conflict with that of his party or Justin. If any asset he possessed would be more vital than stamina, it would be concentration. And of that, he had precious little these days.

He busied himself with paperwork for short spurts, but immersed himself in the gymnasium for hours at a time. He lifted weights until his arms and legs grew rubbery, ran added miles at a pace he thought beyond his capacity, and even, on rainy days, swam laps in the Senate pool despite a lifelong boredom with swimming. Physical exhaustion gave him a few blessed hours of un-medicated sleep—a priceless commodity in the weeks following Carson's thunderbolt.

He avoided Carson, but thought about her often, and one afternoon ran fifty-one laps on the indoor track before realizing that his mind had not left, for a moment, memories of their week in Maine. One morning at 3:00 a.m., unable to sleep, he lay awake wondering why he left her alone during this critical period; the span of days in which she must, of necessity, make her decision. At 6:00 a.m., still puzzled, he arose to begin a brutal day during which he dozed off at dinner with three prominent fund-raisers. He excused himself, went straight home, and fell asleep instantly. But at 3:05 a.m., he awoke with an answer to his reverie of the night before, and it centered on guilt: his own. He didn't trust himself around her, fearing that by his arguments, pressures and pleas, he would add intimidation to his original sins. He stayed away to let her decide, alone, and thereby absolve himself from further guilt in the event she came to regret her decision.

One evening, upon his return to his dark apartment, he called her. She greeted him casually, and within moments they were smiling at his account of recent comments made by Senator Orion, a man without rival as a windbag. She invited Martin up, and he stayed for an hour without mentioning her pregnancy, her decision, or the vice presidency. Thereafter, he saw her with increasing frequency, usually walking up the stairs to her apartment after calling to let her know he was on his way. He would stay for an hour or so, during which they would recount developments in their respective days. He liked seeing her in spite of the tension he felt in every phase of these visits, from the silly wave of his greeting to the studied avoidance of "the problem" in conversation to his awkward good-byes, when he was careful to maintain his distance.

Carson received these visits in the spirit intended, but appeared more relaxed. Like Martin, she never injected "the problem" into their discussions, but her even gaze and ready smile convinced him that she would not shrink from the subject if it popped up. She made him welcome, fixed dinner on occasion, and chided him gently over his loss of weight. Still, there was a distance to her moods, and more than once she asked him to repeat what he had just said. He admired her composure under such stress, and was tempted to ask the source of her serenity.

At 7:48 on a Thursday evening, he heard a knock at his door. He had been home only fifteen minutes, had had no dinner, and was at that moment debating between a quick trip to the sandwich shop in the basement or going straight to Carson's. As he left his bedroom to answer the knock, he mentally reviewed the short list of people who might appear this way, and because Carson had never been to his apartment, he overlooked her as a possibility.

But it was she, and Martin knew at the instant he saw her that she had come to tell him of her decision to bear the child to term. She entered with the same serenity, taking a few calm steps and closing the door softly behind her. She said she would only stay a moment; that she had reached her decision two weeks before but wanted to be certain; and that she was truly sorry for the complications she knew flowed from her choice. "Please understand," she asked. "This is the most selfish thing I've ever done, but I must do it." He merely nodded. "We'll talk again," she promised, giving him a kiss on the cheek as she squeezed his hand. Then she left him, very hungry and alone with his fears.

*   *   *

The following night, Carson called to tell him that she planned to go to Kathy's on Saturday afternoon and return Sunday evening. Martin volunteered to accompany her, with the understanding that he would drop her in Frederick and return to Washington that same afternoon. That would leave Carson at Kathy's without a car, but it created no hardship because Kathy was driving to Washington in her own car with Carson to spend a couple of days shopping. They agreed to meet at a shopping mall just outside Washington so that Carson could change into Martin's car for the trip to Frederick.

The next day, Saturday, Dennis watched the Westchester. Engrossed in the outcome of a college football game on the radio, he almost missed seeing Martin pull out of the garage. If it was another trip to the airport, Dennis still had time to scramble for a date that evening.

After twenty minutes of weaving through traffic, Martin turned into the Seven Oaks Mall outside Columbia, Maryland. Because of the aggressive shoppers in front of him, Dennis fell farther behind than he wanted to be as they entered the parking lot. Dennis lost sight of Martin's car, spotted it, then lost it again. He became oblivious to traffic, nearly causing a collision with a large passenger van which pulled out in front of him. "Get that tank out of the way!" Dennis screamed. The driver of the van smiled, lifted the internationally recognized middle finger, and did not move for at least two minutes. Dennis cursed and blew the horn. When the van finally pulled away, Martin's car was nowhere to be seen.

Dennis circled the parking lot. He stopped and stepped out, raising his binoculars. In the distance, he spotted Martin's car as a woman appeared to enter. His pulse quickened. He had to follow. Fast. He took a circuitous route around the bulk of the traffic. It nearly worked too well, because Martin's car passed directly in front of him, not ten feet away. Dennis slumped at the wheel, lowering his face.

Within moments, Martin guided his car onto the interstate with Dennis two cars back. Dennis used the binoculars to study the backs of their heads, hoping to see some manifestation of affection. But the woman stayed where any passenger would have sat, looking straight ahead.

At Frederick, Martin's car veered off the interstate and negotiated the four turns necessary to bring it onto Kathy's street. As the area became residential, Dennis dropped back. When Martin swung into a spacious driveway, Dennis stopped a block away. Through the binoculars he watched both doors open. The passenger, facing Dennis, carried a small suitcase. They walked to the front door, which immediately opened.

Five minutes later, Martin emerged, returned to his car, backed out, and turned toward Dennis. Dennis slid down as Martin drove by. Dennis raised his head to see taillights pause at the end the block, then disappear.

All of his attention shifted to the trim, well dressed passenger. But he could not maintain this station indefinitely. An occupied car outside an apartment complex in a big city was one thing; a suspicious loiterer in a residential subdivision quite another. He pulled slowly in front of the house, noting the number and "W.R. Fleming" on the mailbox.

Dennis drove to the end of the block to think. Should he continue to watch the Fleming home? The suitcase suggested a stay of more than a few hours. Had Martin merely run an errand? He regretted not being at a vantage point at the mall which would have enabled him to identify the car in which the mystery woman arrived. Most likely, he reasoned, she had been dropped off. If not . . .

His best move would be to return to the mall parking lot after the mall closed. If it was clear of vehicles, he could assume that either the passenger had been dropped off or that someone had retrieved her car. But if there was a car remaining, it could very well be hers. It was worth a shot; he had to return to Washington anyway, by a route that would take him by the mall.

Dennis proceeded to kill several hours by driving aimlessly around Frederick. At 11:15 p.m., he left for Washington after a final pass by the Fleming house, which appeared as it had. Arriving at the Seven Oaks Mall at 11:45 and taking a moment to reorient himself to its layout, he was relieved to see that the movie theaters, outside of which numerous cars were still parked, were located at the opposite end of the mall from where Martin had met his passenger.

As he rounded a retaining wall, his eyes fell upon a light blue convertible parked not far from the spot he remembered as the pick-up point. Fifty yards farther, he saw an older sedan. Did either belong to the mystery woman? He pulled in behind the convertible intending to write down the license number before proceeding to the sedan, but something on the bumper made the sedan irrelevant: on the lower left edge: the distinguished crest of the Westchester.

Chapter 26

Interstate 81 enters Northern Virginia some seventy miles west of Washington, D.C. at the jigsaw piece of West Virginia between Maryland and Virginia. At Strasburg, twenty miles south of Winchester, the apple capital of Virginia, the highway enters the natural crease in the earth known as the Shenandoah Valley. On either side, elevated tendrils of pine-covered earth slope gently skyward as the ribbon of road rolls on toward Roanoke. On the left, Massanutten Mountain rises out of the shadow of the Blue Ridge, essentially as it was during the spring of 1862 when it served as a few squares of rebellious Confederate chessboard, where the gray-clad knights, rooks and pawns of Stonewall Jackson checkmated the Union Army with unprecedented displays of strike and maneuver. On the right, in parallel splendor, lie the Appalachian Mountains, guarding pockets of civilizations so mired in another century that Stonewall's victories may still be greeted there as news.

The drive through the valley had a therapeutic effect on Martin, like a tour of an old neighborhood full of friends and memories. The gentle voters of this valley had supported him in his statewide races, and he in turn had advocated their interests in the national arena. He drove past Harrisonburg toward Staunton, where, on the night he was first elected to the Senate, he had held his victory party, disdaining the traditional sites in Richmond in favor of Woodrow Wilson's birthplace. After Staunton came Lexington, then Natural Bridge, which always reminded him of Allie's rock. And miles past Natural Bridge stood Roanoke, his home. On clear days, he imagined he could see it as he swung onto I-81 at Strasburg. As evening approached, the brilliant mountaintop star which is the symbol of the city beckoned like a porch light.

As he drove toward Roanoke on this evening, the tonic effect of the Valley was not strong enough to overcome the stress of recent events. He couldn't say he was shocked, or even surprised, by Carson's decision. On the ride to Frederick, she had apologized again for the problems it created, but not for her final judgment. And though she had tried to sound unemotional and detached in deference to the crisis her decision precipitated for him, she could not hide her anticipation. Martin could not recall a point in his life when he felt more at a loss than now. Over and over he asked himself a simple question to which no answer came; "What in hell am I going to do?"

Jean would be waiting for him. It had been three weeks since she had called to ask that he address some personal business. He guessed that meant the issue of her role in the v.p. race.

But Jean was not at home when he arrived. A note on the kitchen counter said she had gone to class. Class? Martin fixed himself a drink before adjourning to the den to catch the evening news. He flipped on the PBS News Hour to find one of his colleagues droning forth on the growing instability of the U.S. dollar on the international markets. The scotch on his empty stomach made him sleepy and he dozed off thirty minutes into the program.

He awoke ravenously hungry. As he entered the kitchen to fix a sandwich, Jean arrived. "Excuse me, sir, but you've obviously strayed into the wrong house. Now don't cause any trouble or I'll scream, and if that happens my husband will come running down here from Washington, D.C. to protect me. So go on, hit the highway."

"Hello, Jean." Martin leaned against the counter, his arms folded across his chest and a reluctant grin on his face.

"I'm warning you, sir. I get very angry when strangers rifle my refrigerator."

"I won't eat much."

"You know," said Jean, narrowing her eyes into a squint, "you bear a faint resemblance to my husband. At least I think you do. Wait here while I go into the family room and look at his picture again. My memory's not what it once was."

"As usual, I surrender," said Martin, shaking his head in resignation.

"And that voice. That's another thing. How do you do that—you know, sound like him. If you've got a minute, I want to play some old home movies for you so you can see just how much you look and sound like my husband. It's uncanny."

"May I fix you a drink?"

"Does the Pope smoke a fat cigar?"

He mixed her vodka and tonic. "I'm hungry," he said. "Any thoughts on dinner?"

Jean looked over her left shoulder, then her right. "Are you speaking to me?"

Martin was about to make it clear that he had been referring to the possibility that they could go out to eat, but he was too late. She was already launched.

"You know, I planned this big meal for tonight in honor of your annual visit, and I went to great lengths. I even got a recipe from Margie Williamson down the street. You know we homemakers swap recipes all the time. Why, I've just got recipes all over the house. I've got them stored in the oven, the washing machine, in the toaster, just everywhere. Well anyway, she brought me this wonderful recipe in . . . let's see, 1972 I think it was, and I promised I would reciprocate. Well, here it is 1999 and I figured it was time for me to keep my promise, so I carried one down to her last week. And do you know, she was so grateful to see me. I guess the walker keeps her from getting around very much. She gave me this perfectly marvelous recipe for flaming filet of llama. But the recipe specifies fresh llama, and you know me: if the recipe says 'fresh,' I want it fresh. No U.S. Senator of mine is going to dine on plain 'ole frozen llama. Anyway, the meat market was supposed to deliver it this afternoon and didn't. So no, I have no thoughts on dinner."

"How do you do that?" Martin asked.

"Do what?"

"Make up all that bologna on the spot."

"I have plenty of time to make things up."

"Ok, seriously, what about dinner. Let's run down to Freddie's and see if he's still serving."

Freddie's had stopped serving dinner to the man on the street, but the kitchen never closed for Martin, and the barbecued ribs were, as always, the best.

Meals in public restaurants entailed certain risks for Martin and his elected colleagues. He had accustomed himself over the years to being approached in such settings by constituents with some problem in immediate need of his attention. But because of his genuine concern for the welfare of those he represented, and because he knew they felt better bringing problems to him directly, he accommodated these interruptions at the cost of hundreds of cold dinners over the years.

Jean took a different view. These spontaneous petitions invaded her privacy. It was not enough that her entire marriage had been consumed by politics and that her husband spent virtually all his time in Washington working on their VA benefits, their farm subsidies and their Medicare woes. Was he not entitled to a modicum of privacy at home? Were he and Jean not deserving of some small measure of normality? Were there no limits to what must be accepted with grace and aplomb? For his sake she held her tongue most of the time, ignoring these interlopers, allowing Martin full rein in dealing with constituent sensitivities. And occasionally she would inject something designed to allow Martin a graceful exit.

Jean bitterly recalled 1992, their 20th wedding anniversary, as one of many causalities suffered in the name of public service. She and Martin had travelled to the exclusive Williamsburg Inn, where the rosy glow from a colonial hearth in the lobby set an intimate mood from the moment of their arrival. At dinner, the winsome sounds of a grand piano in the formal dining room added to the luster of a superb roast duck with wild rice. A bottle of Dom Perignon worked its magic as years of living separate lives evaporated with the bubbles in their glasses, leaving behind memories of a younger couple planning, hoping and dreaming in common cause.

As they awaited dessert, a burly man in his late fifties, unsteady on his feet, approached their table. The stranger thrust a beefy hand at Martin, a menacing disquiet to his gesture. "Senator, Sid Nelms is my name and it sure is nice to meet you. And this must be Mrs. Harmon." The beefy hand swung toward Jean. She offered a tentative hand in response, but no smile to accompany it.

Martin greeted Nelms, then wished him a pleasant evening in a tone of finality, a signal that it was time for Sid Nelms to move on. But he stood there, swaying slightly, the fermented odor of whiskey strong. He had undoubtedly spent the evening in the bar. Nelms explained that he owned a local Chrysler dealership which was being destroyed by the slumping U.S. economy. Martin agreed that the recession was hard on everyone.

"Recession, hell! It's a goddamn depression is what it is." Nelm's voice was rising as he railed against foreign competition. "You'd think people in this country would wake up and buy American. But no, they just keep right on putting their neighbors out of work."

Martin commiserated, but Nelms lurched ahead. Jean rolled her eyes as Nelms's voice carried.

"Look, Mr. Nelms, I'm interested in your views, but this happens to be my wedding anniversary. You can understand my reluctance to talk business tonight. If you'll call my office—"

But Nelms ranted on, leaning on the table with both hands to support his swaying frame. Martin saw the maitre d' in full stride toward the table, where he arrived slightly short of breath.

Martin said, "Mr. Nelms was just leaving."

"Yeah, that's it." Nelms sneered. "Blow me off like I was nothin'. Must not be an election year for you."

The entire dining room riveted on Martin's table, the pretense of business-as-usual dropped even by waiters, who paused to stare. Jean sat motionless, frozen in the dual cryogenics of anger and mortification.

The diminutive maitre d' turned resolutely to Nelms and insisted he leave at once. Nelms didn't budge.

"Leave, why? I'm just having a talk with my elected representative, Senator Harper here."

Martin's voice took on the unmistakable edge of a man fighting for control. "The name is Harmon, and I want you to leave now before I call security."

"That's already been done, Senator," replied the maitre d'. "They're on their way."

"Good!" shouted Nelms. "When they get here have 'em ask Harper how much money he and the rest of 'em stole from us last year."

Martin stood up, slamming his linen napkin to the table. The maitre d' blocked his path, apologizing to Martin as he held him back. Nelms raised up to meet Martin's challenge. At the moment it appeared they might come to blows, Nelms turned and wobbled in the direction of the exit. He called over his shoulder, "See you at the polls, Harper!" as two uniformed security guards appeared at the opposite end of the room. They had closed half the distance between themselves and Nelms when Nelms reached the door, thrusting it violently open and disappearing into the night.

Martin turned to Jean, who had sat motionless throughout the ordeal. She wore a look of abject sadness. She raised her champagne glass up to eye level, and in a voice frail with resigned melancholy, said, "Happy anniversary, Senator."

But on this evening at Freddie's there was no confrontation, no strife, no turmoil. Only a friendly crowd and great barbecued ribs.

"Your note mentioned class," said Martin. "What class?"

Jean showed a hint of a self-satisfied smile. "I've gone back to school. Isn't that exciting?"

"What are you studying?"

"I'm taking some art history classes at Roanoke College. It's a real change for me, don't you think? And at my age. If they can't teach old dogs new tricks, it'll be interesting to see how they handle dead dogs."

"We're not that old."

"I feel old. I've felt old for years now. Being around the college hardly makes me feel like a college student again, but it helps. I have a wonderful professor who has that knack of bringing excitement to what could be very dry, proving once again, I suppose, that how you approach something makes all the difference."

"My hat's off to the guy," he said. "If he can make those old pictures of dried fruit interesting, he must be special."

"But there is so much more to it," she countered. "The background of the artist, the conditions under which he worked, why he came to do the work, who taught him, how his work was received by the public. All those things flesh out what you see if you are aware of them."

"Hmmmm," said Martin, chewing a rib.

"Anyway, I'm having a grand time with it. Those classes are my first step in making some changes in my life. After your last visit . . ."

"Jean, it wasn't a visit. I came home for a couple of days. You make it sound like we're distant relatives."

"Perhaps we are," she replied, looking at him evenly. "At any rate, after your last visit, trip, commute—whatever you wish to call it—I thought about everything we talked about. Of course, the prospect of running for vice president scares the hell out of me, but you know what I realized?"

"What?"

"That I'm even more scared of not running; of being here alone with all the kids gone and you gone and drinking a lot and finding myself in some kind of god-awful downward spiral. That really frightens me."

"I'm sure it does."

"So I'm determined to make some changes. These art classes are good for me. Do you know I've spent several days in the studio lately. I even started a picture the other day, my first in years."

"Really?"

"It's dried fruit; I'm going to have it hung in your office." They both laughed.

"What is it really?" he inquired.

"A portrait."

"No kidding; of whom?"

"Of a young woman; late teens, early twenties."

"This woman is sitting for this portrait?"

"No, I'm doing it from a photograph."

"Well, I've always thought you were very talented, Jean. Now, I'm no connoisseur, as we both know, but I've thought your work was wonderful."

"What do you mean you're no connoisseur? With opinions like that, I'd call you one of the foremost art critics in America today."

"And even if it isn't wonderful, it's worthwhile if it brings you pleasure."

There was a silence for a moment before Martin said, "By the way, have you thought through the v.p. question?"

"Let's just say I've thought a good deal about it. As I mentioned, I've been giving my role a lot of thought since you were last here. I haven't finalized anything yet. We still have more time, don't we?"

"Yes," replied Martin, conscious of the fact that Jean had no way of knowing how narrow the v.p. field had become. "Oh, sure," he said, "there's still time."

*　　*　　*

The next morning, Martin arose early but was surprised to find Jean up and about. She had an early art class to attend. Martin sat on the sun porch drinking coffee and reading the various newspapers garnered from the convenience store. Jean appeared in the doorway, dressed for class.

"What time do you need to be there?" he inquired, not looking up from the paper.

"In about fifteen minutes."

"Then you don't have much time."

She hesitated in the doorway, then came into the room taking a seat opposite him. She waited until he dropped the paper slightly, looking over it at her. "Martin, I need to talk with you about something. Remember I told you last night that some changes were in order. You've asked me to consider the vice presidential race and I promised you I would. Now I have a request of you."

"Sure, what is it?"

"Have you ever thought about a divorce? You know, you and me?" Martin didn't move. "Think about it," she said as she stood up to leave. "There's no rush."

Jean had been gone for thirty minutes before Martin made any effort to rise, his mind a blank hostage in the captivity of numbing events. Unable to read, he walked the house in idle distraction, as if reorienting himself. He wandered into Jean's studio, a room he had been in only a handful of times. By a picture window on the far side of the room stood her easel, a cloth draped over it. He raised the cloth to expose a brightly colored acrylic painting; a nearly completed image of a young woman stared at him, smiling, radiant in the glow of youth and promise. He recognized her from her senior college photo, taken a few months before she and Martin were married.

Chapter 27

Martin remained at home for the better part of the day. As he roamed the house, he tried to assimilate the significance of Jean's suggestion. A divorce by mutual consent? Did she want to know if he had considered divorcing her? Was she thinking of divorcing him? Pacing, he waited for her to return from class.

In the early afternoon, Jean called, explaining that she had remained at the college to do some work in the library, and then run errands. She was having dinner with two professors from the college, so would not be home. Besides, she admitted, she simply wasn't up to a serious discussion.

Martin advised her of his need to return to Washington immediately, which she urged him to do. "I need to put my thoughts on paper; I'll sound more logical that way. When I've finished, I'll send you a letter," she promised.

Martin returned to Washington, puzzled. Whatever had seized her had done so since the last time he had seen her. Clearly, this college exercise had boosted her spirits, but a few art history classes should not account for such a radical idea. Martin began to feel that everything he touched, felt or thought had somehow slipped off the edge of late. From a man who enjoyed a precisely ordered world only a few months before, he had traveled a disarmingly short distance into this maze. His journey recalled stories, apocryphal he had assumed, of visitors to the Great Dismal Swamp who strayed only three or four steps off of the beaten path to find themselves lost. He hoped he was not lost.

*   *   *

Jean returned home late to a darkened house, tired but uplifted by the company at dinner. Her companions, both art history instructors, met her on her own ground, exhibiting a minimum of interest in her husband or his politics. They even shared her appreciation for dark humor. She was having fun again.

As she secured the house, she noticed the open studio door. She went in, seeing the exposed canvas of her self-portrait. So Martin had seen her work. She wondered what he thought. If Martin were a painter instead of a politician, she mused, who would he be painting? Himself, perhaps. Or more likely, the woman he met in Maine. She thought back to Dennis Rancour's phone call, reporting that the cleaning crew of the Calm Seas Bed and Breakfast in Pleasant Point had found the gold earrings she had reported missing.

"Dennis, what are you talking about? I didn't lose any gold earrings, and if I did I certainly wasn't in someplace called Pleasant Point."

"It's in Maine. Are you sure?"

"Of course I'm sure. I've never set foot in Maine."

That call confirmed what she had suspected for some time. And rather than depressing her, it had liberated her from any guilt she felt for not supporting Martin in his career. That Martin had taken some comfort in the arms of an unknown woman in Maine was not so bad, she thought. There were worse things, like going through a marriage looking down at the ground. Jean didn't intend to spend another day looking down at the ground.

*   *   *

Martin's situation grew more tenuous with the call from Russell Carrington a few days after his return from Roanoke. Justin was seriously considering a political maneuver with few precedents in American politics—announcing his choice for vice president before the end of the year, six months in advance of the convention and almost a year prior to the election.

Martin conceded the logic in Justin's plan. Aside from the usual platform wrangling, the vice presidential nomination presented the greatest likelihood of masochistic mischief by rank and file Democrats. The skirmishing had begun a full two years before the election and intensified with each passing month. As each pretender to the smaller throne fought for the favor of those closest to the expected nominee, alliances were formed, enemies made and lost, lines crossed and loyalties violated. Justin was determined to head off unnecessary carnage, insuring peace in the party and the best possible odds for the election of his ticket. Announcing his choice would halt efforts by those destined to be disappointed in six months. Better that they and their supporters learn the bad news now, while time remained for wounds to heal and loyalty to the party to reassert itself.

Martin tried to convince Carrington of his excitement. "Tell Justin I think it's a great idea. Christmas, did he say?"

"We're shooting for mid-December. It's not final yet."

"Well, keep me posted."

"You bet I will," said Carrington. "Are you sure you like this plan, because if you don't, speak up. You're a big part of our formula, Senator, and we respect your judgment. If we're making a mistake, tell us now."

"No, no mistake," said Martin.

*　　*　　*

The note beckoning her to Dr. Cass's office uncapped a vial of acid in Anne's stomach. She had been holding her breath since turning in the report of the special task force investigating the Grunfeld leak. She had seen Cass daily, but avoided discussion of the case. She hoped this note did not mean her report had moved to the top of the pile.

"Anne," said Dr. Cass, "we've got to do something about the problem with CalTech." The mention of the word CalTech let loose another vial of stomach acid. "Three of our most active panelists have resigned. It's the Grunfeld business. Turning him down was a blow to CalTech's ego, and the way it happened, with the leak and the press and all the rest of it, left a bad taste. I can't say I blame them. If a confidential submission from one of my premiere scientists had been handled that way, I'd feel like they do. We should probably be grateful they haven't sued us."

Cass said he was thinking of sending her to Caltech for some public relations damage control. When she realized she had been called in to be sent to California, her stomach returned to normal. But then Cass mentioned her investigation, and her blood pressure surged against her temples.

"But our findings weren't all that conclusive," she insisted.

"So tell them that. At least they'll know we made an effort to get to the bottom of it. Think you can handle that?"

"I suppose so."

"Good. I'll call Anderson—he's the department head—to schedule your visit. You ever been to CalTech?"

"Never."

"All the better. Why don't you plan to take a few days out there. You can tour their facilities, then go to the beach or see L.A."

"You drive a hard bargain," said Anne, trying to smile.

*   *   *

Anne's reception by Dr. Anderson could not have been more cordial. He personally conducted her tour of laboratories and classrooms, supplemented with a running commentary on the status of various projects about which he displayed remarkably detailed knowledge. Clearly, he was a man in touch with his department. His pride in his facilities and the use to which they were being put was evident, and she complimented him sincerely.

As they left a cluster of laboratories in one section of the research complex and prepared to enter another, Dr. Anderson turned to Anne to say, "I think you may be particularly interested in the lab we're about to see."

"Why is that?" she asked.

"Because it's Max Grunfeld's lab."

"I see," replied Anne with feigned indifference. She had been waiting for the right moment to raise the subject of Max's grant, but this was too early in her visit.

Max's looked much like the labs she had viewed both here and elsewhere; slightly less tidy, if anything. And deserted. Anderson asked if she had met Max and when she shook her head nonchalantly, he promised to introduce them before she left.

After her tour, Dr. Anderson went over her schedule. "Randy Cass tells me you'll be here for several days, so we would like to show you as much of the school and the area as you would care to see. But don't worry, I'll see that you're not so tied down with us that you have no time for yourself. I'm sure that a bright young woman such as yourself can find lots of interesting pursuits around Los Angeles."

"That's very gracious."

They agreed to meet at 9:00 the following morning. As Anne piloted her rental car along the freeway, she wondered who was performing the public relations work. Either CalTech was displaying far more professional generosity than it felt or NIH had overestimated the impact of the Grunfeld rebuke.

Anne's private, two hour meeting with Anderson was a no-nonsense session during which he painted a clear picture of the wound to CalTech's pride occasioned by the Grunfeld business. Anne went over her report with Dr. Anderson much as she had done with Dr. Cass. As Cass had predicted, Anderson was complimentary of NIH's internal effort to ferret out the source of the embarrassing leak. It was also obvious that CalTech had no thought of maintaining any legal action, preferring instead to move on to positive pursuits. In truth, the university and NIH were far too inter-dependent to do otherwise. As chagrined as he was over NIH's treatment of Max, Anderson was forced to consider the welfare of hundreds of their other grantees as well. But he conceded that the enthusiasm of those in his department for NIH was at an "unprecedented low" and that this was no doubt responsible for the recent declinations to serve NIH.

"To understand fully the attitude here, Miss Harborfield, you would have to know Max Grunfeld as we know him. He is an institution; has been for years. A prince of a fellow, really. The time and energy he puts into his work are an inspiration to us all. Max is what science should be. He has a first rate mind and infinite curiosity, but his big one hasn't come his way; you know, the major discovery that every scientist dreams of—that gets you nominated for a Nobel; that kind of thing. He has come up with a startling theory, as I'm sure you realized from reviewing our grant request. But he needs help, and unfortunately NIH appeared to be about the only potential source of the kind of money it would take. Max is seventy-four now; maybe seventy-five, I forget. He has the mind of a forty year old, but he is not as strong as he once was. Your grant, NIH's grant, would have provided the research assistants needed to take the load off him; let him concentrate on the most important facets of the project."

Anne nodded, while mentally recalling her role in Axe Max. She shouldn't feel guilty, she told herself—her study section had recommended funding. Still, there was the leaked report. She asked if Max had attracted private support and Anderson responded that the impediment continued to be "commercial application."

"But CalTech is helping him, isn't it?"

"Of course," he replied. "All we can, but there is only so much we can do without diverting resources from other projects, which is not fair to those associated with those other projects."

"Then his research is stalled until he finds funding?"

"He comes to work every day, and even with limited resources, I would say he is progressing."

There was a knock on Anderson's door. He checked his watch. "I told you I wanted you to meet him."

Anderson opened his door to reveal Max standing in the hall, his lab coat in its customary disarray. As Anderson made the introductions, Anne was struck by the sparkle in Max's eye. An uncle, with whom she had been close growing up, had that glint.

After an exchange of pleasantries, Max caught Anne off guard with an invitation to join Rita and him for dinner. "My wife is an authentic California cook," offered Max, "and for a native of Boston, that's no small feat."

Having no graceful exit, Anne accepted. Later, at her hotel room, she considered canceling, but it was too late. She tried to steady herself by belittling her fears. Did she think they would invite her to their home under a pretext of dinner and corner her; browbeat or abuse her because she worked for NIH? Besides, they had no way of knowing the degree of her responsibility for Max's rejection. If anything, they should presume she was supportive in that the study section she headed had favorably reported the grant application and recommended funding. She was alarmed over nothing, she told herself.

Max greeted her at the front door, ushered her inside and in the foyer called out, "Rita, the government has arrived. Should I let her in?"

From the distance came Rita's reply, "Is it the state government or that other one?"

Max looked at Anne, smiling, "That other one, I think."

Max led Anne into a modern living room featuring floor-to-ceiling windows fourteen feet high. Rita emerged from the kitchen, having just completed preparation of the meal. She greeted Anne as Max made cocktails.

"To the unknown, whatever it turns out to be," he toasted as they raised their glasses.

Max and Anne plunged into a discussion of science as Rita returned to the kitchen. When all was ready, Rita bid them to a table set for three. Two stark white candles flanked a simple arrangement of freshly cut wildflowers, gathered in an uncut crystal vase. The light cast a lambent glow over the braised chicken in fresh herbs which Rita unveiled. Fresh baked bread and a medley of steamed vegetables in a light teriyaki sauce completed the main course, which was followed by salad, then dessert. The California cabernet was a perfect complement to a meal which Anne swore, in total good faith, was the finest she had ever eaten.

Anne had anticipated the inevitable introductory queries: where are you from?; how large is your family?; where were you educated?, etc. On the drive over, she had rehearsed a few questions to ask in return so as not to monopolize the spotlight. But Max and Rita addressed her like an old friend about whom introductory questions were superfluous. They asked questions, to be sure, but not the ones Anne had predicted. They joked, they needled each other, and when Anne had disclosed particularities of her life, they even needled her, which cemented their intimacy.

In the beginning, Anne had been reticent to say anything of her work for fear of introducing the precise subject she wished to avoid. But Max and Rita freely broached questions related to her work, at the same time managing to skirt the leprous subject of Max's grant application. As they adjourned from the table for freshly ground, French roasted coffee and dessert, Anne knew she was in the presence of two excellent conversationalists, who had learned a disarming amount of information without soliciting it directly. She was, in a word, charmed.

As they walked toward the sitting area of the living room, they passed a marble bust of Abraham Lincoln which occupied a conspicuous place in a nook of paneled bookshelves. Anne stopped to admire and asked its source.

"A gift to Max from the Lincoln task force in Illinois," volunteered Rita. "He helped do a genetic analysis of Honest Abe's DNA back in 1990."

"A gift to us," corrected Max. "You performed some valuable work for the committee as well."

"Really," Rita said to Anne as if an aside, "they sent it to him. His confirmation of Lincoln's Marfan's disease was a highlight of their project."

Anne was thoughtful. "I read about that. So that was you, Dr. Grunfeld?"

"It was a most interesting inquiry, and I had lots of help."

"You had no help," Rita contradicted. "You did it very much by yourself and got less credit than you deserved, as usual."

Max turned to Anne with a sheepish grin. "You see my problem here, don't you, young lady? My wife insists I hung the moon and I have to keep reminding her that I only assisted is its construction," at which they all laughed heartily.

Anne asked a series of questions related to the Lincoln studies. Max responded in the technical jargon which Anne's background permitted her to follow without difficulty. Her dessert went uneaten for nearly an hour. Rita, for whom many of the microbiologic terms were foreign, nevertheless followed his general progression of events from the arrival of the vials to his final report. As he concluded Rita observed, "We felt we had gotten to know Lincoln personally. When the study ended, it was like losing a good friend. That's the reason I am so excited that Max is again doing some work on his DNA."

"How's that?" asked Anne, putting down the first bite of dessert she was about to take.

Max replied, "When we finished the original studies in 1990, the limits of our genetic knowledge prevented us from making some additional studies. But now, with so much progress in the field, many of those inquiries are possible."

"And is that the area you're working in now?"

"Pretty much. I'm dividing my time between Lincoln's DNA in particular and animal DNA in general. As you know, I had planned an extensive progression of experiments on the search for a totipotency trigger in white mice, but that did not work out." Max stated the last sentence as a simple declaration, with no hint of malice. It was his first and only reference to his defeated proposal. Anne felt obligated to at least acknowledge his observation.

"A great many people at NIH felt very badly about the way that turned out." Anne congratulated herself on the phrasing. "So I take it you've abandoned your work in totipotency?"

"Not at all. I'm still very much involved in it. The progress is slow, as you can imagine. Without government support, I am fairly much a one man show. But, slow as it is, the work is continuing, which is the important thing. I'll get there, that is unless the sands in my hourglass run out first. And if that happens, some enterprising young scientists like yourself will come along to finish."

"I remember your proposal, of course. Do you sincerely believe totipotency from a differentiated cell is possible?"

"I do indeed," replied Max.

Anne engaged him further. "Your grant request was for mice studies, but you do concede, do you not, that what is possible with mice may ultimately prove possible with humans?"

"I concede that. The human aspect was not the thrust of my research proposal, but yes, I concede that possibility."

"So," continued Anne, "we might reach a point where a mature living cell could generate a new . . . well, a new person?"

"And not just a living cell," said Max deliberately.

"Then dead cells? You think an old, dead cell could be triggered to produce a new organism?"

"Why not? The formula is all there, isn't it? If there is enough DNA present from which to piece together the entire genetic code, why not?"

"But what about post-mortem deterioration? What makes you think it will function?"

"A problem, to be sure. But with advances in the construction of artificial genes, we may be close to a solution. Look at it this way. You have a small sample; a piece of skin or the root from a strand of hair. Even in such a tiny allotment there are millions upon millions of cells, each containing the formula. If a segment is damaged in one cell, what are the chances that it will be damaged equally in all the cells?"

"Let me be sure I understand you," said Anne. "You're saying that the length of time since death could be overcome, so that someone who could have been dead for a couple of hundred years could be regenerated."

"I say it is a possibility."

"So that someone like Lincoln . . ."

Anne stopped speaking as a grin broke over Max's face, after which he declared, softly, "I say it is a possibility."

*   *   *

The next day, Anne conducted her exit interview with Dr. Anderson before going on to Los Angeles. She thanked him for the chance to meet Max and Rita, whose hospitality she had enjoyed so thoroughly.

"Yes, they are a wonderful couple," agreed Anderson. "And a vital part of our University community. I'm glad you found them as charming as we do."

"I must admit, Dr. Anderson, I had my reservations about going over there last night. I just assumed that someone from NIH would be persona non grata in the Grunfeld household."

"They took it hard at first; there is no denying that. But the passage of a few months has helped. Besides, they are not the type to carry a grudge. If they were, I feel sure they would reserve it for Senator Harmon, who we feel is the real culprit in this episode."

"That was apparent from Dr. Grunfeld's friendliness last night."

"I would be willing to bet," said Anderson, "that the subject of the grant did not even come up. Am I right?"

"Actually, it did, but not by way of sour grapes or criticism of my agency. It came up in the context of his current work in totipotency."

"He told you about that, eh? I am surprised. You must have made a very favorable impression on him."

"Despite his charm I wasn't persuaded on the science. It sounds like he's a long way ahead of his time, and his time may never arrive."

"Possibly," allowed Anderson, "but don't be too sure. I am familiar with his work, including the most recent studies just finished. I cannot go into detail, but I can tell you this: with or without government money, when a man like Max Grunfeld says something is a possibility, it is apt to be a good bit more. Just remember that."

Chapter 28

"Where's the list?" demanded Russell Carrington of the secretary over whose shoulder he had hovered no fewer than five times in the last hour. "Smith will be here any minute."

"Printing now, sir."

"Good. Bring it to me as soon as it's finished."

Five minutes later, the same frazzled secretary appeared at his desk, tossing the one inch stack of paper in front of him with a thud. To his startled glance she returned only a dull stare which seemed to suggest, "Go ahead, say one tiny thing about it taking so long and some ER physician will have to surgically remove those papers from your throat."

"I'm going home," she announced in a voice that matched her stare. "Mr. Smith just arrived in the lobby." She turned abruptly and started out of Carrington's office.

"Oh, Linda," he called after her, whereupon she whirled and rasped through clenched teeth, "What!"

"Thank you," said Carrington, smiling.

It was 9:30 p.m. and Linda had been there since 7:00 a.m.—the fourth straight night of the same grueling schedule with no end in sight. The sin which had landed her this marathon punishment was loyalty to Russell Carrington, whose penchant for secrecy dictated that only a single secretary transcribe the most sensitive campaign documents. And not just any secretary, but one with a time-tested record of keeping her mouth shut and her files locked. News about Justin was going to hit the streets when Russell Carrington said so, and not a minute sooner.

She had been working on the third draft of an invitation list for the announcement of Justin's running mate, set for the night of December 15, 1999, at a gala affair still very much in the planning. Smith had contributed his list, recorded in longhand, and Justin had also dictated names to be included. Carrington's job was to plug omissions which could embarrass his candidate.

Carrington fancied himself a student of war. His instruction in the Marine Corps had been augmented with biographies of the great generals of recorded history. At times, he cursed the fates which had landed him astride the 20th and 21st centuries, for the art of massing troops for lightning swift search and destroy missions had long since died out, depriving him of the chance for glory on the battlefield. Carrington knew that such regrets were his primary attraction to politics, where the art of war was still practiced. In the theater he now readied himself to enter, his army of Democrats would square off against the fortress of incumbency held by the Republicans. All of the elements of war would be at work: attack and counterattack, fire and forced march, desperate charge and last stand defense. In the end, there would be casualties; winners and losers, prisoners exiled into political oblivion and bloodless executions of budding careers.

It would not be easy, for Carrington had never managed anything on this scale. To offset the Republicans' depth of experience, he drew from his knowledge of history a proven technique practiced by his heroes: surprise. The weapon that Washington had used to capture Trenton and that Lee and Jackson had perfected in the flank attack at Chancellorsville could pin the Republicans back, disrupt their supply lines and render moot their battle plans. The early announcement of Justin's choice for v.p. would put the president and his cadre on notice that they were in for the fight of their political lives.

One person who could not be surprised was the candidate himself. That meant Martin had to be primed, readied and in place by December 15th. For the necessary coordination leading up to the announcement, Martin was again called to Chicago. Present for this high-level meeting were five of the six people with authorized access to Justin's plans: Justin himself, Russell Carrington, Howard Smith, Matt Morgan, and Martin (Linda was the sixth).

The meeting began with the upbeat observation by Morgan that as of this date, thirty days before the scheduled announcement, no word of Justin's decision had leaked to the media. Morgan commended those present for their obvious discretion. "A very positive beginning," he noted.

Carrington chaired the meeting, which began with the five seated around a conference table, from which they knew Justin would push away at the first opportunity to commence his customary pacing.

"Ok, listen up," ordered Carrington, like the general he perceived himself to be. "From here on, there's no turning back. Remember, if we can't run a campaign we can't run the country."

There ensued a discussion of the recent world events which the group viewed as relevant to the upcoming race. To a party out of power, its prospects for election are inversely proportional to the economy. The worsening recession continued to boost the confidence of this group, which developed the peculiar habit of cheering bad news. As Morgan put it, "We had better enjoy this doom and gloom now, because 14 months from now these problems will be our problems."

It was Morgan, focused on the ceiling, who raised the question which had been foremost in Carrington's mind for the last two weeks.

"Russ, what's our plan to keep the announcement on Martin under wraps before this shindig?"

"Here's my thinking. The announced purpose will be introduction to the public of all the state party chairmen supporting Justin for the nomination. Since we have no opposition, we should get close to 100% attendance from that group, to demonstrate unity to the rest of the country. Secondly, we announce the campaign staff which will run his race. That's us, folks. Both purposes will be cited in the invitations issued. The crowd which responds will just happen to coincide with the crowd we would want to gather for Martin's news. At the end of the published agenda, Justin will take the podium for a special announcement and tap Martin. If we've kept the lid on tight, the explosion should be deafening." He paused, looking at each man in turn. "Well, what do you think?"

Morgan volunteered, "I like it. Couple of questions."

"Shoot," said Carrington.

"Do we pack three news events into one here? By that I mean are we foregoing the chance to get maximum play for three separate events by combining them. After all, each one is a legitimate news story."

Smith jumped in. "That's true, but I think combining the announced purposes of the meeting gives you more coverage than either would separately, so we get maximum exposure for the true purpose of the whole thing. It's brilliant."

"Louder," joked Carrington, "Justin didn't quite hear that last comment."

"I heard it," called Justin with a chuckle from his path by the window, "and I happen to agree. Brilliant."

Then Carrington added, "But, gentlemen, hear me on this point. The premature release of this information will make us look foolish in trying to make a big deal over something that everyone and his brother already knows. Read your history. As a tactic, surprise is invaluable when achieved. But a plan which calls for surprise is a trap if the beans spill, so let's continue to keep it under wraps, shall we?"

Carrington turned to Martin. "You haven't said much."

"I've been listening, and I have to agree it's a bold, imaginative plan. One thing concerns me. The others currently assumed to be in the running for vice president; are they going to be hearing this news along with everyone else, because if they are, I think we should be prepared for some disappointed reactions as well as some anger."

From the window, Justin was heard to say, "A damn good point, Russ."

Carrington was prepared. "Which is why each of those candidates and their principal advisors have been invited to a very private reception with Justin immediately prior to the big show. He'll break the bad news personally and plead for unity. The last thing we need is a bunch of disgruntled also-rans carping to the press on Martin's big night. Frankly, we'll probably get some, but hopefully it will be a minimum. I dare say we could guess right now the two who will start moaning, eh Justin?"

Justin rolled his eyes and continued pacing.

Carrington again addressed Martin. "So, Senator, are you ready for your big day?" He didn't pose the question as some act of high drama. It was rhetorical, like "hasn't the weather been gorgeous?" But Martin heard another question, the kind that might be asked when the answer had real meaning and futures were affected, like, "is he still alive?"

"Yes, I think so." Then he drew a breath. "After all, it's only the second highest office in the free world."

Into the general laughter Carrington injected, "That's right! What's to worry about?"

*   *   *

Dennis had not remained at the Seven Oaks parking lot to confirm that the light blue convertible belonged to Carson. The sight of the Westchester parking sticker had filled in major pieces of the puzzle. He had considered that Martin's lover might live there, but without hard evidence that prospect seemed no more likely than a number of others. Now he had hard evidence, or thought he did.

But of course he wasn't sure, which was required on a matter of this importance. The woman could be a friend, even a relative although Dennis could not recall Martin ever saying he had a relative living at the Westchester. This woman was strikingly attractive, but so what? Dennis had hardly caught them in bed. He knew in his gut that this woman was neither friend nor relative and was prepared to bet a year's pay that she had been with Martin in Maine.

There was still the not insignificant detail of the woman's identity. He tried a number of the more traditional tricks of the sleuthing trade, at which he was still a rookie. He used a contact in the police department to trace the ownership of the car; no help, it was registered to the company from which Carson leased it. He called the leasing company with a story about being the lessee's uncle, losing her address and needing to reach his niece with news concerning a family member. The leasing company employee found it highly suspicious that Dennis didn't know the name of his own niece, at which point Dennis hung up. For an instant, and only an instant, he considered going through her car while it was parked in the garage. By the end of the week, he was no closer to her identity (and his work at House Agriculture was no closer to being done).

He decided that his cause could be advanced by a photograph. Now that he knew her car, it would be relatively easy to obtain with a camera equipped with a telephoto lens. He resolved to buy one until he priced them and consulted the available credit on his Visa. So he borrowed one from Meg Kildorf, a recent flame who took photographs for a consortium of trade association journals. Unlike his affair with Harriet Storm, this entanglement had not ended cleanly. The young photographer still cared for Dennis, who professed to care for her also but was less than forthcoming about the others he cared about at the same time. The benefit of her intimacy, aside from the loan of the camera, was her willingness to show him the rudimentary techniques for its use. This was fortuitous, as he did not know a lens cap from a hockey puck.

He did not tell Meg why he intended to use it, contenting himself with some vague reference to a hobby. But after several practice sessions, at which he would station himself in his old spot and photograph cars leaving the Westchester parking garage, he became passably proficient. He found the settings required to deliver close-up photos of the driver of each car leaving the security gate. Now he need only wait for the one car that mattered.

Dennis resumed his weekend watch, during which he observed Martin leave the Westchester and return several times. Dennis made no move to follow.

Near the middle of November, after days of patient, boring observation, Dennis got his chance. So anxious was he to capture her image on film that in raising the camera he nearly shattered the telephoto lens on the windshield of his car. As the convertible idled momentarily at the security gate, he squeezed off ten frames of film.

There was no time to revel in the satisfaction, for the convertible was speeding away and he gave chase. She proceeded through Georgetown, packed with tourists and students, crossed Key Bridge, then followed the George Washington Parkway to McLean, where she made straight for Tyson's Corner and its exclusive shops. Remembering his last experience at a mall, Dennis maneuvered directly behind her. As she did not know him, there was no risk of following too closely. She parked, and he proceeded on for a few spaces, pulling in just as she left to go into the mall. He quickly repositioned his camera and managed to fire off five more exposures before she disappeared behind a superstructure for the elevated parking garage.

On the following day, Dennis visited Meg's for the dual purpose of returning the camera and lining her up for the evening. He was in high spirits over ending his siege of the Westchester. Armed with the photos, he would undoubtedly learn the woman's identity.

"You're an angel," he told Meg, squeezing her waist from behind and whispering into her ear. "How's about you and I going out for an evening in Georgetown so we can blow all the money I saved using your camera. Your choice of dining establishments, and make it expensive."

"Dennis," said Meg, unclasping his hands, turning around, and charmed as usual by his syrup, "what kind of economy is that?"

"We're not talking economy here, we're talking food. Great food! Cold drinks! Dancing if I get drunk enough. Fun! We're talking victory here!"

Meg cocked her head to one side. "Victory? What kind of victory?"

"Why, my victory over the modern technology represented by that complicated camera of yours. My victory over photography, of course!"

"Did you win?"

"Look at these pictures and tell me if I won. Now remember, this was done with no prior experience. Am I proud of these, or what?" Dennis laid out the photos on a coffee table, then leaned back on the sofa, his hands locked behind his head.

Meg took time to study each. A professional habit. "I've got to hand it to you. You did good work. These really are fairly good. Who's the woman?"

"I don't know." Dennis feigned a dark and surreptitious countenance, a distant hint of Count Dracula in his voice.

"A secret, huh?"

"No, not a secret. I just don't know. I need to find out, but not tonight. Have you decided on a restaurant?"

"No, I'm still thinking." Then, turning again to the photos, she lifted one up from the table. "Where was this shorter series taken?"

"Tyson's Corner," replied Dennis, stretching and yawning from his semi reclined position. "I guess she was going to do some shopping."

"I'll bet I can guess what she's shopping for."

Dennis cut his eyes toward her. "Right. Can professional photographers read minds by looking at pictures of heads?"

"Not her head, silly, it's her body."

"What about it?"

"She may be going to a maternity shop. She's obviously pregnant."

Dennis jerked forward. "No way!" he snorted.

"Yes way, look at this one." Meg held up a shot from the series of Carson entering the mall. The angle at which the camera captured her did show a telling bulge at her midsection.

Dennis grabbed the photo, staring intently. Later that night, as he and Meg reveled in a posh Georgetown night spot, he experienced a liquor aided hallucination which left him doubled over with laughter. In it, Martin Harmon came before him, hat in hand, to apply for a position with the House Agriculture Committee.

Chapter 29

On Thursday evening, Martin attended a reception at the British embassy for the new charge, Ian Holbrook. As Martin spoke with the Ambassador, he spotted Father Logan at the bar and made a point to seek him out. Weeks had passed since their consultation, and Martin, in greeting him, pressed his hand with added firmness. When he had engaged everyone and consumed his standard one drink, Martin returned to his office to attack his must-do correspondence. The guard waved at him as he entered the elevator, still in his tux. He was alone in his office when he heard a voice in the outer reception area.

"Anyone here?" the voice called. Martin rose tentatively from his desk and started across the floor toward his partly opened door. In the distance he recognized the familiar form of his oldest son.

"Edward!" Martin exclaimed. "Son, how are you? What in the world brings you to D.C.?"

"Hi, Dad," said Edward walking briskly toward Martin with his hand extended. They shook hands heartily. "I took a chance coming by here, and the guard let me pass. Nice threads," he noted, nodding in approval.

Martin straightened his black tie. "My evening uniform. You look wonderful, son. Come on back where we can put our feet up."

Edward Harmon—tall, lean and unmistakably a Harmon in facial features and his gait, a controlled impatience—followed his father back to Martin's office. Martin motioned Edward toward a sofa lining one wall, taking for himself an armchair nearby.

"I didn't know you were coming. You should have called."

"Dad, I didn't know I was coming. I was minding my own business at the firm when one of the guys came down with laryngitis and had to go home. He was scheduled for some depositions here tomorrow so they sent me in his place."

Dreariness, his companion for weeks, left Martin as he studied the handsome, composed man in front of him. "So tell me about Atlanta and your firm. Bring me up to date."

For an hour Edward related news of his personal and professional life. Now entering his third year with his law firm, Edward appeared on the fast track to partner, as evidenced by his recent assignment to some major environmental litigation being managed by one of the firm's two rainmakers. He had even managed his time well enough to acquire a girlfriend, a CPA in a large accounting firm with space in Edward's building. She shared Edward's interest in bicycling down one hundred mile stretches of rural Georgia roads. Edward was easy to talk to; had been since he had been able to form words. He had a natural affability, as did his sister, Allie. So different from Jack, the quiet sibling given far more to thought than speech.

"Dad, you're becoming a hot topic around the firm these days. What's the inside poop?"

The urge to tell him of Justin's offer surged in Martin, but he said, looking away, "Hard to say, son."

"A lot of my friends wish you were a Republican so they could vote for you," said Edward.

Martin laughed. "Well, if the day comes that I climb in the big ring, I hope all those friends of yours will put principle above party and vote for me anyway."

"Yeah? And what about my Democratic friends who think you're a little out of step with the times, Dad. Perhaps 'party over principle' would be a better motto for them, eh?"

"Absolutely true," responded Martin with a grin. "In fact, Edward, I'll give you total discretion to play the principle card or the party card as you see fit. Because if I do climb in the big ring, I want to win."

"Wouldn't that be something," marveled Edward.

"A national campaign is quite an undertaking. I might even need to call on you a few times if you're willing."

"Willing? Dad, I'd be crushed if you didn't call on me, and I mean early and often. How many times does a guy's father run for national office? Of course I'll be involved."

"What about the firm, son? From the rundown you gave me a few minutes ago, it sounds as though you're in something of a stretch drive toward a partnership. I don't want to do anything to jeopardize that. It's too important."

"Vice president is too important. Let's be real here. In exchange for my three month sabbatical, the firm gets a strong tie to the national administration if you get in. That's what I call low risk, large return. And if you lose, no harm done and the firm gets some ink out of the whole experience. I'm sure they'll give me the time, and if they won't, the hell with them."

"Whoa!" cautioned Martin. "Let's not quit your job. Have you talked to your mother about any of this?"

"I went home last weekend," Edward replied. "Mom said you had been there to warn her."

"Is that the way she put it?" asked Martin, shaking his head.

"You know Mom. The limelight of politics scares the hell out of her. And she's afraid she'll let you down."

"She's afraid, I agree. But it isn't a fear of letting me down."

"What then?"

"Winning, maybe. She would have to live here if I win. That scares her." Martin gazed out the window in the direction of the capitol dome, brilliantly illuminated against the autumn night. "Another fear is privacy; hers and yours."

"What's the big deal?" asked Edward. "We haven't done anything we're ashamed of. Nor has Mom, as far as I know."

Martin, clasping his hands behind his head, said, "By privacy I don't mean skeletons in the closet; I mean loss of the ability to come and go anonymously. She values that, as you know. So you two had a chance to hash it out, eh?"

"Actually, four of us hashed it out. Allie came home for a few hours and Jack drove from Richmond and spent the night. We didn't plan it, but it sort of grew into a big family pow-wow."

"I'm sorry I missed it," said Martin.

"It was just as well, I think. Not that anyone said anything they wouldn't say to you directly. Mom had some wine and that, plus the need for everyone to speak their mind—well, you know, sometime people clam up if the atmosphere gets confrontational."

Martin arched his eyebrows. "Did it?"

"Not really. Jack, Allie, and I are as proud of you as we can be. Honestly. Jack doesn't say much, but I know he feels that way. He told me so, in so many words. And Allie, of course, would do cartwheels down Constitution Avenue on Inauguration Day."

"And how about your mother? Is she proud of me?"

Edward hesitated, picking up a pillow from the cushion to his left. "Ah, you know Mom. All bark and no bite." He turned the cushion over, as if examining it for stains. "Down deep I know she's proud. She just keeps it buried under a few layers of complaints. It's rough on her now, being alone so much."

"Did the family reach any conclusions on my fate in my absence?"

"Mom wanted to know how we felt about helping out in the campaign. She warned us what it would be like and told us to check with you if we didn't believe her or thought she was exaggerating. The press, the tabloids, the political blood-suckers; she gave us her thoughts on each. God, she was brutal."

"I can hear her now," nodded Martin, with the trace of a knowing grin.

"She wanted us to look before we leap. She said she assumed our natural instinct would be to sign on with the campaign but she wanted to warn us about what we'd be in for. Maybe she feared you would sugar-coat it for us."

"Good. I'm glad she laid it out as only she can. She's right in what she told you. But there are some other aspects to consider; some positive ones, actually. She doesn't know much about those, or perhaps I attach more importance to them than she does. At any rate, I want to spend some time with each of you talking—"

He was interrupted in mid-sentence by the ringing of the telephone. A glance over at his credenza told him it was his private line. He rose, took three long strides to his desk, and picked up the receiver.

"Martin Harmon," he said with deliberate evenness. It was Carson.

"Well, hello," he said. "No, just finishing up some late paperwork . . . Hard to say, really. Perhaps I can call you back tomorrow . . . Fine, goodnight."

Martin returned to his chair with a casualness he did not feel. "Now, where were we? Oh yes, I want to spend some time talking about the bright side because there is a bright side to it if it happens. But I, ah, won't twist your arms." Martin was having trouble focusing his thoughts. Relax, he instructed himself.

"But we want to help. Jack isn't sure he'll be able to do much; his job is less flexible than mine. But I know he'll try. And Allie has her bag packed; just tell her where you need her and when."

"I appreciate that," said Martin with a resigned sigh. "But where I need Allie is at Hollins and when is most of the time. The social overtones to a campaign hold too much attraction for Allie. And your mother, how is she leaning, or did she say."

"She didn't say," said Edward, casting his eyes back at the pillow, still in his hands. "But I'm sure she'll rally. She said she was thinking over her role in the campaign."

"Yes, I'm certain she is," replied Martin, thinking back to the look on Jean's face when she had suggested he think about a divorce.

Edward tossed the cushion aside and stood. "It's 9:30 and I still have to check into the hotel and prepare for this deposition in the morning. Since it isn't my case, that will take a while. I'd better be going."

Martin walked his eldest son through the large outer door with the seal of the Commonwealth of Virginia fixed firmly in the center. They went into the wide corridor, well lit but empty and silent. At the elevator they paused, but neither pushed the button to summon it.

"How long before you know, Dad? Will it be the convention?"

Martin stared into Edward's gray eyes as if looking at himself. His shoulders sagged as he grasped Edward's arm at the elbow. He started to say something, then checked himself, then said, "You cannot tell your mother, Jack, Allie, or the biker in Atlanta. The decision's been made. I was offered the v.p. spot a couple of months ago, but I'm sworn to secrecy."

Edward's eyes grew wide as he reached to encircle Martin's neck with his arm in a playful hammerlock. Martin did not smile, and his body was stiff and unbending. Edward stammered his congratulations, but a look of mild bewilderment soon showed on his face.

"You don't seem very happy. Don't worry, I won't tell a soul."

"It's not that."

"What then?"

"I have to decide if I want it."

"Want it!" Edward said with the trace of a nervous laugh. "Of course you want it. You've always wanted it. You've put in all this time, all these years. Of course you want it."

Martin looked down. "I've sacrificed a lot to get here, Edward. Perhaps too much."

"You're worried about mom. That's it, isn't it?"

"Mom and much more. I'm wrestling with a lot right now, son. If you're ever tempted by my line of work, make sure you wrestle with it, too. Call me tomorrow afternoon. If you're still here, I'd like to take you to dinner."

*   *   *

"Sis," said Carson, looking up from the classifieds spread before her, "help me find an apartment here in Frederick."

Kathy, lifting a mug of coffee to her lips, replaced it on the counter with a thud. "What!"

"I can't stay in Washington," Carson said, dropping her voice.

They sat at Kathy's breakfast counter. Carson, in a robe and slippers, scanned the paper, circling apartment possibilities.

"Stay here with us," Kathy insisted. "The guest room is large and I'll clear a place for the baby."

Carson cut her eyes from the paper to Kathy. "Are you crazy? There are seven people living here, Sis. You need your kid sister and her colicky kid like you need a brain tumor."

Kathy sighed. "It would be a crowd. Are you sure you want to leave Washington?"

"Positive," Carson replied, tossing her pencil aside. "When Justin picks Martin, all hell will break loose at the Westchester and I don't want to be in the middle of it."

"How will Martin react when you tell him you're moving?"

Carson stood and walked to the French doors leading to the back yard. She squinted as if searching for something in the distance. "Like he responded to my decision to have this child: silently." She turned to face Kathy. "Martin and I haven't really discussed much since that day we talked in your den. He hasn't pressured me, I'll give him that. When I told him, he just nodded."

"What do you think he'll do?"

Carson shrugged. "Run for vice president, get elected, move to the house on that huge hill, and get on with life." She paused. "And send me child support." Then, she threw her head back with a motion that squared her shoulders. "We'll be fine."

"I hope he loses in a landslide," growled Kathy.

"We won't know for a year, Sis, and I'm not waiting for election day to begin the rest of my life."

Kathy cast her eyes down at Carson's expanding midsection. "Some things won't wait," she said, smiling at Carson, who looked down before smiling back.

* * *

The only base left for Dennis to touch could be touched for the price of a plane ticket to Maine, but as he lacked the cash or credit for the trip, it had to await his next check.

Maine is as desolate in the winter as it is lovely in the summer. The harsh winds blowing from the North Atlantic coupled with the frigid New England temperatures insure that the off-season guests at the Calm Seas Bed and Breakfast gather in front of a roaring fire the moment the evening sun hits the horizon. It was late afternoon by the time Dennis entered the foyer to check in. A stocky boy in his mid-teens was laying the fire under the watchful if imperfect gaze of Miss Ruth, seated primly on a Queen Anne settee ten feet or so from the fireplace. Ruth's snow white hair was swathed in a silk scarf tied loosely to the side of her jaw. Plainly, she had not heard him enter. A glance at Dennis by the teen caused her to follow his line of sight to the spot where Dennis stood, a single piece of leather luggage at his feet. She rose to meet him.

"Hello, hello," she called out with an aging quiver in her voice. "You must be Mr. Rancour. Welcome to Calm Seas. I'm Ruth." She extended a frail, veined hand, firm but quite cold.

"Ruth, I'm Dennis. So nice to meet you."

"Your telephone call led me to believe you've never been to Maine before. Am I right?"

"That's true. It's certainly . . . rugged."

"It's what?" she asked, leaning toward him slightly.

"It's rugged," he repeated, somewhat louder.

"Oh rugged, well of course it is; it's Maine, you know. We're all rugged up here. Where are you from, Dennis?"

"Philadelphia originally, but Washington D.C. for so long now I call it home."

"We get some nice guests from Washington. They're not rugged, but they're nice," she said with a wink. She turned toward an old maple roll-top desk in a sitting room just off the foyer. "Let's get you registered so you can get up to your room and wash off some of that highway. Then I want you to come back down stairs because in ten minutes we'll have the finest roaring fire in all New England."

Ruth delivered what she promised. When the fire was in its zenith, she ambled over to the cupboard to prepare the winter specialty of the house, a hot cloved cognac served nightly for as long as Ruth had owned the inn, which was as long as any guest could remember. Her designation for the drink was simply "Ruth's Recipe," a secret blend of spices and at least two other alcohol-based beverages combined and heated to just the right temperature. She beamed as she served it.

Genuine enjoyment by the guests did not prevent a substantial amount of good-natured ridicule from being leveled at Ruth's Recipe. Over the years, a veritable encyclopedia of usages had been suggested by patrons, most of whom would sooner have missed Christmas than missed their week with Miss Ruth. They had, for instance, asked for allocations of the potion to defrost their windshields, cut holes in the Maine ice for fishing, revive dead shrubbery, kill unwanted shrubbery, and embalm favorite relatives. Most guests agreed with Jake Jones, a Texas wildcatter of the old school, who hadn't missed a winter with Miss Ruth in 40 years. Asked his opinion of the brew, he would grunt and then allow that it would "knock the balls off a wooden Indian."

Within seconds of his first sips of the Recipe, Dennis was prepared to swear that Jake Jones had understated the matter. But as the liquid heat warmed him from inside, he melted into the convivial atmosphere created by the fire, Miss Ruth, and the handful of lodgers braving the Maine winter.

The official purpose of this visit was accomplished in a remarkably short span of time after his arrival. As they sipped, Ruth inquired of him how long he planned to stay.

"Only a day," he said. "I wanted to stay here before I booked a week next summer. I know that's probably just an overabundance of caution on my part given the great references this place enjoys, but I'm just a look-before-you-leap kind of guy." Dennis could hardly believe how thickly he was piling it on. Christ, he thought, looking down at his mug, what WAS this stuff anyway.

"It's quite a ways to come for just a day," observed Miss Ruth. "Now tell me again who referred you. A referral isn't required, of course, but we do like to know our guests and to know who sent them to us."

"Senator and Mrs. Harmon. They were here last summer."

"Oh, yes, indeed they were. Such a wonderful couple. Their first stay with us, but I spoke with him by phone several weeks ago. He's made a reservation for next summer, so he and Carson will be with us again. Did you say Senator?"

"Yes."

"What kind of senator is he?"

"Why, a U.S. Senator; didn't you know?"

"I had no idea. Why didn't he mention it?"

"If I had to guess, it was so he could avoid politics for his week here. It is very hard for people like him to get away, if you know what I mean."

"Well, yes. I see your point. How do you know him?"

"I work for him, for Martin."

"Well my, my," she said. "And he never said one word about it for the entire week. All he had to do was to tell me, 'Now, Ruth, I don't intend to be bothered with politics this week' and I would have seen to it. That's the way we do things here. Our guests' wishes come first. Always have, always will as long as I run the place."

"Yep," said Dennis, "that's our Martin. There are rumors he will be running for vice president next year."

"You don't say. What if he got elected? I hope he and Carson would still want to come back and stay with us."

"Oh, yes," said Dennis, on a roll now. "They're like that. This is what they would want in a vacation."

"Imagine that," said Ruth wistfully. "A vice president right here in the Calm Seas."

"And his wife," Dennis injected.

"Of course. And how is she."

"She's just wonderful. Full of life," said Dennis, unable to resist the wicked double entendre.

"Give them both my best when you see them."

"Speaking of Carson, I had the most unusual experience the other day. I can't get over what a coincidence it was. I mean it had to be. A person can't possibly be in two places at once, now can she?"

"Whatever do you mean?"

"You see," said Dennis intimately, warming to his ruse, "I'm an amateur photographer. Nothing serious; just a hobby that gives me pleasure. I specialize in people. The most interesting objects on earth, when you think about it. Don't you agree, Ruth?"

"I quite agree."

"So I take pictures of people, all kinds, all places. Last week I was in Baltimore on business. I happened to look up and see this woman in a car. She was the spitting image of Carson Harmon but I had just left her with Martin at a reception in Washington. I was so startled by the similarity that I grabbed my camera and captured her on film. Here, let me show you." Dennis withdrew from his shirt pocket the photos of Carson at the security gate. "Here, see for yourself. Is that a dead ringer for our Carson Harmon?"

"Positively amazing!" agreed Miss Ruth. "Are you sure, because the resemblance is absolutely faithful to the last detail. I wonder who she is?"

"I don't know," sighed Dennis, "but it proves my point, doesn't it? People are the most interesting objects on earth."

*   *   *

Dennis hailed the flight attendant, ordered his second vodka and tonic, and watched her hips approvingly as she moved down the aisle toward the pantry. He reclined, savoring the contentment of a man holding all the trumps and convinced that the order in which he played them dictated only the timing of Martin Harmon's ruin. The attendant, identified by her badge as Melissa Shaw, returned. He waived off the peanuts but allowed her to bend toward him with the drink.

"Thanks, Melissa." She glanced at him, businesslike, and he, feeling the old cockiness surge after an extended absence, met her glance with his practiced come-on, his eyes hooded just enough to suggest waking up beside her. She smiled thinly.

He vibrated his glass, producing a tinkling of the ice as he pondered his options. Was there, for example, greater satisfaction in alerting Justin Bonner at once, thereby costing Martin the nomination, or in waiting until the convention? He now possessed irrefutable proof of Martin's sins and Justin was politician enough to appreciate the liability he represented. He would drop Martin instantly, possibly without explanation. "That would be good," mouthed Dennis silently as he brought the vodka to his lips and remembered his own dismissal. Martin would reel, confused, victimized, betrayed by the precipitous withdrawal of that which Dennis felt certain Martin was assured. Dennis wanted to be there, to watch Martin's face as Justin brought the hammer down. That was the trouble with Plan A, he decided. He could derive his satisfaction only from Justin's astonishment and wouldn't be a witness to Martin's humiliation. That, he had to see.

Plan B had possibilities. Let Justin tap Martin, let Martin fly around the country for six months becoming a household word and climbing ever higher on the political ladder with major contributors, state party chairpersons, and local party mules. Yes, a fall from that height would make "the splat heard round the world"; a sweet sound indeed.

The plane dropped in an air pocket, nearly spilling his drink. Below, the roads of upstate New York lay in an irregular grid across the undulating landscape. In less than a year, all those roads, no matter how rural or remote, paved, graveled or rutted mud, would lead to polling places, where Americans would cast their votes. Perhaps, he mused, the election should serve as a referendum on Martin's character, a decisive thumbs down from a disgusted national emperor. An early October news conference should suffice; too late for a new candidate, the campaign in disarray, and the ticket headed down because Martin's skeleton had, thanks to Dennis, come tap dancing out of its closet. Yes! Not only would Dennis get to witness Martin's agony, but the nightly news would serve it to him with dinner, over and over for a solid month before the election. He loved Plan C.

By the time the plane touched down in Washington, Dennis was pleasantly high and thoroughly pleased. At the overhead bin, he lingered to speak to Melissa Shaw.

"Any plans when you get off?" he asked. "I'd like to buy you a drink."

She smiled sweetly. "The usual; pick up the kids, fix dinner for Sam. But thanks for asking."

His voice carried an edge. "You should wear a ring."

"Really?" she replied, still smiling. "And you should wear a leash."

Chapter 30

The almost indiscernible tap on Carson's door signaled Martin's arrival. He knocked despite still having the key, the use of which implied license which was not granted, privilege which was not extended, control which was not acknowledged. She admitted him at once.

Although she had seen him the previous day, she was struck by his haggard appearance on this night. To the natural darkness under his eyes, the honest products of long hours on behalf of his constituents, were added swollen pools of sleepless torment. She instinctively placed her hand on his forearm.

"Martin, you look terrible. Aren't you sleeping?"

"Not much," he admitted.

"Want a drink?"

"No thanks. If I start . . ."

"Coffee?"

"Yes, thank you."

He was different tonight, she thought. It went beyond his physical deterioration, which had been gradual for the past several months. With this wasting away had come an erosion of the spirit; an enfeeblement of the essence of the man she had come to know. But the vacant stare tonight troubled her beyond anything heretofore, for the simple reason that she could not deduce its meaning. In the recent past, she had seen those same eyes reflect fear, panic, anger, regret, distrust and frustration. But never nothing.

"How goes the search for Dennis's replacement?"

"Very slow. My fault really. There have been ample qualified applicants. I can't seem to make up my mind."

"You mean you haven't found one with all the qualities you're seeking?"

"No, I mean I simply can't decide. To be honest, I've been deferring it until after the v.p. thing resolved itself."

She was thinking, but did not say, that it would not resolve itself; he would have to resolve it. But the last thing he appeared to need at the moment was a platitude from her about taking charge of his life, so she said nothing.

Then, as if reading her mind with those vacant eyes, he said, "I know it was unrealistic for me to think it would resolve itself. I had to decide"

"Have you?"

He made no response, as if he had not heard the question. "Carrington has been pressing me for a guest list. Pressing hard. It was overdue. The invitations have to go out this week." He dropped his head but said nothing more. Moments later he stood up, walking to the window overlooking the courtyard. Fatigue pulled at him like weights in the lining of his coat. He turned and rested against the sill before speaking. His voice, while subdued, was even and without pathos.

"I have." He paused to stare at an invisible spot on the far wall. "For the past few months I've been struggling to figure out to whom it is I owe my loyalty in this crazy, mixed-up mess, on the assumption that when I solved that puzzle, my decision on the vice presidency would become obvious. My obligation to you speaks for itself. As the father of our unborn child, I owe you and the child my moral and financial support, my presence, my involvement, my name. I owe you both a family. At the same time I owe Jean, for twenty-eight years of marriage, lots of sacrifices raising the children, and the history which is inseparable from us. Then there's Justin . . . I owe him a clear shot at the presidency unencumbered by a possible scandal involving his running mate. And the voters who elected me. I owe them a performance that justifies their confidence. None of the debts can be reconciled. To acknowledge one is to default on the others. That's a depressing realization."

"You haven't mentioned yourself," observed Carson softly. "Don't you owe yourself something?"

Martin smiled, a rueful half smile of sad irony. "I owe myself along with everyone else, and I have selfishly concluded that I must honor that debt first. But I was wrong in thinking that would resolve my dilemma.

It merely prompts the larger question of how to honor that debt. What exactly do I owe to me?" He shifted his feet, looking down at the floor for a few seconds before again finding his spot on the far wall.

Martin told her of the beginning of his interest in politics. In the tenth grade, he'd taken U.S. History from a woman named Masterson, who not only made the colonial period come alive, but the colonial leaders as well. Washington, Jefferson, Madison, and Monroe became his heroes.

"One fact about those men that stuck with me is that they pretty much all went broke, or very nearly." It astounded him that Jefferson sold one of the finest libraries in the world to pay down his debts and nearly lost his home before dying penniless. The same thing happened to Monroe. Their public service cost them everything. These men would leave home for months, frequently years, to fulfill their obligations to the country. They would travel to New York or Philadelphia or Washington or Richmond to sit in legislatures or to Europe as emissaries and ambassadors. They left their farms, and therefore their fortunes, in the hands of stand-ins rarely able to produce what the owner could have produced had he been there. They returned home poorer than when they left.

"You know why they did it? Because they knew that nothing they were attempting to build at home would be worth much without a solid government. To ignore public service would have been to cultivate farms and establish private careers which would be jeopardized, sooner or later, by the lack of a good court system, commercial laws that made sense, fair taxation, defense against invasion, and all the other functions a government performs. So here you had a group of men, ambitious to be sure, who would have preferred to stay at home, build their fortunes, raise their children and be solid citizens, but who knew that unless they left to do what had to be done, nothing they built on their own land would be permanent. Do you see what I'm saying?"

She nodded, understanding all he said, but not why. He paused, his age newly apparent in the deep lines of his face. She had never seen him so intense. Or tired.

"I don't fancy myself as a savior of democracy, but I've worked hard. I hope for the right reasons; the same reasons they did it. But I'm not sure anymore. If I had practiced law in Roanoke, wouldn't the country be in the same state it is today? Did I leave my 'family and farm' to build the kind of country I wanted to live in, or did I do it for me? A year ago I could have answered that question, or let's just say I would have answered it. But now? Am I in it for the average Joe Blow or am I in it for Martin Harmon?

"The last six months have been a nightmare, but for reasons beyond the obvious ones. On a subject on which my position is well known; is spread in the Congressional Record for page after page; is a prime factor in my party's wooing me for v.p.; it turns out I have no such position, or any position at all. Maybe that's true for other issues as well. Maybe that's also true of the positions held by my colleagues, which would help explain why this country finds itself so mired in mud. Are we working to return to our families and our farms, or are we just all jockeying for position. Damn if I know.

"But I do know this. The vice presidency of the United States is but one short step away from some overwhelming responsibility, and it would be criminal for me to assume that nothing would happen to Justin if we were elected. So the decision comes down to whether I'm qualified to be president."

"You're as qualified as anyone in the Senate," said Carson. "Anyone in America."

"On paper, I probably am. My resume may help me get there, but it won't resolve some foreign policy crisis or rally the nation out of this recession. You see, Carson, I was about to put myself into a position where my views are truly going to matter. On one night in November of next year, my opinions, my philosophy, my values would cease being a slogan on a brochure or a sound bite on a ten second ad. Overnight, they would matter, really matter, to hundreds of millions of people."

"Martin, you're not a demagogue. You never have been. And you're not perfect. No one expects you to be. If you expect it of yourself, you're bound for disappointment. Don't you think that everyone elected president or vice president has the same fears?"

"It's not the fear, it's how you deal with it. The airline passenger is permitted to hyperventilate in a crisis; the pilot is not."

"But the pilot has experience."

"That's not what gets him through. It's a deep-seated confidence in his abilities and judgment that gets him through; the same kind of confidence I would need in high national office. To undertake the campaign without that confidence would be the greatest disservice I could render to everyone involved. Most of all myself. That's the obligation I owe myself, and it's the one I'm going to honor."

"Martin, don't—"

"I already have. I called Justin a half hour before I came up here tonight. I made it official. I'm out of the race."

Chapter 31

Justin Bonner stood at the mirror in his Hay Adams suite, angrily looping and pulling the working end of his formal black tie. His face flushed and his eyes bulged from the pressure of his tightly buttoned collar. In the adjoining room Morgan, Carrington and Allen Sutcliffe discussed the meeting, just concluded, in which Carrington had informed Claudia Raines that she would not be Bonner's choice.

"What happened to Harmon?" she had asked.

Carrington shook his head. "Withdrew his name. Don't ask me why because I don't know."

"Russ, I need you," Justin called from the bedroom. Carrington lumbered away, leaving Morgan and Sutcliffe staring awkwardly at each other in silence.

Carrington stood beside Bonner, speaking to his image in the mirror. "No offense, boss, but you look like you're choking to death."

Bonner crooked his index finger, thrust it between the tie and collar, and yanked downward. "See if you can find me another shirt. I can't swallow in this thing." He fumbled with the studs in the starched front.

Carrington eyed him warily. "Allen was your first choice; you should be happy."

"You and Matt convinced me." He frowned at the stubborn third stud. "After we agreed on Harmon, I realized that choosing Allen would have been heart over head; not smart when the stakes are this high."

"You were just being loyal to an old friend. Nothing wrong with that."

"Unless it impairs your judgment. But that's where you guys earn your pay, and you were right."

"Allen will do fine. We'll win anyway."

Bonner shrugged out of his shirt, tossing it behind him onto the bed. The two men made eye contact in the mirror.

"Wonder what happened to Harmon?" Carrington asked for the fifth or sixth time since Harmon's call.

Bonner tendered his pat reply. "He didn't say."

"But it makes no sense. The guy's got it in the palm of his hand and gives it away. Go figure."

Bonner cleared his throat, walked across the room and gently closed the door separating them from the room in which Morgan and Sutcliffe still seemed to be languishing in uneasy small talk. He returned to the dresser.

"He said he was confronting a personal crisis of major proportions. He didn't use the word scandal, but that was the gist."

"No details?"

"None. Said he hoped I never read about it in the newspaper; that if I did, I'd understand why he had to bow out."

"Jesus," said Carrington. "Sounds like he might have done us a favor."

"Exactly, and for that I'm even sadder to lose him. Most politicians I know would have tried to blow smoke in my ear about 'time with the family' or some other bullshit."

"Morgan know about this?"

"I gave him the short version, which is all I have." He checked his watch. "Find me a shirt. It's time to get this over with."

*   *   *

Martin was alone in his apartment on the night of the gala. As he watched various state party chairmen introduced at the dais to applause from the assembled dignitaries, he could not help thinking of what might have been. He fought it for a time, determined not to become a prisoner of second guessing and self pity. But in the end, when Justin rose to make the principal address, the point at which Martin would have been introduced, he could not bear to watch. He turned the set off to stare at the blank screen. And then, for the first time since the night, years ago now, that Allie presented his lucky rock, he cried.

*   *   *

Meg Kildorf had no interest in watching a Democratic tribute to mayors and said so. Not only was she bored by the thought of political speeches, but the hour slotted for the telecast coincided with a National Geographic special featuring some of her photographs.

"We're watching the speeches," Dennis said flatly. "It's part of my job to be up on stuff like this."

"What about my job? I've got eight excellent shots in this special."

"Come on, Meg. They show those over and over. You can catch it next week."

"And I suppose you can't read all about the dumb speeches in the paper tomorrow morning."

"Forget it. We're watching the mayors and that's it."

For dinner, Meg microwaved fettucine alfredo and unceremoniously plunked a tossed salad in front of Dennis, then on his third vodka and tonic. They ate in silence. When finished, he rose abruptly, walked to the living room, and plopped down on the couch as he keyed the remote to the evening news.

Meg cleared the table, washed the dishes, and retreated to the bedroom, slamming the door behind her. Reading a book, she drifted off, only to be awakened by a thundering crash accompanied by shattering glass. She jolted, disoriented at first and sure she was dreaming. She sprang for the door and raced down a short hall. Dennis sat on the couch, his head lowered with his hands over his ears, as if trying to seal off sound. While the TV's audio blared, there was no picture and no longer even a screen, Dennis having thrown his cocktail glass through it at the moment Justin Bonner announced his choice of Allen Sutcliffe as his running mate.

*   *   *

Jean approached Christmas with the intensified nostalgia which always beset her at this time of year. As she cut greenery for the mantel and strung the various lights she had accumulated over a reach of twenty-eight seasons, she tried to push her decision to divorce Martin from her mind. Dwelling on it, she told herself, would spoil everyone's holiday. In the days after, when Edward returned to Atlanta, Jack to Richmond, and Allie flew to Colorado to go skiing, there would be ample time to lament. She consciously blocked the realization which had come over her as she unpacked the ornaments: this would likely be their last Christmas together as a family.

Martin dreaded Christmas, but for reasons beyond the finality Jean sensed, although he felt that also. He returned to Roanoke cloaked in defeat. It was not a comfortable fit, nor did he wear it well. The long drive gave him hours to reflect, and as the Valley opened to him he sought to open himself, to test his spiritual malaise against the objective realities of his life that seemed on the surface to explain that malaise but which, when probed further, masked a deeper, more fundamental defeat. He had lost the nomination, an objective cause of legitimate suffering, but he suffered more from the prospect of looking down the long dining room table at his wife and children. This holiday took on the weight of a reckoning, an accounting for his years away from them. As if they were stockholders who had given him their money to invest, he felt a moral duty to return their trust with interest. "You see, children," he wanted to say, "your sacrifice of a normal childhood has paid off." "Jean," he wanted to boast, "my absence from you and the children has all been to a noble purpose." But he returned worse than empty handed because the circumstances of his defeat would require lies as to how and why the acknowledged front-runner had been by-passed. Press speculation began the morning after Bonner's surprise, but thus far the prevailing wisdom pointed to political realities and not scandal.

Then, just as he neared the Harrisonburg exit, a buried fear broke loose from some mooring deep within him and bobbed to the surface of his conscious thought. What if, for all these years, his family had made no "investment" but merely acquiesced in his life away from them because they loved him and knew he needed it as surely as an owl needs night. How to repay love like that? By taking a lover? By opening himself to a danger he was mature enough to appreciate and wise enough to avoid? "Yes," that fear whispered, "that is the true accounting to be rendered, and the books do not balance and dark questions will be raised, even if unspoken, for which you have no answers."

At dinner that evening he offered an explanation, somewhat rambling and more defensive than it needed to be, about why Bonner had tapped Sutcliffe. Edward, Jack and Allie nodded their understanding, as if to agree that of course the decision was unfortunate but compelling from Bonner's standpoint. Martin almost convinced himself. Jean, seated at the other end, ate little and listened intently.

"Allen is the key to the larger western states." A lie. "He'll patch up some rifts in the party, which is crucial to our chances." Another lie. "I'm a bit controversial with this REA legislation." True, but in a way calculated to help Bonner, so a half-truth worse than a lie.

Jean's face registered doubt. "You told me Allen Sutcliffe was an idiot."

Martin flushed. "I did not. I said he was an ineffective senator for his state."

Jack spoke. "Then why—"

"How should I know?" he snapped. "It's politics. Ask Justin."

"Martin, don't take it out on Jack. Did you? Did you ask Justin Bonner?"

Martin stared down at his plate. "I'm sorry, Jack. Forgive me."

Christmas Day came and went with the usual exchange of gifts, a large family dinner and some spectator sports via television. The following day, the children flew to their respective destinations with a flurry of hugs, good-byes and promises to write, leaving Martin and Jean alone in the house. As he was scheduled to return to Washington the following day, he sought Jean out in front of a winter fire in the den.

"I never received the letter you promised me. Did it get lost in the mail?"

"It got lost, but not in the mail. In here," she replied, pointing to her forehead. "I wrote so many drafts it was revolting. You're the one with command of the King's English."

"Care to try now?"

"Good a time as any, I suppose." She took a deep breath. "I asked if you had ever considered divorce because I've been thinking about it. That can't come as a shock. These past few years have been constant separation. We've grown apart, as trite as that sounds. What we have seems more an arrangement than a marriage. Do you agree?"

"Yes." His face was expressionless; inscrutable.

"The thought occurs to me, often, that whatever sense this arrangement might have made at one time has long since passed. The whole thing seems fuzzy to me now; I can't swear it ever made sense. We've both seen and felt the drift."

"Why didn't we correct it?"

"Because you couldn't and I wouldn't. You've been in Washington chasing a personal dream while I've been here raising the children."

"Lots of children get raised in Washington, Jean."

"Perhaps I've been wrong. But wrong or right, the raising of children is something most women do. Whether we acquire the instinct from genetics or cultural indoctrination hardly matters. The point is, most women grow up with a built-in, pre-programmed goal, which is to raise children. For some women, and I'm one, it keeps them from having to decide about other goals. Then one day they look in the mirror and they look like me, God forbid!"

"Jean."

"Just a joke. The point is, I'm in the second half of my life, chronologically speaking, and I need a purpose."

"You can't pursue a purpose married?"

"Married to you, probably not. The only way to end my isolation is to move to Washington, where I can join you in the pursuit of your dream, but it does nothing for me. That sounds selfish, but it's realistic."

"What will divorce give you that you don't have?"

"Freedom from the pressure of not supporting a U.S. Senator in the manner that 98% of the people around here believe is appropriate. I've been seeing a psychiatrist, Martin. You probably didn't know that. She's very good, I think."

"Has she said you need to divorce me?"

"They don't give advice. They just ask what you think is best, and for that they get $200 an hour. But I shouldn't complain; she has helped."

"I'm glad. I'm very glad of that." A long pause, broken only by the snap of burning logs in the fireplace.

"You've been so silent," she observed. "You, with all the talent for expressing things, have been noticeably silent."

"I wanted to hear your reasons."

"And?"

"And I think you're right. I'm glad we are talking this through, but both of us know the situation so well that there is very little to say."

"What now?" asked Jean, trying to sound businesslike.

"Have our lawyers draw up the papers. You'll have no problems with financial settlement, I can promise that."

"How long will it take? I know nothing about divorce."

"Six months. It's a painless process."

Jean sighed. "No matter how quick or easy, dear, painless is not a word I would use to describe it."

"How do you think the kids will take it?"

"I think they will be upset and will continue to wonder why it didn't come sooner."

The next morning, leaving for Washington, Martin felt resigned melancholy; sadness that twenty-eight years of marriage could be ended in a fifteen minute conference; that an agreement on dissolution could be reached without anger, without tears, without shouting or acrimony or recrimination or any other emotion demonstrating that something important was at risk. He had witnessed more conflict over a check at a business lunch. The sadness followed him all the way to Washington.

*   *   *

As New Year's approached, Martin wrote his children the essential facts: that he and Jean had decided to divorce; that their problems were long standing and unrelated to their children, and that he deeply regretted the pain he knew it would cause them. He closed by telling them that he loved them and that nothing could alter that love. Even as he sealed the last letter, he knew another one would be forthcoming in the spring—the news of Carson and the child. But the shock of the divorce needed to be absorbed first. Within a few days of sending the letters, he received long, emotional phone calls from Edward and Allie, who reassured him of their continued love and support. No word came from Jack.

*   *   *

When Martin abandoned the race for vice president, Carson abandoned the notion of moving to Frederick, where she had put down a security deposit a mere week before he broke the news. She assumed that the chaos she envisioned at the Westchester would be rendered moot by his decision to withdraw.

His withdrawal shocked her. She would have bet money against it—had done so, in fact, by making the security deposit. She took no joy in it, but some relief. In the ensuing days he had resumed his nightly visits. His appetite returned, she noticed, and he appeared less fatigued. But down and listless as well.

Carson spent Christmas with Kathy, who showered her with infant clothing, new and used. Her due date, only ninety days away, rushed toward her, its approach confirmed by heightened anticipation and swollen ankles.

On January 26, 2000, Carson celebrated her thirty-fifth birthday. Alone. Martin was in Omaha honoring a long-standing political commitment she had urged him to keep. Kathy was ill and "not about to expose you to this god-awful bug." Carson took a cab to a Georgetown restaurant, where she squeezed sideways into a booth, laughing at her bulky awkwardness. Over soup, salad and hot tea she thought back to her thirty-fourth, when she and Martin had driven to a small inn twenty miles into West Virginia, talking as they drove of politics and their passion for each other. No politics now, and no passion; instead, as the prods from tiny knees and elbows reminded her, something new, unexpected and entirely irreplaceable.

*　*　*

The loss of both his chance at national office and his marriage, within a forty-five day span, hit Martin hard, and he was tempted to blame Carson. She feared as much, and during their evenings together, friendly and always platonic, she looked for signs. One such evening, as a light snow fell and muffled sounds of snarled traffic made them glad they were off the roads, she made an offhand comment about the severe temperatures in New England at this time of year.

Martin snapped at her. "If you mean New Hampshire, I'd readily endure the cold."

She looked at him, startled, then said softly, "Maine is up there, too."

Martin, seated, hung his head and covered it with his hands. He said nothing, cradling his head and staring at the floor. Then, he looked up and grinned at her faintly. "We should go back some day."

"I'd like that," she replied.

"If there's any bright spot in this dismal mess it's relief from the fear of finding reporters on the doorstep. Now that I'm just another senator, I doubt there is a single soul in Washington outside this room who cares about what has happened to us, or what will happen." In that assessment, he was off by one.

*　*　*

A mile away, Dennis also sought comfort in defeat. His failure to cost Martin the nomination, to be the blunt instrument in his demise, left the kind of bitter aftertaste that no quantity of vodka purged. Why Justin had passed Martin over was a mystery, but whatever the cause Dennis's carefully constructed scenarios for gratification had crumbled overnight. But Martin still had a problem, and in that problem Dennis saw redemption.

He resumed his stakeout of the Westchester; since he now knew Carson's car, this vigil would be relatively brief. Absent were both the binoculars and Meg's camera, replaced by a GPS transmitter the size of a quarter. He had purchased it on the underground economy from "Benny," a small-time cocaine supplier. On her first trip out, he followed and idled across the street as she parked at a supermarket off Massachusetts Avenue. He waited until she was inside, then parked in a space nearby. His path into the store logically took him by her car, at which he dropped his keys. Bending over, he attached the transmitter to the undercarriage by means of a magnet attached to its reverse side. Then he proceeded toward the entrance, appeared to change his mind, and returned to his car.

The receiver, also purchased from Benny, was a hand-held computer programmed for the District. Once oriented, it produced a display of street coordinates nearest the transmitter. Dennis waited for her to emerge from the market and followed her back to the Westchester.

Her excursions during the week interested him only in one particular: her pre-natal checkups. He needed the coordinates for her doctor, but reasoned that they would become obvious. For the next few weeks, he kept the receiver close by at all times. When the faint "beep" alerted him to a change in her car's position, he noted the final destination and length of stay on a small pad he kept in his pocket.

By mid-February, a pattern formed. Every other Thursday morning, she drove to Chevy Chase, parked for periods between thirty and forty-five minutes, then returned home. A medical center or complex, he surmised. He drove there, confirmed his guess, and returned to Meg's without feeling any need to identify her specific doctor; his or her identity was irrelevant.

Dennis waited for the interval between visits to shorten to one week, signaling the approach of delivery. In March, as buds on the cherry trees began to ripen in prelude to their April splendor, she went to Chevy Chase on three consecutive Thursdays. Then the visits stopped.

BOOK 5

BETHESDA'S CHILD

Chapter 32

At a private hospital in Frederick, Martin stood at the foot of the bed looking down at Carson, sleeping peacefully in the narcotic haze of the anesthetic administered when a Caesarean section had become necessary. She would awaken disappointed that she had been unable to complete the delivery naturally, but fourteen hours of labor was enough. When the attending physician commanded that the surgical procedure be initiated, she was too weak to object. With a feeble smile mustered between excruciating contractions, she had signaled her resignation.

He studied the profile of her face, pale and spent from her effort. Perhaps he imagined it, but she seemed to harbor beneath her silent exhaustion an unseen glimmer of anticipation, like a child asleep on Christmas Eve. It was as though a subconscious instinct had left her to journey down the hall to the nursery, there to view the newborn in all his pinkish splendor, and return to the bedside to await the awakening of the physical mother.

Charles Martin Cox, or "Casey" as he would be known, was eight pounds, four ounces of pure boy if his primal scream at birth was any indicator. Because of the Caesarean, he had been spared the trip down the birth canal, leaving his head perfectly rounded and his features smooth, unlike his comrades in 201 East who had endured the pressure required to expel them and bore the marks to prove it.

As he stood over her, eager for her to regain consciousness so that he could impart the superlatives he had already assigned to Casey, he felt a tap on the shoulder.

"Mr. Harmon?"

"That's right."

"I'm Dr. Gaffney, the baby's pediatrician. I understand you're the proud papa."

Martin nodded. "I've been waiting for Carson to wake up so I can tell her some details about our son." He searched Gaffney's face for signs that the doctor recognized him. If he did, he gave no indication.

The doctor beckoned him with a silent finger away from the bed into the hallway outside. When they were out of earshot of the room, he said:

"This is nothing to be alarmed about, but my physical examination of the baby revealed a small problem. I want to emphasize 'small,' so don't get too excited."

"What is it?" demanded Martin.

"The baby—what's his name?"

"Casey."

"Casey has a slight hip displacement on the right side. I took some X-rays and it appears the hip socket is modestly deformed."

"Meaning what?"

"Meaning nothing of practical significance for the first few months. Once he starts to walk we'll need to keep a close eye on him to see how he compensates for it. It's correctable by surgery, but we don't want to do that to an infant. I've seen several of these. Sometimes the hip realigns itself naturally despite the structural imperfection in the socket. When that happens, the child walks and runs normally with no surgery required. We hope that happens with Casey. If it doesn't, that is, he begins to favor one leg creating a hitch or limp, we'll have to evaluate it. But the important thing for you to remember is that his condition poses absolutely no threat to him. At worst, we have a situation which may require corrective surgery when he gets to be two or three years old. Other than that, he's healthy as a young horse and in fine shape."

"Thanks, doctor. I'm relieved, to tell you the truth. You had me going there when you first motioned me out of the room."

"I understand. Tell you a short story. Early in my career I examined a newborn with some fluid on her lungs. She couldn't breathe very well so we put her on oxygen for a few hours; nothing serious. I went to report to the parents, and found the father by the mother's bed, just as I found you. I was in something of a rush and I knew the mother was heavily sedated, so I lowered my voice and told the father the problem. Do you know that even through the anesthetic the mother thought she heard the word 'death' when what I really said was 'breath.' It's the first time I ever observed someone unconscious become hysterical, and the last time I briefed a parent at bedside."

Martin laughed. "We all learn from our mistakes. Thanks for looking after Casey."

"Don't mention it. I'll check on him every couple of hours. Please give your wife my congratulations."

Martin gazed at him steadily. "She's not my wife, but I'll tell her." He cut short an apology by Dr. Gaffney. "Don't worry about it. I'm not," he reassured him.

Martin returned to the bedside, where Carson began to stir. Taking her slender hand protruding from the bed sheet, he bent to whisper, "Great job, mom." She managed to open one eye before relapsing into sleep. Minutes later, she again stirred, this time turning her face toward the ceiling and opening both eyes. She smiled weakly at him. He repeated his praise.

"Well, is it Casey or Heather?" Her lips barely moved.

"It's Casey and he's beautiful."

Her grogginess evaporated as a wide grin broke over her. "I have to see him."

Martin summoned a nurse who quickly made the short trip to the nursery, returning with a rolling bassinet in which lay Casey, in peaceful repose. As Carson watched in wide-eyed transfixion, the nurse raised Casey from the bassinet and carried him across the room, placing him into Carson's cradled arms. She studied him before turning her face to Martin. She said nothing, the joy unmistakable in her eyes. She turned back to Casey, still sleeping, his tiny mouth puckered to emit an occasional wisp of breath. Tears welled to the size of raindrops, rolling over her cheeks. One managed to roll off, landing on Casey's forehead. He gave a start, a squawk turning into a full scale cry, his new lungs bursting in protest of virgin sensations. As he worked himself into an indignant fit, Carson laughed, while the tears continued. "It's definite," she said through sobs and shorter bursts of laughter, "I'm going to keep him."

Martin was not about to cast even the smallest shadow on her happiness by relating the hip problem. He left that to Dr. Gaffney, who briefed Carson the next day. She took the news calmly. Weakened by the surgery, she slept for the better part of the next two days. On the third day, she pronounced herself ready to take a more active role in mothering, but the doctors kept her two additional days as a precaution. Five days after Casey's birth, mother and son went home.

The changes in her 17th floor apartment reflected the changes in her life. In January, she had begun decorating the spare bedroom as a nursery. The former contents of this room; her computer, her reference books, and the other accoutrements of her consulting business, were removed to the living room so the nursery focused on Casey and his needs.

Martin hired a cook to prepare evening meals; Theresa Mendez, wife of Pablo Mendez, the long-time chief of security for the Mexican Embassy. An excellent cook, she had routinely accepted assignments such as this one to help defray the cost of putting the two Mendez children through George Washington University. The demand for her services justified her high rates, and Martin felt fortunate to secure her at any price. She was a petite woman, standing a bare 5 feet, but as one of her former employers, a Congressman from Oklahoma, put it, "Don't let that little lady fool ya'; she cooks a lot bigger than five feet." She arrived at 4:30 p.m. daily to begin her preparation. More often than not, she stopped on her way at a market to purchase the fresh fruits and vegetables that were the foundations of her meals. She baked her own bread.

Theresa was but one fixture in Martin's effort to reorganize his work habits. Gone now were the nightly rounds of cocktail parties, receptions and dinners. He rarely accepted invitations to these, preferring to leave his office at 5:30 p.m. to arrive home by 6:00. He would stop off at his apartment, change into casual attire, and proceed upstairs to Carson's where dinner would be served at 6:30 sharp. After dinner, as Theresa tidied the kitchen, he and Carson reviewed the events of the day over coffee. At about 9:00, he returned to his apartment, where he read reports, studies and background material for projects engaging his time at the Senate. At 10:30, he went to bed.

Carson's day took on the changes she anticipated with the responsibility of a newborn. She was determined not to fall behind on her consulting contracts, meaning she had to take full advantage of the periods during which Casey slept. The luxury of Theresa was addictive.

Casey fulfilled her fondest hopes as a new mother. The precision with which he slept, ate and awoke each day was uncanny. After the first month at home he slept through the night. After his bath, he would coo, gurgle and sigh in the way unique to infants. He cried rarely, but fiercely when he did so. As the weeks passed, Carson took joy in the milestones marking the first few months of life; the lifting of the head, turning over, clutching her finger in his tiny fist. This was, she told herself, everything she had hoped it would be.

* * *

Dennis learned of the birth in the vital statistics reported in the Frederick Gazette during the week following Casey's delivery. When the signals from Carson's car ceased, he scanned the Washington Post for weeks without encountering a single new mother named Carson. When he remembered Kathy, the logic of delivering in Frederick was obvious and he readily found mother and son listed. But not father.

"No," muttered Dennis with a self-satisfied smirk as he clipped the notice. "This is one vote the senator from Virginia doesn't want to be recorded on."

Dennis alighted from the cab at the entrance to the Russell Senate Office Building as he had done enumerable times preceding his relegation to House Agriculture. The security guard flickered in recognition, started to wave him through, then thought better of it and asked his destination. Dennis gave the guard the plainly wrapped rectangular box he carried casually in one hand and appeared indifferent as he shook it.

"What's this?"

"Little gift for the senator," answered Dennis with sing-song boredom in his voice. The guard returned it as Dennis cleared the metal detector.

The halls of Russell brimmed with a sense of purpose that seemed to infect even the tourists. The pace here was one of throttled haste, where everyone was already five minutes late for wherever they were going. Congressional aides, coatless with shirts or blouses rumpled and ties askew, hurried in quick-step with their sheaf of paper or armload of committee reports, each more or less convinced of his or her importance to the country. Dennis could recall when he felt that way. Now he moved in counterpoint to the bustle, more like the mail carts that still pack-muled correspondence among the offices. This was a day to be savored, not rushed through.

He paused at the entrance to Martin's suite. On the open door was mounted the seal of the Commonwealth of Virginia: Victory, standing with her foot on the chest of the supine vanquished oppressor; "*Sic Semper Tyrannis*", or "Thus always to Tyrants." Today would be Martin's day on the ground, looking up at him. He stepped inside the office, nodded at a receptionist he had never seen before, and continued past her desk like he belonged. At Ellen Fry's desk, he stopped.

She looked up from the appointment book spread before her. Most executive secretaries now kept appointments on computer, but Ellen still clung to the security of ink on paper at her elbow. Her surprise at seeing him was undisguised.

"Dennis . . ."

"How's it going, Ellen? Is he in?" He followed her glance to the box he carried, enjoying the discomfort she was embarrassed by but unable to hide. Good, he thought. She was listening for the tick-tick-tick, and not all explosions produced noise, as she was about to learn. He smiled, gently tapping the corner of the package on the front of her desk.

"Five minutes, Ellen. That's all I need."

"I'll try, Dennis, but you know what it's like."

"Yeah, I remember," he retorted, making no effort to hide the irony. "Three minutes." He flipped the box into the air, sending it end over end, then caught it on the descent. "Two and a half, and that's a promise." In the old days he could have charmed her into anything, but now he needed simple access. With a stern unabashed look toward the package, she slipped away.

"Fromang here?" Martin asked, not looking up. Under Secretary of State Donald Fromang, suspended in traffic, had called to push their meeting back half an hour.

"No," said Ellen, her pause so gravid that he raised his head and his eyebrows simultaneously.

"Trouble?"

"Dennis. He says he only needs a minute or two."

Martin rolled his eyes. "Tell him I'm busy."

"He worries me. He's acting . . . strange."

"Would you feel better if I got rid of him?"

"He's got a package."

"His lunch," said Martin, impatiently tossing his pen onto the desk. "Tell him to come in, but warn him I'm expecting Fromang."

She shot him a tight-lipped smile and disappeared. Moments later, Dennis entered.

Martin stood, buttoning his coat as he rose. Dennis never expected to see his coat unbuttoned again. They shook hands stiffly.

"Sit down, Dennis. How have you been?"

Dennis remained standing. "Well enough to get an offer from Randall Stevens."

"Ah; the special election in Montana. AA?"

"Provided my references are in order."

"I haven't blocked you, Dennis."

"You haven't helped."

Martin folded his hands on the blotter in front of him. "We have history. Perhaps he won't ask."

"He already has."

"As before, I won't respond. He'll probably hire you anyway."

"No." said Dennis, his tone hardening. "You will respond. You will recommend me."

Martin shrugged, leaning back. "I can't—"

Dennis flipped the package, until now held down at his side, onto the desk. Momentum skittered it across the blotter and off the opposite edge into Martin's lap. "A gift," said Dennis, nodding toward the box. "Open it."

Martin laid the package calmly on the desk. "I'm preparing for a meeting. Good luck with Senator-elect Stevens."

"I went to a lot of trouble. Open it."

Martin sighed. Extending his arm, he drew the box back. For a moment it looked as though he would tear into the wrapper, then he hesitated. "I can't accept gifts, especially when accompanied by a request for a favor."

"It's a token, under twenty-five bucks. I know the rules."

Martin tore at the brown paper, determined to end this pointless pursuit. At the sight of the word "cigar," he froze.

Dennis stood before him, rocking from heel to toe. "Imported Havanas; I have a source. I lied about the twenty-five bucks."

Martin stared as the color in his face drained into a body suddenly limp and old.

Dennis reached across the desk, flipped the lid, and pointed. "One missing, I confess. I smoked it the night I found out Carson was expecting." He plucked one out, peeled the cellophane, and clamped it into the corner of his smile. "A good looking woman. Is Charles a family name?"

"Leave Dennis. Now."

For the first time, Dennis sat. "Not without that letter of recommendation."

"We've discussed that." But his voice was without power.

"Not over a friendly cigar, we haven't." He lowered his and pointed the moistened end toward the box.

Ellen Fry's voice came over the intercom. "Senator, Under Secretary Fromang is here."

Martin hesitated, thinking how an immutable force in the universe compelled the most sensitive secret to be placed in hands most calculated to do damage. Call it the First Law of Enemies. Dennis, of all people. But this result obeyed a rough logic; an enemy possessed the motivation to dig, and there was no reason to believe an avenging angel any less potent than its counterpart. Besides, if not Dennis, someone, as he had known since the night he accepted her invitation to dinner, shutting the door on his instincts as he flew out of his apartment and telling them not to wait up. Now here sat Dennis with the bill for his folly. Pay up? Or buy time. He turned his head toward the intercom. "Ask Fromang to have a seat."

Dennis grinned affably and nodded approval. "A two paragraph letter on your Senate letterhead. That's all I want. I won't bleed you."

"It's blackmail, Dennis. I hope you've thought this through."

"It's politics."

"Your bitterness will eat you up."

"It might," Dennis conceded. "On the other hand, what I know could swallow you whole."

"How did you find out?"

"Miss Ruth, though she doesn't realize she spilled the beans; you two made quite an impression."

Martin swung back to his credenza and touched a button. Ellen entered just as he thrust the cigar box into a drawer. "Ellen, type this letter now." He dictated as she wrote. "And tell Fromang I'll be with him momentarily."

She left. Martin stared at Dennis in silence. Dennis did not meet his gaze, focusing on a spot on the desk and occasionally shifting the cigar from one corner of his mouth to the other. Ellen returned, placed the letter on the blotter, and stood by as he signed it.

"I won't need a copy," Martin said, dismissing her. When she was gone, he shoved the letter across the desk.

"It could be stronger," said Dennis, glancing over it.

"It could be truthful," he countered. "Then where would you be?"

Dennis rose. "No worse than I am now. No worse than I've been since you fired me for no good reason. I did a damn fine job here, so you're getting what you deserve. See you around the Senate dining room." He turned and walked out, leaving Martin with the sinking certainty that he had just paid a steep price for a very short reprieve.

Chapter 33

When the Democratic National Convention opened in San Francisco on July 16, 2000, Martin sat in Carson's apartment watching on TV. Carson, having just put Casey down for the night, entered in her bathrobe and sat next to him on the sofa. From the kitchen came a steady clatter as Theresa stored the dinner dishes, and the last aromas of her zesty baked salmon lingered in the room.

Carson had approached this moment with curiosity, knowing that for Martin the convention was tantamount to a party to which he had been uninvited. She glanced at him often, but he watched in dispassion, as though he had come no closer to being part of the pageantry than the voter next door.

"Wishing you were there?" she asked.

He shook his head slightly in response. "I'm better off right here. And the Party's better off, too. Besides, I want to be here."

As the governor of Ohio began the keynote address, Theresa waved good-night and Martin went into the kitchen, returning with two bowls of frozen yogurt. As he resumed his seat, Carson asked if he had given any thought to running for re-election to the Senate. "Two thousand-two will be here before you know it," she reminded him.

"I want to run," he acknowledged, "but I'll have a hell of a time getting re-elected after the divorce."

"When will Jean file?"

"'I got a call from one of her lawyers yesterday. They plan to file next week."

"The public won't blame just you," she offered.

"No, but Jean won't need their votes in two years."

"Maybe," replied Carson, squinting her eyes as if she had heard glass shattering, "our luck will hold and none of this will become public."

Martin turned and reached spontaneously for her hand. "No chance. The divorce is public, of course." He paused. "And there's something else I haven't told you. Just after Casey's birth, Dennis came to see me. He knows everything."

Her face lost its color as she absorbed the ramifications. "So we're going to see it all in print; the tabloids, just like Sis said."

"More than likely."

Carson turned away, her eyes half closed and her head moving from side to side in dismay, but she did not withdraw her hand. "What's stopping him?" she demanded. "Why hasn't he told the world by now?"

"Because I did something I shouldn't have done. I bought his silence with a letter of recommendation. He's now the AA for Randall Stevens, a new senator from Montana."

Martin's free hand rested on the robe which covered her thigh. It had been almost a year since he had touched her intimately, and the cotton of her robe burned his hand. Her smell, a mixture of soap and Casey and the faint aroma of the salmon, pummeled his senses.

"So now we're trapped." she said. "Today a letter, and who knows what tomorrow? Can he be trusted to keep quiet?"

"I'm sorry to say he can't be trusted for much, especially something this explosive. Plus, we have no way of being sure that others don't know. Dr. Gaffney, nurses at the hospital—any of them could report what they saw."

"Then we should deal with it now," she said decisively.

"I've been thinking the same thing. I'm ready if you are." She gulped faintly but nodded. He squeezed her hand tighter as he reached up and placed his free hand beside her face. "The next few months could get very ugly, and if I could do anything to spare you and Casey, I'd do it. That includes leaving the Senate."

Deep inside, at her core, emotions flared—emotions familiar but forgotten. Perhaps his offer to leave the Senate ignited them, or perhaps it was more subtle; a growing reassurance that what they had shared before Casey had been real and honest and human. Her breath grew shallow, and without taking her eyes from their riveted fix on his, she took his hand from her face and slid it down to her breast, swollen with milk. She heard him groan as he parted her robe and covered her exposed flesh with his tongue. She groped for him, and heard herself groan as he tore off the robe and then her panties. In a fury she mounted him, arching her back in a frantic quest for release, which came instantly for them both as, over her bare shoulder, the governor of Ohio pledged a united Democratic Party in an all-out war for the White House.

*   *   *

At the end of July, Jean filed for divorce in the Roanoke Circuit Court on "no fault" grounds, assuring that no causes for the breakup would become matters of public record. Six weeks later, a judge's clerk would preside over the burial of the Harmon marriage. He would serve as the undertaker of that corpse, signing and sealing a legal benediction as part of a day's work. The interment in a steel gray morgue, properly indexed, proved swift, simple and silent; the death had occurred many years before.

The divorce made headlines in Roanoke and throughout Virginia. Major dailies carried stories featuring Martin's career, his prominence in the Senate, speculation over his near miss for the nomination, and the possible impact of divorce on his political future. No hint of scandal surfaced.

Despite seven months to reconcile himself, Martin felt despondent for days after the stories appeared. But as time passed, a new freedom encroached on his continuing regrets. He and Carson had, by unspoken agreement, rarely talked of Martin's marriage, and there was much he had to tell. Now that the divorce was final, he felt the sharing of those thoughts and emotions were no longer such a violation of Jean's privacy as they were part of his own personal history, sorely in need of revelation.

On a sunny fall afternoon, Martin and Carson went hiking on the Appalachian Trail. Casey, separated from Carson for the first time, slept peacefully at Kathy's. For reasons neither could recall later, they began discussing, between short breaths and out-of-condition sighs, Martin's marriage. They talked for several miles. At the end, within sight of the car, he said: "It takes two people to kill a marriage. The fault was mine as much as Jean's. I want you to remember that when I ask you to marry me, because I'm far from a perfect mate."

"Are you going to ask me to marry you?"

"I plan to. Do you plan to accept?"

"I do. When were you thinking of asking?"

"I was thinking I just did."

"And were you also thinking I just accepted?"

"I was."

"Then you're a very smart man, Senator, and I'm a very lucky woman."

*   *   *

Max wanted a Nobel Prize badly. He had wanted one since his triumph over his ancient battle with cancer, and at times he chided himself for wanting it so badly. He rarely mentioned it, and then only to Rita, but he thought about it often, especially now that his career was in its winter. But he took comfort from the fact that a man of his age could still find himself daydreaming occasionally; still picture himself bowed before the Swedish Academy to receive a medal which, more than any other, confirmed monumental achievement by the recipient.

He made inordinate strides forward in the summer of the year 2000. In the assemblage of the Lincoln DNA, he could realistically envision the project completed. Dr. Anderson stayed abreast of the milestones in his work, expressing the opinion that the successful assemblage of a complete Lincoln cell would give him an irrefutable claim to a Prize. In point of fact, the successful assemblage of a complete cell of anyone dead for 135 years would be equally compelling, but the use of Lincoln's cells would give the accomplishment a star quality it might otherwise lack.

But could he finish? Anderson saw signs that Max's age was catching up to him. The evidence was not to be found in the quality of his work but rather its quantity. He was simply slowing down in obedience to the natural laws of aging. Anderson could feel himself slipping under the spell of the same gravity. All the resources Anderson could divert to Max were sent his way. Colleagues familiar with his quest took time away from their projects to put in time at his lab, most often performing the routine labors of graduate assistants, but indifferent to their demotion in support of a fellow scientist on his last run for the roses. Max was deeply moved by these gestures. When he strolled through his lab to find fifty or sixty-year-old degreed colleagues patiently at work on menial but necessary tasks, he would pat them softly on the shoulder in silent thanks.

Lincoln's DNA was a curious project in that much of it depended upon sequencing and coupling work which was relatively routine. Edison said "Genius is ten percent inspiration and ninety percent perspiration." The sequencing and coupling work was the perspiration. A well trained graduate assistant could do it provided he followed Max's exacting instructions and maintained his level of concentration on the details.

Max made the major tactical and strategic decisions, in consultation with his associates. His role was the "ten percent inspiration." He could do the sequencing and coupling; had done it before and was not afraid to do it again to finish the job. But it was here that his flagging stamina came into play, for he simply could not sustain his concentration for the relentless hours required. As a result, his contributions tended to be sporadic. He might spend a full ten days charting the next step, outlining the scope of the work, setting standards for his assistants, and laying down time lines. Then, with the exception of monitoring progress and being available for consultations, he might be essentially free for the next month or two while the detailed work was performed.

This hiatus in his duties was most fortuitous, for it allowed him to pursue his studies on totipotency. The totipotency work was the exact reverse of the Lincoln DNA project, for it completely absorbed Max's intellectual faculties but required less of the labor which fatigued him. In other words, for totipotency, Edison's maxim was reversed: genius was ninety percent inspiration and ten percent perspiration. Thus the two separate projects were hand in glove, Lincoln requiring Max's brain but others' labor and totipotency demanding Max's brain and little labor.

In the late afternoon of a summer day which had seen steady progress on both projects, Max arrived at home in an ebullient mood. Rita, who had just returned from her daily swim at her health club, called as he entered the foyer.

"Max, there's a letter from Anne. It's in your study."

Max fixed himself a cup of hot tea. Upon entering his study, he lit a cigar and put on a Chopin disc which filled the room with the music he loved. On his desk he found the letter from Anne, dated two days before. Regular correspondence from Anne had been a pleasant outgrowth of her visit the previous fall, beginning with the long thank you note they received after she returned to Washington. Rita had replied, expressing sentiments that the evening spent with Anne had been equally enjoyable for them. Then came an exchange of Christmas cards accompanied by letters. Since then, Anne had written about once a month with Rita and Max alternating their replies. Reading the letter, Max felt the urge to respond. He left his easy chair for the chair at his desk, where he wrote the following:

August 21, 2000
Pasadena, Ca.

Dear Anne:

Received your letter this afternoon and find myself in an expansive mood so thought I would make the most of it before it passes. Rita and I are delighted to hear of your promotion at NIH. To have a position of that authority at your age is quite remarkable. We shall both be amazed if you are not running the whole show before long. Congratulations! Why, if NIH keeps making intelligent decisions like this one, I may have to revise my opinion of the entire operation! The Lincoln project, about which you have been kind enough to express so much interest, is now about sixty percent complete. Most of the credit belongs to my associates, who have pitched in to help an old man along. It is painstaking work, at times bordering on drudgery, but the progress is steady and encouraging. Good news also abounds on the totipotency front. I have been engaged for some time now in a rather detailed analysis of the chemical structure of the "trigger agent" which I believe to be responsible for this phenomenon. After comparing that structure to that of the relevant chromosome, I have constructed a fundamental hypothesis which may explain the triggering effect on the organism. The next step will be the experiments to test it, which I anticipate beginning next week. It all makes for a very exciting period in my professional work. Enough of my endeavors. Rita joins me in extending to you an invitation to visit us should you find yourself back on the West Coast. By all means consider us a haven from the harsh Washington winter, now only months away.

Fondly,
Max

In Washington, Anne read the letter, returned it to its envelope, and opened the locked drawer in her desk. She smiled as she placed it with her Grunfeld correspondence, kept for sentimental reasons, but she was not unmindful of its potential economic value if, as she suspected, Max succeeded without the assistance of her agency.

Chapter 34

On November 7, 2000, Justin Bonner was elected president of the United States. His margin, as a percentage of the vote, was almost as narrow as Martin's in the REA vote, but as with Martin, victory was victory. Martin celebrated. He had campaigned hard for the ticket in Virginia and throughout the South, where the Democrats had done well, carrying key states.

In December, six weeks before Justin's inauguration, Martin got a call from the president-elect himself. Could he, Justin wanted to know, stop by for a chat?

The transition team, organized into 'squads' by the ever-militaristic Carrington, occupied the top four floors of an office building on Pennsylvania Avenue near 18th Street. A guard directed Martin to the top floor, where Secret Service personnel patrolled the halls. An unsmiling agent frisked him, herded him through a metal detector, and ordered him to prove he was the U.S. Senator he claimed to be. Satisfied, the agent escorted Martin to a conference room in a corner office, where a secretary seated him and brought coffee. After she left, closing the door behind her, Martin stood and walked to the window. In the distance, he saw the Washington Monument and regretted never having taken the time to ride the elevator to its apex. The sight entranced him, so when the door behind him opened and Justin entered, Martin was not immediately aware of his presence. Justin boomed a friendly, "Hello" and Martin, startled, moved to greet him.

He certainly looks presidential, thought Martin as they shook hands. Justin's navy wool suit, blue shirt with French cuffs, and pale yellow tie seemed a fitting uniform for a man with tough battles ahead. Martin remembered reading an account by a Kennedy advisor who described the edge, the subtle but distinct distance, he perceived in Kennedy's demeanor on the morning Kennedy awoke as president-elect. Martin felt that distance from Justin, but their conversation was friendly and unhurried. They talked of the campaign, Martin complimenting Justin's strategy in refusing to debate the incumbent, and Justin praising Martin for the effort which put Virginia in the Democratic column.

At length, Justin turned and motioned Martin toward a chair, taking for himself one across the table. Instantly, the president-elect turned serious, saying, "I see Bill Lucas has plans to run against you next time."

"So I'm told. He was a popular governor; he'll be tough to whip if I decide to run."

"Precisely why I asked to see you," Bonner said. He got up and went to the window, where he paced. "Martin, a president can't do much without Congress. Ask my distinguished predecessor. Now, I could put you in the Cabinet, and I will if you ask, but where I need you most is in the Senate—in 2002 and beyond. I hope you run for re-election. We've got some legislative wars ahead of us, and I can't think of a better man to have on our side."

"Mr. President, I'm very grateful for those words."

"The gratitude is mine." Bonner corrected. Walking to the table, he leaned over, humility cushioning his voice and his manner soft and forgiving. "The single most important decision made in this campaign was not made by me or my staff, but by you. We all have our Achilles heel; some sin or foible which would cost us a race for dog-catcher if the voting public knew about it. Hell, I've got one or two myself, and don't think I won't spend a sleepless night or two in the White House hoping and praying that what's dead stays buried.

"But a nominee for this office is put in a unique and, I don't mind saying, uncomfortable position of being a goddamn hypocrite of the first magnitude. I require men such as yourself to come to my aid without baggage, knowing full well I've got my own. It's not fair, but it's the system. No doubt your decision was part—hell, mostly—looking out for yourself, but my gut feeling is that you also considered me and my campaign. Not everyone would have. Our self-interest, our ambition is usually so strong we just whistle on past that graveyard. Allen didn't contribute much; not a fraction of what you could have. But neither did he embarrass me, so I won. I'm grateful."

Martin nodded. "My motives weren't all that altruistic, but what you've just said means a great deal."

"Good," said Bonner. "Now, let's talk business. Your reasons for withdrawing are your own. But if it impacts your ability to run for re-election to the Senate, then I want to help. Clear?"

"Perfectly."

"I don't want to pry, but I read about the divorce—"

"Yes, that's part of it. The rest gets complicated. A couple of years ago I became involved with a wonderful woman here in Washington. Just about the time you selected me for the ticket, I found out she was expecting. We had a son in March."

Bonner didn't flinch, maintaining an even stare as though he had just been briefed on some third world coup d'etat. "That's a bitch, politically speaking." Martin nodded faintly. "Does anyone know?"

"Dennis Rancour, my former AA. I fired him a while back and he took it pretty hard. He confronted me a few months ago, demanding that I recommend him to Randall Stevens or else."

"Has Rancour asked for money?"

"Not yet. He insisted he only wanted a job equivalent to the one he lost, but who knows?"

Bonner drummed his fingers on the table, a pensive tilt to his head as he looked past Martin. "Your choices are to let Rancour force you into retirement or to call his bluff, lay it out in the open, and take your chances with the voters."

"Virginia's a pretty conservative state."

"Hell, they're all conservative when it comes to scandal. But voters can also have remarkably short memories. You've got two years and a president that wants you in the Senate. Think it over." He winked, evoking a reluctant smile from Martin.

"I'll consider it," Martin declared. "I've been happy in the Senate. It's still the arena, and I belong there."

"Yes, you do," replied Justin Bonner, unable to suppress a grin. "And Martin, remember this. I made three trips to Montana stumping for Randall Stevens. If I ask, he'll sweep the bus depot in Helena naked, and he'll sure get rid of Rancour. You just give the word and consider it done."

*   *   *

On January 15, 2001, five days before Justin Bonner took the oath of office on the steps of the Capitol, Carson and Martin married in a private ceremony at St. John's, the pale yellow church trimmed in white on Lafayette Square. Father Logan presided, wishing them a "long and loving union" as he pronounced them husband and wife. They walked from the church to a waiting limousine, which Carson entered. Martin paused to stare at the Hay Adams directly opposite the church before looking left across the square to The White House. Then, he ducked into the car and was gone.

On the day following the wedding, Martin's office issued a press release announcing the event and advising that the couple had left for a honeymoon in an undisclosed location. The second paragraph contained the following: "The couple also announces the birth of their son, Charles Edward Martin, on March 16, 2000, in Frederick, Maryland."

The text, published in the Washington *Post* and every other daily newspaper in the country, produced the violent storm of outrage Martin had feared. The Denver *Post* labeled him a disgrace, the Atlanta *Constitution* cited the bastard birth as further evidence that the country was being guided by a "moral compass on which all directions are labeled north." Bitter recrimination came from Christian action groups, several of which were headquartered in Virginia. The Republican Party of Virginia published Martin's "political obituary" and proposed a recall vote to be held as soon as signatures could be gathered. Every major editorial in the state demand his resignation. Condemnation would have been total but for the one-sentence statement issued by President-elect Justin Bonner, expressing confidence "in my friend, Senator Harmon."

Dennis followed the furor with the nervous dread of a midwest farmer watching a tornado tracking inexorably toward his barn. The day after Bonner's inauguration, he was fired in a phone call from Randall Stevens, whose sole explanation was that Dennis had managed to make "a very powerful enemy." And this time, the doors to government service would be locked for at least four years.

*   *   *

In April, on the same day President Bonner confronted the first crisis of his new administration when the Chairman of the Federal Reserve quit in a violent clash with the White House over fiscal policy, Max sat in his office reading an article in Nature detailing a major advance in computerized DNA sequencing. He was deep in thought over its possible applicability to his Lincoln project when he stood up to go to the water cooler and stumbled momentarily. Lightheaded, he sat down. He rested a moment, got up slower, experienced no difficulty, and forgot it until the following week when, in his lab, he felt a tingling numbness in his left arm. Alarmed, he drove home. In the driveway, as he prepared to leave his car, he slumped over the wheel, sounding the horn. Rita ran from the house, flung open his door, and helped him to the pavement, where she administered CPR until the medics arrived.

The heart attack Max suffered was relatively mild. He stayed in ICU for forty-eight hours before his cardiologist ordered him moved to a private room. Tests showed some arterial blockage, prompting discussions of surgery. When he was safely through the crisis, his doctor felt secure enough to kid him.

"Come on, Max," he said, "let me open you up. A chance to cut is a chance to cure."

Max scoffed and rolled his eyes at Rita, standing with the doctor at the end of his bed. "It's the way you say 'chance' which concerns me."

Max vetoed surgery and the doctor, professing disappointment, acquiesced. Seven days after he was admitted, Max left the hospital.

His recuperation at home put Rita in fear of a second attack. He paced, smoked, and grouched at the nurse hired to attend him, and read when not pacing or grouching. "I need to be at the lab," he muttered over and over.

The day before his release to return to work, Anne came to visit. She brought him a banzai tree and a small box of chocolates. Rita let him keep the tree. Max scolded Anne for coming "three thousand miles to see a wrinkled old fossil," but patted her hand repeatedly during the forty-five minute talk at his bedside. Her visit touched him, coming as it did on the heels of her new responsibilities at NIH and at her own expense. When Rita learned she had just checked into a motel, Rita insisted she check out again in favor of the Grunfeld guest room.

The next morning, Max awoke at dawn, ready for work. He was surprised to find Rita and Anne sitting on the deck, drinking coffee and watching the sunrise. Rita suggested that Anne might wish to accompany him to work. "A great idea," said Max.

They entered the building which housed Max's lab together, but were soon parted by the rush of people pressing to welcome Max "home." Colleagues, most of whom had visited him, some only a day or two before, besieged him in spontaneous if dignified celebration. With handshakes, shoulder claps and words of encouragement, the team hailed the return of its captain.

In the happy confusion, Anne found herself next to Dr. Anderson, who greeted her warmly. Together they watched the well-wishers escort Max down the corridor toward his lab. Near his door, Max turned to wave at Anne over the heads of his friends, and she waved back in acknowledgement.

Dr. Anderson invited Anne into his office, where they spoke frankly of the improvement in the Caltech-NIH relationship since their last meeting.

Anne credited Max. "His offer to serve on that study section was a class act. NIH was impressed."

Anderson, seated behind his desk, agreed, then added, "He looks wonderful. Lots of color, a spring in his step—he looks like he's good for another twenty years."

Anne nodded, then crossed her legs and lowered her voice.

"I learned something over coffee with Rita this morning. Does he have a realistic shot at a Nobel?"

Anderson looked off as if surveying the horizon, contorting his mouth in an exaggerated pucker. "I should think he does. The Lincoln project is a winner."

"What about the other one—his totipotent mouse."

"Even more spectacular. Max might now be working on his second Prize if . . ." Anderson cleared his throat as he cast a nervous glance at Anne. "Sorry," he said, "I didn't mean to open old wounds." Anne flushed as Anderson returned to his subject. "I've been urging him to drop his mouse studies; he needs to concentrate all his energies on Lincoln if he's to finish."

"Well," said Anne, squaring her shoulders, "it's not as though he is on some deadline."

Anderson stood and walked around his desk. Even leaning against its edge he towered over Anne, seated in front of him. "Oh, but he is," Anderson said. "And this heart attack won't help."

"I guess," said Anne, re-crossing her legs, "if he were to—you know, die, they would still have to give it to him since he started the project and did so much of the work."

Anderson frowned and shook his head. "I'm afraid Max's chance will expire when he does. The Nobel isn't awarded posthumously."

On her flight back to Washington, Anne said a prayer for Max and, less directly, for herself. She touched none of the food placed in front of her by the flight attendant. In listening to Dennis Rancour, she realized, she might have cost Max his reward, and the thought took her appetite.

Chapter 35

In the year that followed, Martin survived.

He survived calls for his resignation by insisting that voters, not editors, had elected him for a six-year term.

He survived a recall petition orchestrated by Republicans despite an opinion from the state's Attorney General, also a Republican, that an incumbent U.S. Senator was immune from recall. What saved Martin was not the legal uncertainty but his own perceived vulnerability. Bob Lucas, the former governor who had announced against him prior to the revelation of the scandal, appeared to have an uncontested nomination until the storm broke. Then, with Martin on the ropes, every Republican hopeful in the state jumped in, confident that the nomination meant certain election, either against a new Democrat in the event Martin was swept aside, or a mortally wounded incumbent should he prove crazy enough to try for a third term.

Lucas opposed the recall, igniting a fratricidal war. He preferred to organize and run his campaign against the emasculated Democrats stuck with their vulnerable Senator. Other Republican aspirants pushed the recall, certain that success would cripple the Democratic Party in Virginia for decades to come. Eventually, the issue of recall became a "line in the sand" among the Lucas forces, who felt that he had staked his credibility and leadership on the issue and that defeat boded ill for the nomination battle ahead. His rivals came to view it, less from conviction than political expediency, in precisely the same terms. If they forced a recall, they could dispatch Martin and Lucas at the same time. Both sides stood toe-to-toe at the line in the sand, with the result that recall momentum slowed, then stopped, a victim to squandered good fortune.

When it became clear that Martin would finish his term, the scandal made its way from front page to back, propelled along by more current controversies. In the spring, the director of the state's welfare program was indicted for embezzlement. In August, the state's Attorney General was involved in a hit-and-run accident in which a teen was severely injured and alcohol was suspected, but never proved. A politically active Christian ministry lost its tax exemption.

In late October, a poll confirmed Justin Bonner's wisdom; while voters had not forgotten Martin's mistake, many had mellowed and a few had forgiven. While still a loser to every Republican matched against him in the poll, the margins had narrowed. Martin was by far the biggest contributor to his own rehabilitation, working tireless hours, canvassing the state, and never missing a single vote in the Senate. The president appointed him to chair a commission on domestic violence that yielded positive press.

A curious but undeniable fact was the continued esteem showed Martin by his colleagues in the Senate. While few sought public identity with him out of concern for their own careers, in private and on the floor they were more forthcoming. Perhaps they, like the president, hoped the dead stayed buried or perhaps they appreciated, as only insiders could, the rude harshness of an ever-blurring distinction between a politician's private life and public service. In any event, the depths to which he sank in the public's eye during the nadir of the scandal never destroyed his effectiveness in the Senate and he told Carson more than once that this fact alone sustained him on days of doubt.

Dennis, during the same period, developed a mentality close to that of a prisoner, confined to the dungeon of his personal history and guarded by the Washington establishment that banned him. He grew steadily depressed. When his initial inquires about employment on the Hill met with stony rebuff, he correctly perceived the search as futile. He tried the trade associations, usually a ready market for those with strong ties to Congress. But in his second interview, his attention was drawn to a fundamental disqualification: ethics laws prevented him from lobbying his old employer for two years. He would have to tunnel elsewhere to escape.

He enrolled in a life insurance training course which promised a minimum monthly draw against future commissions. Vanguard Life specialized in a high volume of cheap hybrid term policies with disability riders and, if a buyer lived long enough, some modest pension benefits. A cold-call, dialing-for-dollars business that Dennis hated almost from the greeting by the company's founder at the initial session. But he did it, and for a time his innate gift for smooze kept him afloat, while each month the rising tide of production quotas threatened to engulf him.

His spiritual ration during his days with Vanguard was the simultaneous pillorying of Martin Harmon in the press and media. Every time he saw a reference to the "lame duck senator from Virginia," or read speculation as to "Martin Harmon's successor," or heard a late-night Letterman or Leno jab at Martin's folly, he mentally chalked up on his prison wall another day, bringing him one day closer to parole or pardon; the day Martin left the Senate because of him.

But at some point in the late summer or early autumn, Martin's free-fall stopped. Dennis sensed it. He could smell revival in the air, as pungent as the aroma of a street vendor's griddle. It coincided with Dennis's departure from Vanguard, a victim to the ever rising quotas matched against his flagging energy. And it was at that precise point that Dennis began to hate.

He hated Martin in a way fatal to rationality or compromise or pacification. He hated him for a reason beyond their personal histories of who did what to whom. His was hate on a more fundamental, profound, and dangerous level, for Dennis had slipped over an invisible ledge which divided his self-interest from Martin's. He no longer cared what happened to himself; only Martin's fate would determine Dennis's success or failure. Martin's sin? The fuel for this white-hot fury Dennis carried in a lead-lined subconscious? Martin had, unknowingly and without intent, held Dennis up to the mirror of his own existence. Both men were casualties in the war of American politics. Both received wounds diagnosed as fatal. But one would survive, and Dennis knew with murderous certainty that it would be Martin. Why this was so absorbed him less than the naked fact. He supposed it was something in their backgrounds, perhaps their familial relationships, or their genetic makeup or their religion or ethic or God or who knew what, and what difference did it make anyway? The cold, unmitigated reality was that Martin possessed some intangible that had been denied Dennis and for which there simply was no substitute. Martin's constitution or character enabled him to suffer, to endure, and then to triumph, as surely as wings enabled a bird to fly. Dennis, rooted to the ground, lacked wings, and watching Martin loop and soar above provided the starkest contrast imaginable. Dennis hated Martin for those wings.

*   *   *

New Year's Day, 2002: Martin, Frog and Jason, the more sports minded of the twins, relaxed in front of a wide-screen TV in Frog's family room, more or less absorbed in the fourth college bowl game of the day. Scattered about them were the staples of this time-honored tradition—half munched popcorn, bowls of the obligatory servings of black eyed peas, the recipe for which had been in Carson and Kathy's family for years, and glasses of soft drinks and beer. Frog stretched out in a recliner, a beer can concealed discreetly by one leg of his chair. Kathy prohibited drinking from cans, a rule Frog routinely ignored. Beer just tasted better from a can. He did not flaunt the violation, however, keeping the can out of her sight as often as possible.

Martin, dressed in casual slacks, an open shirt and the new sweater Carson had given him at Christmas, sat at the end of a couch near Frog's chair. They had whiled away the better part of the day, cheering or booing teams to which they had no particular loyalty, but feeling the instinctive need to take sides.

"This quarterback for Alabama will never make it in the pros," opined Frog. "Too short. Those pro defensive lines average what, about six feet five now? Average! This guy's got a cannon for an arm, but at five feet eleven I hope he's planning on getting a degree because he'll need a job after college."

Martin was about to agree when an ear piercing shriek arose from the hallway. Moments later, Casey came trucking into the room in full toddler stride, his cousin Tim in hot pursuit. Casey squealed through his giggles. The slight limp which his parents had begun to detect in his walk did not manifest itself when he ran. At the orthopedic appointment next week, they would get an updated report on Casey's hip displacement, but if the hip pained him, he didn't show it.

Casey rounded the corner of Martin's end of the couch and headed for the opposite end, where he grabbed at the back of a cushion while throwing his legs up, so that he rolled onto the couch giggling hysterically. Behind him Tim stayed far enough back to menace Casey without actually running him down. Tim reached Casey, whose head was now buried in cushions, making monster-like growls to enhance Casey's happy terror.

He bent over and tickled him furiously, at which point Casey squirmed away and darted toward another room. Tim looked up at them in weary resignation, saying, "He never gets tired of this game," and resumed his growling. Casey's retreating squeal could be heard several rooms away.

"Senator, you've got a real live wire on your hands in that one," observed Frog.

Martin nodded. Casey, almost twenty two months old now, did have boundless energy. He also, according to Kathy, who professed elephantine powers of memory for events of her early childhood, looked exactly as Carson had looked as a toddler. Her hazel eyes, like Casey's, had been there from the beginning, merely darkening a little as she grew older, as his were certain to do. He had her blonde hair which, if he followed her development faithfully, would begin to darken about the time he entered school. And the face was every inch his mother's. The only discernible trace of Martin above Casey's neck appeared to be his ears, as the lobes on Martin's were longish like Casey's, whereas Carson had almost none, a feature that had made getting her ears pierced as a teenager more of an ordeal than that suffered by her friends. Casey's body seemed to favor Martin's, as his waist and legs both appeared rangy, although he was not yet definitively developed to form hard conclusions.

But one verdict was in which no one who came into contact with Casey disputed: he was all boy. From the day he had taken his first step he required constant monitoring. Carson began to swear he had supernatural powers, so adept was he at being in a particular place and with the turn of her back for a fraction of a second showing up somewhere else. He fell early and often, seeming to lead with his chin at every opportunity. But he would not stay down. Even as she struggled to hold him still long enough to get a Band-Aide on his beleaguered chin, he would be fighting for the freedom to trip over some new obstacle or to hurdle some new fascination. How he kept up his pace was a source of continued bewilderment to Carson, who pondered how she would ever keep up with two children, even if it was possible to have another.

But the fury of Casey's day yielded a benefit at night: at bedtime Casey was out cold. It did not matter if Carson was singing to him or a thunderstorm raged outside; when the appointed moment came his eyes closed and he was asleep until morning.

Dawn brought Carson's favorite part of the day. Casey awoke sweetly, looking around his room as if searching for changes since falling asleep. He seemed in no hurry to get up or to eat. For periods which sometimes lasted an hour, he would contemplate the toys surrounding his crib or the clowns which entertained on the wallpaper. Through clear, bright eyes rounded for maximum observation, he studied his world and the people in it. When Carson appeared over him, he would gaze at her in infant wonder before smiling a smile which never failed to weld her to the moment. If she left him for a minute or two, he could be counted on to lie quietly until she returned, secure in the knowledge that he was the focus of her universe. After he was changed, fed and bathed, his mood changed. It was as if he had dressed for work. He had clean clothes, a full stomach, and it was time for some serious hell raising. And he would take off, not stopping again until it was bedtime.

In the late afternoon, Kathy entered with an exaggerated flourish, walking in front of Martin and Frog to a spot directly in front of the TV.

"Gentlemen," she said, "I have an announcement."

Frog called out, "Hey, kid, you're in the way. It's late in the game," as he craned his neck.

She moved slightly to further obstruct his view. "Don't you 'hey, kid' me," she said, hands on her hips. "And don't interrupt me while I'm making my announcement."

"We'll be quiet," offered Martin.

"Thank you. I'm glad to see we have at least one considerate man about this house." She cut her eyes toward Frog. "One of the finest dinners in recorded history will be served at 7:30. Both of you bleary-eyed football fanatics will be in attendance. You may consider that an invitation if you wish or an order if you must. It matters not to me. What matters to me is your presence at the table."

"Kath, be reasonable," moaned Frog. "That will be during the last quarter of the Rose Bowl. USC and Michigan are ranked one and two. It's for the title. The game of the year—maybe the decade."

"Rose Bowl, Smose Bowl," countered Kathy. "How can they tell it's the game of the year when the year is only one day old?"

"Don't ask me, that's just what they say."

"Well, you don't have to live with 'they'; you do have to live with me, and if you want any peace in the new year, you'll be there at 7:30, and I don't care if you miss the Lions playing the Christians!"

Martin laughed. "I'll talk some sense into him."

"Ok," surrendered Frog. "We'll be there. I guess I could tape it."

At 7:30, the two families sat down to eat. Martin felt certain that an afternoon of snacking would rob him of any appetite for the meal, but he was wrong. The dinner before them was close to Kathy's advanced billing. Martin and Frog paid tribute to it in the coin of the cook's realm: requests for seconds. Over coffee and ice cream, the talk turned to Martin's re-election announcement, scheduled for January 3rd in Richmond.

"When did you decide?" Kathy addressed Martin over the rim of her cup. Steam rose, partially obscuring her eyes and lending the question an oracular depth.

Martin and Carson exchanged glances. "Last month," he said. "I'm still substantially behind in the polls but . . ." He trailed off, as though going over yet again the arguments in favor of this race that had all the attributes of a quest.

Kathy brought her cup down decisively on its saucer. "Then why go through it?" The edge in her tone told him this question had been building in her, festering like some splinter. "Why put Carson through it, and Casey?" She dropped all pretense of curiosity, accusing him of the very selfishness which had preyed upon him during recent weeks.

Carson spoke, canting her head to one side as if to acknowledge, gratefully, Kathy's concern while at the same time leaning imperceptibly toward her husband. "A mutual decision, Sis. It's something we both feel we need to face, together. It won't kill us if we lose, and it won't erase the ugliness if we win."

Martin broke in. "I don't blame you for suspecting that this re-election bid is a super-ego at work." He surveyed Kathy and Frog in his glance, but could have been addressing invisible others as well. And himself. "For twelve years I've held my own in one of the most demanding jobs in the world. I was elected to be hardworking and effective, not perfect. Running is something I have to do."

The following morning, they arose early in preparation for the trip to Richmond. They would spend that night in a suite of rooms at the Tyler Hotel, on the steps of which Martin would deliver his announcement the following day. After dinner the night before, Carson had stressed again to Kathy her right to remain in Frederick, removed from certain controversy. "Not a chance," Kathy had responded.

The cars were packed, the house on the verge of being secured, and all nearly ready for departure as Carson looked around for Casey.

"Where did he get off to?" she asked no one in particular.

"He's around back with the kids," Kathy offered. "I'll go get him."

As Carson, Martin and Frog made small talk in the driveway, Kathy disappeared into the back yard via the gate at the side of the house. Moments later they heard a mixture of loud voices, including Kathy's, calling "Casey! Casey!"

The three adults exchanged looks of puzzlement and followed Kathy's route to the back yard, where they found everyone engaged in a search. Casey was nowhere to be seen.

"Tim, you were playing with him. Where did he go?"

"He was right here, Mama."

"Well, he's not here now. Did you leave him alone?"

"I just went in the house to the bathroom, that's all. Then I came back and he was gone."

Kathy turned to the other children in the yard. "Surely someone saw where he went. A toddler can't simply vanish into thin air."

"Maybe he went into the house," Mark suggested.

They went inside. They looked behind doors, in closets and under beds—every place they could think of where a small boy could hide. No Casey.

"Sis, what could . . . ?"

"Don't worry," Kathy said. "We'll find him. He's got to be here somewhere."

They returned to the yard, fanning out to cover all the shrubs, hedges and plants, and calling "Casey! Casey!", with more urgency now. Carson searched in the extreme back, where she and Tim had buried George two years before.

They looked everywhere but up, where Casey stood, at the railing of the tree house in the very back of the yard. He watched them in silent amusement, as if their increasingly frantic darting and bending among the bushes was a game that he might like to play too. Carson was about to panic when she happened to look his way and spot him, a mischievous grin spread upon his face.

"Oh, my God!" she exclaimed as she ran toward him at full stride. "How in the world . . . ?"

The members of the search party reached the base of the tree at about the same time. Casey beamed down at them from his perch some twelve feet off the ground.

"Don't move, honey!" ordered Carson, near tears. "Just stay right there until Mommy comes up for you."

Frog and Martin positioned themselves under the spot where Casey would be likely to fall in the event he lost his balance. Neither really expected to have to play outfielder to a falling infant, but they were ready if called upon.

Carson scampered up the horizontal wooden slats that, nailed to the tree, comprised the ladder. In seconds she was at Casey's side, lifting him into her arms. Only then was she able to calm herself and say to the still smiling Casey, with an anger negated by relief, "Charles Martin Harmon, don't you ever scare me like that again! How on earth did you ever get up that ladder?" Casey made no reply, as though his climbing method was an infant trade secret protected by patent. Moments later mother and son descended into the relieved crowd below.

"I just can't get over it," Kathy said, laughing. "Tim couldn't climb that tree until he was almost three! I can't believe it."

Carson, still visibly shaken, clung to a seemingly unperturbed Casey. "Funny how fast you can be reminded of what's really important," she murmured with a nervous laugh, hugging him tighter.

Chapter 36

The Tyler Hotel on Grace Street in Richmond stands as a Georgian-style monument to lost causes. Originally constructed in 1842, its owner intended it as an enduring reminder that tobacco paid for groceries in the Old Dominion and always would. But when the Tyler was half completed, he ran out of cash, effectively reducing the grand statement to a footnote that any source of money dependent on sunshine and rainfall was as enduring as the weather that produced it. The six stories originally planned were revised to four, with a discernible waning of construction materials and attention to detail on the upper floor and the roof, where wood replaced the more expensive slate specified in the design.

On the other hand, the foundation, front portico and lobby had been built during the season of plenty, when imported marble steps set the tone for what was anticipated to follow. On those steps in 1861 Jefferson Davis had announced to a feisty throng the Confederate victory at Bull Run. Two years later, the same steps supported mourners during a candlelight vigil for Stonewall Jackson, dying in Guiney Station some forty-five miles away. Grant burned Richmond and with it the Tyler, but the steps endured and when the hotel was rebuilt in the 1920's, blackened streaks seared into the marble memorialized a spirit of defiance treasured by Richmonders.

It was that spirit which led Martin to choose the Tyler as the site for his re-election declaration. Like the Confederacy, he faced long odds and he knew it. He would plant his feet on the marble steps, look Virginians in the eye, confess his sins, then ask for their vote. He did not expect to win, but he didn't have to. The race would be his expiation.

On the marble steps workmen struggled to level the dais. Two burly men tilted the heavy podium as a third placed wooden blocks he had scavenged from an equipment shed. A royal blue coverlet, emblazoned with the seal of the Senate, would hide the blocks from view. Ben Palmeroy, recently hired to direct Martin's campaign, supervised the placement of microphones in front of the dais while a florist waited patiently for access to position sprays around the sides and base. Palmeroy's personal supervision of a detail like staging showed just how critical this announcement was to Harmon's re-election. Police, muffled against the chill, used fluorescent tape to establish a cordon in front of and along both sides of the steps, and on either side of this boundary mobile network trucks were parked, their roof-top satellite dishes trained skyward. Spectators began gathering inside the cordon, shifting from foot to foot to stay warm.

A debate between Palmeroy and Harmon over the presence of a banner behind the candidate occurred the week before. Martin took an uncharacteristically hard line against the huge "Re-elect Senator Harmon" banner Palmeroy had envisioned.

"I want a simple, direct announcement," Harmon had stated.

"Senator, you can't launch a campaign on an apology. The flags have to fly and the banners have to wave and the balloons have to rise. It's the only way."

"Ben, you came highly recommended and after Richmond we'll run this campaign your way. But I'm coming before the people of my state with my hat in my hand. I want a dignified, low-key stage from which to present the same kind of message." Then he paused. "And that's final." Palmeroy shrugged and canceled the banner.

The Jefferson suite on the third floor overlooks Grace Street and the front entrance. From a tall window, Martin peered down at the preparations underway below. The podium rested beneath the portico, blocked from his view, but as he watched the crowd building inside the cordon, police scurrying to keep traffic on Grace Street flowing, network cameras and newscasters positioning themselves for the one location triangulated to take in the entire drama, his blood quickened, his pulse raced, and his stomach reverted to the nervous hollowness he associated with the moments before kickoff in his football days or the vote in the Senate on the REA.

Behind him, Carson changed Casey into a blue and white sailor suit as Kathy, at the mirror with a comb, grappled with a rogue curl. Frog sat on the bed reading the sports page, outwardly as calm as he would have been at home in his den.

"How is the crowd?" Carson asked as she tried to thrust Casey's arm into a sleeve.

"Decent," Martin replied without turning from the window. "It's only 11:30; still time for a full house."

Ben Palmeroy entered, out of breath. "The elevators are slow and jammed. I took the stairs." At the window, he conferred with Martin about a request by a reporter for an interview after the announcement.

Martin agreed. "Fisher's never been one of my fans but dodging her will make her mad."

Palmeroy had just left the suite when a slender hand tapped on the jamb of the open door. Martin looked over to see Anne Harborfield.

"Anne," he said, smiling and striding toward her with his hand outstretched. "Don't tell me you drove all the way down here for this."

She took several tentative steps inside, looking about awkwardly. "The least I could do."

Carson rose and introduced herself, Kathy and Frog. "And this is Casey," she said, pointing toward the back of the sailor headed toward the kitchenette.

"I came to wish you luck," Anne said. "Now that I have, I'll leave you in peace." She was gone as quickly as she had appeared.

As Martin returned to the window, Carson, walking beside, touched him lightly on the arm. "You see. There are hundreds, thousands of people out there like Anne. They won't desert you."

Martin, his mind now on his speech, nodded mechanically but drew adrenalin from Anne's gesture and Carson's reminder. He had more friends than he realized, and he would need every one, starting in about twenty minutes.

*   *   *

Dennis awoke with a blinding headache and a squeamish stomach. At the medicine cabinet he felt for aspirin, popped five, then stumbled toward the kitchen where he opened a beer and guzzled down the tablets. He sank onto the floor as a means of steadying himself. The apartment was silent. Meg had left near dawn for a bike ride with "friends," although in fact it was a lone friend, a male, and she sensed a mutual attraction.

From the floor Dennis surveyed through bloodshot eyes the rubble of his existence. He had no job and no decent prospects. His wallet held seventy-eight dollars and again, no prospects. He lived at the sufferance of Meg, a woman of tolerance but one he knew was approaching her limit. His clothes were dated and could be moved in two armloads. He had no insurance; medical, dental, auto, or even burial. A repossessed car and some credit cards he carried for show completed the picture. Almost. He abused alcohol and saw no relationship between that abuse and his problems. Well, perhaps he did see, but the hell with it. Booze, he told himself like a mantra, was an effect of his demise, not its cause. The cause was Martin Harmon.

His head reeled. Bracing himself on the counter, he slowly rose to his knees, paused for balance, then continued until standing. He twisted open the cold tap, bent over the sink, and lowered his head under the faucet as the chilly water streamed down his face and neck. His legs wobbled. He needed to lie down.

Passing the vanity in the bedroom, he caught sight of himself in the mirror. His eyes looked like fire ants on a mound, his cheeks were bloated and dark patches above them spoke of enough sleep but no rest. He needed a drink.

He pulled on corduroy pants, a black wool sweater over his tee shirt, and running shoes. Ten minutes later he occupied a stool at Ray's Country Club, a dingy dive of a pool hall and bar two blocks from Meg's and just over the "red line." A Bloody Mary cost him $8.25 but the pounding in his head subsided to a muted throb.

Dennis glanced at the clock above the bar. Eight a.m. In four hours, Martin Harmon would announce his bid for re-election. His knowledge of polls and Harmon's vulnerability told him Harmon couldn't win, but his instincts, dulled but not destroyed, told him the opposite. Perched upon a vinyl stool at this beer-and-benediction bar, Dennis was consumed by the inevitability of Harmon's survival, as if the results of their personal struggle were already chiseled into marmoreal certainty. He, the third generation Rancour, would fair no better than his ancestors. Something in the Rancour chemistry preordained defeat and it would be Dennis's fate, his duty, to walk in formed footprints breaking no new ground.

He gazed around, his eyes bleary. Places like this dump, and worse, would be his future, while across town new carpet would be ordered for the Senate offices to cushion the steps of men like Martin Harmon. He tossed a quarter on the bar and returned to Meg's. In a closet he rummaged through his athletic bag until his hand struck cold metal. He withdrew a .38 Special, thrust it into his pants, pulled the sweater and a dark jacket over the bulge and headed for the bus station.

*   *   *

"It's time, Senator," said Ben Palmeroy as he entered the suite.

Martin nodded, slid three-by-five cards into his coat pocket, and adjusted his tie. Through the windows, heavily draped and closed against the January chill, came the muffled chant of "We want Harmon!" from below. Palmeroy had worked hard to organize that "spontaneous" show of support, and he hoped it sounded heartfelt.

Martin was not fooled. A cynical smile crossed his face for an instant, then disappeared. He parted the drapes and looked over the crowd now filling the space inside the cordon and pressuring its limits. Frosted breath puffed forth as supporters hit the first hard syllable of his name. "Har'mon!" He was about to release the drape when he saw, in the midst of the throng, a bare-headed man glance upward for an instant. Martin tensed reflexively just as Carson, in coat and gloves, approached.

"Martin, what's wrong?"

He maintained his frozen stare.

"Martin . . ."

He turned to her, distant. "For a moment . . ."

"What is it?"

"Nothing. I'll tell you on the elevator." He donned his overcoat and wrapped a cashmere scarf around his neck. "Let's go."

Martin and Ben Palmeroy walked out together, followed by Carson taking measured steps to match Casey's. In the elevator she stared at Martin expectantly but he was all business and whatever had engaged him moments ago now seemed far from his mind. At the lobby, he took her arm and they started toward the wide majestic doors leading to the portico. He stopped short when he heard a shout from behind.

"Dad!"

He turned to find Edward and Allie striding toward him. Allie, ignoring Carson, approached her father and kissed his cheek.

"We got tied up in traffic. We'll be watching," she said in her breezy fashion. "Give us hell." She grabbed Edward's arm and pulled him toward the door before Martin could utter a word of introduction. Edward gave a thumbs up and called, "See you afterwards," as he retreated.

"How wonderful," Carson whispered, visibly moved. Martin nodded.

Arriving at the massive brass doors Martin, Carson and Casey walked together to the dais. Cheers arose and chants of "We want Har'mon!" renewed as he surveyed the crowd, packed in front and to both sides. Palmeroy had done a good job whipping them into an expectant campaign fever. The rest was up to him.

He raised his arms for silence. "Friends and citizens of the Commonwealth, before I begin I want to introduce two very special people in my life; my wife Carson and my son Casey." Carson waved briefly in acknowledgement of restrained applause. "I know you've read about them in the newspaper but I wanted you to meet them face to face and for them to meet you.

"Twelve years ago I came to you on a day much like today and asked for your vote and your trust. You gave me both and saw fit to renew that trust six years ago. To serve as your senator is the highest honor. I have done my best for you and for Virginia.

"Some of you feel I breached your trust for reasons that have been widely reported. You may decide to hold me accountable at the polls, which is your privilege under this grand system we call democracy. To you, I offer an apology but no excuses." He paused to gage the impact of his candor. Some looked away; they were here out of curiosity, and he would not get their votes.

"Today, I announce my candidacy for a third term. I do so not as a referendum on any human failing for which I might be charged but on the record of a dedicated legislator who loves his job, his state, and his nation."

Applause interrupted, feeble at first but growing from those in front and spreading through the crowd. From the middle of the mass, the man in a dark jacket began edging his way toward the dais.

"Let me review my record, of which I am extremely proud and which I believe merits your vote in November."

As Martin ticked off his legislative credits, the man in the dark jacket pressed forward, careful to keep his head down and his eyes on the feet of those he wedged past. With each stirring of the crowd he seized the chance to shoulder past another row.

Behind Martin, Casey grew restless. He pulled away from Carson, who clasped his hand tighter in restraint. He sat, or tried, but she scooped him up and held him as Martin neared the end of his speech.

Dennis also sensed the end. His efforts were no longer subtle, drawing hostile stares from those he elbowed through. His migration forward had also angled right so as to eliminate the protection offered Martin by the bulky dais. He gained the second row as Martin concluded.

"With God's help and your vote, I can finish the job you elected me to do. I ask for that chance."

The crowd around Dennis raised their voices and their arms, clapping and shouting approval and encouragement. Martin responded with waves of both arms, thanking them. He turned, motioned to Carson, who approached with Casey still in her arms. The three faced the crowd. As Martin turned to acknowledge the cheers to his left, his eyes fell on Dennis, now making no effort to avoid him. As Martin's congenial grin turned to sober recognition, Dennis raised his gun and fired three shots in rapid succession.

At the instant Martin saw the gun, he turned away from Dennis, simultaneously pushing Carson and Casey violently backward. With the shots echoing in the portico, he felt a sting in his side, then his neck as he, Carson and Casey tumbled downward. He seemed to fall forever, and the jarring landing he braced for did not come. Faces, out of focus, appeared above him, a circle of strange people shouting and pushing each other and asking him questions. He tried to rise, fearful of hurting Carson, but an excruciating pain seized his left side and he could not move.

Carson never saw Dennis. The look on Martin's face as he turned to shove her displayed no terror but only determination. She reeled backward with the force of his push, instinctively bringing her free hand to protect Casey's head as they fell. As she landed, her head snapped back, striking the marble with a sickening thud. All went dark as Martin lay across her legs and Casey lay quite still in her arms, pinned between her and the cold surface of the Tyler's portico, stained with fresh blood.

Chapter 37

Martin's first sensation following the shooting was euphoria brought on by morphine. Unable to move his neck, his hand groped at the traction collar enclosing it and forcing him to stare directly at the ceiling. Less tactile but more serious were the broken ribs and internal bleeding. His peripheral vision surveyed the room as his mind strove to rationalize why everything seemed white and clean.

After what seemed days, but could have been minutes, a man and a woman approached his bed wearing medical coats and name tags he could not read.

"Senator, can you hear me?" the woman asked.

"Yes," he responded in a conversational tone.

"Do you know where you are?"

"No."

"MCV—Medical College of Virginia. Do you remember what happened?"

"I fell. I . . . pushed her."

"You were shot."

"Shot?" Martin thought hard, or felt as though he did. Somewhere in the back of his mind he could see a dark spot, weightless and infinitely distant. "Where?"

"Once in the neck; that's why you can't move your head. And the other in your side. That one broke a couple of ribs, but no vital organs hit," she assured. "You'll be fine. Lucky you moved quickly."

He sighed. After a pause, he became animated, his eyes darting and his lips beginning to quiver. "What about Carson?"

"Senator, your wife is in a room down the hall. Like you, she has some injuries. She broke her leg in the fall and she has a concussion. Her CAT scan is being read and we'll know soon if she needs surgery."

He smiled weakly at them. "How did she like the speech? Did she say? I'll go see her."

The doctors exchanged professional looks. "Later." She patted his hand. "Sleep for a while now."

They seemed nice enough, he thought through the morphine. He wondered why they had come to see him. He closed his eyes to get a better view of the black spot. Soon he lapsed back into sleep, for how long he could not determine. He was dreaming. The black spot was moving around now, up, down, now here, now there. It should stop, he thought. It should slow down so he could look at it closely; hold it. But it would not stay still, preferring to continue its erratic caroming.

Voices came to Martin, remote and hushed. They were talking about him, he knew, although he could make out none of their words. Then closer. "Ok, 50 milligrams. Call me if he wakes up." The spot again. There it was, low on his mind's horizon, like a black sun dawning in the west. It must have some meaning if it . . . . Suddenly, he bolted up, or wanted to, but he couldn't move. There it is. That's it. A jacket. Dennis!" A nurse was beside him. The animation in his open eyes signaled calamity.

"Relax, Senator. Stay calm. You're beat up pretty bad."

"Where's my family," he demanded, attempting to summon forth the authority his voice normally commanded; the air of imperative that would send a staffer scurrying to do his bidding.

"Let me get the doctors for you."

She disappeared from his vision, to be replaced moments later by the same two doctors from earlier in the day? The month?

"Senator, I see you've—"

"Where's Carson? Where's Casey?" he insisted. "I need to see them."

The doctor's eyes shifted from his as she dropped her shoulders and buried her fists in the deep pockets of her white coat. Perhaps she did it intentionally, as an advance messenger of tragedy sent to alert the senses that a shock of unspeakable proportions was about to be inflicted. Her hesitation, only a second in duration, made that which followed superfluous.

"Your wife is recovering. Your son was very severely injured, I'm afraid. The bullet which struck you in the neck passed through, lodging in the boy's skull. We've done all we can for him here, but it has not been effective."

"Is he dead?"

"He has a flat EKG. We can maintain life support systems for as long as necessary, but we hold out no hope for him. I'm very sorry."

"Does my wife know?"

"She is still disoriented. We'll brief her as soon as she is physically and mentally able to handle it."

"I'll tell her," said Martin, "but you'll have to find a way to get us together. When can I see her?"

"Let me see what I can do." She turned to leave, then hesitated. "The waiting area is full of reporters. A Mr. Palmeroy wanted to see you when you feel up to it." He lifted his hand at the wrist, as if to push it all away.

On the same floor of an adjoining wing, Carson lay motionless in bed. The IV above her head dripped its steady syrup into a shunt in her arm. Her eyes, blackened by the impact, were closed evenly. Her right leg, set and elevated, throbbed like a deep bruise. She stirred slightly, giving a quick wince before settling back. Her eyes remained closed, in no hurry to expose her to the world into which she would all too soon awake.

The following morning Martin was wheeled down the hall to Carson's room, where he waited for her to come out of her drug-induced somnolence. Late that evening, with Martin barely able to see her from his prone position and with Kathy at the end of her bed, she rallied. Some minutes later, a cry pierced the stillness of the deserted hallway outside the room. The tortured, anguished cry of a mother's soul being torn from her body; the inconsolable grief which comes as emptiness moves in to fill its place.

Carson did not go to Casey's room for two days. On the third day, when she was able to walk with crutches, she took Kathy to visit his bedside. Like all modern hospitals, MCV is highly compartmentalized. There are areas for those just entering the world, those about to leave it, and those recently departed. Then there is an area for those with conditions that blur the lines. Casey, defying classification in the first three, made his home in the fourth.

As they entered, the battery of digital gauges, monitors and machines gave the room an arcade quality. At the end of wires, tubes, shunts and masks, was the comatose form of Casey. Bandages concealed his features. Carson's eyes fell upon the wires leading from the creases of the bandages to a monitor above and behind the bed. On the screen she saw the telltale verdict displayed as a horizontal beam of impersonal green light; a perfect, unbroken line running east to west. She turned away, unable to negotiate the remaining distance to Casey's crib. She would come closer tomorrow, she told herself. Today, she had done all she could do.

Carson, more mobile than Martin, came to his room each morning and remained most of the day. Kathy took up temporary residence in the Tyler Hotel, visiting three times a day to provide comfort where none could be found.

Edward, Jack and Allie came to visit, taking turns reading newspapers to their father, who tired easily. They each spent time with Carson as well. Edward seemed particularly drawn to her, while Jack's reserve was apparent. Jean remained in Roanoke, but talked with Martin by phone and sent Carson a short but intimate note of condolence.

A conversation Martin and Carson dreaded came sooner than expected. Three doctors and a hospital administrator came to discuss "the options regarding Casey." Dr. Stampers, the neurologist attending Casey, led a group which, despite their practiced professionalism, would clearly have preferred to be somewhere else. Stampers appeared to be Carson's age or younger. Severely thin with a chalky complexion, she sat on the end of his bed, composed but very tense.

"Senator, Mrs. Harmon, we understand how difficult this is for you. I won't presume to tell you I know how you feel, because frankly I can't imagine it. I'm sure I speak for my colleagues as well." She gave an oblique sweep of her arm to draw her companions into her declaration. "At some point, and I stress that it doesn't have to be today or next week or any fixed time, we are going to have to make some decisions regarding Casey. We have gone over the prognosis with both of you in some detail and I see no point in reviewing that in light of the fact that nothing has changed. Do you?"

Martin uttered, "No," barely audible to their visitors. Carson shook her head slightly but said nothing.

"Our job as doctors is to keep Casey alive by whatever means are available. We intend to do that job to the best of our ability. As you know, his condition is maintained by advances in technology. Thirty years ago, we would not have been confronted with this problem. But today, it is upon us, and we need to deal with it. There are two basic options. We can keep Casey alive in the sense that he is presently alive for as long as you wish, or we can withhold the systems that are preserving the status quo. As his parents, the choice is yours. My personal advice, for what it's worth, is to let nature take its course free of the machines. It's so very, very difficult, but the sooner done the quicker the healing process can begin for both of you. If there was anything to be gained from hanging on, I would not hesitate to recommend it. My colleagues are in accord with this recommendation."

She stopped speaking for a moment, bringing a hush to the room. Through the closed door, faint, muffled sounds from down the corridor could be heard as nurses and patients carried on the business of living. Carson thought of Tim, when his rabbit, George, died. "Sometimes these things happen and we don't know why," she had told him. "You gave him the best life he could have had." Finally, Martin used the limited mobility in his neck to look toward her. "It's up to you."

"No," she said softly. "The answer is no, not yet."

"I understand, Mrs. Harmon. Please don't feel rushed. As I said, there is no time limit on this decision."

In the days that followed, Carson recovered sufficiently to leave the hospital. She returned home, grateful beyond words to Kathy for arranging matters in Frederick to allow Kathy to stay in Washington. The door to Casey's room, while closed, yawned at her as a gaping pit in the earth. She cursed the fact that passing it was required to get from her room to the living area, and once she left her bedroom in the morning she would not return until bedtime. When avoidance was impossible, she turned sideways, as an acrophobic would approach a railing over a precipitous drop. The thought of entering the pit made her knees weak.

As Martin recovered, an unofficial but defined pattern asserted itself. Ben Palmeroy visited him early each morning, bringing newspapers and messages from well-wishers. Also, contract offers from agents, publishers and film studios. From Palmeroy he received his first tangible account of the assault. The Richmond *Times Dispatch* devoted an entire supplement to the tragedy. A photo spread captured the critical minute in exposures seconds apart. He saw himself at the podium, arms extended above his head in acknowledgement of the crowd's applause at the end of his speech. An arrow pointed to Dennis, then in the second rank about to break through in front. Turning to beckon Carson. The three of them acknowledging cheers. The gun visible as Dennis extends his arm. Martin sees him. Turning toward Carson and Casey. The shove. Falling. The crowd around Dennis frozen; seconds later, chaos. Then, a later photo of Dennis in custody. Another of Casey being wheeled from an ambulance into the ER. The accompanying story reported Dennis being held without bond, a court appointed attorney, and rumors of a suicide watch at the jail and an insanity plea at trial.

An hour after Palmeroy's departure, Ellen Fry, commuting daily from Washington, arrived to help him carry on the business of being a senator. Having prioritized the correspondence, messages, committee work and reports, she was able to dispose of the most pressing in a session lasting about ninety minutes. She left then, in deference to his rationed energy. After lunch, Kathy and Carson visited for an hour or so until other visitors, mostly constituents but occasionally a senator or colleague from the Hill, stopped by in a parade tightly monitored by his doctors. In the evening Carson came alone, sitting with him while they watched the evening news together.

When the news broadcast ended, they went together to see Casey. Standing with her beside his bed evoked memories of standing together at his crib at home, watching him sleep. Carson was silent during these visits, and he wanted to know her thoughts, but he never asked, preferring to let her bring it up, which she never did. She was so subdued when she returned, on some nights not uttering another word until time to say good-bye. On these occasions, she pretended to read, but he was aware that hours passed without her turning a single page in her book.

On a morning just after Ellen left with her marching orders for the day, Dr. Stampers appeared in Martin's doorway.

"Do you have a moment, Senator?"

"Sure, come on in."

Martin, having just reclined the bed in the wake of Ellen's departure, returned it to a position which permitted him to maintain eye contact with his visitor.

"It's been two weeks. I was wondering if you and Mrs. Harmon have had a chance to talk. If not, I was going to suggest that she avail herself of some very fine counselors here at the hospital. They could help her. Do you think she would be interested?"

"I really don't know. I've been reluctant to press her on anything, but it sounds like a solid idea to me. Would you like me to suggest it or would it be better coming from you as a medical recommendation?"

"I'll see her tomorrow when she comes to visit Casey and suggest it to her then. I just wanted to get your feeling on it before I broached the subject."

"I appreciate that."

Dr. Stampers got up to leave.

"Doctor, I suppose there is, you know, no change with Casey."

"Absolutely none," she replied.

*　　*　　*

In an afternoon on which frigid arctic wind blustered and howled about the windows, Martin awoke from a nap to find Anne Harborfield, her normally pale cheeks apple-red from the wind. She was standing beside his bed watching him, as a sentry might eye an object she was charged with guarding but did not expect to move.

"Anne, how are you?" he asked weakly.

"Hello, Senator. I feel so guilty for not getting by before now. How's the recuperation coming along?"

"Better every day," he replied, shaking off the grogginess of his nap. "Perhaps it's just as well you waited to visit, though; I tire easily, I find. I'm afraid my earlier visitors left with the feeling that they didn't get much for their time here."

"I promise I won't stay long, but I had to let you know I'm thinking of you and your wife. The *Post* reported your son's condition. I'm so very sorry."

"It's a painful time, Anne. Thanks for your concern. Tell me what's new with you. How are things at NIH?"

"Couldn't be better. I was told last week I'm about to be promoted again. Care to guess the position?" She tried to suppress a smile.

"I don't suppose it would be a guess on my part. You've been promoted to fill the spot left by Dr. Cass's retirement, haven't you?"

"You know I was, and I have you to thank for it."

"Now, hold it. You got that job on your own. NIH knows talent when it sees it."

"Thanks, but I have a strong hunch those phone calls from you before the holidays didn't hurt my chances any."

"Don't overlook Dr. Cass himself. His recommendation carried a lot more weight than any two cents I put in."

"I have thanked him as I am thanking you now. I owe you both an enormous debt of gratitude."

"Just work hard and do the best you can. That's all the thanks I need."

Anne stared down at her hands, folded together in front of her. "I want to tell you something but I don't know how to go about it."

"Why? Just tell me."

"It's so personal, especially now. I'm just afraid to even approach the subject, frankly. If I said the wrong thing I'd die."

"I'm a big boy, Anne. Tell me what's on your mind. What's it about?"

"It's about your son."

Martin sighed. "What about him?"

"This is going to sound so crazy; so off the wall. That's why I hesitate to bring it up. You know how people in stressful situations, really desperate ones, will do anything they think might help; like people with terminal cancer will go on weird diets or pay huge sums of money for strange 'miracle drugs' that are nothing more than sugared water; that kind of thing. You know what I'm talking about?"

"Sure. It's sad to see people so desperate they'll do anything. There has to be a special spot in hell for those who prey on the hopeless."

"Exactly, which is why, when I tell you what I'm about to tell you, I want you to keep in mind that I realize this goes on, and if I thought for one moment this was some kind of hocus-pocus, I would never even bring it up."

"Bring what up?"

"Max Grunfeld."

"What about him?"

"You remember him, of course."

"Sure. He had the research project that was shot down by NIH right after the REA was enacted."

"Exactly. NIH sent me to California a couple of years ago to meet with the people at Caltech, where Grunfeld works. Dr. Cass thought I could cushion the blow to their egos after we turned Grunfeld down. I met him while I was out there. He and his wife, who is a charming woman, had me to dinner. We became friends and have corresponded routinely since then." She paused, as if having second thoughts about continuing.

"And?" prompted Martin.

"And he's working on a couple of fascinating research projects. He sends me progress reports. He's been hard at work on a concept called 'totipotency.'"

"I remember the term; something about growing a tail in a mouse or something."

"That was part of the early research. Applying the concept to humans was the biggest argument against his project in the grant hearing. But since he receives no NIH funding, he's very open about the thrust of his work."

"What does he have to do with Casey?" The question was benign, with no hint of impatience.

"About forty-five days ago, he wrote me that he had progressed to a point that he was going to experiment with living human cells taken from his grandson. He was very excited about it. Two weeks ago, I received a note saying—wait just a moment, I brought his letter so let me quote it directly." She fumbled in her purse. "Here it is. He says, 'I must immediately confess to the awesome implications of these recent tests. Man's ability to recreate himself in his own image is at hand. I for one believe I would make a terrible God.' That's the part I wanted you to hear, about 'man's ability to recreate himself.'"

"Are you suggesting that Grunfeld's work with these mice somehow holds out hope for Casey?"

"I warned you it would sound crazy."

"But Grunfeld is speaking in generalities. He could be making absurd claims without much to back them up. Isn't he getting up in years? Sounds like delusions of grandeur, or worse."

"But I have more than generalities. His letters have been fairly detailed, except he protects his potential patents by declining to name the critical chemical agents he employs. Take my word for it; his claims do appear to have a scientific basis."

"So you're suggesting that by some new genetic process Grunfeld is patenting, he can recreate a person; a live human being."

"I'm saying that is what he is claiming and that from what I know personally about him and his work, his claim cannot be summarily dismissed."

"I see. Well, thank you, Anne. I appreciate your bringing it to my attention."

"Senator, I can see you are skeptical. If I could put myself in your place, I know I would be too. It is not my purpose to convince you. All I am trying to do is alert you to something I thought you should know. When I heard about Casey, the thought occurred to me that it offered hope."

"Thanks, Anne. I can see this hasn't been an easy mission for you. Your heart's in the right place. Let me think about it. If I have questions, I'll call you. Why don't you leave me your home number."

After she left, Martin pondered the implications of her message. Even if Grunfeld was a century ahead of his time, the point was that somewhere someone was actively working on such a project, and that one hundred or two hundred or five hundred years from now, there could be hope for

Casey. It seemed an absurd concept to him, but was it any more absurd than others that he took for granted? Frankly, he still found the concept of airplanes absurd, and look at what one hundred years of progress had done for them. If he were lying in the same hospital bed in 1902 rather than 2002, would Anne have been able to convince him that she would, within her lifetime, be able to eat dinner on a coast to coast flight? Or that microscopic video cameras could be sent through his veins to perform diagnostic procedures? Or that Casey could be kept alive on machines indefinitely? Was it possible that one hundred years hence, Grunfeld's process could be as refined as flipping a switch to light a room?

That evening, following Carson's return from her pilgrimage to Casey's room, Martin felt the need to talk about him; to address the decisions which Dr. Stampers knew were inevitable; which he, Martin, knew were inevitable. Yet the thought of adding one more burden to this unbearably sad woman was too much for him. He would have to wait until she was ready. He had to give her time to let go. But would she? The worst part of it had been alluded to by Anne: the absence of hope.

Anne had risked broaching the Grunfeld business because "it offered hope." If Martin ever doubted the power of that elixir before, he could no longer. Seeing Carson across the room, broken and distraught yet trying to maintain her equilibrium, wrenched him, like watching an elegant quarter horse with a broken leg attempting to stand. He could comfort her, console her, but he could not offer what she wanted most: hope.

Martin debated sharing with Carson Anne's revelation. False hope, he knew, was insidious cruelty, whether offered by a priest or a scientist. In the end, he decided to relate Anne's message. All hope involved a leap of faith, he reasoned. Neither he, nor the priest, nor the California research could spare her that leap. It would be up to her if she wished to take it.

Chapter 38

"But why?" Carson demanded of Anne. "Why won't he meet with me? Doesn't he understand what's at stake? Won't he even talk with me?" They sat in the Harmon apartment at the Westchester, meeting for the first time. Anne found she liked Carson, whose posture was so erect, her carriage so assured, even under the weight of loss. Carson was too absorbed in Casey to register any impressions of Anne.

"I don't have a good answer," lamented Anne. "I can only tell you what he said; that the totipotency work is still in the research stage and has no practical application at this time."

"I can't believe it! That sounds like a banker turning someone down for a loan." Carson buried her face in her hands, the strain of recent days threatening to overwhelm her. The redness around her eyes spread toward her cheeks, raw with the dryness of the Washington winter. She had put on makeup, for the first time in days, an hour before Anne's arrival, but then she had spotted a key ring that had been a favorite teething toy of Casey's, and she had become upset and her eye shadow had run and she had washed it all off, startled to see how dreadful she looked.

"It does sound cold," Anne agreed. "But he's not a cold man. I'm sure there must be more to it than we realize."

"I'm sure there is," Carson sighed. "There are always reasons not to do something. Would it help if I called him?"

Anne shook her head slowly. "I don't think so. He sounded firm. He was very sympathetic. I got the feeling he was very frustrated because he can't help."

"But he can help, or at least you seem to think he can."

"Mrs. Harmon, please. I'm not sure he can. He's the best judge of that. The only one, really. Perhaps I made a mistake in telling your husband."

"No, you didn't. I'm very grateful. If a mistake has been made, it's probably mine in putting so much on this. I just have no other option."

*   *   *

As Max turned the corner on the hall leading to his lab, he spotted the trim, well dressed young woman leaning against the door jamb and slowed his pace, surprised to find his mental image of Carson Harmon so faithful to the person awaiting him. But he was not surprised to see her. From the newspaper accounts of the shooting and Anne's description of the tragic situation, he could hardly fault her for forcing this confrontation.

Max fumbled with his keys as he drew closer to the lab. The scuff of his footsteps and the jangle of metal echoed in the corridor, deserted as usual early on Sunday morning. Carson heard him approach and turned to meet him.

"Dr. Grunfeld?"

"Yes."

"I'm Carson Harmon. Anne Harborfield called you about me. Please don't be mad at me for showing up on your doorstep like this. I just had to see you."

Max unlocked the door to his office and held out his arm as a signal for her to lead. When she was seated, he offered her a soft drink. She declined.

"How was your flight?" he asked.

"No turbulence, if that's what you mean. You may have read I broke my leg. Sitting on a plane for that long was no fun. Let's just say I'm glad to be here face to face with you."

Carson stood and walked to the wall where the Faulkenberg award hung. She studied it as Max studied her from behind his desk. Her eyes roamed to the other frames before coming to rest on Max.

"I know why you're here, of course," Max said. "I presume there is no change in your son's condition."

"None."

"And how is your husband, Senator Harmon?"

"Much improved. He's scheduled to leave the hospital in a day or two. I was hoping he would be out in time to come with me. Then I thought that might not be such a good idea with . . . well, you know." Carson lowered her eyes, her unfinished statement hanging in the air.

Max leaned back in his swivel chair, the creak of the old springs loud in the hush between them. "With him being responsible for blocking my grant?"

Carson looked at him directly. "Yes. That. Anne has said some wonderful things about you, so I was hopeful you had forgiven him."

"Anne's a dear girl," he replied. "And as for your husband, there is nothing to forgive. I'm sure he was doing what he thought was right, although I believe the REA is a misguided law. Don't tell him I said that; he has enough on his mind. I harbor no ill will toward him, though, if that worries you. Revenge drains the energy, and I need all my energy for my work."

"Anne tells me your work is rather spectacular. I'll confess I wouldn't know." Carson left her spot by the wall, returning to her chair but standing behind it.

"Not many people know what Anne knows. If they did, we would be besieged."

"What do you mean?"

Max brought the chair upright and took off his glasses, rubbing the bridge of his nose in a weary massage. "I mean that there would be masses of people coming to us for miracles we don't possess." He replaced his glasses before placing his palms flat on his desk. "Let me give you an example. A colleague of mine in biomedicine was the subject of a rumor about a cure for AIDS. This was several years ago before the cure was found. A paper he wrote for a medical journal was interpreted by some university professor somewhere as containing a cure, even though my colleague denied that it was a cure and further stated that the test results were inconclusive. Anyway, this friend of mine suffered the tortures of the damned for a full year because of this misinterpretation."

"You mean because it held out hope for them a lot of sick people contacted him?"

"Contacted?" Max raised both hands toward her. "They practically assaulted him." He clenched his outstretched fists as if they held the lapels of his friend's coat. Then, he relaxed, letting his hands fall limply to the desk. "Not maliciously, of course. They were desperate, which was understood. But my friend was helpless; helpless in the face of all these suffering people. Some offered him money; incredible amounts of money. They would do anything. When he explained that it was all a misunderstanding, they were devastated. It was very hard on him, and the more he turned away the worse he felt. And there were a few who didn't believe him; who thought he was holding back for reasons they could not understand."

"I see your point." Carson said, with businesslike formality. Then she reached into the pocket of her suit and took out a white handkerchief, which she absently twisted around her fingers. "You are afraid that if word of this got out you would be put on the same spot as your friend by people like me."

Max shrugged, then added softly, "It's a possibility. And that is only one of my concerns. There are others, more serious ones actually. I am also worried—"

"Dr. Grunfeld," she interrupted, holding the back of her chair for support and leaning toward him. "My only child, the only child I'll ever have, is lying brain dead in a Richmond hospital. My husband and I must decide when and if to withhold his life support systems. I'm going to make that decision now. Today. I'm going to make it on the basis of what you tell me about your research. I am no scientist. I cannot argue with you, challenge your assumptions, dispute your conclusions or contradict your judgment. That leaves me bound by your word, which will be final as to Casey. If you tell me there is absolutely nothing that can be done, I'm going to let Casey go and begin a long healing process that may never be completed. I am putting it to you this way because I want you to be certain, very certain, that any objections you have are worth the price of Casey's future. And mine. Is it absolutely, completely hopeless?" Carson held her breath.

Max, who had not taken his eyes from hers for an instant as she spoke, now gazed to his left, at the door leading to his lab. He drummed his fingers softly on the top of the desk. He had, in the back of his mind, known it would come down to this. She had framed the question in an exquisitely poignant way, but Max had posed the same question, less artfully but no less forcefully, to himself. There was only one answer to give. He turned his gaze back to her.

"No," he said softly. "I can't say that it is absolutely, completely hopeless."

Huge tears welled in Carson's eyes. "I swore I wouldn't do this," she said, bringing the handkerchief to her cheeks.

"Now listen to me, young lady. Don't go jumping to any conclusions. There is an awful lot of ground between 'absolutely, completely hopeless' and even a decent probability. Nor have I said I would try to help."

"At least it's something. No hope is just so . . . hopeless. Anne mentioned a recent breakthrough of some sort."

"I'm very excited about it." Max motioned for her to follow him into the lab, where he paused beside a bank of glass cubicles, each containing a white mouse. He pointed to the donor mouse as he explained how the duplicates of the donor had been produced and took her through the essential steps by which cells differentiate.

"About the time," he continued, "that I applied for my ill-fated NIH grant, I discovered the process by which a mature cell could be 're-triggered,' or made totipotent. I discovered it, but I didn't understand it. I saw it happening, but I didn't know why. That's why I needed the grant."

Max tapped softly on the glass as if to greet the captive mice. The mouse on whose cubicle his finger rested retreated, then came boldly forward. Max watched the mouse, while Carson looked at Max.

"How do you get from mice to people?" she asked.

"Good question." The mouse in the adjoining cage came forward. "At the risk of sounding flip, it's all the same biology, physics and chemistry. The laws of genetics are the laws of genetics."

"Meaning you could use the same process to re-trigger a human?"

He turned to look at her. "Not quite. Adjustments must be made for the human recipe, which contains forty-six chromosomes. Mice have only forty. That is where my recent breakthrough came." Max explained the patterns found on chromosomes in mice or in people, and talked with obvious relish of Chromosome #5. "I lived with that chromosome for years. It is the only one I really know, which is fortunate because that is where I found the gene pattern I was looking for. If it had been on any other chromosome, I might well still be looking."

"Have you tried it out? With people, I mean."

"I've performed some experiments on some cells from my grandson. The results are encouraging."

"Would it be silly to ask if duplicating your grandson is a risk?" She managed a brief, nervous laugh.

"Well, I have duplicated him in a literal, genetic sense in that I have re-triggered some cells and seen the totipotency effect. But I suspect you mean growing a person, correct?"

"That's what I meant."

Max smiled patiently. "I think you're forgetting the mother's role in all this. Once a totipotent cell is produced, it must be implanted into an enucleated egg. That is one from which the nucleus has been removed. The egg must be planted in the mother and then the embryo carried to term, just as any other baby would be born."

"Is that difficult, implanting the cell?"

"Not at all. It's essentially in vitro fertilization, a process that has been around for years. Now, don't misunderstand. There are many things that can go wrong at that stage, but the process itself is old technology. That's the easy part."

"Why use cells from your grandson? Why not your own?"

"Mine are old," sighed Max, and at that moment Carson thought he did look quite old. And tired. "I could use mine, but the younger the cell, the better the response."

"So you would anticipate a very good response from a twenty-two-month-old cell?" she asked, a touch of optimism unmistakable in her voice.

His answer was halting, "Possibly."

Her face darkened. Max gave a final tap on the glass and walked toward his office. She turned and followed, afraid of the signal sent by his abrupt movement. He held the door as she entered, then closed it gently behind her. Still facing the door, his back to her, he said, "Mrs. Harmon, this research is completely experimental at this stage. What I've told you may encourage you, but believe me the risks are enormous. I'm thinking in particular of a deformity, perhaps a hideous one."

Carson winced. The possibility had not occurred to her. "Can you tell before things go too far?"

Max turned around and walked past her to his desk. "We can use diagnostic tests that are currently available to detect quite a few deficiencies. I suppose any truly terrible genetic disorder would show up, but we don't know what to expect here because we'll have no data from prior efforts."

"Then you'll try it?"

Max raised his eyebrows as his jaw dropped slightly. "I didn't say that."

Carson pointed her index finger at him. "You did; you said 'we'll have no data.'"

Max eyed her finger coldly and snapped, "What if this effort produces a freak of nature? Can you imagine what my liability would be, aside from the moral responsibility I would feel?"

"I'll sign a release."

"Not worth anything," countered Max with a dismissive wave of his hand.

Her eyes narrowed and her voice, strong in its clipped determination, said, "I'll give you my word."

"Mrs. Harmon, I would do anything to help you. Believe me. But I'm not God. My advice to you as a father and as a human being is to let Casey go."

"As a mother and a human being, I can't. Will you try?"

"I said earlier that I wouldn't depress you by telling you the odds, but I think you need to know them if you are seriously contemplating this. In my opinion, your chances are no better than one in one hundred thousand, maybe more."

Carson smiled slightly, in a way that could only be understood by someone who had already beaten odds far greater.

Chapter 39

It is the year 2006, one year after Max Grunfeld was awarded the Nobel Prize for the reconstruction of Abraham Lincoln's genome. Carson Harmon sits on a bench outside the main entrance to Fair Lawn Memorial Park, some five miles from Kathy's home in an area marking the outer sprawl of Frederick's growing population. She comes often to this place, where in spring she watches the dogwoods and the jonquils repel the last gasp of winter. She will not enter the cemetery, for it holds the last remains of her child under a cold marble monument inscribed:

Charles Martin Harmon
Born March 16, 2000 Died January 3, 2002
Rest in the Peace of Angels

She fears the spirits which pervade the tombs inside the low, flagstone wall which separates her from the cemetery and the living from the dead. Her healing, so late in beginning but now nearly complete, must be guarded at all costs. Like so many survivors of tragedy, she forces herself to look forward.

The cemetery is built on a series of rolling hills wreathed by the wall. From the bench, she cannot see the tomb, hidden as it is by the undulations of the land of which it is a part. But with the passing of half an hour, she will begin to scan the horizon above the wall for her husband,

Senator Martin Harmon, whose familiar silhouette will appear to her inch by inch in the distance as he walks the hill leading to the entrance. The flowers which accompanied him to his grave-side homage will be absent on his return. As his shoulders and limbs are ever so gradually exposed to her view, she will stare intently, as she always does, at his arm, and she will follow that arm down to make certain that at the end of it, in his hand, there is another hand, smaller and engulfed. It will be the hand of a boy, and she will watch them walk toward her, a father and son normal in every respect save the slight limp of the child.

THE END

Edwards Brothers,Inc!
Thorofare, NJ 08086
19 January, 2011
BA2011019